Brian Moore

Brian Moore was born in Belfast in 1921, educated in Ireland, and then immigrated to Canada in 1948. He made his mark in 1955 with the publication of *The Lonely Passion of Judith Hearne*, which won him the Authors' Club First Novel Award. He was given a Guggenheim Fellowship in 1959, and in 1961 he received a grant from the U.S. National Institute of Arts and Letters. More success followed with the publication of, among others, *The Luck of Ginger Coffey, I Am Mary Dunne, The Doctor's Wife,* and *The Mangan Inheritance*.

Gillian Saward

Gillian Saward was born in 1934 at Maidstone, Kent, England and immigrated to Canada in 1948. She studied at H. B. Beal in London, Ontario, and the Instituto d'Allende in San Miguel, Mexico. She currently lives in Toronto. Her work has been shown in many exhibitions in private and public galleries in Canada and several abroad. She is the recipient of several awards and grants and is represented in many private and public collections.

New Press Canadian Classics

Distinguished by the use of Canadian fine art on its covers, New Press Canadian Classics is an innovative, much-needed series of high-quality, reasonably priced editions of the very best Canadian fiction, nonfiction and poetry.

New Press Canadian Classics

Matt Cohen *The Expatriate*

Mavis Gallant *My Heart Is Broken*

Anne Hébert *Kamouraska*

David Helwig *Jennifer*

Robert Kroetsch *Badlands*

Brian Moore *An Answer From Limbo*

Michael Ondaatje *Coming Through Slaughter*

Leon Rooke *Fat Woman*

newpress CANADIAN CLASSICS

Brian Moore

An Answer From Limbo

General Publishing Co. Limited
Toronto, Canada

Copyright © 1962 by Brian Moore

All rights reserved

No part of this book may be reproduced or transmitted in any form or by any means, electronic or mechanical, including photography, recording, or any information storage or retrieval system, without permission in writing from the publisher.

First published in Canada in paper by PaperJacks in 1973

General Paperbacks edition published in 1982

ISBN 0-7736-7019-X

Printed and bound in Canada

To Jacqueline

When the answer came to me, it reminded me of my schooldays when, out of nowhere, you suddenly knew that Ankara was the capital of Turkey. Or in algebra you found out what x was. Because I knew one thing, everything else was simple. Simple as genius.

And yet, this morning, before it began to fit together, I seemed to be in a low curve on my life's graph, a curve which fell to its lowest point at breakfast when I opened a letter from my mother, a letter which carried me back, not to the Ireland she wrote of, but to Home, that Moscow of my mind, forever shut in from the rest of the world; forever shut out. There, in the house where I was born, I could see my mother as young, pretty, quick to laugh, quick to scold. In that memory she had nursed me; when things were wrong, she made them right. It seemed impossible that the woman who wrote this trite, lonely letter could be the mother I remembered; impossible that she, not I, was the child now. Yet two weeks ago Ted Ormsby wrote to say that the allowance I am sending her is no longer enough for her to live on. It is none of his goddamn business, of course, and I might have forgotten his warning. But now, with my mother's handwriting in front of me, I was uneasily reminded of my duty. I put the letter down. The spindly table at which I breakfasted trembled with the adjacent tremor of the washing machine. I remember thinking that here in New York I was doing that which my mother would frown upon: eating in the kitchen. Opposite me, my wife Jane was reading *The New York Times*, unconcerned by the way the children were messing with their breakfast eggs. My children's table manners would appal my mother. They appal me.

'That a letter from your mother, darling?' my wife asked.

'Yes.'

'How is she?'

'She seems a bit down in the mouth. Of course she's never been the same since my father died.'

'Who died, Daddy?'

'Nothing, Lisa,' Jane told the child. 'It's just big people's talk. Now eat your egg up, sweetie.'

Jane does not like to talk of death in front of the children. My mother would have had them on their knees saying rosaries for the souls of the deceased. What would my mother say if she knew that they have not even been baptized? She is a total stranger to my present life.

So her letter, due notice of her claim on me, was left on the plate with my other unpaid bills. At the time I merely supposed that I would have to increase her allowance and I resented that. Resentment is, perhaps, a key to my character, but before I am condemned, I ask, is it fair that I, of all her children, should be elected as her sole support? My brother Rory, who was ten years older than me, heroed out when his parachute failed Somewhere Over Germany, back in 1945. My elder sister Sheila ran off to Australia with a feckless veterinarian and has been breeding like a rabbit in the outback ever since. My younger sister Moira is wedded to Christ and poverty in a Manchester convent and my father, Dr Charles Grattan Tierney, died four years ago after an illness which destroyed his life's savings as surely as night unravelled Penelope's loom.

Which leaves me. Yet of all my family, I alone, under the natural law – no, no, let me explain it in another way. As a child I feared that I was stupid and cowardly and thought that I would be a disappointment to all who knew me. I read a great deal and like many unsure children I had a taste for tragic endings. But in my reading I discovered that to fall from the heights of tragedy, heroes must first scale the peaks of achievement. In books I searched for a suitable daydream. When I was fourteen we were asked to write an essay about our ambitions in life. I wrote all night. I was, for the first time in my life, inspired. I wrote that I would become a great poet, that I would devote my life to the composition of a masterpiece and that, at the age of thirty, coughing blood in a last consumptive frenzy, I hoped to die, my gift still clear and unmuddied. This essay I submitted to my English master who, the following day, came to my desk, took my ear between his nicotined thumb and forefinger and led me before the class to read my essay aloud. O, what a fine foil I must have seemed for the exercise of his lumpish pedagogic wit; what a perfect victim with which to win amusement from a class of captive boys.

But that schoolmaster is dead now. I can no longer hate him for his use of me as hunchback for his sallies. Nor can I hate my classmates for the larger diversion they staged after school. Why should I? At the time, the incident seemed the greatest triumph of my life. After class, that day, a much larger audience assembled as I was dragged to the school drinking fountain, ducked under it and held until water ran down my spine, dripped into my trousers, trickled down my skinny legs to fill my socks and shoes.

After the ducking, I was forced to read my essay once more. I was to be stripped of my pretensions, to be taught that lesson I had been too long in learning. But I learned nothing. Soaking wet, my clothes torn, I read my essay, but with pride now, screaming out that I would do everything I had promised in it. And my classmates, watching my pale face and trembling shoulders, hearing the true fanatic in my thin, defiant scream, turned away, uneasy of me. Because conviction, even a wrong conviction, makes the rest of us uneasy. For the first time in my life I had won. My own unsureness died and for the remainder of my years at school I grew in the wind of my classmates' disapproval. Their doubts that day made me victim – the victim I still remain – of my own uncertain boast.

For I have not yet become great. I who boasted that I would never settle for the ordinary avocations have settled instead for – what? I have written, yes. Prose, not poetry. Six of my stories have been published in small literary magazines. Yet the novel with which I hope to fulfil my prophesy lies in a drawer in my office, a loved but ailing child, its life endangered by my fitful labours. True, I have escaped from the provincial mediocrity of my native land and now live, in exile, in the Rome of our day. Yet my employment in New York is as an editorial slave on a publication so banal in title and content that I cannot bear to reveal its name, and if asked why I do it I must talk of bills; clothing bills, food and rent bills, medical bills, kindergarten bills, my mother's allowance, those bills in which I monthly drown. And I can tell you that at night, in a harsh, recurring dream, I stand again beside that freezing fountain, reliving that moment when, by their fear of me, my classmates gave me a taste of what my ambitions might bring me, when suddenly, haphazardly, yet with no possible alternative routing, my course was set towards a destiny I have not yet accomplished. In that dream, I weep.

So, journeying to work this morning I sat glum in the subway's jiggle. Shall I describe myself and get it over with? I am pale with a Napoleonic lock of hair which falls over one eye. An American film director whom I met one night in a bar in Palma de Mallorca offered to cast me in the part of a drunken young Calvinist divine because, he said, I have 'a noble, guilt-ridden stare'. The following morning when I went to his hotel he professed not to remember his offer but I still hold his description of me as a compliment. It is true that my paternal grandmother was a Scot. I am tall with large hands which stick out of the cuffs of my suits. One of my eyes is larger than the other and not quite so brown. I give up. Can I describe myself by saying that women do not trust me, as I discovered on my first summer in America when, to supplement my earnings, I tried to sell encyclopedias door-to-door? Customs men ask me to open my bags. Policemen have told me to move along.

This morning, slack on the subway seat, wearing scuffed suede boots, a wrinkled cotton corduroy suit and buttoned-down blue shirt, I sat mum as though filled with a vision. In reality I was doing sums, translating dollars into pounds in an attempt to see how small an increase in my mother's allowance I could get away with, debating for the umpteenth time the chances of renting the empty back bedroom in our apartment to some Columbia student (female), daydreaming fitfully and lasciviously about the pretty Negro girl who sat opposite me, switching my thoughts abruptly to the 'profile' of a prizefighter on which I am supposed to be working, plotting out my next paragraph in the few blocks between Grand Central and my office and vowing as I went upstairs that I would finish a first draft that morning.

But by noon, having written only two bad pages, I went out to lunch. For some weeks now I have been avoiding my colleagues and have journeyed down to Greenwich Village where I lunch in Howard Johnson's and walk the streets afterwards in foolish nostalgia for a Paris I never knew. In Howard Johnson's, safe from interruption, I ordered baked beans and knackwurst and opened an old copy of *Partisan Review*. But as I flattened out the spine of the magazine, someone slipped into the opposite seat of my booth.

'Hi, Brendan.'

He knew he would find me. I knew he would find me. Through some telepathy of failure we know each other's paths, resting places, drinking wells. Yet which of us is the hunter? I feel it is he. But in my need for his company am I not bird to his snake?

His name is Max Bronstein and he is twenty-seven years old. This morning he was wearing sandals, sunglasses, green *chino* trousers and a red shirt imprinted with a design of yellow birds. Recently he has grown a beard which somehow mocks this Beat fancy dress, giving him the look of a rabbinical student who has mislaid his *yarmalke*. He lives with a cat in a one-room apartment in the West Village, is a sometime free-lance writer of articles for the magazine which employs me, and a twice published story writer for the small literary magazines which have published my own work. A gregarious solitary, a joker for his supper at other people's tables, and above all, a giver of unasked-for advice.

'So, Old Buddy,' he said. 'Where've you been this last week? You hear my news?'

'What news?'

'My novel. Gardiner Key's going to publish it.'

I did not believe him.

'Fifteen hundred dollars advance,' he said. 'I'm having drinks with him at the Algonquin this evening. They've already had a great report from Carnovsky and they're going to send advance copies out to all the other important critics. Here – I'll show you the letter.'

He passed it over. I read it. God! It was true. I looked up at him and saw him smile, a cur's smile, ears flat against his skull, ready to be stroked or to snap. From here on in, anything I said would be taken down and used in evidence against me.

'Congratulations,' I said. 'That's great, Max.'

'It *is* great,' he said. 'It just shows you. Stick at it and sooner or later your talent will be recognized. You know what I'm going to do now, Brendan? I'm going to take that advance, get out of New York and start right in on another novel. If I go up to some neck of the woods, I figure I can live six months on that money.'

'You could,' I said. 'I couldn't.'

'That's right,' he said. 'The wife and kids. Still, you've got to remember Tolstoy's remark. "No man can know life who has not been a father."'

'Where did he say that?'

'Someplace. I must admit though, it's tougher for a married man.'

'I've got my mother too –' I began, but he did not listen, he was giving his order to the waiter.

'Ham steak with an egg on the side, glass of milk, English muffin and coffee, right? What's that, Brendan?'

'Nothing.'

He removed his sunglasses and put them in a plastic case. 'You know,' he said. 'You should finish up *your* novel.'

'I can't afford to.'

'Wait,' he said. 'I have an idea.' He smiled, showing the steely prongs of his dental bridge. 'How's about if I mention your name to Key tonight? He's on the lookout for good young writers.'

Screw you, I said in silence. But wasn't this an omen? No longer was it Max, *mon semblable*, filled with the same day-dreams and bitternesses, no longer was it Max, two years my junior, with two published stories against my six. No, from now on it was Max Bronstein whose novel would be published by Gardiner Key, praised by Carnovsky, whereas I – it was not fair.

Be that as it may, there was no escaping it. Things had changed. After lunch, Max, who normally scuttles off in clock-watching terror, dawdled on the pavement and casually suggested that I take the afternoon off. He knew I must say no.

'Come on, man.'

'No. I have to go back to work.'

'Work? Who needs it?' he said. 'Come on. How about one beer at the San Remo?'

'No.'

'Well then,' he said. 'Be seeing you, slave.'

Even his walk had changed. How often had I taken leave of him, watched him, a sad young rabbi shuffling unwillingly to *shul*, his destination the soulless cubicle of some pulp editor or that lonely one-room apartment on West 12th Street, that room which the bitch-goddess could be counted on not to enter, where his ginger cat, seeing him come in, would stiffen its legs in boredom and sink back to sleep. Yet just look at him now, prancing gaily into traffic with no backward look, disappearing among the crowds on 8th Street, a solid four-star winner.

How many works of the imagination have been goaded into life by envy of an untalented contemporary's success? More, I would wager, than by any sight of talent rewarded. As I watched Max go, I was seized by a trembling, a trembling which mixed both rage and joy for there, prancing away from me, inciting my envy, was a two-legged proof positive that I could and, by God, I would, write a far, far better book than Max Bronstein ever dreamed of. I saw my novel as a banked fire which needed only this flame of rage and resentment to spark it into genius. My life in America has been caught up in marriage, in parenthood, in the pursuit of a wage, in the foolish vanity of the few short stories which I published here. My novel has been subordinated to these dilettantish things. I shall be thirty years old next December. I can no longer coast along on 'promise'. Performance is the present imperative. I must be ruthless. I have only one life; I must do something with it. Time, I must find time.

And in that moment, at the corner of 6th and Greenwich Avenues, the answer came. Ankara is the capital of Turkey. My mother.

When Mrs Eileen Tierney got off the bus at her stop, she put the little bag inside her coat. It was a BOAC overnight bag which the clerk had given her when he made out her ticket. She did it because Dromore Estates was all eyes, eyes which had nothing better to do than mind your business for you. She walked up the main path, took a left turn, then a right, then another left. Even after four years here she still had to think of her bearings because all the little bungalows were look-alikes. As she turned off into the path leading to Number 49, the shower of rain which had held off all afternoon began to spit down at last. It was lucky for her that she'd dodged it.

She put down the little bag in the front hall and saw that there was a letter from Moira. Asking for those shoes again, most likely. She would read it later. And now? The evening waited, a blank page that must be filled. The evening paper would not take half an hour to read. She had taken back all her library books, she was as far ahead in her packing as she could go, all her bills were paid, her letters written and posted and tomorrow was the soonest she could say her last good-byes. Well then, what else could she do that would be useful? There must be something, there always had been.

But there was nothing. At least, living with Brendan, there would be the two children, they would keep her busy. There would be a television too. And she would be able to help Brendan's wife. 'Jane,' she said, trying it aloud. Who was Jane? The sender of some four polite letters a year, letters giving thanks for the sweaters for little Liam and Lisa, talking about the weather, offering good wishes, closing 'with love'. But what does 'love' mean, what am I to her, some old woman she has never seen, her husband's mother, a person of a different faith?

She felt dizzy. She went into the little sitting-room, drew the blinds and sat down. She opened the letter from Moira. The Convent, Pinks Lane, Manchester, Lancs. What a funny address. And the letter was signed, as always, 'Sister Teresa', that name the Church gave her when it took away her allegiance to her family, her nice auburn hair, her right to buy a cup of tea or say good morning to a man. I know. It was supposed to be a vocation, but was it just that she was not pretty? I wept when she went in. I lost her then. Teresa in Christ has no earthly cares, she teaches slum children in Manchester and is not allowed to write home in Lent. Her letters are all I have left of her and are they her? Would you ever think this was written by a woman of twenty-eight, this letter so innocent of the world, the letter of a schoolgirl asking for her Christmas treat, telling of the term doings, excited over little things? Will I ever see her again, my Moira? Maybe not.

She would rest a few minutes. She still felt dizzy. Dr Brady, who was attending her, had urged her to lose weight. She had arthritis in her joints. She sometimes had trouble getting her breath. No doubt about it, she was hypertensive, her blood pressure was over 200. She had been a nurse, a theatre sister, when she married Grattan. Now, she tried to remember the name of the instrument – a sphygmo-something, sphygmomanometer! That pleased her. There was nothing wrong with her memory. Just rest a minute – The tall dark man came along the deck holding on to the rail, head bent into the wind. He wore a tweed hat and a heavy overcoat with an Ulster cape. He had a dark pointed beard and in his fingers was a dead cigar. He came down the narrow staircase into the saloon where the stretcher cases were and, as he did, he fitted his pince-nez on his nose. It was 1926. In an hour the pilgrimage would dock at Calais and she, who had come along to help nurse the chronic patients, sat deathly seasick on a bench by the wall. The reporter and photographer from *The Daily Sketch* were there. There was a blind of lights as they took the photograph of the dark bearded man kneeling beside one of the stretchers, freezing him in time: Dr Charles Grattan Tierney, medical officer in charge of the Irish pilgrimage to Lourdes. He was frozen in a photograph: he could not hear her when she called him, but Brendan came. He had no business there: he was not born yet. Yet he was twenty and wearing his brother Rory's suit. He said the suit was hand-me-down, it did not fit him properly. She said not to worry, he would have his own suits soon. She knew Rory would be dead. Brendan asked her to come to New York. She told him he had no business in this cabin: he was not even born. She asked him if his children were Catholics but he did not hear her. She called for Grattan; Grattan would not be afraid to ask Brendan. Grattan came and took off his pince-nez which were clouded by the heat of the saloon. He untied the cape of his Ulster. She felt she would die of seasickness, but he did not seem to notice. He told her about the reporter and photographer. 'English, of course, and absolute pagans. Oh, Eileen, pray that we have a miracle on this pilgrimage. A miracle that, as a medical man, I can testify to.' He only wants his name in the papers, she thought. Brendan takes after him. I did not always love him, and now it is too late. I hope he is in heaven. She was all alone now but not in the cabin, she was sitting in the Café de la Paix in the Place de l'Opéra in Paris. She wore a cloche hat. Grattan sat down at the table. He had not yet grown his beard. He ordered coffee and cakes in French and the waiter answered him in English. Grattan was furious. He was proud of his learning. He had won a gold medal in French in his second year at the National University of Ireland, he told her. She knew he had told her this before. She loved Paris. She wished he would take her to one of those naughty places, but was afraid to ask him because before he went to bed each night he knelt down to pray. He said when they would have children, they must say a family rosary in the evenings. They knelt down then in the Café de la Paix and the children joined them. Moira was devout, Rory could not remember the names of the Joyful Mysteries, Brendan fidgeted and leaned over to her, right in the middle of the rosary, and said he knew Paris, he would show her anything she wanted. She asked him point blank if he had ever been in those bad places, bordels they called them. He laughed at her and said was she daft but she knew by looking at him that he had been. Grattan came back from his surgery. He was older now: he had trimmed off his beard but had a heavy grey moustache, stained brown with nicotine from endless cigarettes. When she asked him about bordels he said that sometimes he almost believed she had a filthy mind. She hated him for saying that. She had a filthy mind: it was not fair of him to say it. She saw him lying on a bed in his blue suit. There were calla lilies at his head. He looked young. There was a fine arch to his nostril that she had not seen before. It was his last disguise. The coffin bumped into the wallpaper and left a mark at the turn of the stairs. She hated to pass that mark. She meant to have it fixed, but was he really gone or was he still upstairs? Was that him ringing his bell?

It was the doorbell. She got up, went out, and switched on the hall light. She opened the front door. 'Well, hello, Ted,' she said, genuinely pleased.

'Am I interrupting you?'

'No, not at all, come on in. I just dozed off for a second.'

Ted Ormsby came in, pulling off the flat little English cap he habitually wore. He removed his much-used raincoat and hung it up on the hallrack. He was a tall man in his forties with curly greying hair and very thick-lensed glasses. He wore an expensive tweed jacket, grey flannel trousers and brown suede boots. Mrs Tierney knew that he was a Socialist, a teacher of English in a Protestant boys' school and, at one time, her son Brendan's best friend. Her husband had thought him a bad influence during Brendan's university days, but this opinion had not affected Ted's regard for her, or hers for him. During Grattan's long illness Ted had helped in dozens of ways from preparing tax forms, to bringing in coal once a week from the shed at the back of the house. When Grattan died, Ted helped her move to Dromore Estates. Mrs Tierney, who had known few Protestants in her life, had been surprised to discover that of all the people she was leaving behind in Ireland she would probably miss Ted most.

He came in now, walking in the aloof, hesitant manner of the almost blind. He found his usual chair, peered through his thick-lensed glasses until he saw her sit, then sat himself, crossing his long legs, taking out his pipe and tobacco pouch, holding them up apologetically to receive her permission to smoke.

'Get your tickets all right?'

'Yes, Ted, I got them today.'

'Everything in order?'

'Yes. The timetables were just as you wrote them out for me. I have a three-hour stop in London.'

'Did you get your seat number on the transatlantic flight? I reserved a seat for you at the back of the plane. It's safer.'

'Yes,' she said. 'I have it in my purse. And thanks very much, Ted, for all that you've done.'

He dropped his head and began to fill his pipe in embarrassed concentration. She was delighted he had come and, in expectation of his visit, she had laid in four bottles of Guinness. Remembering them, she got up and went to the kitchen, returning with a bottle and glass on a tray. His embarrassment deepened. 'O,' he said. 'O. Thank you very much. Have you eaten yet? I wasn't disturbing you?'

'No, no.'

He poured the Guinness carefully, matching the foaming head neatly to the brim of the glass. 'Tell me, Mrs Tierney. Now that you're leaving. What. I mean. What do you feel about leaving Ireland and going to live in another country?'

He watched her as he spoke, although with his weak eyes, he could not see the details of her face. He waited, half afraid of what she might tell him. He felt very much responsible, for this move to America was, he believed, his own idea. He was conscious of the responsibility it put on him: conscious of the dangers to this woman in rejoining a son whose world and whose ways were so opposed to her own.

'Well, Ted,' Mrs Tierney said. 'As I've told you I've nobody left here. My husband had no close relatives and in my own family there's just my sister Agnes in Derry, we haven't seen each other in fifteen years. And besides, I've always loved travel. I was dreaming just now of a trip we made to Paris once.'

'This will be very different,' he said. 'You know that, of course.'

'Yes, but won't that be the joy of it? I'm to be envied, I think.'

'I mean,' he said. 'You and Brendan may not always see eye to eye on things.'

'I know. Brendan was always very independent. But we'll manage.'

He nodded and drank a long swallow of Guinness. He had come to say something but now, facing this old woman he was fond of, he wondered if he had any right to invade her privacy. Three months ago, visiting her in this bungalow, he had come across a weekly grocery bill and seen that she ordered only bread, tea, milk, corned beef and tinned salmon. He made discreet inquiries. A post office clerk he knew told him of the money order she regularly cashed. Brendan's. Typical of her that she would not think to ask for more. And, although he hated interfering in anyone's dealings with their parents, Ormsby had written Brendan a note, hinting that the cost of living had gone up here and that maybe his mother was finding it hard. He had known before he wrote that in some way he still acted as conscience to Brendan. He had not expected this turn of events: that Brendan would invite his mother to live in New

York. So he felt responsible for this thing. He had something he must say to her.

But could not say it. He finished his Guinness. Perhaps he could take her out, buy her dinner and tell her then? As soon as he had conceived this procrastination his moral code rejected it. He would take her to dinner, but he would speak now.

'Look, Mrs Tierney. This is hard to say and I hope you won't misunderstand me.'

He stopped, took a deep breath and sucked on his pipe.

'Yes, Ted, what is it?'

'Well. I mean. Well, it's occurred to me that if you go to New York you might feel committed. Do you understand?'

'No,' she said.

'Well, you might feel obliged to stay there. Even though you were homesick.'

'O, I won't be homesick.'

'But if you were, do you see? If you didn't like it over there. I don't know how to put this, but an aunt of mine left me a little bit of money not long ago. So. If you wanted a loan at any time. I mean. Supposing you wanted to come back again. I'd consider it an honour to help you.'

'Isn't that nice of you, Ted,' she said, moved with no warning for wasn't it amazing that this man, no kin of hers, quite different in his way of thinking, could say such a thing and mean it. 'I'll remember that,' she said and smiled at him, but O, she could never take a stranger's charity, he didn't know her at all if he thought she could ever call on him for one penny piece. She noticed he had finished his Guinness and got up to give him another.

'No thanks,' he said, and stood up himself. 'Now that you're on your feet, put on your hat and coat and we'll go out and get a bite to eat.'

'O, no.'

'O, yes. I came here to take you out for a farewell feast. You mustn't disappoint me.'

He hushed her protestations, made her agree. He waited while she got ready. In his near-sighted way he went up to the window and, stooping, peered at the objects on the ledge. He picked up a framed photograph, brought it close, and saw a face, a Napoleonic lock of hair over one eye, the hard young eyes accusatory. Brendan as he had known him, a face seen in lecture halls and saloon bars, a face which never smiled but went from angry gravity to wild, excessive laughter. A portrait of the young man as artist. Was it only a decade ago that Brendan had come, as a shy undergraduate, to offer his first stories to F. E. Ormsby, editor of *North*? Was it only ten years since he and his young friend Brendan had made those hilarious sorties to *épater la bourgeoisie* at Belfast literary soirées? This photograph was the familiar Brendan, but who was Brendan now?

The features of the photograph jumbled and fused. Seven years ago in Lavery's Saloon Bar: heat of the coal fire behind them as they drank; smell of damp tweeds, nicotine, porter. Brendan was back from his year in Spain. Two of his stories had been published in England. Had he changed, even then? He was talking about a girl he had met.

'I'm in love with her, Ted. I have it bad.'

'She's a pretty girl,' Ormsby said, handing back the photograph.

'That's the trouble. If I let her go back to New York on her own, some Yank will propose to her the minute she gets off the boat. That's why I'm going with her.'

Ormsby's head went up. '*You're* going?'

'Yes. I got my visa at the consulate in Barcelona. I'm going to join her at the end of this month. We're to be married as soon as I get off the boat in New York.'

'O.' Grey light from the leaded pub window struck against the lenses of Ormsby's glasses, blinding him. 'And bring her back here?'

'No. She's getting a job there, a good job. She does magazine illustrations.'

'And what about you?'

'Jane knows a lot of people on the magazines there. She thinks that with a few published stories under my belt I'll be able to find something. Anyway, I don't care. There must be all kinds of journalistic work to do in America.'

Ormsby sipped his Guinness, listening to that young, confident voice. He licked foam from his moustache. 'Yes,' he said. 'The Blue Bugloss.'

'What's that?'

'Cyril Connolly's remark. Journalism. A dissipater of talent.'

'Journalism,' Brendan said, 'is inevitable in my case.'

'But why? If your wife has a good job?'

'Jane wants children.'

Ormsby felt behind him, found the bar counter, put his pint down. 'She wants children,' he said. 'Do you?'

'Not particularly.'

'Then why?'

'I told you. I want to marry her. If children are part of it, that's all right too.'

'Why not go back to Spain, Brendan? It would be cheaper.'

'Spain, Spain, I've been to Spain. You suggested it, remember? The trouble with Spain, Ted, it's the solution of your generation, not mine. The idea of living in some foreign funk-hole just because it's cheap belongs to the thirties. This is the fifties. Times have changed. A writer today must be at the centre of things. New York is the centre.'

'Balls. In New York you'll need so much money just to exist, you'll be forced to work like a dog to get it. If you marry this girl and have kids and get a job in a place like New York you're finished as a good writer.'

'But I love this girl.'

Through his glasses, as he turned towards the fire, Ormsby saw a red blur. The coal's reflection heated his cheeks. 'I thought,' he said, 'your writing was more important than anything else.'

Behind his back, Brendan's laugh; an angry, gleeful shout. 'Still the romantic, aren't you, Ted? Always wanting a cause to die for.'

'And what about you, Brendan, have you no cause but yourself?'

'Causes? Colonialism, the class system and all that. Don't you realize, Ted, that those aren't real causes any more. The trouble with today's causes, they're bound to succeed. The Welfare State isn't a cause any more in these islands. Even in Ireland it's inevitable.'

'We can still hurry it up.'

'Go ahead. I can only get excited when the odds are against me.'

'Who's the romantic now?' Ormsby said bitterly. 'Three-quarters of the world's people don't have enough to eat, yet you –'

'That problem won't be solved by revolution and you know it. Just as the fact of the atom bomb can't be charmed away by pacifists.'

'Brendan, for God's sake stop trying to rationalize your selfishness. All you care about now is getting into bed with some Yankee skirt. When I think that I used to believe your palaver about writing and the sacrifices you were going to make for it.'

'So F. E. Ormsby is disappointed in me, is he? I always knew I'd be a great disappointment to my friends.'

'Don't flatter yourself.'

'And don't underestimate me, Ted. I published those stories, didn't I?'

'And on the strength of them you hope to find a hack journalist's job in New York.'

'I'm going to New York because I love Jane and I don't want to lose her. Love is important too, or don't you agree?'

'O, yes,' Ormsby said. 'The world's well lost for love.'

'Don't laugh.'

'I'm not laughing.'

'All right then. Don't worry about me selling my writing soul or whatever. When the chips are down, I know my writing's the important thing. I'll be perfectly willing to sacrifice anybody or anything for the sake of my work. You'll see.'

There are moments in conversations when the truth comes in like death: the friendship does not recover. This, Ormsby remembered, was one.

'Yes, Brendan,' he said. 'I believe you. You'll sacrifice other people, all right. But will you sacrifice yourself?'

The question, asked seven years ago, had returned no answer. And now, looking at this room, luggage packed, this mother rescued by a stranger's word, the question posed itself again. Why had Brendan sent for her? How would he use her?

Behind him, Ormsby heard Mrs Tierney's footstep. He replaced the photograph.

Jane Tierney dreamed of dark ravishers, young and fierce, who loomed in her thoughts like menacing yet exciting phalli, their silken white shirts disturbed at the openings by crisp black curls of body hair, who wore suits of impossible cut, gold watch bracelets and religious medals on silver chains, who used cheap cologne, whose olive-complected smiles revealed white predators' teeth. Men. With them, in fantasy, she performed unnamable acts and, willing yet afraid, was humiliated, robbed, degraded, defiled. Men who used their mouths as lyres of love, their tongues as navigators of every hidden orifice, their hands as cruel, yet gentle, tamers of flesh. Men who smoked dark cigars, men to whom desire came in improbable places, who performed the act of love with relish on tables, in trains, at high noon and in an open boat at dawn. Men. Not Brendan.

Sin was, to Jane, an archaic word. Sick was its current usage. But in the disparity between dream and reality she had a sense of wrongdoing, a vague guilt that foolish fantasy could rear so terribly large in the midst of fact, that, in considering the spare back bedroom which must now be fixed up for Brendan's mother, she could recall the dozens of times she had in her imaginings provided it with an entirely different tenant, a French, Italian or Mexican student from Columbia University, a dark-complected, amoral, fierce young man, hungering and unfulfilled, to whom in the hot afternoons while Brendan was safely at the office she gave her body in a dozen abandoned positions.

But now, when she looked at the room, she compensated for those absurd dreams by becoming creative and inspired and at once she saw what was wrong, what had always been wrong with this room. It was cluttered. The thing to do was make it seem larger than it was by creating a feeling of space and light. All right. She started by moving out all the children's junk. She painted the walls white. She bought a Japanese bamboo blind on Fourth Street, a single unboxed Continental bed (where else but Macy's), a rectangular mirror from a Second Avenue junkyard and a small, unpainted dressing-table and chair from Bloomingdale's. Over the bed, a Noguchi rice-paper lamp, and for colour and contrast a gay red cotton bedthrow with black Chinese characters on it and just one print, a little Hokusai. She did it all herself, kept the door locked until she had finished and on the Saturday before Mrs Tierney was due to arrive, she called Brendan in and showed it to him.

'How do you like it, darling?'

'Well,' he said. 'Yes, I like it. But will she?'

'Why not? I think it's beautiful.'

'Yes,' he said. 'But maybe she should have an arm-chair in here.'

'Good arm-chairs cost the moon.'

'I know. But perhaps you could pick up a second-hand one somewhere. Something she could relax in.'

'But it will destroy the room. Do you realize I did the place this way because besides being attractive and functional, it was cheap?'

'I know,' he said. But he did not seem convinced.

It was so inconsiderate of him: she felt like crying. She took refuge in the bathroom at once, because the children were at home and she didn't want them to see her in tears. How could you explain things like this to four and five? It wasn't like him not to appreciate her efforts. There was not going to be an arm-chair in there. Definitely not. It would spoil everything.

The bathroom was large and still luxurious, with a seven-foot tub, real tile and two full-length mirrors. The apartment was on Riverside Drive, once an elegant address but now running down, although Jane had proved to her own satisfaction that taste and simplicity could work wonders with any place provided the proportions had once been good. When she thought of the time and trouble she had taken hunting all over New York for the right things at the right price. And now, out of the blue, he talked of a second-hand arm-chair in that room.

She sat on the toilet seat and let the tears come. She could see herself reflected in the mirror, her hair in long braids, a sight just now, a fright. She could be harsh in judging herself because most men found her attractive. She had her private reservations: she worried that her breasts were too small and her bottom a little too lush, but she had her own style, she knew that; and that style extended from her clothes and make-up to her surroundings; it was her; it was important to her as a person and she'd thought it was important to him too. But a second-hand arm-chair would ruin everything.

'Jane? Are you in there, Jane?'

'Yes.'

'Come on out, darling, I'm sorry.'

Let him wait. When she remembered that in a week or so *she* would be the one who was going to work in this family, not him, when she thought of what they were giving up for the sake of his talent, having his mother over here, when she thought of that, the nerve of him. Let him wait.

'Jane?'

What was the use. She unlocked the door. After all, she had done it for him, she had done it to help *him*, didn't he realize that, didn't he have any gratitude? It was *his* mother this was for, didn't he see that? So why must he bring up arm-chairs, when he knew she hated rows. When he knew she always gave in. It wasn't fair.

'Look,' he said. 'Forget about the arm-chair.'

O, no, he wasn't going to get away with it that easily. 'No,' she said. 'If you think it needs one, then we'll have to get one.'

'No, darling, you're right. It would spoil the room.'

He had admitted she was right; that was something. 'On the other hand,' she said. 'Your mother probably *would* need an arm-chair. I'll find some suitable horror.'

'Good. It's just that I hope she sits in here a lot. After all, we don't want her on top of us all the time.'

She looked at him and thought of Louise's remark. Louise was her best friend at Swarthmore and now was art director for a very big group of women's magazines. Louise had been just wonderful when Jane mentioned that she wanted a job, in fact she had immediately offered Jane something in her promotion department. Perfect. But then, chatting on the telephone, this had happened:

Louise said: 'But what about the kids? Who's going to look after them while you're at work?'

'Brendan's mother, didn't I tell you? We're bringing her over from Ireland to live with us. She can have the spare bedroom.'

'O dear,' Louise said.

'What do you mean, Louise?'

'I mean is he crazy about her? Oedipal and so on?'

'He's quite the opposite,' Jane said. 'At least I think so.'

'But poor you, you don't know, do you?' Louise said. 'You'll just have to watch how he reacts.'

So now, watching his reaction, Jane decided that even getting an arm-chair was worth it, if he didn't want his mother on top of them. 'All right, darling,' she said. 'Leave it to me.'

When I saw that room, Japanned by Jane, I began to feel afraid. Anyone who can conceive of that Zen shrine as suitable for my mother will never understand my mother's world. Will I myself understand it?

These worries came at dawn this morning as I journeyed alone to meet my mother at the airport. Her world. It once was mine. But when did my world become an island? The answer: when my island was no longer the world. That was Ireland in the summer of my twenty-second year, that year in which I got my B.A. and, planning escape, began to work as a clerk at the American Air Base near my home.

Escape to what? To write, I thought. But was it really that?

A six-year-old boy says he will be a fireman when he grows up. His parents smile. They know he will not be a fireman, not if they can help it. It is a stage all children go through. At fourteen he says he wants to be a writer. His parents smile. It is a stage some children go through. At seventeen he says he wants to be a writer. His suits are permanently too small for him; he is shaving twice a week. It is time to have a serious talk. He says he wants to be a writer. An adolescent phase, no doubt, but still it's a hint that perhaps he is not cut out to be a doctor or an engineer. At eighteen, he is writing poems for the undergraduate magazines. Everyone is worried. Professor O'Neill is asked to have a talk with him. He says he wants to be a writer. It is now a family joke. Good evening, Shakespeare, Mother says. Don't disturb the Muse says Sister to her Boy Friend as they come into a room where letters are being written. Why don't you write something for the films? says Mary Meenan, black-eyed and beautiful but O so dumb. Writer, writer, Father says, why don't you grow up, teaching jobs aren't to be sneezed at, let me tell you. Do you think I spent good money so that you could get a perfectly good Arts degree and wind up clerking for some American Air Base? Look at your cousins, both doing well, making something of themselves, I want you to do at least as well, is that unreasonable?

Yet I loved my family, yes, I loved them all. I said I was saving to become a writer. But now, looking back, perhaps it was not the need to write which made me leave home, so much as the need to run. Wasn't it simply that I was twenty-two, that fifteen and seven made twenty-two, seven years of telling lies to keep the religious peace, seven years of observance without belief, seven years of secret rage at each mention of my 'immortal soul'? Wasn't it the need to run which made me save every penny I earned that summer and in November, when the money was in the bank, book my one-way passage out?

The night boat sailed for Heysham at nine. I ordered the taxi for eight. My sisters ran down the path to put the bags in. My father (he had written me off as a failure) frowned and shook hands, advising me to drink no tap water. My mother, my pious, quick-tempered mother, wept; warned that Mass must be attended; offered to pray for a success she knew would never come, for, in two months, this foolishness out of me at last, she was sure I would come back up the avenue, tail between my legs. Wave a last good-bye, see her wave blurrily at the departing taxi lights, then turn blind from the evening darkness, back into her brightlit hall. Blind to my smile of rage and triumph as I settled back on the taxi seat. Blind: not knowing I had gone forever.

The night boat's hooter echoed up the lough: fog closing in. In the third class amid the returning poor who work on English roads and in English kitchens, who live in slums and send their postal orders home. Old hands had bagged the benches: the rest of us sat on our suitcases. Bottles of stout went around and a pale girl in black (home for a death in the family?) sang in a choir-loft contralto: 'Come back to Erin, mavourneen, mavourneen.' Faces drugged with sleep and whisky farewells turned to listen. The last channel buoys slipped past the porthole. Ireland invisible. At sea. Voices took up the girl's wistful chorus until three young labouring men, ruddy and primed with porter, countered with 'The Long And The Short And The Tall', and the passengers, finding this more to their taste, cheerfully blessed all the sergeants and double-you-oh-ones. I did not sing. A war song, Rory's war and Rory dead, a war I was too young for, a war I hated just for that. Beside me a man in a greasy suit took out a Baby Power, drank, then passed it on. 'This your first time across the water, lad?'

'Yes.'

'What line of work are you in?'

'A writer. I'm going to be a writer.'

'Ship's writer?'

'No, just a writer.'

'Would that be good wages?'

'I don't know.'

I did not know. Next morning it rained, it rained at Crewe, it rained all down the Midlands and was still raining as the boat train met the trailing entrails of London and slowed into Euston Station, the journey over, the emigrants out in a banging of carriage doors, an embrace of welcoming pals on the platform. They ran off: I was alone with my suit-case, alone in my choice, a writer I had said, but was I? Ahead lay the channel boat, the Spanish border and, at Barcelona, another boat bound for Ibiza where, for three pounds a week all found, I would have time to find out. Ibiza, Ted's suggestion, where, my eyeballs still bright with the after-image of my father's frown, my mother's tears, my schoolmates' uneasy jokes, I would write. Write them all wrong.

Rage and revenge. But was it really a rage to write? Eight months later, shivering in a steerage deck chair on the night boat to Mallorca, I offered a light to an American girl. A week later I lay beside her on the damp sands below the city of Palma watching dawn dilute the floodlights on the cathedral across the bay. I told her I loved her. Her name was Jane Melville, and in September she must go back to a job in New York. And what did that do to my rage to write?

Back at home, Ted Ormsby sent my stories out, got them back, sent them out. The temperature of my hopes fell with each rejection, the symptom of my fear remained constant – return to Ireland, loss of Jane. I was down to my last five pounds and uneasily debating the ethics of living off her American traveller's cheques on that morning when she ran under the Moorish archway of the Plaza Mayor, a letter in her hand. I can remember my sudden and shocking tears, yes, tears of vindication and relief as I read that letter ... happy to publish your story ... payment enclosed ... promise ... high hopes ... see more of your work.

There, in that long ago Spanish square, I was freed. With that letter I believed that I had paid back my ducking at the fountain, erased my father's frown, my mother's angry words. With that letter I was baptized in a new communion. With that letter, I left my parents' world forever.

Yet now, seven years later, have I really been freed? Am I not still waiting to prove that the world has been wrong about Brendan Tierney? Did I come to America because of my need to write, my need of Jane, or simply my old need to run? I do not know. But this morning, as I got off the bus at the airport, as I went through a door which opened by electric eye, and rode up on a moving staircase to the observation lounge, I knew that it is this world I care about, this world of moving staircases, electric eyes, efficient loudspeakers. Exile now means exile from this. My island is no longer home.

As I stepped off the moving staircase, numbers changed on the electrically-operated arrival board. A voice announced that BOAC flight Five Three Nine had just landed. 'Passengers will shortly pass through immigration and customs.' I went to the windows of the observation lounge and looked down into the sealed off customs area below. I looked at a young couple carrying a baby in a plastic basket, at a British bowler and duffle coat, a schoolboy in a too-short blue blazer, an irascible German, a Slavic blonde, a dumpy little woman, a Negro clergyman, a Kensington matron, an American student and then – shock of recognition sudden as a floodlit mask veering up in the darkness of a funhouse – I looked back at the dumpy little woman who stared about her, lost (as a child, lost in a park once, I had wept for her) – my mother.

I did not wave. I could not. I stood rooted in the sight of her as stranger. Small and old, grey hair under her hat, wearing a badly-fitting suit of green tweed, carrying a scuffed leather travelling case. I watched her hand her customs declaration to the officer and then look up, lost – saw her faded prettiness, dark circles under her large, sad eyes. She looked up at me, did not know me. She said something to the customs officer and then moved towards the customs gate. I turned away, ran down the staircase to catch her. Was I, to her, equally a stranger?

*

Mrs Tierney, worried that she had come out the wrong door, looked around the terminal but could not see Brendan or – but, was it –

Is it –

Ah, no, it isn't – yes, it is!

Brendan?

But, in those dark glasses, is he blind or what? His nose, that lock of hair, it *is* him –

Sees me? He's smiling – he's coming over –

Brendy!

He was older, not a boy any more, a man, what was he doing wearing dark glasses, looking like some Dago Dan you wouldn't trust your girls with?

'Brendan,' she said. 'Is it you?'

'Didn't you know me, Mamma?'

His arms held her. His lips (he had not shaved) touched her cheek and, close to tears, no man had held her since Grattan's death, she held this, her last man, half laughing, half crying. 'How would I know you?' she said. 'Is it a tin cup you're earning your living with?'

'The glasses,' he said. 'I forgot I had them on.'

He took them off. She smiled at him, then remembered the black man who had taken her luggage, where was he, had he run off? She was glad of Brendan: this place was foreign from the first go off, what with niggers in red caps asking for your bags. She had never before in her life spoken to a black man.

'Listen, Brendan, there's a porter took my suitcase, a nigger, could you find him? He had a red cap on him, number 47 it was.'

'I'll find him,' Brendan said. 'But look, Mamma, don't go calling him a nigger around here. People wouldn't like it.'

'What should I call him?'

'A Negro. Or coloured, that's the polite word.'

'Coloured, then,' she said. Why was it the first word he said to her had to be telling her she was in the wrong? 'I'm coloured myself,' she said, trying to make light of it. 'I'm red as a lobster.'

He smiled: she had won him back. He patted her shoulder and told her to stay put; he would check. Check, that was a Yankee word. She looked around the great terminal, dazed, tired, excited. She had dozed a little on the plane but had not really slept, her feet were killing her, but never mind, where was Brendan's wife? Not here. Ah, she probably couldn't leave the children. Did they have a maid? She had never thought to ask.

There he was with the porter. Waving to her, telling her to come.

She went. It was good to be down. Sacred Heart of Jesus, I give Thee thanks.

Her knee was a bit stiff, getting into the taxi. She knew Brendan noticed it for he asked, at once. 'How are you feeling, Mamma?'

'I have a wee touch of arthritis in my left knee. It stiffens up sometimes.'

'But otherwise you're all right?'

'O, I'm grand.'

The taxi moved out under lights suspended from long aluminium stalks, past vistas of glass, poured concrete and steel, past a file of airport buses, past a modern chapel with an airplane propeller on its wall, past a glass and concrete heating plant which revealed intestines of huge, multicoloured machines, past aircraft in long parade rows, past a confusion of signs, into the swirling patterns of traffic circles and a highway's several lanes. She was reminded of an H. G. Wells film she had seen years ago, a film in which men in white togas directed the world from sterile operating theatres. But this was the future made present and real: nothing sterile about it. There was a rim of dirt on the taxi-driver's collar, and the taxi itself was dirty, its cheap plastic seat covers cracked.

'Jane couldn't come,' Brendan said. 'She had to take the children to kindergarten. She should be home by the time we get there.'

'Brendan,' she said. 'I hope I'm not going to be a bother to you.'

'Why would you be? You'll be a great help to us.'

'With the children, do you mean?'

'Right.'

'Do you have a maid?'

'No,' he said. 'Maids cost a fortune here. Besides, now that Jane's going back to work, she wouldn't want to trust the kids to a stranger.'

(Work? Why was she going back to work?)

'So you see, you'll be a great help, Mamma. We'll talk about it.'

She might as well say it to him now, say it and get it over with. 'Brendan. Now, listen, I just want to mention something while we're by ourselves. Now, listen, if it becomes too much, I mean if you ever feel you need the space – you know what I mean – I want you to promise you'll tell me.'

'Why would I want the space?'

'Well, there are all sorts of reasons. Besides, Jane might not be happy with this arrangement, having me living with you. So, Brendy, if ever I wanted to go home to Ireland, you wouldn't be angry, would you?'

'Of course not. But don't tell me you're homesick already?'

Homesick? Easy to see he doesn't know Dromore Estates, how could anyone be homesick for that wee misery of a place?

'Ah,' she said. 'When you're my age, it's the past you're homesick for.'

'Yes, but I suppose you'll miss your friends?'

'I have a first cousin living here,' she said. 'Here in New York.'

'A cousin?'

'Frank Finnerty, a first cousin on my mother's side. He left Ireland when he was about your age. I have his address, I must look him up.'

'That would be the Donegal side of the family?'

'Yes,' she said. 'Would you remember Donegal at all?' He was so far away from her now, a grown man with an American accent, wearing a funny shirt with buttons on the collar, the kind she remembered were in style at home thirty years ago. Hard to think of him as that wee Brendy who, aping his country cousins, ran barefoot in the fields each summer on his uncle's farm, hard to see in this man in dark glasses that Brendy who collected hard chestnuts and British Empire stamps and who came to her once (informed by a classmate called Jim McTurk) to ask if it was true that babies were born through the belly button in a lady's tummy. What kin was that boy to this stranger? But then, she thought, who's talking, what does he see when he looks at me? I must seem like Methuselah to him. 'I suppose I look a lot older since you last saw me?'

'No. You look fine.'

Fine, that's a Yankee way of putting it. But he *is* a Yank now. And anyway, wasn't he always different from the rest of us, even as a wee boy, his nose always stuck in a book, afraid of his own shadow, but with a terrible stubbornness about him. Wanting to be a writer. She remembered when he first said that. He couldn't have been more than twelve at the time.

'How is the writing coming along?' she asked him.

'Fine.'

'I always read your articles in the magazine.'

He looked out the taxi window.

'Wasn't it lucky, the way you got the job with that magazine, and you just an immigrant here.'

'I'm thinking of quitting the job.'

Gracious God, what did he mean, was he sacked or what? Was that why Jane was going back to work?

'You see, Mamma, I want to finish my book.'

'A book?'

'A novel.'

'O. And would you be well paid for that?'

'Pay has nothing to do with it. I'm sick and tired of writing magazine junk.'

'But won't you miss the salary it pays you?'

'Of course. However, Jane's job will take up most of the slack. We'll make out.'

'But when you've finished the book I suppose you could always get your job back, couldn't you?'

'I never want to see that place again. When I think of the years I've wasted there, I feel sick.'

Was his wife going to support him forever, was that what he meant?

'You can't serve art and mammon,' he said. 'I'm tired of being a Sunday writer. I need to devote all my time to it. Having a family to support is one thing. But there are more important things.'

Important, what could be more important than looking after your wife and children? O, you haven't changed, my boy, you're the same stuck-up wee fellow, thinking yourself a cut above the rest of the world around you. Is it any wonder I've worried about the way you're living, a fellow who can say the like of that?

'Brendan? Do you still go to Mass?'

'No.'

'And your children?'

'Look, Mamma, we might as well get this straight once and for all. My children are not being brought up as Catholics.'

Suspicion was one thing: knowledge was another.

'Well,' she said. 'Are they Protestants, then?'

'Of course not. As Joyce once said, I'll not forsake a logical absurdity for an illogical one.'

Joyce, who's Joyce, some girl? Never mind. Control yourself.

'As a matter of fact,' he said. 'The children are not anything. They're not baptized.'

My grandchildren.

'Mamma, are you all right?'

Dizzy. She could not see. She lowered her head for a second and the blackness cleared. She pretended to look out of the window. 'What's this we're coming to?' she asked. 'A tunnel?'

It was the Midtown Tunnel, he said. He went on to talk about it, but she hardly heard him. To chase her thoughts she looked out at the cars: she had never seen so many cars in her life and now, roaring in the long lavatory-tiled tunnel with the policeman on the wall looking down, a whine of tyres, ruump, ruump, ruump, until they came up and out into the air again, cars in front of them, cars behind them, cars coming to sudden jouncy stops before the traffic signals, their back lights starting up like mad red eyes. It was as though this city were made for cars, not people. Even the buildings seemed built to car scale and she had a sudden silly vision of cars roaring up the skyscrapers' stairs, running into rooms where there were beds for cars, nurseries for the little cars to play in –

Pagans. Not baptized.

Everything was so high, so tall. Even London was human compared with this huddle of great upended cartons, a man was like a fly beside them –

My grandchildren are heathens.

Dirt. Grey grime over so much of it, wastes of paper blowing about in the gutters and yet the people passing were clean, their clothes pressed –

Not baptized.

Glimpsed for a moment, an old boozer lying in a doorway, the only poor man in all this crowd, but only for a moment, for the taxi swung up on to a ramp and on to a bridge, a high road running along the river, and she saw big ships – the *Queen Elizabeth*, Brendan said – and then off that high road into a very grand avenue with great buildings like the side of Buckingham Palace. This was his neighbourhood, he told her, and she was impressed, for surely it must be one of the best parts of New York. Canopies, and even doormen in uniform. Why did they not have a maid if they lived in a place like this, how would Jane earn enough to support all of them, including her?

Jane, what sort of person is she?

'Here we are,' he said. 'Home.'

As she stepped out of the taxi she looked up and there was the number 468 over the entrance transom. 468 *Riverside Drive*, an address she had written a thousand times, familiar to her as any prayer. Yet now it was not words on an envelope, it was a real place, a place where his wife waited upstairs, a place with a dark lobby, bald plush reception benches, a smell of strong disinfectant and, when they got out of the lift, over-filled bags of refuse outside each door. Brendan went ahead, put down her suitcases and took out his keys. Behind that door his wife waited. Behind that door.

She was not tall as Mrs Tierney had thought from her photo; she was like a pretty little gypsy, her dark hair drawn up in a bun, wearing a loose purple smock and black trousers which were so tight around her hips you could see the ridge of her panties underneath. She had a large smiling mouth which was very wet as it kissed your cheek. She seemed shy, not sure of herself, younger than Sheila or even Moira. How could you be afraid of her? Jane.

'Let me take your coat, Mrs Tierney, did you have a good flight? Shall I take your hat too? O, it's so great to see you. And how do you find Brendan? Is he very changed?'

'Sure, I didn't know him at all, when he met me,' she said, smiling. 'With those dark glasses on him I took him for some Jew man.'

What was wrong? Jane was looking at Brendan as though somebody had hit her, what were they both looking so funny about?

'Mamma, Jane's mother is part Jewish.'

'O.' She felt the blood rise to her cheeks. 'O, I'm very sorry, Jane. I didn't mean any harm. It was just...' But just what was it, how could you explain a boner like that?

'Come on,' Brendan said. 'Let's have some coffee.'

Which was *not* the way to deal with it. Furious with herself for saying such a tactless thing, she was twice furious with Brendan for not having warned her.

'This way,' he said. 'In here.'

Here meant the kitchen, they ate in the kitchen, who would have thought it? But something must be said – something – anything – to hurdle this awful start. 'Isn't this nice,' she heard herself say. 'How nice and bright. I noticed the sky as we were coming in. So clear, such a change after home.'

Jane smiled at her, a heroine refusing a blindfold. Brendan said something harmless. The talk staggered up on its feet and went on in weary pilgrimage, talk about the flight, talk about the children, talk about New York, talk that was like the meeting of three strangers in a dentist's waiting-room, talk to pass the time until they could decently get free of each other.

And so, having swallowed a cup of coffee and eaten a small piece of toast, she said she would like to change. It had been so hot on the aeroplane. Jane rose, still trying not to show what showed so very plain and led her down to the far end of the flat to open a door into a small room, white as a hospital ward, with a single bed, a teetery wee dressing-table, an old stuffed armchair, no proper curtains on the window and 'This,' said Jane, 'is yours. I hope you like it.'

Brendan carried in her suitcases and Jane gave her a set of clean towels. Then amid thanks from her and their reassurances that they would see her soon, the door closed and she was alone, listening to their footsteps going away. She heard them whispering: she could not catch what they said.

*

'I'm sorry, darling.'

'Don't be silly, Brendan, there's nothing to be sorry about, it wasn't *your* fault.'

'Well, she didn't really mean any harm, you know. It's not her fault either. She just doesn't know any Jews.'

'She does now.'

'Come off it, Jane, you're not Jewish.'

'I'm one-quarter Jewish. And your children are one-eighth Jewish, remember. What's going to happen if she fills them full of anti-semitism?'

'She won't. I'll speak to her. Let's be fair, darling. Remember your grandmother Levinsky and *her* remarks about the drunken goyim.'

'That's different. My grandmother had cause.'

'Your grandmother came from a backward environment, that was why she thought all Christians were drunks. And my mother comes from a backward environment too. Same thing.'

'Excuse me, Brendan, it's not the same thing.'

'All right then, what do you want me to do about it? Send her back home?'

'Did I say that? Did I say anything? Didn't I keep a smile on my face?'

'Shh! Is that her?'

*

It was her. She made as much noise as she could, coming out of that strange room so the un-understood voices would know she approached. In the bathroom she locked the door, then took off her blouse and mopped her neck and shoulders with cold water. She would not think of what had just happened with Jane: she would try to think of something nice. She was going to meet her grandchildren in a minute, the only grandchildren she would ever see. (For Sheila's children in Australia, who would ever lay eyes on them?) O, I hope they take to me, she thought, remembering that, as a rule, children did not like old people. Her own children had always hung back when Grattan's mother, old Mrs Tierney, came to see them. Funny to think that to Brendan's children she would look as old as old Mrs Tierney was to Brendan. But I am as old, she remembered. The bill for living is that everything comes to you in time. How vain I was once, how glad that I was a pretty girl: yet now, what difference does it make? Now I am that old body I sometimes find standing between two mirrors in a shop, with humpy shoulders and grey old curls forever coming undone at the nape of my neck. What relation am I to the girl I was, the woman I was, the Eileen Moynahan I have been all my life?

She was tired. It was five in the evening by her watch: here in America it was only noon. She began to dry her neck and face, thinking of that five hours she had gained. If only it were that easy to gain back time, people would be like the Flying Dutchman, sailing on forever. But the Flying Dutchman sailed on because God doomed him to sail on. Like me.

What a codology! What was she doing standing here with a face on her as long as last week's washing. What did she think this was going to be, a picnic? Surely she was old enough to know that nothing was perfect in this world, no, nor never would be. Now get your blouse on you, fix your hair and put a smile on your phizzog. Go out there and talk.

*

Jane, on her way out to pick up the children at kindergarten, came out of the kitchen and saw her mother-in-law sitting in the living-room with Brendan. As a senior in college, Jane had once attended a lecture on stage design given by a very talented queer. First, the queer set up a little stage model, very elegant, very Louis Quatorze. To show how the set worked he began to move little cardboard court figures around on the stage. Then, in the centre, he suddenly placed a tiny, bowler-hatted figurine, representing a Victorian pork butcher. 'See?' he said, with a cold smile. 'You must always be careful. Look at this little man. One false note. If you have one false note, your cosmos crumbles.'

That derisive comment and the students' laughter came back into Jane's mind now as she looked into her living-room and saw, dead centre, that old woman with her untidy grey curls, ill-fitting suit and sensible black shoes, an anti-semite with an Irish brogue, a Legion of Decency sort of person, someone's baby sitter waiting to be driven home. But this person could not be gotten rid of after an exchange of five dollars and a few moments talk about what time the children went to bed. This wrong note was here *forever*.

Brendan, sitting opposite his mother, did not look any happier than Jane felt, but after all, Jane thought, it's his mother: not ten minutes ago he was trying to excuse that inexcusable remark of hers. And that, come to think of it, was the most terrible part of this visitation. She would no longer be able to confide in Brendan. She could hardly tell him, for instance, that the sight of his mother sitting in her living-room almost made her want to puke, now could she? He was a man: there were some things only another woman could understand. Jane looked again at Mrs Tierney's untidy grey head and, sick, went out to fetch the children.

*

It was past one when they returned. Mrs Tierney, sitting in the living-room, heard the apartment door open. A quick rush of feet in the hall. The boy entered first. He was four years old: his skin more delicate than any woman's; his eyes, beautifully lashed, wondrously large. Yet all was dirt, the yellow playshirt, the robin's egg blue trousers, the new blue sneakers stained with finger paints. His voice was high and yawling, reflecting to perfection the naked self-love of his years. 'Dad?' he yelled, racing into the room, skidding to a stop, struck dumb at the sight of his grandmother.

'Hello, Liam,' she said.

Outside in the corridor, a voice whispered. 'No, I don't *want* to, Mummy,' and as Mrs Tierney turned towards it she heard Jane's urgent whisper and saw the child unwillingly propelled into the room. She was tall for five, a lumpy child with freckles, wearing a dress already too short for her, staring at her grandmother with sullen panicky eyes, then turning to Jane. 'Can I have my lunch now?'

'Say hello,' Jane commanded.

'Hello.'

'Hello, Lisa,' Mrs Tierney said.

'Mummy, can I have my lunch now?'

'Just a *minute*,' Jane said.

The little boy had moved closer. 'She's older than Willa Mae,' he said.

'Willa Mae is a baby sitter we have sometimes,' Brendan explained.

Mrs Tierney smiled. She stood up. 'Wait, children,' she said. 'I have something for you.'

She went to her room. Gracious God, American children, every single word you heard was true. Savages. They did not look like Brendan (or the mother, for that matter). The boy was the good-looking one: God help the wee girl. She took three packages from her suitcase and went back to the sitting-room. 'This is for you, Lisa. And this is for you, Liam.'

And then, shyly, for suddenly the present did not seem the right thing at all, she offered the third to Jane, saying 'It's just something I picked up at the last minute.'

She had knitted a sweater for Lisa; she hoped it would fit. A sweater for Liam but a little toy car in the package too, for boys never cared about clothes. For Jane, not something she had made herself, but something on which she had spent money she could ill afford, an Ulster linen tablecloth with a damask design of pink roses. Now, seeing this room, she knew it was not right. Jane did not look as if she ever served afternoon tea, let alone put on a cloth for it.

Jane opened the box, did not remove the cloth but stared at the pattern, then held the box out for Brendan to see. 'How nice,' she said. 'Look, Brendan.'

'That's Irish linen, isn't it, Mamma?'

'Yes. It's what they call a damask pattern.'

'I didn't know they had them in colours.'

'They usen't to have them,' Mrs Tierney said. 'But this is a new sort, very popular, the man told me.'

She saw Jane frown: it was not popular with her. She heard her own voice back in Robb's in Royal Avenue telling the shopman, she would have preferred the plain white one but the shopman urged the other, saying it was what all the Americans bought.

'I could have it changed for a plain white one, if you'd prefer that?' she asked Jane.

'O no, this is very nice. Isn't it, Brendan?'

He nodded. Ashamed of my taste. He fingered Lisa's sweater. 'Did you knit this yourself, Mamma?'

'Yes. I hope it fits.'

The little girl took the sweater from Brendan, held it up against herself. 'It fits,' she said. 'Thank you very much, Granny.'

Mrs Tierney could have kissed her.

Afterwards (Brendan had gone downtown: Jane was giving the children their lunch in the kitchen) Mrs Tierney went back into the sitting-room. She had never seen a room quite like this, with its canvas and wood chairs, its long black modernistic sofa, its gooseneck lamps like a dentist's surgery, and enormous paintings of potato-headed creatures on all the walls, painted by Jane who had signed her maiden name. Jane Melville. (Was that a Jewish name?) Books galore and magazines, ashtrays every place and three half-empty bottles of spirits on a side table. But for all the untidiness, all the objects strewn about, the room made her think of a room on a stage: it was not real. There was not one thing in it from their family homes, not one thing which looked as though it had belonged to someone else before them. And yet she remembered sending them some silver as a wedding present; she remembered a silver christening mug she sent for the little boy, and a large Beleek vase Brendan's aunt had sent and surely Jane's family must have given her something, furniture or something? Where was it? Had they hidden it all or sold it? Were people in America ashamed of their past?

If so, she decided, then this present they're so proud of

doesn't say much for their taste. No carpet on the floor, just coco matting, the sort of thing you'd put in a maid's room; sofa cushions of cheap cotton corduroy and so on. Never mind my own bedroom that looks like a hospital ward, the whole flat is the same: modern, skimpy, cheap. No wonder he never sent me a decent allowance, no wonder he's putting his wife out to work.

He wants to write a book. She will earn the dollars. I am to mind the children. Yes; I am to mind his little pagans for him. Did he bring me across the ocean to show me where I failed?

The stranger who is my parent is asleep. 'She's asleep,' a voice said to me in the phone booth in Eddy's bar. I could hardly hear it. Four subway workers on nearby stools were discussing baseball loud, clear and drunk. It was as though someone whispered to me, wakening me after a car crash, and in the joy of finding I was still alive, I did not understand what was said. 'Speak up,' I said, into the phone. 'What was that you said?'

'She's gone to sleep,' Jane's voice told me.

'To sleep?'

'Of course, to sleep. There's five hours time difference, remember? It's eleven o'clock at night, her time. O, Brendan, where are you? Why did you run out like that? She's your mother, after all.'

'I'm sorry,' I said. 'I just couldn't talk to her any more. Look, I'll finish my drink and hop on the subway.'

'When shall I get dinner? Will seven-thirty be all right?'

'Fine,' I said although, privately, I didn't think I could make it. After all, Pat Gallery had just bought me three drinks: I couldn't very well walk out on him. Besides, my friendship with Dr Patrick Hubert O'Sullivan Gallery is a very complicated one. He is a successful surgeon who was once a poet and now, as a hobby, he edits and helps finance a small literary magazine. He is, moreover, an Irish American of invincible sentimentality and fierce loyalties and one of the few people in New York who think of me as a writer of fiction who is temporarily engaged in journalism, rather than a journalist who has occasionally written short stories. This, I find gratifying. What I do not find gratifying is the outrageous stage Irish brogue he uses in conversations with me. As I went back to the bar, he lapsed into it. 'Well now,' said he, 'and did you phone Herself?'

'I did,' said I, despising myself for the equally spurious Irishry which creeps into my speech during these Hibernian communings.

'And so?' he said.

'My mother has gone to sleep.'

'Well then,' said he. 'Not a thing to worry about. Here. Put this under your collar.'

He leaned forward to pick up the brimming martini glass and I noticed, as so often before, how thin his hair is under that undergraduate crew cut. With surgical exactitude he placed the glass within my reach, refusing to let me pay.

'No,' he said. 'Today's a big day in your life. You're organized now. Ould mother on tap to mind the childher and Herself off to make an honest dollar in commercial art. You're all set now. And one day I'll be bragging that I knew you when.'

He fixed me with a drunken glare, as though he had just sighted a cancer on my cheek, then clapped his arm around my shoulders.

'You know why I say that?' he asked. 'I say that because you've finally demonstrated that you have the first requisite of genius. Know what I mean?'

I said I did not.

'Ruthlessness,' said he. 'Sheer goddamn ruthlessness, that's what. Until now, I had my doubts about you. Sure, sure, you have talent. Those stories you wrote weren't leprechauny crap, they were good. But the hard fact was you were a young fellow with a hack writing job, you were married, you had two kids. You didn't show any sign of that single-mindedness, that fox-that-eats-his-grandmother drive that every great artist must have. Gauguin lighting out for the south seas and to hell with his kith and kin. Or Arthur Rimbaud spitting in his ould mother's eye. You know what I mean? But you've changed.'

'How have I changed?' I asked him. 'Haven't I spent all afternoon hiding in this bar afraid to face my mother?'

'Ah, but you did bring her over here, didn't you?'

'Yes.'

'And you're sending your wife out to work to support you, aren't you?'

'Yes.'

'Well then,' said he. 'That's what I mean. I couldn't do that in a million years. Take me –'

He always wants you to take him.

'– Take me, I was a good poet once. And my wife's a darlin' girl, oh, a darlin' girl. But she hired out to marry Gallery the doctor, not Gallery the poet. And Jaysus, a poet's supposed to give up all for love. So I did. I gave up poetry. Now, you'd never do a thing like that, would you?'

'No,' I said. 'I wouldn't.'

'Exactly,' said he. 'Ruthless, that's just what I mean. Now I'm a surgeon, I cut people up. I'm a helluva cool surgeon, you ask them down at Saint Vincent's, they'll tell you I'm a cold one. But although I can cut people's guts out, I'm chicken. Not like you. You came in here today, pale as plaster, and you told me your mother's just arrived and she's like a stranger to you and you're worried if she'll be happy here. What have I done, you said. But you're play-acting. You don't care. You brought her here without ever asking yourself whether she'd be happy or not. And the only reason you're afraid now is because you're worried your little scheme isn't going to work. You don't give a damn about your mother, really. All you care about now is finishing your book. And that, Brendan, I envy you.'

Did I believe him? A part of me wanted to. But my mother must have been lonely since my father died: here, she will have her grandchildren, she will be living in a family. I didn't act just for selfish reasons, did I? Or did I?

'Eat?' Eddy asked, coming down the bar. 'You want potato chips?'

'And two more martinis,' Gallery said.

I stood up. 'Not for me. I've got dinner waiting.'

But Gallery reached out, grabbed my arm and turned his drunken face towards Eddy. 'This Irish sonofabitch,' he said to Eddy. 'This sonofanIrishbitch has decided at long last to do what the good Lord put him into this world to do. Write. And you and I, Eddy, you and I are going to be proud of him.'

I admit that, be it delivered drunk or sober, such talk is blood on my bones. Sick as I am for the world's unconditional surrender, I can listen to this line until the cows come home. But even as I basked in those warm and foolish words I saw that elderly stranger standing lost in the customs enclosure; I saw Jane's face when that Irish voice said 'Jew'; I remembered that it was ten past seven and so, ignoring Gallery's appeals to stay and have another, I said good-bye and made for the street. The bar door shut. A gust of warm air huffed down Seventh Avenue, ruffling the feathery coat of an Afghan hound which led a tall homosexual home; ballooning two cellophane-covered suits held aloft like a prize catch by a passing delivery boy;

whipping the skirts of a little secretary tight about her hips; blowing my own forelock down into my eyes as I hurried down the subway steps. Down I went, clicking through the turnstiles, down another flight of steps to the platform where, suddenly numb with martinis, I found my face in the mirror of a candy-vending machine. Was it a ruthless face? Was it Van Gogh who will lop off an ear? Or the face of a false Stephen Daedalus dreaming impossible dreams of bound volumes in all the great libraries, including Alexandria?

But the train came in and I shoved with the crowd, swayed among packed bodies in the sickeningly fast uptown rush, sprinted across the platform to catch the local at Ninety Sixth, coming out hot and weary at Columbia amid a downrush of homegoing students, to meet once again that warm city wind which drove my forelock into my eyes. I turned towards home, ruthless and dedicated, my loved ones sacrificed *ad majorem Brendan gloriam*, ready at last to begin my life's work.

But as I turned the key in the apartment door my domestic persona popped up like Banquo's ghost. A man's voice said: 'And now it's time for most of you to go to bed.' My years as paterfamilias told that his was the ringmaster of Terrytoon Circus, and thus commanded by the television authority, my children obey as they would never obey me or Jane. I heard Jane's voice saying that they could have one glass of milk and that she didn't want anybody getting up for anything later as she and Daddy were going to eat dinner very soon. I felt triumphant and relieved. I was home on time.

Then I remembered my mother. I went down the corridor. The door of her room was slightly ajar and there was no light inside. I saw myself in the taxi, telling her that my children were not baptized. I remembered how she put her head down as though she were ill. O God, I thought, I don't want to see her again. I wish she had never come.

But as these fears took me I seemed to hear her voice, chiding me in childhood for my fear of going upstairs in the dark. 'Come on, Brendy. There's no devils there.' Gently I pushed open my devil's door. In the reflected light from the corridor she lay, small and solid under the blankets, her face towards me. A hairnet covered her grey hair: her skin, slightly flushed, seemed soft and babyish. For the first time since Idlewild I recognized a relation – the mother of that young mother who once was mine.

She had nursed me, this woman. When things were wrong she made them right. I must speak to her. I must tell her I was sorry for running out on her this afternoon. 'Mamma,' I said softly. 'Mamma?'

I listened. There was a faint snoring sound.

'Mamma?' I said again.

The snoring stopped. Her large dark eyes opened, blind against the light. My panic returned. Quickly, I shut the door.

The sun came through the bamboo blind, half lighting the room. Mrs Tierney's mouth and nose felt dry. She turned her head on the pillow and saw her little alarm clock beside the Chinesey paper lamp. Five past six. She reached out and took up her watch. Five past eleven. That was Irish time. Here, no one would be up yet. Wouldn't it be a good idea, seeing she was awake and rested, to get up and get their breakfast? She rose, went in to wash, then, returning to the bedroom, put on a flowered print dress, a bit too good for housework, but still. She might as well look smart, her second day. Quietly she went into the kitchen where, after some puzzling, she got the hang of how the coffee pot worked. She had set the table by the time the coffee perked. There was a sound of children's voices. She went into their room.

'Shh,' she warned them, as they stared at her from the double-tiered confusion of their bunk beds. 'We're going to make your mother's breakfast as a surprise. All right?'

Four stared at five for guidance and five decided it was a good game. With a yelp she was out of her bunk and getting dressed. Mrs Tierney felt a quick sense of joy. It was so easy to manage children at this age: you made it all a game.

'What does everybody eat for breakfast?' she asked little Liam, as she began to dress him.

'Mummy has coffee. Daddy and us have a boiled egg.'

She oversaw their washing, then led them to the kitchen.

When Jane, blear with sleep, rose to the sound of the alarm, and rushed into the kitchen to make coffee, she found all three of them at table.

'What's going on here?'

For a moment, looking into her dark eyes, wide as a child's in the moment before tears, Mrs Tierney thought, O Lord, I've put both feet in it again, what was I thinking of? Imagine how I'd have felt if my mother-in-law took over my kitchen and my kids her second morning in the house?

But then little Lisa said: 'It's a surprise, Mummy. We made your breakfast as a surprise.'

And Jane smiled. 'Did you, darlings? How nice of you. Thank you.'

So it was all right.

*

Although, as Jane later told Louise, in that first moment of entering the kitchen she felt like the captain of battleship *Potemkin* faced by the mutinous sailors on the afterdeck. There they were, grandmother and children, completely in agreement, completely in charge. Fantastic. 'But you know,' Jane said, 'suddenly I wasn't in the least bit jealous – O, I suppose I was, just a tiny bit – but the moment I saw that it was all right and that the kids liked her, I was happy. Really I was. Of course, I'm still worried about her anti-semitism and the fact that she's Catholic. But after all, that's a chance you have to take with anyone who looks after your children. And she does want to make herself useful and that's the main thing, don't you think? For instance, the first morning, I took her with me to the kindergarten and the next morning she wanted to take the kids herself. Naturally, Brendan and I don't want to rush her, I mean we'd sort of planned on giving her two weeks to settle in and see New York and so on. But she, my dear, she's the one who wants to get started. And so, as Brendan's giving up his job on Friday, we just don't see any point in delaying things any longer. What I mean is, if you have no serious objections, I'd *love* to start work next week?'

That was what she told Louise (at the party four days after Mrs Tierney arrived) but was it really why she wanted to get out of the apartment and start work? In talking to Louise you had to remember that Louise had never been married, was in analysis, and obviously had great difficulty relating to men and children. She was the last person in the world to understand how the presence of another woman could upset the balance of things. Besides, Jane was going to work for Louise. She wanted Louise to think everything was all right.

However, even from the beginning, there were these maddening little incidents. Take the business of tea. On Tuesday, the day she arrived, Mrs Tierney drank coffee without a murmur. On Wednesday, Brendan asked if she wouldn't prefer tea. 'Well, yes, I would,' Mrs Tierney said. 'But it doesn't really matter. I mean, don't change things on account of me.'

Well my *god*, Jane thought, don't be ridiculous, we have tea. She got up at once, found some teabags, stuck one in a cup and put water on to boil. 'I can't find the pot, I'm afraid,' she said to Mrs Tierney. 'But any time you want tea, just use one of these. I must find that pot, though. Brendan says teabags are a horror.'

'I've never tried them,' Mrs Tierney said. 'But I'm sure they're quite all right.'

'Well, look,' Jane said, 'from now on, if there's anything you want, don't wait to be asked. Help yourself. And if there's something we don't have, I'll order it for you. All right?'

All right. That afternoon when Jane came back from downtown she found Mrs Tierney waiting for her in the living-room with a silver tea service, hot buttered toast, and thin little bread and butter slices. 'I just made us a cup of tea,' Mrs Tierney said. 'I found this teapot on a top shelf in the kitchen. I hope you don't mind me using it.'

The service, last seen tarnished and wrapped in newspaper, now gleamed in reproach. 'You know,' Mrs Tierney said, pouring, 'when I came across it, it was like finding an old friend. It was my mother's, you see, and I always believed I'd sent it to Sheila.'

'No, it was your wedding present to us,' Jane said. 'I should have remembered. But it was so lovely, I never wanted to use it.'

'O, you might as well use things, my dear. The things I put away, there they were staring me in the face after my husband died. I remember thinking what good are they to me now, why didn't I enjoy them while I could.'

She was so bland, so old shoe about it that Jane could hardly be sure that she'd dragged out and polished up the service as a reproach. But this, Jane discovered, was the most infuriating thing about her mother-in-law. You could never be sure what was accidental and what was not. It was like the business of dust. The day after Mrs Tierney arrived Jane, noticing a crust of dirt on a windowsill and worried that Mrs Tierney had noticed it too, made some reference to the difficulty of keeping things clean in New York. All right. The very next morning she discovered her mother-in-law, duster in hand, cleaning off the edges of picture frames and flicking around inside light fixtures. 'O hello, dear. You're right about the dust. It must be awful trying to keep up.'

Was it a reproach, or was it simply that the woman could not sit still? 'Can I give you a hand with anything, Jane? Is there something I could do?' Or worse, much worse, when Jane finally settled down with *The New York Post*, there would be a rattle of dishes from the kitchen or a sudden thunder from the washing machine. 'No, no, please stay where you are,' Mrs Tierney's voice would say. 'Finish your paper. Let me.'

But you couldn't let her do everything and that meant Jane was forced to help her in a series of chores that normally she wouldn't have done. Something had to give. Tomorrow (Friday) would be Brendan's last day at the office and any complaint now might look as though Jane were trying to back out and god knows, that was nonsense, she was not backing out, if only he knew how excited she was at the thought that next Monday she would be at work in the promotion department of Vanity Magazines, doing something creative for godsakes, after five years of parks and prams and diapers. No, it wasn't a question of backing out, it was a question of getting him to tell his mother what was, and what was not expected of her. But it must be done diplomatically.

So when Brendan came home that evening Jane took him into the bedroom and tried to explain. Diplomatically. 'I know she means well, darling,' Jane said. 'But it's simply too much. It's like having a cleaning woman around with not enough work for her to do. She makes me feel guilty, for godsakes.'

'She's only trying to be helpful,' Brendan said. 'She's probably as nervous about the whole set-up as you are. Give her a day or two and she'll settle down.'

'Settle down to what? To some perennial spring cleaning? Honestly, darling –'

'Shh.'

'And that's another thing. Look at us, whispering in here like two kids. I mean, this is our apartment, not hers. Why should we have to whisper? I mean, she's always in the living-room, she just *sits*. Last night she sat all evening. I couldn't even read, for godsakes.'

'Well, what can *I* do about it?' he said. 'I can't tell her to go and sit in her room, can I?'

'She could watch television there. You could move the set into her bedroom. Okay?'

'Okay.'

'But do it nicely,' Jane warned. 'We don't want her to think she's not wanted.'

'Don't worry,' he said. 'Come on. Let's have our drink.'

Drink time was normally, for Jane, the really blessed moment of the day. The children were out of the way watching television and mostly she and Brendan got a tiny pre-dinner bun on while he told her about the doings at the magazine. But with that false note in flowered rayon dead centre in the room it was true that the cosmos crumbled. Instead of their normal chat there was a perfectly dreary guided tour of New York given by Brendan with his mother asking *inane* questions about America and both of them going on about Ted this and Seamus that until Jane thought she could scream. Yet as soon as Jane had escaped to the kitchen Mrs Tierney thundered right in after her with: 'Could I help you, dear? Is there anything I can do?'

After dinner it was even worse. It had taken Jane years to get Brendan into the habit of helping with the dishes. His mother broke him overnight. 'O come on, let me have that towel, Brendan. Go and sit down. Let me.'

He let her. And once again Jane was stuck with her.

After dinner, when she and Mrs Tierney had tucked the children into bed, they came back into the living-room. Brendan was reading. 'Darling,' Jane said. 'Perhaps your mother would like to look at something on television?'

'Would you, Mamma?'

'Well, yes, that would be very nice.'

'We could move it into your room?' Jane said.

'But I wouldn't want to monopolize it,' Mrs Tierney began. 'Maybe you two want to look at something?'

'We never look at television,' Jane said.

'O. Well, in that case . . .'

'I'll move it for you,' Brendan said. He went into the children's room, got the TV set and carried it into Mrs Tierney's bedroom. Then he came back to Jane.

'Satisfied?' he asked.

Why did he always make it out to be *her* fault?

I used to have a dream in which I, the lowly editorial slave, walk down the corridors of my place of employment for the last time. There is a murmuring in the cubicles as I pass the receptionist's desk and enter the office of Mackinley Downes, editor-in-chief. There is a further murmuring as Downes' voice is heard, first reproachful, then entreating. He offers me a raise in salary; he paints a vivid picture of my possible future with the magazine. Finally, in a last effort to keep me, he proposes a year's leave of absence. All his offers are ignored. I resign. Envious eyes follow me as I walk to the elevators, my parting bonus cheque in hand.

But yesterday fact did not fit fantasy. No eyes noticed my passage along the corridors and when I entered Downes' office, the receptionist told me to wait. When, finally, I was admitted to the Presence, he motioned me to a seat, finished a telephone conversation and then, tall, thin and languid, leaned back in his red leather chair, looked at me in puzzlement and said: 'Yes?'

Humble, forelock-tugging Tierney. 'I just came in to say good-bye, Mr Downes.'

'Oh, yes,' he said. 'That's right, you're leaving us, aren't you?'

'Yes.'

'Yes,' he said. 'Harkness told me. Something about you wanting to write a book, wasn't it?'

'That's right.'

'And you've been with us how long? Four years?'

'Five.'

'Mnn. Is this a fact book you're planning?'

'Fiction.'

'Mnn. Have you got a publisher, an option, or something on this book of yours?'

'No, not yet.'

He shook his head very slightly, Mr Worldly-Wise marvelling at youth's folly, then leaned forward and touched the intercom button on his desk. 'Suzy,' he told the box. 'Phone accounts and tell them to get up a five hundred dollar bonus cheque for Brendan Tierney in editorial. Yes, now.'

He switched the intercom off.

'Thank you, Mr Downes,' I said.

He shook his head again, as though correcting me. 'No, no, don't thank me, that's the usual thing around here. A hundred for each year you've been with us. How long do you think it will take you to finish your book?'

'I don't know. I hope I'll do it in six or seven months.'

'Mnn. Well come back and see us whenever you get it out of your system. You never know, we might have something for you. If not on staff, then on a contract basis.'

'Thank you.'

The interview was over and suddenly I realized that I was no longer in his employ. I was alone and I did not want to leave. 'Perhaps you'll need some fixes on the last piece I turned in?' I said to him.

'See Harkness about that. Anything else?'

'No, Mr Downes.'

'Been nice talking to you,' he said, standing up.

Unnoticed in the corridors, I went up to accounts and collected Downes' going-away present which was some two hundred dollars more than I'd expected to get. But I did not feel exultant. Not at all. I went back to my desk, packed some stolen office supplies in my overnight bag and began the rounds of my colleagues' cubicles. I had already made sure that all of them knew I was leaving. 'So you're quitting the whorehouse,' they said. 'Out on your own, eh, Brendan?' They shook hands, they smiled, they talked vaguely of having lunch some day. Keep in touch, they said. But no one had organized a farewell party; no one even asked me downstairs for a farewell drink. They were busy; they had a 'book' to get out. I left at three, hours before closing time. Once outside the building, it was as though I had never worked there.

I did not go home. I went down to the Village, to the small sour room in a loft building which Max and I had discovered a month ago during one of our aimless walks. There, on an old trestle table, was my typewriter, a writing board and several pencils. On the shelf above the tiny, grimy window were folders containing drafts and chapters of the novel which is now the substance of my hopes. I unpacked my stolen supplies and laid them out neatly. I must begin at once. But O God, O God, will I succeed? Will I be able to revenge myself on the past by transforming it into a world of words? I sat down at the desk and opened a folder. I began to read the opening chapters. How jumbled, flat and stale they seemed. Words, not worlds. Jesus, why didn't my classmates drown all my foolish ambitions under that school fountain? If I am wrong, if I am setting out to do something I am not fit to do, then am I not assuming the most despicable of roles? For who is more contemptible than the false artist, posturing through life as he spews out his tiny frauds? What spectacle more degrading than the lives of these Village Rimbauds, covered in the vomit of sickly pastiche, crying out their genius and their purity from mouths filled with rotten teeth? Am I now to be one of them?

I could not read; I could not write. I left the workroom and wandered towards Washington Square, mingling near the fountain with the phony folk singers, the adolescent Brooklyn Bardots, the sad, small-bearded Negro A-trainers, the coffee house poets clutching the latest copy of an illiterate Beat review, the few twenties' leftovers (fraudulent Heming-Pounds, boozers bloat in their puffy greybeard cheeks), the abstract daubers hurrying to basement galleries with their latest pastiche of other men's scrawls. And there, the living Christ of all my own fears, coming towards me on the sidewalk was Pelardy, hand in hand with the inevitable sixteen-year-old girl.

He wore a white tennis shirt, white duck trousers, white sneakers. His face was tanned to the colour of a good light cigar, so that at twenty paces he looked my age or younger. All his art is in that look for he is over forty, an advertising copywriter who is a night-time teacher of courses in creative writing; a Village whoremaster whose fame rests on four published short stories and the promise of a novel which he boasts will re-create the conscience of our time. Meanwhile, aware that editors and publishers are not immune to the national cult of youth, he has successfully, for a decade, impersonated twenty-nine. We had met at David Dortmunder's parties. He waved to me as he passed.

'Hi, Brendan.'

'Hi.'

They moved on. I heard him say to the girl: 'That guy's an Irish poet, a grandson of O'Casey. He's a junky.'

At forty, a false litterateur supported by my wife, my novel still promised and not delivered, shall I walk the Village streets inventing colourful lies about other nonentities for the titillation of some credulous child?

Think of Max Bronstein, I kept telling myself. Max was a Village failure. Max has less talent than you and yet he has broken out of the cage of meaningless jobs. Think of Max. But for once the thought of Max did not work. Instead, as I went towards Seventh Avenue and my subway, I saw the slight, hopeless shake of Mackinley Downes' head as he touched the intercom button and ordered up my bonus. Even the five hundred dollars did not cheer me. In my black mood it seemed the last real money I might ever receive.

And then, O God, when I got home tonight. My mother was in the children's room reading them a chapter of *Winnie the Pooh.* The children's supper was on the stove. The apartment was as neat as if a cleaning woman had just left. But there was no sign of Jane.

'Where's Mummy?' I asked Lisa.

'In the bathroom, Daddy.'

Bathroom equals tears. And why not? Everything else had been awful today. I knocked on the bathroom door and heard a splashing of water. For a moment I dared to hope that everything was all right. Perhaps she was just taking a bath. 'Jane?'

Another splash. She opened the door, naked and wet, her hair in rollers. Behind her, the room was thick with steam, its mirrors clouded. My hopes rose until I saw her face which had the sulky look of a child who has just slapped another child and knows it will be punished. 'Come in,' she said. I followed her in, shut the door and watched as she got back in the bath, sliding down among the soapsuds, her lacquered toenails surfacing at the far end. She stared at them.

'What's wrong?' I said.

'Nothing. Let's have our drink in here tonight.'

'Are you crazy? It's like an oven in here.'

'It has advantages. It's private.'

'God,' I said. 'Don't tell me you've been having a row with Mamma?'

'No row. She's just taken over, as usual. I'm not needed.'

I sat down on the toilet seat. 'Take it easy,' I said. 'I've had a lousy day too.'

'What happened, didn't you get a bonus?'

'Yes. Five hundred.'

'Well, that's far more than you expected. What are you complaining about?'

'I'm not complaining. I'm worried.' And, foolishly, I told her about my interview with Downes and my fears for the book. Foolishly, I say, because at once she sat up in the bath and asked: 'What do you mean? Don't you think your novel will be a success?'

'I hope so. I don't know.'

'You don't know. Don't you realize that unless it's a *huge* success we're all in the most *huis clos* situation ever invented?'

'What *huis clos* situation?'

'You and me and your mother, that's what. I'm not blaming *her*, but do you realize that unless you make a lot of money with this book, she's going to be with us for the rest of her days? Isn't that true?'

'Yes, I suppose so.'

'Well then, don't even think about the novel failing. And please go and get us a drink.'

I did not move. 'And you were the one who said you believed in me,' I said. 'You were the one who talked about my talent.'

'But I still believe in you, Brendan.'

'No, you don't. You want me to write a lousy best-seller. Money, that's what you want. We're not on the same wave-length, are we? *Et tu*, Jane.'

Immediately, she saw her mistake and with feminine arrogance she saw only one way to right the hurt. Give the boy some candy. She got out of the bath, dried her breasts and tummy on a bathtowel, let it slip to the floor and stepped into me, wet arms around my neck, lips presented to be kissed. 'I'm sorry, darling,' she muttered. 'I didn't mean that.'

But all I could think of was that nobody in the world is attractive with metal rollers in their hair. I did not want to kiss her, but I am married. I kissed her. 'Come on,' I said. 'Let's get the kids tucked in and then we'll have our drink.'

'Your mother will take care of the kids,' she said, biting away at my left ear. 'Come on. Lie down on the floor.'

'But it's too goddamn hot in here. I'm limp.'

She kissed me again. 'Five hundred,' she said. 'That's great, darling.'

'Yes, it is. Now get dressed and get rid of those damn rollers.'

'I can't. It's Dortmunder's party tonight. My hair isn't dry yet.'

'Do we have to go to Dortmunder's? I don't feel like it.'

'Well, I do. It's that, or sit with your mother. Besides, I've asked Louise to come with us.'

Louise. I loathe Louise, but this was no time for argument. 'All right,' I said. 'But for godsakes get a move on. Get dressed and I'll make the drinks.'

I got her arms off my neck and left the bathroom. I went into the kitchen and found my mother washing dishes at the sink. I moved past her to get at the ice trays and as I did, I noticed two rings which my mother had laid aside while she scrubbed. One was her wedding ring; the other was a man's signet ring. I picked it up, ran my thumb over the indented letters C.G.T. *Compagnie Générale Transatlantique*? Then, guiltily, I realized that the ring was my father's, that the letters stood for Charles Grattan Tierney. It seemed to me a measure of how little I really knew my father. I turned to Charles Grattan Tierney's widow, bent over the sink, scouring a saucepan with steel wool. How would my father have dealt with a naked, amorous wife with metal rollers in her hair?

'Mamma,' I said suddenly. 'What was father really like?'

Her hand paused for a second, then resumed its scrubbing motion. 'Your father?' she said.

'I mean,' I said. 'Was he at all like me?'

Again, that momentary pause: she stared at the saucepan's insides. 'Yes,' she said. 'You often remind me of him.'

'How?'

'Well. You're very set in your opinions. So was he.'

Was that true? How would I know? My father was thirty-nine when he married and would be seventy-nine if he were alive today.

My father, I remember, liked walks. He liked the seaside. I can see him in white ducks and blue blazer, wearing the black beret he bought at Lourdes, an incongruous, heavy, jaunty figure on the blustery promenade at Portstewart. As a medical student he had been on a walking tour in the Norwegian mountains and in the attic at home there was an iron-tipped shepherd's staff marked Halverson, Trondhjem. In the attic too were a bag of old-fashioned golf clubs, a set of fretwork tools and many pans and trays of photographic developing apparatus. But when I knew my father he had given up such things. He liked to read. Once a week he would send Sheila or me to the Carnegie Public Library with an attaché case full of books for exchange. He admired Hilaire Belloc, Maurice Baring, Shakespeare; certain plays by George Bernard Shaw. He enjoyed the books of Clarence E. Mulford, A. E. W. Mason, W. W. Jacobs and Sir Arthur Quiller-Couch. He despised the works of Somerville and Ross (a travesty of Ireland), James Joyce (a sewer), Oscar Wilde (a blackguard) and John Millington Synge (bunkum). In the years before he discovered the public library, he filled his house with second-hand books, and hidden in the back shelves I once found a shilling edition of Maurice Dekobra's *The Madonna of the Sleeping Cars*. He was a Grand Knight of Columbus and thought highly of his own powers as an orator. He was a Fellow of the Royal College of Surgeons and fond of signing himself as such. He did not sympathize with failure. He addressed his sons as 'sir', and his daughters as 'miss'. When faced with my mutiny he would say: 'Don't look at me in that tone of voice, sir.' It became a family saying.

My father listened to the B.B.C. news each night at six and again at nine. In their heyday he had said good things about Mussolini and Franco but not about Hitler whom he considered a blackguard. He considered the English Royal Family a subject for derision but dearly loved a Prince of the Church. He was a very bad driver and had fourteen accidents in, respectively, a Ford, a Morris, an Austin and a Vauxhall.

He was religious. He kept a picture of the Little Flower of Lisieux beside his bed. He was patriotic. As a boy he had known Sir Roger Casement. He never forgave England for the things he had seen. When he died, I was in America and, by his lights, I had not been a success. I feel that he thought me stupid. In addition, I alone of all his children had disputed his views on religion, politics and literature. I considered him out-dated and wrong-headed. He considered me a 'pup'.

I have, however, kept his photograph with me through all my travels and once or twice have tried the experiment of putting it up. It shows him, heavily moustached, wearing a medical society tie and a stiff white collar, three inches high. I cannot endure his stare. Yet why, why? Is this how he lives on in me, in snapshot memories and in trivia, in adolescent judgements now calcified into history? Was it for this that he sired me in the fiftieth year of his life?

I do not know. I know only that if I were granted the wish to bring back to this world for one hour any human being I have known or read of, I would put in the call tonight for my father. We would not be friends. I might be shocked at his bigotry, his vanity, his platitudes. But there, standing in the kitchen, holding his signet ring, I suddenly, desperately, wished that he were with me. I wanted to tell him that I am about to change my life. I wanted to prove to him that he was wrong, that I, of all his children, will do him honour. O, Father, forgive me as I forgive you. Father, I am your son.

Mrs Tierney thought they would never get off to the party that night, what with Jane taking hours to do her hair (after coming to the table in curlers!) and Brendan seeming to be in the sulks about it. However, when they left at last, she felt as though she were on holiday. It was the first time she really had the apartment to herself so she did something she wanted to do, but something she was not proud of. As soon as she had put the children to bed, she locked the apartment door and then spent a leisurely hour going through the rooms, opening drawers and closets. She had always been curious: she was a looker into medicine cabinets in other people's bathrooms. She tried to excuse herself this time by telling herself that, as next Monday she would have the running of this place, she should find out where things were. But that was not the reason: it was nosiness and she knew it.

They were a funny pair: fond of their comforts. Furry slippers, back rests for sitting up in bed, throat sprays, nose and eye droppers, half finished boxes of pills. Jane had three negligées, eleven pairs of shoes, slacks, dresses and skirts galore. There in the bedroom, looking at the closets stuffed tight, the jammed drawers filled with underthings, stockings, slips, sweaters, scarves, fifteen men's shirts and enough ties to dress a regiment, scent, foundation creams, electric fan, nail scissors, toe clippers, a jewel box stuffed with outlandish necklaces, atomizers, sunglasses, purses, Mrs Tierney felt a bitterness rise in her; they were not hard up at all; they did not go wanting for one blessed thing. She thought of the little bungalow on Dromore Estates; she thought of the saving it would cost her to buy one pair of black shoes which Moira, snug in her convent, wrote to ask for as a Christmas present – O, and when she remembered the presents these ones had sent her; cheap blouses, a dress that was badly finished, ugly earrings; when she remembered that, it was hard to be fond of them.

They were well named, she decided. The darlings. That was her private name for them, what with their darling this and darling that. Look at those back rests would you. Brendan not thirty and her even younger. Back rests, as if they had one foot in the grave! Bohemians my eye; they were as set in their ways – 'Is it drink time yet, darling?' 'Is it time to do the dishes, darling?' – as two old grannies. Bohemians, it's their children, not them, who are the Bohemians. Wild savages those children are, but whose fault is that when Jane treats them as equals. 'Never even your wit to the child,' as the saying goes. Sure aren't they only children, don't they want somebody to make up their minds for them, is Jane daft that she can't see that? O, well. On Monday I'll have the looking after of them. Then they'll see who's boss.

She went into the living-room and looked out at the city. Out there, somewhere, was her first cousin, Frank Finnerty. She must go and see him: he lived alone. What an awful city to be alone in. It occurred to her that she had never seen a funeral passing in the streets. It was gloomy standing there, so she went back to her own room and switched on the television.

The Zoomar lens went down to the white square, came in on three hundred and twenty pounds of mountainy man, wearing galluses, long johns, a ragged shirt and a beard which fell on his obese breasts. The bad Zulawski Brothers both came at him, bouncing off the ropes like chimpanzees. They crashed into the mountainy man and rebounded. The hillbilly then waddled across the ring, took hold of one Zulawski, then another, dragged them to centre ring, a head under each of his fat arms, then knocked their skulls together. The cameras moved to a reaction shot; front row faces, screams of joy; a woman, open mouth filled with half-masticated popcorn, eyes ecstatic in her hate.

Mrs Tierney changed the channel. And they said the Irish were backward.

On the new channel, an old film. Norma Shearer in an Empress Eugenie hat, talking to a servant, then going down a long, curved staircase. Her skirt was long. Mrs Tierney put it in the Thirties. She remembered how she had hated those hats over one eye: they never suited her. Four men in dinner jackets in some club, no, it was a library; library doors opening, joining the ladies, all in evening dresses. In those days you went to the pictures to see another life: smart clothes, butlers, balls, handsome men, lovely houses. Then out into the rainy street past groups of collarless men in caps and mufflers, standing on the corner, men who had spent all morning in the public library keeping warm by pretending to read. Shawled women coming up the entry behind your house, picking over the dustbins for an empty bottle or some rags. Grattan telling of the Saint Vincent de Paul Society, the things he had seen, six people to a room, people who lived on bread and tea and dripping, always in bed to keep warm. Shipyard workers who went from apprenticeship to a life on the dole. In 1935 the mounted policemen charged down the streets. Martial law. Religious riots, my eye, the papers did not tell the truth: Orange and Catholic alike were looting the shops for food. The Government was afraid. That was the Thirties, the real Thirties. Not Norma Shearer in an Empress Eugenie hat.

But she watched the rest of the film. It was early: she had nothing else to do. Was Brendan still in the sulks, she wondered, now that he was at his party? And what would their party be like?

In the narrow trough of David Dortmunder's kitchen, a bag of ice cubes lay beside the sink, its mouth open like some strange brown fish. I looked at it, then passed on to the bottles of cheapest bourbon and vodka, the jumbo soda water bottles, the carton of cokes. A cheap party, drink delivered at the last minute from the Greenwich Village store which advertises as 'The House of Instant Booze'. And I, Tiresias Tierney, had seen it all, had been interchangeable host and guest, had walked among the lowest of the dead at these dead gaieties. I plunged my hand into the dead fish mouth, secured an ice cube and dropped it into my glass. I picked up a bourbon bottle, poured thickly, then watered the result from a dripping tap which had stained the sink's enamel brown. I was, I realized, drunk.

I turned to leave the kitchen but stopped, for what was the point in moving from the point of instant booze? Beyond, in Dortmunder's long, dun living-room I could hear the static of endlessly familiar talk; the integrity (or duplicity) of Adlai Stevenson; the phony sex in New Wave films; the psychiatric records of certain literary figures; a tirade against the educational system. The people were familiar as their subjects; a critic of literature who worked for an advertising council; a sociologist who wrote articles deploring *kitsch* for little magazines which deplored *kitsch*; Pelardy, the promising young writer of forty; a labour lawyer; an unpublished playwright; and Dortmunder, my host, a marginal producer of documentary films. And their women. I used to be smug about the fact that my friends were not my fellow workers; that all of them, in their separate ways, might qualify as 'intellectuals'. But tonight, no longer a magazine slave, I felt superior to them. Do you understand this? I say it: I am ashamed of it, but I must say it. They were ticks. 'Ticks,' I said aloud. 'Ticks on the back of literature.' Said, the phrase pleased me until I realized I was mentally filing it for future use. I was no better than they. I was disgusting. 'Disgusting,' I said aloud, as I walked out of the kitchen.

'What's disgusting?' asked Dortmunder.

'Me. Us. Don't you think there's something disgusting about parties like these?'

'I would think nothing should be disgusting to a writer,' Dortmunder said in his fatuous way. 'After all, a party like this is part of human experience, no matter how trivial.'

I looked past him, hoping to find someone to talk to.

'I mean, they should be grist to the writer's mill,' Dortmunder said.

But there was no one else out there: they were all bores, all disgusting. 'I tell you,' I said. 'A statement like that is really disgusting. If there's one thing that makes me want to puke it's this idea of writers going out to look for experience so that they can write about it. That's journalism.' I said. 'Documentary,' I added, for Dortmunder's benefit.

'Now wait, Brendan,' Dortmunder began.

'What's documentary?' said Dortmunder's wife, a pretty but dull girl who dislikes me intensely.

'Now wait,' Dortmunder repeated. 'I mean a real writer is not a reporter in the sense that he's looking for the sensational or the newsworthy. He's merely recording experience as it comes to him.'

'Exactly,' I said. 'And do you find him more admirable? Standing by his wife's bedside watching her face contort, the better to record her death agony. Taking mental notes so that he can write about it later. Poor bastard, I feel sorry for him.'

'Why for him? Why not for her?' said Dortmunder's wife.

'Because he can't help doing it. He's not human: he's a writer. He can't feel: he can only record.'

'But to write about life,' Dortmunder said. 'You must, in a sense, stand apart from it. You must have a streak of the sociologist, the documentary observer, even. Now take Zola –'

'Why take Zola?' I said. 'Zola is a footnote. And why must you turn everything into a literary reference?'

'Brendan's right. Experience is a trap.'

I did not have to look. It was Max's voice. But when I did look, Max had come with a girl: not the sort of girl you saw at these parties, but an expensive girl, wearing an expensive, tightly-fitted orange suit and a white silk blouse with so many buttons undone that I immediately started up a lustful prayer that she drop something on the floor, then stoop to pick it up. I could not believe that this girl was with Max, Max who repelled even ugly girls with his first damp hand-shake, lonely Max whose room contained a pair of Japanese binoculars with which, each night, he checked on lighted windows across the yard. Yet the girl had her arm in Max's arm. And there he was, late to the party, coming on now with a new and frightening assurance.

'Yes,' Max said. 'The writer who relies on experience is only a photographer.'

And the gorgeous girl (model? actress? débutante?) listened as though he were Socrates.

'Take my experience,' Max said. 'It was useless because it was pure cliché. Most experience is, of course. My mother, well, my mother is the classic Jewish Momma, so eat a little, so be sure you don't catch cold. And my father, my father's another fictional stereotype, the Jewish mystic who got caught up in the woollen waste business. I could go on – my vulgar uncles in the clothing trade – I can even produce a *zeide* from Rumania. They've all been done, you see. There are a dozen writers all alive and using this same material. And wort of all I was born in Brooklyn. Brooklyn, the greatest cliché of them all.'

'There he goes, the old agitator, old Lev Davidovitch Bronstein,' said a tall fellow who had come up while Max was lecturing, a fellow in blue jeans, dirty sneakers, never mind him, I thought, who is this girl?

'Hi, Jack,' Max said. 'You just get here?'

'Yes, and let's cut out,' the fellow said. 'I know a better party.'

'Jack,' Max said, pointing to Dortmunder with an embarrassed smile. 'This is our host. Besides, we just got here.'

'Suit yourself,' the fellow said, ignoring Dortmunder who had his hand up for shaking. 'What about you, Gigi?'

'I'll wait with Max,' said the gorgeous girl.

'Okay, but if you change your mind, the party's at Plimsoll's.'

'Wonderful,' the girl said. 'You may see us.'

'So long, Trotsky,' the fellow said to Max. He went out of the room without further good-byes.

'Who's that rude bastard?' Dortmunder asked.

'Why, that's Jackson,' the gorgeous girl told him.

Jackson. I don't have to tell his second name, do I, for isn't Jackson-Bloody-Clayburn a member of American royalty, that blood line of Tallulahs and Tennessees and Trumans whose day-to-day doings people in New York follow more closely than the lives and deaths of their own kin? Dortmunder and Mrs D. turned reverently towards the door. Jesus had walked there. And I, observing this, felt my envy unloose me. 'You mean the playwright,' I said, turning on the gorgeous girl. 'The lousy Broadway playwright.'

But gorgeous girls fear me not. She smiled as though I were cracked. I cracked in her smile. A girl in glasses who had just joined the group spoke up in answer. 'I agree,' she said. 'But you've got to admit he has a certain talent for writing stage monologues.'

'His plays are junk,' I pronounced.

'They get marvellous reviews,' said the gorgeous one.

'Only proves they're junk.'

The gorgeous one turned to Max, faint smile on full lips. 'The man sounds jealous.'

'*Jealous*?' (I was shouting now.) '*Me*, jealous of the Jackson Clayburns of this world? Jesus, Max, where do you find these people? I thought you had more integrity.'

But Max, ugly Max, merely smiled.

'Do you hear me, Max?'

'I hear you, Brendan.'

'Girls in orange suits. Parties with Jack-son. Jesus, Max, what's happened to you?'

The orange-suited girl looked at Max, shrugged, then turned and walked across the room. Max followed her. And I, dulled, drunk, my mouth opening for another blast of invective, watched that girl go, watched that magnificence of buttocks undulate towards the door, hips that like twin melons move, bye, bye, blackbird.

Drunk, but not drunk, the girl gone, Max gone, the rest of the room drifting away from me, all except the girl in glasses, who was she, who cared? I turned back towards the kitchen to get another drink but there was Jane standing at the kitchen sink, deep in chitty-chat with her dike friend Louise, probably moaning to Louise about the hardship of having to put up with my mother who is only trying to help her, who at least knows enough not to eat dinner wearing those goddamn metal hair rollers. Furious now (for why should Jane make me feel guilty?) I pushed my way into the kitchen and without speaking to either of them, I half-filled a tumbler with bourbon and pushed my way out again, looking for Max, anxious both to castigate and apologize, vaguely aware that I was in some way in the wrong, yet fully convinced that in some way I was in the right, that I must tell Max, *mon semblable* . . . what? I mean, Max, who's that girl you're with, eh? Listen, Max, I know you'll keep your goddamn integrity, but if you were me and I were you, what would you think of a guy who came on the way you did just now, just because his goddamn novel is going to be published. I mean, Max, I'm a writer too, I just quit my job, you should treat me with more respect, goddammit, and remember, I'm writing a novel too, a far, far better, you know, you'd better watch out, highhatting me, your book isn't so goddamn great, do you hear? You and your girls in orange suits!

But in the dead smoke, in the stale busy movements, in the huddle of talkers in that long, dismal room, I saw the critic who worked for an advertising council; the sociologist who wrote about *kitsch*; I saw Pat Gallery and Yvonne, I saw Paul Pelardy, I saw Dortmunder and Dortmunder's wife, I saw a fund-raising agency employee who was writing a satire on fund-raising agencies.

No Max. No orange suit.

So I drank my bourbon, feeling it hit me in the head, dulling me, lulling me. You're drunk, drunk, drunk, I reproached myself and because you're drunk tonight you'll feel guilty tomorrow. I thought you had given up this nonsense, what's the matter with you, why do you come to these ingatherings of the envious and parade your own envy and hatred? You are a clown, Tierney, a comic but unpleasant figure. Are you afraid to finish your book, is that what's the matter with you? Afraid to go down into the marketplace with it, as Aquinas said, or was it Aquinas? Sober up, you undignified slob. Go home.

In penance, I went to the bathroom. I opened the bathroom door. The light was on. As I closed the door behind me, a girl looked up from the washbasin. She wore a mauve sweater and a cheap black skirt. She was putting stuff on her lips.

'Sorry,' I said.

'No, it's all right, I'll be through in a minute. Don't go.'

I nodded, reasonable in drink, then sat on the laundry hamper and looked at her. She bowed her mouth with lipstick, and smutched her lips together, rubbing the stuff in. I found the gesture sexual. She curled two fingers into her hair and fluffed it up over her brow. 'You know,' she said. 'You were right about Jackson Clayburn. The trouble is, you *did* sound jealous.'

I was still looking. I found her pretty. Not beautiful like that orange-suited one, but pretty in a practical, possible way. I looked at her back, at her buttocks, at the backs of her legs. I looked at her face in the mirror. Young. She had finished fluffing her hair and now she took a ring from the washbasin and put it on her marriage finger. She reached on to the shelf above, found her glasses and put them on. And when she did this, I remembered her. The girl with glasses. The one who spoke while Clayburn – no, after Clayburn left.

'Now,' she said. 'I'll get out of your way.'

'No, stay. Want a cigarette?'

She sat on the edge of the bath. She took off her glasses. In my drunken state that seemed to me a very touching thing for her to do. 'You see,' I heard my drunk voice say. 'I wasn't jealous of Clayburn. I was angry at someone else.'

'Do you mean Max Bronstein?'

'How did you know?'

'O,' she said. 'I know Max. I saw you looking at that girl of his.'

'Did you?' I said brilliantly. I offered a cigarette and lit it for her. 'I'm a writer too,' I said.

'I know.'

'I don't mean magazine articles,' I said. 'I've written stories for the little magazines.'

'Yes,' she said. 'I've read your work.'

'You're a liar.'

'I did too. I remember a story called The Jugglers. It was terrific.'

'You're marvellous,' I said.

'You shouldn't be jealous of Max,' she told me. 'You're a better writer than he'll ever be.'

'Thank you. What's your name?'

'Guinevere.'

'You're a liar.'

'No,' she said. 'That's my name.'

For some reason this was hilarious, Guinevere, and I opened my mouth to laugh, but laughing, remembered that when I laugh I show my bad back teeth. I stopped laughing. 'You're a queen,' I told her.

She ignored this. 'Tell me,' she said. 'Why haven't you written more stories? Was it marriage that stopped you?'

'How do you know I'm married?'

'Your wife is Jane Melville, or used to be. Our children are in the same kindergarten.'

A leaden sobriety sank me. A friend of Jane. Our children in kindergarten. Jane must have told her about my stories: Jane always told everyone. It was because of Jane, not because of my stories, that she was talking to me.

'You didn't answer my question,' she said. 'Was it the responsibilities of marriage and earning a living?'

'I suppose so,' I said. 'But the fact is, I'm writing a novel.'

'That's what all non-writing writers say.'

'But I mean it,' I told her. 'I've quit my job and I've imported my old mother from Ireland to look after the kids. Jane is going out to work next week and now I'm going to finish it.'

'That's wonderful.' She stood up and in the small bathroom she was almost touching me. She looked at me, waiting, a frank, lustful stare in her myopic eyes. I put my arms around her, tongued her, felt her tongue me, ran my hands down her thighs and stood here, rocking back and forth in the narrow space, kissing, becoming excited, wanting to lock the door.

'Somebody in there?' a voice said.

We separated. She looked at me as though I should do something, so I went to the door, opened it and said; 'Go away, will you?'

It was Pat Gallery. And a few feet behind him was Jane, talking to Louise. Confused, I came out of the bathroom, closed the door and whispered to Gallery: 'Go away, will you, Pat? There's somebody in there.'

'You mean you?' Gallery said.

'No. Somebody else.'

'What are you up to, Joxer Daly?' Gallery said, beginning to laugh.

I dragged him away from the door. 'Shh. There's a girl in there.'

'Well, glory be.'

'Shut up.' I turned back to look at Jane and Louise. They were watching me. At that moment the bathroom door opened and the girl came out behind me. Adding one and one and the bathroom, my wife did a doubletake, which, for horror and shock, would have done justice to a Theda Bara silent.

'O, there you are,' the girl said to me. 'How about us going to the kitchen and getting a drink?'

(Summing up for the defence: 'Look, darling, I went into the bathroom, the door wasn't locked, and there was this girl, she knows you and the kids, she said she was nearly finished in there and asked me to wait. Of course, there was nothing to it, just some talk and then Pat Gallery knocked.')

'Are you coming?' the girl said.

(Anyway, what was Jane getting excited about, the whole thing was an accident: she was blaming me without knowing the facts.) Virtuous, wronged, mistrusted, I took the girl's arm, led her past Jane and Louise, through the living-room and into the kitchen. 'What will you have, Guinevere?'

'Vodka,' she said. 'With anything. Tell me. If you believed in something would you be prepared to give up everything for it?'

'Believe in what?' I said, pouring vodka into smudged tumblers.

'Well, in your writing, for instance.'

'Absolutely.'

'I mean, would you give up everything. Family – children even?'

'Of course.'

'Then why didn't you do it?'

'What is this? A Congressional Committee?'

'O, listen to me,' she said, removing her glasses and staring at me with naked myopic intensity. 'I want to inspire you. Or perhaps I want you to inspire me. I'm a writer too. I think talented people like you and I should have courage to do the difficult thing. We've got to be ruthless, don't you think?'

Ruthless. There was that word again. So she wanted us to inspire each other to give up our families, did she? By God, I'd inspire her. Drunkenly, I peered up, and saw the cord which hung down from the light bulb. I'd give her ruthless. I reached up and pulled the cord, pulling darkness down upon us, fumbling for her, finding her, rocking to and fro in that narrow space as we kissed each other, inspiring each other.

'Brendan?'

I froze.

'Brendan!'

It was Louise's voice. I turned towards the kitchen door and saw a woman's figure in silhouette. 'Light's broken in here,' I lied.

'Jane saw you put that light out,' Louise's voice said. 'She's leaving.'

With the girl I moved from the darkness of inspiration into the dull living-room light. Louise said: 'Brendan, you should be ashamed of yourself. And you too, Jean.'

The girl shrugged, put on her glasses and smiled at me. Louise walked away.

'Jean?' I said. 'I thought your name was Guinevere?'

'No, Jean Revere. Brendan, what are you going to do?'

With her glasses on, she was not pretty. I thought of Jane, weeping, running out to a taxi. This girl was phony – a fool. What was I doing?

'What are you going to do?' the girl asked again.

'Good night,' I told her and turned away, pushing through the living-room crowd. Pat Gallery, loud and jovial, came up to me in the hall. 'Hey, Brendan –'

'Seen Jane?'

'She just left. Brendan –'

I did not get my coat. I dodged around Gallery, opened the apartment door, ran down the staircase in great jolting leaps, knees buckling as I reached the ground floor. Down the front steps into the empty street that was wet with rain, slick, warm with a hint of summer. She was not there. Perhaps, even now, she was signalling for a cab up there where the street intersected with Eighth Avenue? I rushed past a line of parked cars, running in a winded, gasping burst of speed until I reached the intersection. But she was not there.

Aimless as a loose jib, I came about in flapping confusion. Where now? Opposite me was the White Horse Tavern and as I stared drunkenly at its black-painted façade and old-fashioned windows, reminiscent of Irish and Scottish pubs, I was caught in a sudden wash of nostalgia. I forgot Jane, I forgot the present. Over there, just across the street, was the simple provincial life I had left behind. Over there Ted Ormsby waited, pint in hand, ready for an evening's talk. Over there. Home. Across the street.

I stepped off the sidewalk in stumbling haste. I went towards the windows and looked in.

Two boys wearing yellow mohair sweaters leaned against the bar, inward turned in longing looks of love. A bull-faced woman with bangs, drunk in a corner, disputing bitterly with a bearded fellow who wore a black shirt and a silver medallion on a long silver neck chain. A woman in a white nurse's coat drank gin with a small Indian man. And seated near the window, an elderly garbage scavenger, mad, muttering, raised his matted head: met my stare.

I drew back. That ache for home, that wash of boggy sentiment, was boozy and false as the dreams of old Kerry men, downing two-for-thirty shots of gasoline bourbon in those few Third Avenue bars which were not yet the martini haunts of *New Yorker* sentimentalists. Home was here: it was on Riverside Drive where my mother guarded my sleeping children, where Jane, weeping and furious, would soon arrive.

Uncertainly, I came about again. Back down the street a girl in glasses wanted me to inspire her to desert her husband and children; back there a drunken doctor called for literary ruthlessness; a film producer turned all of life into a literary reference; an advertising copywriter lectured on 'creative fiction'. The literary life in New York was a vast charade in which people pretended to be other than they were. Their ambitions remained private fantasies: they had neither real beliefs nor the courage to implement them. Was I one of them? Was I really serious about my manuscript? And if I was, why was I drunk, kissing strange girls, then running through the streets in search of my wife? Why wasn't I working tonight? Was I really prepared to be a Flaubert, labouring a life away at Croisset in an endless search for the right words; was I prepared to face the future of Gide's lonely old writer man in the endless solitude of some hotel room? Was I ready at last to redeem my long ago boast, my dripping scream of defiance under the school fountain? Or was I just an envious journalist, a drunken, self-deceiving fool?

O, no, I am not a drunken fool. I have given up my job. I have burned certain boats. Next week I start again. This time, I shall finish the book and go down into the literary marketplace for whatever fate awaits me. I will not fail. I will put my life in order. I will be ruthless.

I stumbled into Eighth Avenue, semaphoring wildly. A cab careened in a half circle and came to a stop ahead. I ran after it.

At eleven, Mrs Tierney shut off the television, said her prayers, then got into bed with a book. It was a novel by Neville Shute, the sort of story Brendan would turn up his nose at, but a good yarn all the same. She had picked it up because it was about Australia and now she lay back holding it at arm's length, reading about Australia and the atom bomb. It was very hot in the bedroom: it was always hot here – Screaming with laughter down on the strand, two children ran through brackish seaweed in a wide zigzag towards the fine sand and the sea. The tall dark man, whooping like a Red Indian, chased them, all three growing smaller and smaller from the dune where she stood, far away now, just three black specks running close to the frothy burst of long breakers. She knelt down and opened her picnic basket; it was a new wicker one and she was proud of it. She laid out the little primus stove, the white enamelled cups and plates, the knives and forks, the condiment jars, all of it a set. She unwrapped her fruit cake from its wax paper cover, then the ham sandwiches, aware that he was watching her. It was a joke: he was only twenty; he was Grattan's cousin and going on for the priesthood. Of course she never let on that she knew he had a secret crush on her. She leaned across him to put down the plate of sandwiches and as she did her skirt caught on the tripod of the primus and rucked up to show her stocking top and her bare thigh. She disengaged the hem of her skirt from the primus tripod but could not help looking over at him to see what effect the sight of her leg had had, could not help teasing him when she saw his face, red with blood. 'What's the matter, Denis?' she asked, and chucked him under the chin. He pulled back as though she had hit him, then, suddenly, caught her by the shoulders, threw her down on the heathery dune (the heather scratched her neck) and kissed her, rolling and rolling with her there in the grass under the blue picnic sky. And what would have happened if the sky had not changed, clouding dark as though in anger at what it saw, spitting down the first drops of a shower of rain? 'Denis, stop, stop,' she whispered, breaking free. 'It's raining. They'll be back.' Fear made him relax his grip but she did not move again, she lay beside him, she pretended to be in a faint for he was handsome and, although she knew Grattan and the children would be back any minute, she wanted him to kiss her again and he did. At first, she lay limp but then, unable to stop herself, kissed him back in that lustful way. It was not Denis she was kissing, it was Rory, her own son Rory who is dead, who was not on the dune but down there, a wee boy, playing with his Daddy on the strand. I am dreaming. A dream . . . God forgive me, it was my own son I was kissing in that dream. The awful things I have done in dreams.

The book by Neville Shute had fallen on the floor. She leaned out of bed and picked it up. *On the Beach.* I dreamed of a beach. Real life sins are bad enough but the sins in dreams are terrors. What kind of a horrible person am I?

She lay, looking up at the white ceiling, listening to the long screams of an ambulance on Broadway. Why do I dream that dream, so hot and pleasant and full of sin, and always some nightmare in the end? Why did I lead Denis on that day, I was the older one, I was the occasion of his sin. Only the rain saved us. Five minutes more and Grattan and the children would have been on top of us. I said a prayer of thanks for the rain and then I remembered that I was making God my accomplice. I could not pray after that. I could only ask His forgiveness but will He ever forgive me, will He? And Denis, the next summer when I met him in Dublin, saying in that cold voice in the student digs that it was because of me he had lost his vocation. I took a soul from God's service, yes I did. And He paid me back, the year after that I had a miss, three misses in a row and until Brendan was born I thought I would never have another. Seven years between them. And all that's happened since – Rory killed, Grattan's illness, Sheila running off, Brendan and his unbaptized children – all that is paying me back. Even Moira. You took her from me and put her in a convent. The priests are wrong: You are not all-forgiving. You never forgive.

There was a noise at the front door. She heard the door open, then shut with a slam. Quickly, she reached over and turned off the little bedlamp. Footsteps went down the corridor to the kitchen. Suddenly it came to her that those footsteps might not be Jane's or Brendan's. She thought of the children's open bedroom door: what if they saw a stranger and screamed?

Nervous, but not afraid (for she kept her mind on the children) she got up, put on her dressing-gown and went to look.

False alarm. It was Jane: there was no sign of Brendan.

Jane did not see her. Alone in the kitchen, Jane hurried about and as Mrs Tierney watched from the darkness of the corridor, she put two scoops of ice cream in a glass dessert bowl, opened a tin of peaches and put two peach halves on top of the ice cream, then took a can of Reddi-Whip from the refrigerator and gunned a jet of whipped cream over the peaches. To the cupboard now for a jar of maraschino cherries, four of which she used as decoration on the cream. She took a spoon, sat down in front of the concoction and ate three gulping spoonfuls of it. Then stopped, looked across the kitchen at the refrigerator. Her head dropped. Her shoulders trembled. She began to weep.

I should go back to bed, Mrs Tierney told herself; this is no business of mine. But despite her resolve, she moved towards the kitchen door. 'What's the matter, dear?'

Jane stiffened, but did not turn around. 'Oh, it's you,' she said, still looking at her plate. 'How . . . how are the children?'

'They were grand. No trouble. How was your party?'

'So-so.'

'I heard you come in,' Mrs Tierney said. 'Only I wasn't sure if it was you. Where's Brendan?'

Jane masticated another mouthful of dessert before answering. 'He's still at the party.'

Not a good sign, Mrs Tierney thought. Better leave her be. 'Well, dear, I'll leave you to your supper.'

Still, Jane did not look at her. She crouched over her plate, a pretty child in a backless black dress, a dark-skinned child, her dark hair fluffed out in a bouffant helmet, her shoulders hunched, scapula bones sticking out slightly as she bent to devour another mouthful of the dessert. She wore a necklace of jagged yellow stones, an antique silver bracelet and a thin platinum wedding ring. She seemed too young to wear that ring. She stuck her spoon in the ice cream mound, scooping and assembling pieces of fruit. She raised the spoon to her mouth but as she did, she paused, and, for the first time, turned to look at her mother-in-law. 'Good night,' she said in a sharp, dismissing voice and as Mrs Tierney met that glance she saw in Jane's eyes the spiteful look of a child just before it bangs its dolly's head on the floor. Frightened, Mrs Tierney turned and went out of the kitchen door.

'Wait,' Jane said.

They were going to talk after all. Woman to woman: it would be all right.

'Do you know your son well?' Jane said. 'I mean, do you know things about him that I don't know?'

'What do you mean?'

'You've known him longer than me, that's what I mean.'

'But only when he was growing up,' Mrs Tierney said. 'Sure, he's nearly a stranger to me now after all these years.'

'Was he selfish when he was a boy?'

'Well, yes, I suppose so. He was always very wrapped up in himself, even as a child.'

'He still is,' Jane said. 'He only thinks of himself. Sometimes I think he hates me.'

As she said this, mascara, mixed with tears, ran from the corners of her eyes. Mrs Tierney offered a clean handkerchief from the pocket of her dressing-gown. It was accepted.

'Tell me,' Jane said. 'What would *you* do if you found your husband necking with another woman?'

Mrs Tierney thought of Grattan, of his dislike of being kissed or touched. She saw him put his face up for a duty peck: felt the brush of his heavy moustache. Grattan kissing some strange woman? It was silly. She laughed.

'What's so funny?' Jane said, staring at her.

'Well,' Mrs Tierney said. 'My husband was very prim and proper. I couldn't imagine him doing that.'

'And Brendan? Could you imagine him?'

'Brendan?' Wee Brendy? Yet he was her blood: she had imagined worse of Sheila, Sheila who would not hear no about that drunken boy friend of hers. 'I'm not sure,' she said. 'After all, that's a side of him I wouldn't know, would I?'

'But you're not surprised?'

'No, I suppose not.'

'Well, I am,' Jane said. 'Who does he think he is? I've got a good mind to take the kids and walk out.'

Mrs Tierney looked down on that dark head: there was no compassion in her look. 'And why?' she asked. 'Is he not worth fighting for?'

'He's changed,' Jane said, beginning to weep again. 'He never used to be like this, who does he think he is, it's not as if he were great in bed, I'm a lot better in bed than he is, he's got no reason to treat me this way, there are lots of men who're crazy about me, I could have done this to him a dozen times. If he thinks I'm going to stand for it, he's out of his mind. I won't, I won't.'

Weeping, her whole body convulsed, she laid her head down on the table. The ice cream mess was getting in her hair. Tentatively, Mrs Tierney advanced her hand to move the bowl, but stopped. Imagine discussing being in bed with your husband in that way. They have no dignity, Americans. But everything is different here. There is no law that says they must stick it out in a marriage. Would I have stayed with Grattan if there were no laws to hold me? Maybe not.

'Jane,' she said. 'Come on, Jane, pull yourself together. Here now, sit up. Would you like a damp cloth for your face? Wait, I'll get one.'

In the bathroom she wet a clean face towel. As she wrung it out she heard the front door open. Jane must have heard it too for the sobbing stopped. Mrs Tierney stood undecided, cloth in hand, wishing she were home, not here. It was their private affair. She let the cloth drop in the sink and quietly left the bathroom, intending to go to her own room. But in the corridor Brendan lurched past her, knocked on the bedroom door. 'Jane? Jane? Darling, let me in, I'm sorry ... Jane? ... Want to talk to you ... Jane? ... Open up!'

His good blue suit was rumpled, his black knitted tie was half undone, his white shirt unbuttoned at the collar. His dark hair was tousled more than usual and his face seemed pale and ill. He was drunk. He turned from the door and went swaying into the living-room. Mrs Tierney went towards her own room but, as she did, her footsteps sounded on the bare corridor boards. In the living-room, Brendan turned around and saw her. 'Mamma?' he said. 'Come here a minute.'

'No, Brendan, it's very late. Good night.'

'Mamma?'

*

'Mamma?' I said, and there she was, in her old grey bonnet, with a hair net on it, waiting old Dobbin for the fray, in her old blue dressing-gown, waiting for a dressing-down –

– And I, pouring whisky, was Macbeth, Macbeth who heeded the muses' song sung by lying witches, Macbeth alone on his battlements, the hour late, the owls crying, Macbeth who, disturbed by his lady's strange behaviour, summons a Wayting Gentlewoman. 'Come here,' I said to her. 'Come here, my Wayting Gentlewoman.'

'What are you talking about, Brendan?'

'Come here, mother dear, mother o' mine. I want to talk to you. Unless I can set my house in order, all plans are void.'

I poured whisky, drank some and went to the window. Out there across the Hudson I saw the far Jersey shore. Over at Palisades Park the fairground lights were out. I felt my Birnam Wood had come. 'Tell me,' I said. 'Have you spoken with my lady?'

'O, stop it, Brendan. You're squiffy.'

'Squiffy?' I found the outdated slang hilarious. I roared my laughter, the hour late, the owls crying. 'I am drunk, mother, drunk,' I said. 'My wife has locked me out of the nuptial chamber. Now, why did she do that, do you think?'

'You should know why.'

'Ah. So you and Jane have had a little chat?'

'Brendan, this is none of my business. I'm going to bed.'

'Fortunately, you have a bed. I have none.'

'Do you want me to put some blankets on the sofa?'

The heavy liquid rolled in my glass. I drank from the goblet. Dulled, drunk, much drunker than an hour ago and why? I had not had any drinks since the kitchen kissing. 'No,' I said. 'No blankets. Macbeth hath murdered sleep.'

'What are you talking about? You're squiffy, you should be ashamed of yourself. Now, will I make up a bed, or do you want to try Jane again?'

'No. Not Jane. No bed.'

'Then good night. And I'd stop drinking if I were you.'

'Wait,' I said. 'Please wait. I want . . .' (And what did I want, I wanted someone to talk to, I wanted to explain, turning over new leaf, you see, mother, listen to me, Mamma dear, I want to talk to you, lay my head upon your breast) . . . 'Please,' I said. 'It's still early.'

'It's not early, it's late. And tomorrow I have to go to early Mass.'

'Ah yes. Mass. If only Mass were the answer.'

'Mass *is* the answer.'

'Ah, Mamma, Mamma. There are far fewer things in heaven

than are dreamt of in your philosophy.'

'How do you know?' she said. 'Who told you what there is in heaven?'

'Nobody. That's the trouble. That's why I've made writing my religion.'

She smiled. 'You call that a religion?'

'Well, it's an act of faith that by my own efforts, some part of me will survive the undertaker.'

'Brendan, that's no religion, that's pure vanity. Would you tell me something? Since you haven't done anything great until now, what makes you so sure you'll do something great in the future?'

'Trust you, mother dear. Trust you to tear me down.'

'And trust you to blow yourself up. Who do you think you are? Shakespeare? And what does it matter?'

'Of course it matters.'

'Not to God, it doesn't.'

What was the use? I went to the sideboard and made a fresh drink. 'It's not my night,' I said. 'Jane locked in her bedroom, and you and I in an argument.'

'I'm sorry, Brendan. But you started it, not me.'

'All right, I started it. But do you ever think of my problems, Mamma? Do you think it's easy to go through life not knowing why I'm here or what I'm here for?'

'No, I suppose it isn't,' she said. 'But who's to blame for that? Your father and I did our best to teach you why.'

'Stop it,' I said. 'It's no use our talking, is it? There's no communication between us any more. Let's face it, we don't even live in the same world.'

'O, Brendan,' she said. She looked as if she would cry, and drunk and angry as I was, I felt like crying too.

'I'm sorry,' I said. 'It's not your fault. It's my fault.'

'If I were you,' she said. 'I'd stop thinking about yourself for a minute and think of your wife. I'd go and apologize to her.'

'But she won't let me in.'

'Try again.'

I raised my glass to drink.

'And stop drinking,' she said. 'Brendan, what's going to happen to you if you drink like that?'

'I'm stopping,' I told her. 'Now. And if I haven't done anything great until now, just you wait and see. Yes, wait, my old

Wayting Gentlewoman. And Max Bronstein and Jackson-Bloody-Clayburn and those orange-assed beauties of theirs can wait too. I'll show them.'

'Brendan!'

'I'm sorry.' I put the whisky glass on the side table, took off my tie and my jacket. 'Tomorrow,' I said, very grave, very drunk, 'I will have a hangover that will take all day to cure. Jane will sulk; the children will be noisy. But to-morrow will be my last wasted day. On Sunday, I'll be a changed man. You'll see. From now on, no more wasted days. Now, I'm going to get some sleep.'

'Will I get you a blanket?'

'No.' I went to her, took her in my arms and touched my forehead against her. 'Good night,' I said. 'And turn the lights off, will you?'

I lay down on the sofa, unlaced my shoes and put my feet up. I saw her by the door, old and heavy in her blue woollen dressing-gown, her grey hair in a hair net. Happy in her faith.

'Good night, Brendan.'

The light went out. From the window I saw the reflection of the street lamps on Riverside Drive. Beyond the street lamps, the night river flowed down to the sea. I sailed on that dark river, sailed to sleep.

*

Jane woke at three and found herself lying face down on the bed, still wearing her party dress. He was not in the bed – he had gone out, back to that girl. He had left her. An anger, so terrible it made sense of nonsense, sent her out into the corridor looking for him, wanting to kill him. There were no lights on in the apartment. He had gone. How could she kill him if he had gone? The injustice of this made her want to weep, but she had no time for weeping. She ran into the kitchen – wreck of her ice cream dessert, chairs awry, nobody – then down the hall, fumbling for the living-room switch. One Christmas her parents had gone off to Bermuda, leaving her and her sister Barbara behind in school in Poughkeepsie. She had a terror of being left behind.

Yet now, as she switched the light on, she saw his jacket on the floor, his shoes on the rug and him on the sofa, asleep. He had not run off. He moaned as she put the light on, muttered something in a talking-in-his-sleep voice. Dreaming of that girl perhaps? 'Brendan,' she said. 'Brendan?' She shook him.

He sat up as though she had said the building was on fire. 'What's wrong?'

'Brendan, you know what's wrong.'

'O,' he said. 'That.'

She stared at him. She began to cry.

'Look,' he said. 'I'm sorry. I don't know what got into me, but whatever it was, it's not important. It was Max, I think. I was angry at Max and so I just got mad at everyone.'

'You didn't seem very mad at that girl.'

'I'm sorry, darling. I *am* sorry.'

She knew it had begun, the litany of atonement. They made their ejaculations and responses as devoutly as monk and nun, knowing all the extravagant declarations by heart, confident that they could pray back into their marriage its act of faith, its bond of submission, its vows of obedience and trust. Within minutes they were hovering in a choice of two rituals which normally terminated such devotions – an act of love or a mutual analysis of faults. And tonight, because it was late, because he had been drinking, because she had seen him kiss another woman and must reassert her sovereignty, they moved at once to the first rite, her hands stripping him of his shirt, his hands raising her up, undoing the zipper of her dress, easing the dress from her shoulders, her hands at his belt buckle, his hands at her bra, her hands on his genitals, his hands on her thighs, hands on waistbands, hands on flesh, shut eyes, mouth on mouth, bodies moving in a fevered trance as though the act itself were an act of communion, a taking unto each other of all faults, all transgressions, all blame.

But soon she was bored. He was so predictable. Sex to him was a certain foreplay, one position and a ritual termination by lighting a cigarette. He was Anglo-Saxon in his attitudes: never the dark ravisher. Yet the act of sex was the only solution she knew for rows, tears and disappointments. And, once satisfied, he would be ready for the more subtle inquisition she intended.

And so, as they lay smoking cigarettes on the living-room floor, naked and warm and quiet, she moved the litany into its second stage; beginning with the oath of allegiance.

'I love you, Brendan.'

'Love you too.'

'Do you? Would you really rather sleep with me than with a

new girl?'

'Of course.'

'Then why did you neck with that girl tonight?'

'I was high. Besides, I told you, I was mad at Max.'

'Were you jealous because he had that fancy dish with him?'

'What dish?'

'You know very well what dish. I saw you talking to her. That model.'

'Was she a model?'

'Why? Are you interested?'

'Of course not.'

'You *are* interested. You wanted to sleep with her and, because you couldn't, you turned to that Revere creature.'

'Don't be silly.'

'But it's true,' she said. 'It's true.'

And so, guiltily (and to shut her up) he began to make love to her again, the tempo slower, his only desire to please. And she, her mission half-accomplished, allowed herself to relax and be rewarded, enjoyed it as she had not enjoyed his frantic first time. He was no dark ravisher, no black curls of male hair irritated the nipples of her breasts. But at least, it was being done unconventionally on the living-room floor in the dark, in the middle of the night.

'What was that?' he said.

They listened. He jumped up. 'One of the kids?'

It was a heavy footstep, not a child's. It went to the bathroom. The bathroom door shut. Caught, they moved around in the dark, grabbing at clothes, furtive as burglars –

A bathroom noise, thunderous in the night silence. The door opened. Mrs Tierney appeared briefly in the light from the bathroom, snapped the light off, then went back up the corridor to her own room. Her door shut.

'Goddammit,' Brendan said. 'Just when we were getting somewhere.'

'It's like living in a goldfish bowl,' she said.

'Come here.'

She dropped her clothes and crossed the room, moving deliberately in front of the window. She looked down at the street lamps, the empty street, feeling a faint disappointment. No feral stranger stood on the corner to admire her surprisingly ripe body; no dark ravisher dropped his cigar and stared up, eyes hot with desire. But perhaps she did not see him; perhaps he lurked beyond the line of trees overlooking the river, watching?

'Jane, for christsake, will you come away from the window?'

'Coming,' she said. But she turned again towards the window, showing the stranger all of her, teasing him there beyond the trees and (without realizing it) teasing Brendan too, for he came up behind her and pulled her away from the window, wincing as she suddenly bit his hand.

'For christsake, Jane, that hurts.'

'Then flog me,' she said. 'Beat me.'

But of course he did not: he never understood such things. He kissed and fondled her conventionally, and in a few minutes reached across her, groping for his cigarettes. Why was he such a lousy lover? On Monday, she would be working in an office downtown. What sort of men did they have in Louise's office?

He slapped her on the bottom. 'Did anyone ever tell you what a lovely fat ass you have?'

'It's not fat.'

'It is.'

'Anyway, I don't have to take my glasses off before I kiss a man,' she said. 'What did you two do in that bathroom?'

'Nothing. We just talked.'

It was a lie, of course, but who cared. She wasn't even jealous any more. She moved her head and looked out at the street lamps' reflection. Beyond those lights, in the dark, some mysterious dark ravisher lay in wait. He would carry his prey down to the waiting boat, his hand over his victim's mouth as the boat slipped down the night river to the sea. What sort of men worked with Louise? Monday she would wear her yellow silk to the office. She looked young in it.

A park is a world fenced off from all others. At the playground in Central Park near the Tierney children's kindergarten, Mrs MacAnaspey, by far the most regular of the bench-sitters, had spent two weeks observing the comings and goings of the newcomer. The children she knew already. The mother, a beatnik type who used to accompany them, she had long disapproved of.

But the newcomer was more promising. And so, on a warm day when all the benches near the playground were taken, she saw Mrs Tierney approach, then hesitate as the two children ran off to the swings. Mrs MacAnaspey removed a batch of newspapers from the bench beside her and beckoned to indicate that she held a seat.

As Mrs Tierney sat down, Mrs MacAnaspey was forced to shift slightly on the bench and so, in her lap, Bubbles was disturbed. His little eyes, invisible beneath the long white hair which covered his face, sought the cause of this annoyance. He voiced his protest.

Mrs Tierney, smiling her thanks, saw Mrs MacAnaspey's ringed hand move to comfort the little white dog which lay like a muff in her lap. A widow she was, surely, in her uniform of black shantung coat, black chiffon dress, black stockings and shoes, and a necklace of small pearls on her raddled neck.

'Now, Bubbles,' Mrs MacAnaspey said. 'Be good.' She turned to Mrs Tierney. 'Warm day, isn't it?' she began.

'Yes, it's a lovely day. What a nice little dog you have.'

'Yeah, he's a sweetheart. Aren't you, Bubbles?'

'It's a toy terrier, isn't it?'

'No,' Mrs MacAnaspey said. 'This dog is a Maltese dog. That's the name of the breed. Not Maltese Terrier but Maltese Dog. That's a very old kind of dog, it used to be the pet of royalty. If you go to the Museum of Art, you can see this dog in those old Spanish paintings sitting on the lap of kings and queens. Bubbles is a royal dog.'

'O, is that so?'

'Yes, and he's a great little guy, he is,' Mrs MacAnaspey said, fondling Bubbles' head. 'Those your grandchildren over on the swings?'

'Yes.'

'I used to see them with the mother,' Mrs MacAnaspey said. 'I know everybody comes in this park. This guy,' she said, fondling Bubbles' head. 'He likes this place. And he's the boss, you know. I mean, what he wants, I want. If he eats, I eat. If he don't eat, I don't eat. You're Irish, right?'

'Yes, I am.'

'I heard you talkin' to the kids the other day, I said to Bubbles, she's Irish. My late husband was Irish from Boston. I'm German stock, both sides. You born in this country?'

'O no, I just came here a month ago.'

'No kidding. You hear that, Bubbles, she just came over a month ago, how about that, Bubbles? Your husband come too?'

'No. He's dead.'

'Yeah, the men go first, right? And kids, you might as well forget. My daughter lives in California. Last week she calls long distance to say hello. Before that, we hadn't heard from her since Easter, had we, Bubbles? So she calls to say hello but she wants me to ship her out something from Hammacher Schlemmer. They call when they want something, right, Bubbles? See that man over there, the one with the scarf around his neck?'

'Yes, he comes here a lot, doesn't he?'

'Yeah, he lives right across the street. Three coronaries he's had since two years. You visiting here, or you plan to stay?'

'O, I'm planning to stay. My daughter-in-law is working now, so I have my hands full with these children.'

'They work you hard, eh? She looks tired, don't she, Bubbles?'

'It's this heat,' Mrs Tierney said. 'I'm afraid I'm not used to it.'

'Heat, she says. Hear that, Bubbles? Beginning of May she finds hot. Wait till summer. Hot. You'll die.'

Bubbles sat up, peered at Mrs Tierney. He sniffed her and his tongue, no bigger than a primrose petal, slipped out and licked her wrist.

'You like her,' Mrs MacAnaspey said, delightedly. 'Well, if you like, I like. Eh, Bubbles?'

So they became friends.

With Mrs Katherine Duke, the introduction was made through Lisa. Lisa was running with her ball, bouncing it, and it bounced right into Mrs Duke's leather-brown face, lodging itself in the blinkers of the sun reflector strapped around her dyed chestnut head. Mrs Tierney came up and apologized at once. Mrs Duke had already noticed that Mrs Tierney did not allow the children to run around a person's bench yelling their heads off the way their mother used to. Neither did she allow them to cover themselves with mucky sand, nor did she buy them candy and ice cream every hour as some young mothers did. Mrs Duke, who did not discuss her own age, even with herself, knew very well that the society of younger people made you feel younger, but confided to Mrs Tierney that somehow she felt more at home with the manners of an older generation. Her only daughter was married to a man in General Foods and lived abroad. Her daughter, she told Mrs Tierney, thought of her as a contemporary, and called her Kitty, and sometimes, as Mrs Tierney listened to this line of talk, she found herself wondering if Mrs Duke was not the youngest mother ever to conceive a child. Certainly, she could not, by her own account, have been much over fifteen at the time. Mr Duke lived in Pittsburgh where Mrs Duke had lived until the divorce. She showed Mrs Tierney his photograph once in a clipping from a Pittsburgh newspaper. He looked quite old.

Mrs Duke only came to the playground on sunny days, but on these days she came early and stayed late. Her lunch, which she brought with her, invariably consisted of a carton of yoghurt, four dried figs and a vitamin pill. She told Mrs Tierney that she did Swedish exercises two hours each day and that at night she covered her face and neck with a special paste. She had a man friend who took her to concerts and ballets and who sometimes sat with her in the park on Saturdays. He was very tanned himself and were it not for his grey hair he could have passed for a boy in his twenties. He owned an antiques store in the East Sixties and was, according to Mrs Duke, a person with the most exquisite taste.

Mrs Duke did not speak to Mrs MacAnaspey. Once, when Mrs MacAnaspey observed Mrs Tierney in conversation with Mrs Duke, she remarked to Bubbles in a loud voice that some people should act their age.

The one park regular who was on speaking terms with all the others was Mrs Hofstra, a plump, maternal person who wore odd ceramic necklaces designed and executed by her own hand. Her husband, an automobile dealer, had done very well and as they now had a full-time maid, Mrs Hofstra, at the age of fifty-five, had embarked on a painting class, a creative writing class and a course in ceramics. However, each Monday, Wednesday and Friday afternoon she interrupted her multiple studies to bring her grandson to the park so that her daughter could attend social welfare classes at Memorial Hospital. Mrs Hofstra was the first park regular to nod to Mrs Tierney and the only one who did not seem exclusively interested in talking about herself. Mrs Hofstra wanted to know Mrs Tierney's impressions of America, her views on Ireland, her experiences as a mother and her opinion of Picasso. Mrs Hofstra was interested in Picasso.

'Such a creative person,' she said. 'At eighty he has the body of a young man. And do you know why, Mrs Tierney? Because his creativity has kept him young. There's a close connexion between creative activity and keeping young, you know.'

'It's a pity we can't all be geniuses then,' Mrs Tierney commented.

'Ah, but you miss the point,' Mrs Hofstra said. 'I mean there are such wonderful creative opportunities all around us. I had no idea myself, I was just like you, until I investigated. Now, take this painting class I go to. We do mostly abstract work, and do you know, some wonderful spontaneous explosions have come out of our group. We have painters who never even knew they were creative until they tried it. And it's the same thing in our creative writing class. My dear, you've no idea how much joy there can be in sitting down and really *writing*. Now, that might very well be your forte, your son being a writer. After all, genius is inherited, you know.'

'Well, not from me,' Mrs Tierney said. ''Deed it's all I can do to write a letter.'

'But how do you know until you try?' Mrs Hofstra asked. 'After all, take Picasso. Supposing he'd never tried? He'd be an old man today, quite unknown, living in some Barcelona slum.'

'But isn't he an old man anyway?' Mrs Tierney wanted to know. 'I thought you said he was eighty?'

'Ah, but he's not old, he's young,' Mrs Hofstra said. 'He looks young and he feels young and he's still producing. That's what counts.'

'But he's eighty,' Mrs Tierney said. 'He may feel young and all that but he's an old man. He's not long for this world, no matter how he feels.'

'Negative thinking, my dear. Creation is the opposite of death, isn't that so? If you do creative things you rejuvenate yourself, now doesn't that make sense?'

'But supposing you have no gifts for it?' Mrs Tierney said. 'I mean, most people are just ordinary.'

'Ah, but how do you *know*?' Mrs Hofstra asked triumphantly. 'There are wells of creativity in nearly everyone. I can tell you in my own case, I was astonished.'

Mrs Tierney was reminded of Brendan's blather. They saw the truth who wanted to. She liked Mrs Hofstra, though. Mrs MacAnaspey and Mrs Duke were good crack to listen to: Mrs Hofstra you could talk to. And God knows, she needed someone to talk to this last while.

It had been three weeks since that drunken party and she must say Brendan had kept his nose to the grindstone ever since. He was hardly ever in the house, always down at that room he worked in. Jane too was out at work now, and it was fare thee well Sweet Morgan's Braes to any notion that Mrs Tierney was over here for a holiday. It was like having four children in the flat instead of two.

'But they ask you to do too much,' said Mrs Hofstra who had inquired at length about Mrs Tierney's duties and activities. 'You have no time for yourself.'

'Time for myself? O, sure after my husband died I had far too much time for myself. The days are short now, that's the main thing.'

'Of course, artists can be very demanding,' Mrs Hofstra said. 'Still, I envy you living with your son and his wife. You must have such interesting conversations.'

Mrs Tierney looked over at the playground area. Conversations? Little Liam was at the top of the slide. Lisa was on a swing. Conversations? Supper with the children and into my own room with the telly by eight at night. Conversations. Do you think Lisa's getting a cold? Would you be an angel and run

Liam's bath for me? Conversations. Are you tired, Mamma? I hope the children haven't been too much for you. We're going out, okay? Thank you then, we won't be late.

Her first cousin, Frank Finnerty, she must ring up. Some night when she was not tired, next week perhaps. Meanwhile, the only conversations she had were in the park. But that was nice: it was so nice coming up the path, seeing all the ladies there, wondering which of them you would grace with your company.

'Well, look who's here, Bubbles,' Mrs MacAnaspey would say. 'It's that lady you like. How are you, dear? Warm today, isn't it?'

'Shocking.'

'Yet it's only seventy-five in the shade,' Mrs MacAnaspey said. 'It's not the heat, it's the humidity.'

Seventy-five degrees in May, already far warmer than it ever was at home, and all her clothes were Winter and Spring. She would have to get a couple of summer frocks. Money, that was awkward here. At home, little as she had, it was hers, she had the spending of it. But here, Brendan would hand her twenty dollars to buy food then wave away the change as if she were some servant looking for a tip. It was mortifying. She sat down beside Mrs MacAnaspey and took Lisa's ball and Liam's water pistol before sending the children off to the swings. There was something dead about the air in this city. She always felt short of breath.

'Those kids,' Mrs MacAnaspey said. 'They got better manners since you took over.'

On the past two weekends Jane, home from her office, had swooped down on Lisa and Liam as if they were orphans, playing games with them, giving them treats, undoing all the discipline Mrs Tierney had taught them during the week. But this motherly attention never lasted more than a few hours. Once out of motherhood, Jane did not want back in. Not full time, anyway. She makes me laugh. Going on, on the blink of tears, because I made them pick up their clothes and put them on the chair. 'Do you not think they're too young for that?' said she. 'Too young?' I said. 'They're never too young to learn good habits.' And about their feeding problems, as she calls it. There are no feeding problems among the black babies in Africa, are there? As my old aunt used to say: 'If you don't know the road to your mouth, you can want.' O, it's hot. This air is dead as bad breath.

'Of course it's the neighbourhood that makes a difference,' Mrs MacAnaspey said. 'I mean, kids in a good neighbourhood don't act tough. Now your neighbourhood, Riverside Drive, used to be one of the best. That was before the Puerto Ricans moved in below. Now, it's as much as a person's life is worth to walk down some of those blocks at night.'

'O, I don't think they're so bad,' Mrs Tierney said. 'I saw crowds of them at Mass last Sunday. After all, they're Catholics, same as we are.'

'Catholic?' Mrs MacAnaspey said. 'They're the kind of Catholic would strangle you with the rosary beads for one dollar in your purse.'

The Catholics here were not very tolerant, Mrs Tierney had noticed. The priests preached sermons on Sundays that hardly had the word God in them but plenty about the communists and the Chinese and so on. And that bishop on television, all decked out in his crucifix and cape and biretta and telling jokes, some of them not in the best of taste. There was nothing very holy about him, was there? As for Mrs MacAnaspey, she always had the hard word for everybody.

'Gran? Granny?'

It was Lisa, pale and running, what was it now, it was always something with these children, they were terrible babies for their age. 'What's the matter, Lisa?' she said.

'Liam fell. Over there.'

Mrs Tierney started up; there was a man carrying Liam out of the playground. As she went towards them she saw dirt on his face, dirt mixed with blood, a big cut on his forehead and him pale as death.

'He was on the slide,' the man said. 'Standing at the top, waiting his turn. One of the other children pushed him and he fell off the ladder.'

The ladder? She looked back. From the top it was a good ten feet. The nurse in her took over as she lifted him out of the man's arms. The child was not even crying. He was in shock. 'Did he fall on his head, or did his body break the fall?' she asked as she lifted Liam's head, looked into his eyes, looking for pin-point pupils. There was some retraction: she could not be sure.

The man was not sure either. He had seen Liam fall but had not noticed how he fell.

'Did you see him, Lisa?'

'No, Gran.'

'It's just a cut,' said Mrs MacAnaspey who had not risen for fear of disturbing Bubbles. It crossed Mrs Tierney's mind that people who love dogs do not love children. She turned her back on Mrs MacAnaspey and, carrying the child, went to the drinking fountain and washed the dirt from the cut. It was not deep but the child looked concussed. There *could* be a fracture.

'Is he hurt?' said Mrs Duke, coming up, her face oily with sun tan lotion.

'Get me a taxi, would you?' Mrs Tierney said. 'Where's the nearest hospital? Lisa, go and get your ball and my handbag. Come straight back.'

While they waited for the taxi, Liam vomited. It was not a good sign. Where was the taxi, why didn't they hurry up, where was the nearest hospital, what if the child went into a coma and died? Brendan was at the other end of the city, Jane was down at her office; there was no one to look after the child but her. She must keep her head. The child began to cry and this reassured her. 'There now, Liam,' she said. 'There now. We're going to make that cut all better, don't you worry.'

In the taxi, she held his face against her bosom. Lisa, little, ugly Lisa, sat bolt upright on the seat beside her, not saying one word. She remembered babbling to the pair of them about getting a bandage on the cut, it wouldn't hurt, they would just let the doctor see it. She told the cab driver to go to the extern department. 'You mean the Admitting?' the taxi driver said. O gracious God, let them not admit us, let them tell me it's nothing and send us away.

She gave the driver a dollar as the cab slowed down and was out and up the steps and along a corridor, holding the child before her like a sacrifice. There were some Puerto Ricans clustered in the corridor and a nurse came along, looked at the cut on Liam's head, then told Mrs Tierney to 'go into that room and wait. Leave the little girl here.'

'Lisa, dear,' Mrs Tierney said. 'Go and sit on that bench. We won't be long.'

But they *were* long. In the little examination room there was no doctor, only a Puerto Rican mother, small and dark, with little gold earrings and a dress with a crinoline and on her lap a crying baby, dressed in a party dress with little gold earrings, same as the mother. Liam began to cry too. 'You're a good boy,' she told him. 'You're a very good boy. It won't be long.'

The intern (he must be an intern, he was too young for a resident) wore a white barber jacket and came without a nurse. He looked at the Puerto Rican baby first. 'Take its clothes off,' he said. The Puerto Rican woman did not understand, so he went out and got a porter who could speak Spanish. 'How long has the baby been sick?' he asked, through the interpreter. 'Since a week,' said the interpreter. 'Jesus Christ,' said the intern, under his breath. He turned to Mrs Tierney. 'What's wrong with this little fellow? Did he cut his head?'

'He fell off a ladder at the top of a slide,' Mrs Tierney said. 'He fell on asphalt and he's vomited.'

'Nurse?' the intern called. 'Take this boy's temperature.' He turned back to the Puerto Rican baby, naked now except for its earrings. While he examined the baby, the nurse came in, cleaned off Liam's cut and took his temperature. Mrs Tierney tried to see what she wrote down, but could not. Liam seemed hot.

The doctor told the interpreter to admit the baby and tell the mother to wait. He then turned to Liam, took his pulse, examined his ears with an auriscope, looked at his pupils, stethoscoped his chest and asked: 'How're you, old pal? Does it hurt anywhere? Show me where it hurts.'

Liam said: 'I cut my face. It hurts me.'

The doctor patted him on the cheek, then turned to the nurse. 'This one for X-ray,' he said. He walked out of the room before Mrs Tierney could speak.

The nurse began to bandage the cut. 'Do you have Blue Cross?' she asked.

'I don't know,' Mrs Tierney said. 'Is that insurance?'

'Don't you know what insurance you have?' the nurse said snappishly.

'I'm his grandmother. I'd have to get in touch with his father.'

'Well, if you haven't got Blue Cross, you'll have to go up to the office.'

Mrs Tierney felt her temper rise. 'Nobody's going to run

away,' she told the nurse. 'I have two children to look after, one of them waiting outside. I'll go later, if you don't mind.'

Dumpy, dowdy, old, with a brogue; yet you never could tell with people, the nurse decided. She turned on me like Park Avenue. 'Well,' the nurse said, pettishly. 'It's the regulation. Just so long as you do before you go. Now take the little boy outside and sit on that bench. We'll call you for X-ray.'

The corridor was more crowded and noisy than ever but Lisa, thank heavens, was sitting where she had told her. There was a very short wait during which Lisa got fidgety and then an elderly Negro in a white jacket came up and said: 'Bring the boy in here, please.' She made Lisa keep their seats, then carried Liam into the X-ray room. The Negro (she had thought him an attendant but he was the radiographer) gave her a rubber apron to wear. He then positioned the child for skull X-rays. Liam was balky at first, but after the third one he lay so still that Mrs Tierney felt her heart begin to hammer. Perhaps this was drowsiness, the beginning of coma. She tried to remember her old training but the details were not clear. The elderly Negro smiled at her, showing his pink tongue, then winked reassuringly behind his glasses. 'Okay now,' he said. 'You just take him outside and have a seat. Take me a few minutes to get these ready.'

Lisa was still there, thank God. They had to wait. She watched Liam, talked to him, watched for signs of sleepiness. A coma, then death, the child dead. O God, to face Jane and Brendan, their child dead. He must not die, O Lord, he must not die, I will do anything You ask of me, give me any penance but do not let him die. O Mary, I pray to you, a mother, ask your Son to spare him.

'Can we go home now, Gran?' Lisa asked.

'Soon, dear, soon.'

If he dies, she thought, he cannot go to heaven. He will go to Limbo; that's the place for children who have never been baptized: in Limbo they stay for eternity, never in the sight of God. O, Brendan, Brendan, why didn't you baptize him, what do your silly notions matter now, you can write all the books you want but you have failed in your duty. Limbo.

O my God, she prayed. Spare him. If you spare him I will right this wrong, I promise You, I give You my solemn promise now.

'I want to go home,' Lisa said, beginning to cry. 'Why can't we go home?'

'It won't be long, dear,' she said. 'Liam, is your head sore? Liam? Are you sleepy? Liam, look at me.'

But he turned his face away and closed his eyes. The nurse passed by together with a girl who carried a clip board. 'That woman over there,' the nurse said. The girl with the clip board squatted down in front of Mrs Tierney and began asking about Blue Cross, address, father's occupation, telephone number, mother's occupation, business address. She said the X-rays would cost thirty-five dollars. Then she went away.

'Liam?' Mrs Tierney said. 'Are you sleepy, Liam?'

In case of emergency, the catechism said, and why hadn't she thought of that before? Baptism. In case of emergency any layman or woman can do it. I baptize thee in the name of the Father and of the Son and of the Holy Ghost. Water, all that was needed was a little water to sprinkle on his forehead and to say the words –

'Lisa dear,' she said. 'Would you go up there to the desk and see if you can get a glass of water and bring it back to me? Will you do that, dear?'

But as Lisa went to obey, the elderly Negro came back down the corridor with the young doctor. They went into the X-ray room and before Lisa had reached the nurse's desk, they came out again. The doctor came over to the bench where they sat.

'Hello, there,' he said. 'Well, we've taken X-rays and we have wet plates on them. They're not final, but I don't think there's any fracture. Just take him home, keep him quiet and in bed and if he gets worse bring him back here at once. Nurse!'

The nurse came.

'Give them an appointment for the day after tomorrow. We'll take another look to make sure.'

'Right,' the nurse said. She took out a pad and wrote on it.

'Keep him quiet,' the doctor said. 'He'll be all right.'

'Thank you, doctor. Thank you.'

The doctor nodded and turned away. As he moved back to the examining room Mrs Tierney saw him pass Lisa who was coming slowly up the corridor with a paper cup full of water. The nurse gave Mrs Tierney her appointment slip and said: 'All right now, you can take him home. Did you give your address to the office?'

'Yes.'

'Okay then.'

'Thank you.'

Mrs Tierney put the slip in her purse, hooked the purse over her arm, then bent down and lifted Liam up, no longer so afraid of disturbing him. 'All right, dear,' she said. 'You're all right.'

'Here's the water, Gran.'

'Thank you, dear, but I can't take it now; my hands are full. Would you like to drink it?'

'But it's for you, Gran.'

'No, it's all right. You drink it. We're going home. We'll have a nice cold drink at home.'

I no longer go out to lunch. Instead, I walk three blocks from my cell on West Eleventh Street, buy a sandwich and a container of coffee and go straight back to work. I am living, not in New York, but in a world of my characters. I take wrong turnings, I cross against the lights, I am in danger of being run down. This morning, for instance, I got out at the wrong subway exit and found myself on Fourteenth Street. Yet even this mistake seemed meaningful for, because of it, I walked past Loew's Sheridan Theatre, a place I do not normally pass. On a wall, between the loud poster attractions of *Alias Jesse James* and *Gunfight at Dodge City*, I saw a small plaque:

GEORGES CLEMENCEAU

THIS TABLET IS TO COMMEMORATE THE RESIDENCE IN AMERICA OF FRANCE'S GREAT WAR PREMIER. FOR SIX MONTHS IN 1870 HE LIVED, PRACTISED AND TAUGHT MEDICINE ON THE SITE NOW OCCUPIED BY LOEW'S SHERIDAN THEATRE

I read that with joy. It was an omen. Headbent past the Silver Dollar Diner, crossing West Twelfth Street, came the Tiger, living, practising and teaching medicine, going up into the second balcony of Loew's Sheridan Theatre to write a socialist pamphlet; a Tiger burning bright with future promise of revolution, justice for Dreyfus, the taxis of the Marne, *Les Splendeurs et Misères de la Gloire*. Yet here at the corner of West Twelfth, he turned no heads, he was, like me, an unknown immigrant. In fact, he was just about my age. (In this, my thirtieth year, I have developed a sudden awareness of other people's ages. People used to be older than me, or young like me. Now, they are sometimes younger than me. If so, I do not want to hear what they have done. Conrad did not begin until he was thirty-eight. We all salute the Pole.) I turned towards my workroom, composing my own plaque.

Omens. I watch for them now. In the past three weeks they have all been good. Today's meeting with Max Bronstein was one, although, when he dropped in this afternoon, I was ungracious and curt.

He wore a short black raincoat, a ridiculous green hat and new yellow shoes. He was smoking a cigar and a cigar in Max's hand is as unnatural as it would be in a baby's. It was about four o'clock in the afternoon and I could see that he was slowed by drink.

'Hi, Old Buddy. Working?'

'I was.'

'Good, how's it coming?'

'It's coming.'

'Great.' He sat down precariously on the edge of my trestle table, almost spilling the manuscript sheets. I caught them in time. He clicked loose his dental bridge, and did a surreptitious cleaning job with his tongue. He removed his omnipresent dark glasses and put them in a case. I noticed it was no longer a plastic case.

'I've just had lunch with Gardiner Key,' he said.

'O.'

'We talked about you.'

'O.'

'What's the matter, Brendan, you mad at me, or something?'

'No. I was working.'

'Sorry,' he said. 'But I thought you'd want to hear this.'

'How's Jackson Clayburn?' I said in a surly voice.

'Him? Yes, that's right, I haven't seen you since that night. Look, man, Clayburn's just a jerk. I know that.'

'But he lines up pretty girls for you, is that it?'

'I remember now,' he said. 'I was with Clayburn's chick and you were giving me a lot of hazz about how success corrupts people. I'm not successful, for christsake. My book isn't even published yet.'

'But it's going to be published, isn't it?'

'Right. And so will yours be, when you finish it. Listen, when I had lunch with Key today Sidney Gerston was there, he's the firm's senior editor. That's what I came to tell you about. I mentioned your name and Gerston had read one of your stories. He was interested, man.'

'Interested in what?'

Max did not answer. He went to the window and threw his cigar into the alley. 'Cigars make me sick,' he said. 'Key gave me two. Want the other one?'

'No.'

He clicked his bridge again. 'Well, anyway, I told Gerston you were writing a novel. I said you'd been working on it for two years and you were finishing it now on a full-time basis. You are, aren't you?'

'That's the general idea.'

'Anyway, Gerston was quite excited, he wanted to see it. He said if they liked what you showed them they might be able to help you with an advance. He wanted your phone number, but I said I'd better speak to you first.'

'Why?'

'Well, I haven't seen you for a while, I thought you might have another publisher in mind. I didn't want to embarrass you, man.'

'Very funny.'

'No, I'm serious. If you're interested, I'll put you in touch with Gerston right away. If he likes your book why not ask him for fifteen hundred bucks? You'll get it. I did.'

'Which story of mine did Gerston read?'

'He didn't say. But he knew your name, all right.'

Now, fifteen hundred dollars means the difference between finishing my book in comfort and finishing it on the ugly scrimp of a budget which leaves no leeway: it means an end to Jane's frowns every time I buy a bottle or suggest a club steak for dinner. But, more than that, it will be proof that I am not writing into a void. Which story of mine had Gerston read? I began to feel excited. I looked at Max, Max with his stray's uncertainty, Max who had thought of me in the moment of his own good luck, *mon semblable*, whose first success had, in a way, inspired all that I had done since. I had been unfair to him: nothing had changed between us, he was still the same old Max, Max-who-phones-in-the-night. At that moment, I knew he was my one true friend.

And yet (do you understand?) I did not want to ride on Max's coat tails; I even resented his trying to help me 'All right,' I said, as though I were conferring a favour. 'You can give him my phone number, if you like.'

'Great. Now come on, let's go out and have a drink.'

'No thanks.'

'Why not?'

I did not tell him the real reason which was that I remembered the day, months ago, when he had called me a slave because I refused to drink to *his* success. 'Because I'm working,' I said. 'I'm not interested in boozing these days. This,' I said, pointing to my manuscript. 'This is what interests me now.'

He sighed. 'Sure,' he said. 'Of course.'

'How about you?' I asked. 'I thought you couldn't wait to get out of town to hole up with your new book?'

'Yes, I'm going soon,' he said, with his painful, uncertain smile.

'What's holding you?' I said. 'Second novel nerves?'

He reached in his pocket and put on his dark glasses. 'Thanks, Old Buddy,' he said. 'Thanks a lot, Old Buddy.'

The door shut and I heard his slow step on the wooden staircase. Why had I treated him like that, why didn't I call him back, apologize, thank him for his help and go off to drink beers with him at the San Remo? What's the matter with me?

*

It was not fair. He could not see TV. Lisa could. He was sick. Silly old Gran said no. He must rest, Gran said. It was not fair. He wanted to see TV. 'I want to see TV,' he shouted.

He listened. They had all gone and left him. 'I want to see TV.'

Lisa came in. 'You shut up,' she said. 'You're sick. You're supposed to be asleep.'

'I want to see TV.'

'Gran says no.'

'I hate old Gran. Where's Mummy? I want Mummy.'

'Yah, yah, yah,' Lisa said. She went over and shut the door. 'Yell, yell, yell,' she said. 'Nobody hears you now.'

He began to cry. It was not fair. He was sick. He had cut his face. He was at the hospital. He was sick. 'GRAAAN?' he yelled.

'You shut up,' Lisa said. 'Poor old baby goofy boy. If you shout you'll be sick again and then you'll be dead.'

'You're dead,' he said. She was too big. It was not fair. 'Dead yourself,' he said. He cried.

Lisa sat on the windowsill. There was a smudge on her glasses so she took them off and wiped them on the edge of her skirt. She was glad he was not dead. She was glad he was not in the hospital. Mummy and Daddy would give him everything if he was in the hospital. If he was dead they would be sorry. He only had an old cut on his head. He was a little faker. Everybody thought he was great, but she knew he was just a junky old boy. Gran liked her better than him. Gran didn't think he was so great.

'Gran likes me better than you,' she told him. 'Gran says I help her.'

'Yah, yah, yah, yourself,' he said hopelessly. He began to pick at his bandage.

'You leave that alone. You're not supposed to. I'll tell Gran on you.'

But he did not leave it alone. He would pull it off. 'If you pull it off, you'll bleed and if you bleed you'll be dead and if you're dead they put you in a box and throw you in the garbage,' she told him.

He stopped. He looked at her. 'How do you know?'

'Because I do. And then the garbage man comes and throws you in the garbage truck with all the old ka-ka and pi-pi and stinky old food and stuff and they take you out to a big dump and set you on fire.'

'But I'd come back and tell Mummy,' he said.

'You couldn't come back, silly. You'd be all burned up.'

'Anyway, you never had a cut on your head,' he said. 'And you never had to go to the hospital. I had to go to the hospital.'

She saw herself in a white hospital bed, with boxes of candies and Daddy and Mummy leaning over her and everybody looking sorry and saying poor little Lisa. And he would have to wait outside, nobody would care about him.

'You weren't really in the hospital,' she said. 'They didn't *keep* you there.'

She got up and skipped a jacks course across the room. Nobody would care about her when they came home: they would be in here oogly-pooglying over poor little Liam. She felt like scratching him but contented herself by giving him a pinching look and nipped her fingers a few times to make him afraid.

'If you pinch me, I'll tell Gran,' he said. He was afraid, all right. But she heard the doorbell ringing. She skipped out and shut the door on him. Gran came out of the kitchen, wiping her hands, going up the hall to answer. Gran looked afraid. Why was she afraid: it was only Mummy. Mummy never used her key; she always rang the bell. Why was Gran afraid of Mummy? Gran was a big person.

'Hello, Jane. Did you have a good day?'

'Hello. How's everything? Is Brendan home yet?'

'No. Liam had a little accident.'

'An accident?' Mummy said. She looked just the way she did when you told her you had done a bad thing. 'What accident?'

'He fell off the slide and cut his head. Now, don't worry, dear, it's all right. It was just a little cut, it didn't even need stitches. I took him to the hospital.'

'The hospital?' Mummy said, sort of screaming.

'Yes, I was afraid he was a little concussed, but they took X-rays and he's all right. The doctor said to keep him in bed for a day and see how he does.'

'O my God,' Mummy said. 'Where is he?'

And started running down the corridor, never said hello Lisa, or anything, just ran in to see her dear little Liam who only had a cut on his head. Gran came after her, but Gran noticed and said: 'Hello, dear. Are you not watching television?'

'No,' Lisa said.

'Well, you can help me in the kitchen in a moment.'

Then she went into the room. Mummy was on her knees by the bed, kissing him. 'Poor darling,' Mummy said. 'Poor lamb.' And Gran stood there, watching Mummy and Liam. Lisa saw that Gran was afraid. She was still afraid. Why?

Then Mummy started to cry and Gran said: 'Jane, Jane, there's nothing to worry about. He's all right.'

Then Liam started to cry. He *would*. 'What happened, darling?' Mummy said. 'Tell Mummy.'

'A boy pushed me,' Liam shouted. 'A boy pushed me.'

'He did not. You pushed him first,' Lisa said.

'How far did he fall?' Mummy asked Gran.

'Right off the very top of the slide,' Lisa said.

'But who was looking after him?' Mummy said.

'He was on the slide hundreds of times before,' Gran said 'I was sitting talking to a lady, that Mrs MacAnaspey I told you about.'

'But weren't you watching?' Mummy asked.

'I didn't see him fall, if that's what you mean,' Gran said.

'That's why I took him to the hospital. I wanted to be sure there were no fractures.'

'What's a fracture?' Lisa said.

'Never you mind,' Gran said. 'Come on now. Come and help me make Liam's supper.'

But Lisa let her go by herself. Mummy was hugging Liam again. 'My poor darling,' Mummy told him. 'You might have been killed.'

'I'd be dead and in the garbage,' Liam said.

'No, no, darling.'

'Yes, and the garbage man would burn me all up.'

'Who told you that?'

Lisa moved up behind Mummy. She looked right at him. If he told he'd be sorry. She would tell on him, a thing he did. He'd be sorry, she warned him. He looked at her and he was afraid. He knew he couldn't tell. He looked around and he shouted out: 'Gran told me. Gran told me.'

Mummy got very stiff. Still on her knees, she turned and looked at where Gran had been. But Gran wasn't there. She was in the kitchen. 'Said what, darling?' Mummy asked. 'What did Gran say?'

'Said if I pull the bandage I'll be bleeding and I'll be dead and the garbage man will put me in the garbage and burn me up.' He was shouting. He always shouted when he told lies.

But Lisa saw that Mummy believed him. 'That's not true, darling,' Mummy said. 'Mrs Tierney? Mrs Tierney, can you come in for a minute?'

Gran came back from the kitchen. Lisa was glad. Now he would get it, the little liar.

'Tell Granny what you told me,' Mummy said. 'About the garbage.'

But he was afraid. He began to cry.

'What's the matter?' Gran asked.

'He says you told him that if he took the bandage off, he'd bleed and die and the garbage men would take him away.'

Gran laughed. 'Where do they get these notions? Now, you know I never said that, don't you, Liam?'

But Mummy believed him. Lisa saw that Mummy believed him. 'Now, now,' Mummy said to him. 'Don't cry, darling. Nobody's going to put you in the garbage. I wouldn't let them.'

'He's not himself, poor wee thing,' Gran said. 'Now, be a

brave boy, Liam. Stop crying. I'm getting you a lovely supper. Lisa, do you want to come and help me?'

'Okay,' Lisa said. She might as well. Mummy was hugging that little liar again. She went with Gran into the kitchen.

'Here's a tray,' Gran said. 'Put a paper napkin on it and a spoon and fork. It's for Liam.'

'No,' Lisa said. 'I don't want to.'

'Why not?'

'Why is everything for him? Why do I have to do everything because I'm the big one?'

'Lisa,' Gran said. 'Would you not be annoying me; I'm not feeling well. Help me or don't help me, I don't care.'

Gran was going to cry. She had never seen Gran cry. Mummy cried sometimes, but Gran was really old, old people shouldn't be crying. 'O, all right,' she said. 'I'll help you.'

Gran sat down on the chair by the kitchen table. She blinked her eyes but she did not cry. Then, without any warning, she reached out and pulled Lisa towards her. She pressed Lisa's head against her bosom and held her there, rocking to and fro. 'O, child,' she whispered. 'Child.'

Explosive Pink, Embroidered Faille, Jane wrote, using a Futura Display lettering which she did not care for but which Louise loved. And, make no mistake about it, what Louise wanted, Louise got. You could be best friends with someone for years, but try working for them. Take this rush job. Three-quarters of an hour ago a sullen CCNY kid from Louise's floor had slapped a copy envelope on Jane's drawing-board. Clipped to the envelope was a slip of pink memo paper.

FROM: *Promotion Editor*
TO: *Jane Tierney*
This is a MUST GO *for the printer first thing tomorrow. Return for my approval. Louise.*

No apology, not a word. The job couldn't possibly be finished before six-thirty at the earliest. And this was the night Jane had promised to let Brendan's mother go off to church.

Vito Italiano, the promotion art director, came out of his cubicle, snapping his fingers for the messenger. 'Double iced coffee,' he said. He looked at Jane who was the only other person in the office at the time. 'You want one?'

She shook her head. No use appealing to him, he was Louise's right hand, a swarthy, ambitious young bully in pink shirt, tight Continental trousers and black Italian straw loafers. But no fag. Jane had heard stories. And, lately, she herself had seen signs.

He came up behind her and she felt her back muscles tense. 'So, what are you working on, huh? What's this?'

She took a breath and held it as she completed the letter M. Although all the windows were open, there was a dead, heavy feeling in the room, as though a thunderstorm would break at any moment. The messenger had gone (could Italiano have sent out for coffee on purpose?) and they were alone. He waited until she had completed the M, then leaned into her, under pretence of checking on her work. Shocked, she felt the hard bump of his crotch press against her buttock. She moved aside and at once he became impersonal: the boss. 'Rush job, eh? Better get it back upstairs tonight.'

'I'm trying to do that,' she said. 'If you'll excuse me.' She took a breath and began to letter a B.

'They're such a drag, these rush jobs. If only Louise would get herself organized and give us some warning.'

She was surprised. She had never heard him criticize Louise. She began the letter R.

'I mean, you might have had a date tonight.'

She ignored this. She finished the R and shifted the tracing paper. At that moment, he moved up behind her, took the cheeks of her buttocks in both hands, jiggling them as though he were weighing fruit. Her temper lit. 'You *stop* that,' she said. 'You just stop it, do you hear?'

'Stop what?'

'I'm not going to stand for it, do you hear? I'm going to report you. Now, go away and leave me alone.'

He did not answer. He stood facing her, and smiled and smiled and was a villain. His skin was dark in a way that had nothing to do with the sun. His teeth were large and white. His shirtsleeves were rolled up and she saw an animal coating of black hair, thick on his forearms, curling over his linked gold watch band. As she stared at him, she remembered her shock at the assured, cruel way his fingers had seized at her flesh. 'Go away,' she said; but this time, her voice was shaky.

He laughed. For one outrageous moment she thought he was about to throw her down on Patsy Armstrong's desk and bite her in the neck. Impossible, of course – in the first week she had worked here, she had given up her fantasy of an office affair – but, as she looked into his eyes, wasn't he, why hadn't she seen it before – but wasn't this man the flesh and blood of all those dark ravishers she had dreamed of?

'I've been watching you, Janey. I've been watching you from the first day you came in here. You're the only real woman around.'

As he said this, the CCNY kid came into the room with a container of iced coffee. At once Italiano changed. He said, in his normal voice: 'By the way, I'd better pass on that job before you send it upstairs again. Okay?'

'But I won't get it finished before six-thirty or seven.'

'That's all right. I'll drop back around six-thirty.' He turned and walked to his cubicle. Patsy Armstrong and Dick Duryea came in and began to tidy their desks. Perspiration, damp and cold, made Jane's dress cling to her shoulder blades as she reached for the tracing paper again. It was five twenty-five. In a few minutes they would all leave for the day and at six-thirty Italiano would come back alone. And then what? If you can't trust yourself, she thought, there's only one thing to do. Get out of here now. Go straight home.

But if she goofed on this job, then what? She had a clear and chilling picture of herself, back where she was a month ago, sitting in the park, watching Lisa and Liam play in the sand muck. Back to dishes and dullness, to the boredom of motherhood's daily drudge, the feeling that life was passing you by, the cheat of being in a middle-aged routine while you were still young. Good-bye to the weekly pay cheque of one hundred and thirty dollars after deductions, and would anyone, except Louise, have been so generous about salary? Which was why, as Italiano and the others left the office, she went on patiently lettering CHINESE WILLOW WAND DIET, trying to make each letter as perfect as she could. And then, in sudden guilt, she remembered Mrs Let-Me. She picked up the phone and dialled home.

'Hello, who is it?' said her mother-in-law's voice.

'It's me. I meant to call you sooner. I'm afraid I won't be home in time to let you go to church before supper.'

No answer. A put-upon silence.

'Maybe you could go after supper?' Jane suggested.

'Confessions are only from five to seven.'

'Well, I'm sorry, but it's not my fault. They gave me a rush job to do.'

Silence.

'Anyway, I'll be home as soon as I can. How are the kids?'

'They're all right.'

'Have they had their supper yet?'

'No, not yet. I was just reading them a story.'

'O. Well, I won't keep you then. Good-bye.'

Silence. Then Jane heard her replace the receiver. Doesn't that damn woman realize that it's me, not Brendan, who's bringing home the family bacon? Her and her put-upon voice. Her and her church. Her and her sadistic tales that terrified the kids, and her bland incompetence at minding them. Mrs Let-Me

Tierney. Always underfoot. What was the word for that? Ubiquitous. Yes, that was it, she was ubiquitous.

And the worst part of it was, you couldn't expect any sympathy from Brendan. He didn't understand. He would never understand this thing about Italiano. He'd never see how you could get into a situation even though you didn't *want* to.

She held her breath and lettered an O, remembering that Giotto, when asked by the Pope for a sample of his art, took a brush and described a perfect circle. But she could try forever, her circle would never be perfect; nothing ever seemed to turn out just as it should, not her looks, not her sex life, not even her kids: nothing ever had and perhaps nothing ever would. It was all very well helping out while Brendan finished his book but what would happen after that, what if Mrs Let-Me just went on living with them? What sort of perfect circle could the future be with that one horrible false note right in the centre of it.

Now, stop that, she warned herself. One thing at a time. But she could not stop it. How would they ever get rid of Mrs Let-Me, short of deporting her like some gangster who had stolen their happiness? Of course, Brendan had promised it wouldn't be forever. But had he ever really thought of it, had he?

She held her breath, lettered a T, and put in a final period. Hastily, she checked copy. If Italiano decided to be picky, he could force her to do the whole job over again. And he would be picky. If.

Still, it was ten to seven: it was finished and he had not come back yet. Perhaps, if she took the copy up to Louise's office, Louise might still be there and could clear it herself? In sudden hope Jane stuffed all the copy into the envelope, clipped the rough to it and went out into the corridor. Nobody could expect her to wait all night, now could they? She rang for the elevator, then noticed that it was already on its way up. As the implication of this entered her mind, the elevator came level and the door slid open. Vito Italiano smiled at her.

'I thought you weren't coming back,' she said.

He winked. He knew what she thought, his wink told her. 'But I am back. Now, let's have a look at that work.'

They went to her desk. As they approached it, she handed him the envelope, leaving him to open it himself. In that way she avoided his leaning over her. But his smile, as he accepted the envelope, told her that today all her thoughts were known to him. From his black, raw-silk blazer he took an expensive Mont Blanc pen, carefully touched up a few details of the lettering, then checked the rough against copy. He turned and looked at her in a meaningful way then, smiling, signed his approval in a neat italic script. 'There you are,' he said. 'Now, why don't you run upstairs, drop this on Louise's desk, and then we'll go out and have a drink.'

He handed her the envelope and the rough.

'But, Vito, it's very late –'

'Come here,' he said. His hands gripped her bare forearms. He was strong. He pulled her to him and kissed her and the copy envelope fell from her hands to the floor. It was not at all like her dreams for she was not taken against her will. She buried her face in his awful pink shirt; she clung to him; she kissed him back; found herself shaking with lust; was surprised when suddenly he released her.

He bent down, picked up the copy envelope, and handed it to her. 'I'll wait for you,' he said. 'Hurry.'

Obediently, she turned and went towards the elevator, walking as though her shoes did not fit and her high heels were broken. In the elevator, she leaned her forehead against the cold aluminium wall. She entered Louise's office, a small room containing an escritoire on which, in feminine clutter, were photographs of Spencer, Louise's Siamese cat; of Roddy, Louise's handsome little nephew; and of Louise herself, as seen by a famous fashion photographer. On the wall behind this desk, other photographs stood to attention in neat black and white rows, photographs of fashion models and designers, all overwritten with best love to Louise. On the windowsill and indeed on all the ledges and protuberances of the room were African violets and Japanese dwarf trees, each of which received Louise's daily care. From the ceiling, a large white French bird-cage hung from a golden chain. Inside it a mobile of Japanese paper birds, motionless in the hot, dead air.

Standing in this room, Jane saw it anew. This was success in the world of jobs. From this escritoire Louise could command Jane to work late, could unwittingly set in motion something that could change all of Jane's life. From this sterile lair, less an office than its owner's true home, a dark ravisher could be unleashed. It was not fair. It was not fair because Louise had no right to have this power, Louise was just a stuck-up Lesbian spinster, pretending that those picky little plants of hers were children, putting up her handsome little nephew's picture in a false front of normalcy – but where, Jane asked, where is the other nephew's picture, the ugly little one I met you with in Saks that day? How dare you, Louise, how dare you get me into this mess.

But of course, there was no sense blaming Louise for what had happened. There was no sense blaming anybody for some sick thing that was hidden inside you all these years just waiting its chance to come out. For she had kissed him, she had clung to him, he could have done anything he wanted with her. Imagine. Vito Italiano, with those christly clothes, the kind of man you wouldn't be seen dead with, had never been seen with in your entire life. Yet now, he was waiting downstairs. And if she went back down, she was done for.

Carefully she placed the rough and the copy envelope on Louise's escritoire. She had done nothing wrong. Last month Brendan had done as much, if not more, in the kitchen at Dortmunder's with that creepy Revere creature. Now, we're even, right? At the moment I've nothing to feel guilty about.

If I go home.

And if I go back down to him?

She turned and ran out of Louise's office. As she shut the door, the French birdcage swayed on its chain, the Japanese paper birds stirred and twirled on their thin wire mobile. She ran to the elevator which was still waiting, its door open. She got in, hesitated, and then as though shutting her eyes and picking a number in panic, she pushed her finger on a button. The elevator went down, past Italiano, down to the ground floor. She ran across the terrazzo entrance hall and out into the seven o'clock quiet of the street. She turned and looked up at the fifth floor of the building as though she feared that some dark face watched her. She saw no one. She ran like a fugitive towards Lexington and her subway.

Past the stone lions, down the steps of the Public Library, oblivious to the late afternoon sun and the crowds of people moving along Fifth Avenue. I had checked on a reference and now I was writing in my head. I was in a hospital with my hero. A nun moved off, clothed in white, (samite? Mystic, wonderful) going to find out if this young man's seed had seeded. Would it be a boy or a girl? My hero did not care, he did not want a child, he was not yet ready for fatherhood. The nun came back. 'Not yet,' she said. My hero turned away, remembering Dostoievsky, the blindfold on his eyes, waiting the crash and buffet of the soldiers' bullets. Hoofbeats in the courtyard and a Czar's sudden pardon. 'Not yet. Live on,' my hero said, echoing the words of the firing squad's commander.

I realized I had spoken these words aloud in the middle of Forty-Second Street.

I realized it because a fat woman in a blue cotton dress, wearing a beanie hat on which some Times Square souvenir-seller had stitched the word FLO, arm-linked to her husband, a tall old fellow in a transparent nylon shirt, brown slacks and deerskin loafers, who wore a camera which announced him as a tourist, and a beanie hat which proclaimed him JOHN: both stopped, gaped at me, then exchanged uxorial glances of complicity. I glared, wanting to say something which would prove that I was not mad, that I do not, as a rule, talk to myself; something which would turn their ridicule of me into instant, unquestioning respect. But what could I say? Dumb, glaring, foolish, I watched them edge past me and then, cursing them, went on towards the subway. My hero had fled: I was left with myself, and myself seemed ridiculous.

At Fifty-Ninth Street several Negro boy scouts got on the subway. Some carried drumsticks, some fife cases, some the mouthpieces of bugles and trumpets. They were in a good humour. A tiny boy sat beside me, fiddled his drumsticks like a woman knitting, and began to beat out on his little black knee-cap, the rhythm of some march. In Barcelona once, in the

Tibidabo amusement park, I wandered into a penny arcade filled with quaint-seeming relics of Edwardian mechanical marvels. I fed a *jeton* into a musical box over which Confederate and Union flags were erected. Behind the glass, marionette pickaninnies and mammies danced jerkily up and down to the sound of tinny banjo music and the grinding of mechanical gears. On a platform above the dancers were larger figurines representing the players in a nigger minstrel band and one of these, a little blackamoor, beat his sticks on a flat drum with the same sinewy jerkiness which my seatmate now displayed. But having started the machine, I remember noticing that the nigger minstrels were, in reality, monkey-featured and on closer examination of the plantation dancers, discovered them to be similarly simian, a repulsive joke on the part of the music-box maker. Foul Spaniards who had built this thing! Yet when I inspected the back of the machine I discovered that it was made fifty years ago in Trenton, New Jersey. In fifty years how much has changed, here in America? How can my little seatmate salute the flag in two-fingered innocence, how can he sing Land of the Free? But who's talking? Didn't young Brendan Tierney of the Catholic Scouts of Ireland once raise his hand in salute to the trinity of Father, Son and Holy Ghost, didn't I sing Faith of our Fathers, sittingcross-legged on wet duckboards where the Mountains of Mourne sweep down to the sea? Yet if scout Brendy Tierney were to sit down in the subway beside me, his merit badges sewn on his sleeve, what password could I give him to prove our common identity? We change. Scout Tierney is dead in me, as Brendan Tierney, the wage-earning paterfamilias, is dead. The man I am become in these past weeks is kin only to that old writer who, some day, sitting on a balcony in Nice or San Francisco, will try to think back to this year and this place, to the moment when he was truly born. But will he remember me? Will he remember the agonies, the uncertainties of these past weeks, will he recall the excitements, the depressions, the feeling that this book is a tunnel through which I must crawl on my hands and knees? Yet I cannot, I would not, escape from it. Is this the drive that Pat Gallery talked about? Am I become the fox-that-eats-his-grandmother?

Cold, vulpine, (a wolf in Macy's summer clothing) I entered my lair, going up in the old, slow elevator, loping along the corridor, filled with a dedicated resolve to eat dinner early and go for a long, lonely walk in the hot summer streets. But when I unlocked the apartment door, both of the children ran wild in the hall. The apartment itself was noise, heat and confusion, the last place in the world for a writer to gather his thoughts. My mother was in the kitchen making supper. And where was Jane?

'O, Brendy, I'm glad you're home. I have to go down to the church and Jane just phoned to say she'd be late. I've made the children's supper. Will you see that they eat it?'

'But what's your hurry, Mamma?'

'There are confessions between five and seven. It's half past six now.'

(And what does she have to confess, for Christ's sake? The murder of my evening?)

'Hello, Daddy.'

Liam, wearing that hospital bandage on his head. My beloved son. I pick him up and kiss him.

'Shouldn't Liam be in bed, Mamma?'

'O, he's all right. He's full of beans, there's no sense keeping him in bed.'

My mother comes out of the kitchen, putting on her hat and a pair of white gloves. I watch in gloom.

'Their supper is on the table, I won't be long.'

'When did Jane say she'd be home?'

'She didn't say. She said they'd given her a rush job at the office. Good-bye, children. Good-bye, Brendan.'

Did Flaubert ever sit in a kitchen watching two small children mess their way through tinned corn, hot dogs, tomato salad and ice cream? Did Dostoievsky ever pour chocolate milk? Or were they able to ignore things like that, simply because their powers of concentration were real and mine are not?

The telephone.

'The telephone, Daddy.'

'I know.'

'Well, aren't you going to answer it?'

I went into the living-room. Pat Gallery's voice.

'Brendan? Listen, Yvonne and I are taking Charlie Lupus up your way to eat at the Great Shanghai. I have a bottle here. Can we come in and have a drink on the way up?'

What would James Joyce have said?

I said yes.

*

When Mrs Tierney came back from church the apartment was Bedlam. Jane was not home yet; the children were running in and out of the rooms like wild Indians and there were two strange men and a girl in the living-room with Brendan, all on the tear by the looks of them.

'O, there you are, Mamma,' Brendan called to her. 'Come on in, I want to introduce you. This is Dr Pat Gallery and this is Charles Lupus, he's a doctor too.'

'Beware of him, he's a psychoanalyst,' said the girl.

'And this is Yvonne, Pat's wife. My mother.'

'Sure and it's a pleasure to meet you,' said Dr Gallery in a stage-Irish brogue. 'Sit you down, Mrs Tierney, sit you down. Will you have a wee drop of the craythur with the rest of us?'

The other doctor, a small thin fellow with a bow tie and a short haircut, nodded hurriedly as though he had been interrupted, then turned back to Gallery's wife who was red-headed, pretty – and a little tight, Mrs Tierney guessed.

'No, what I meant is,' he said, 'of course there have been phallic females all through history, but it's only in America, in this century, that they've achieved a cultural dominance on the mass level.'

'No, Charles,' Gallery's wife said. 'I can't let you get away with that. If there's one thing I'm tired of, it's the way you analysts reduce every female aspiration to simple penis envy.'

Mrs Tierney, not sure that she could have heard right (did Mrs Gallery say *penis*?), looked over at Brendan, who, catching her eye, interrupted his conversation with Gallery and came up, taking her by the arm, saying in a whisper: 'Look, Mamma, I wonder if, before you sit down, you'd just throw the kids into a cold tub? Give them some toys to play with. Jane's not home yet and I don't know when these people will leave.'

'All right, Brendan.' She let him lead her towards the door. 'But I can't put the kids in together. They're too old for that.'

'O, come on, Mamma, they're only babies.'

Well. As she went down the hall calling to the kids, she felt her face burning. Of course they were only babies and did she have a dirty mind? She would not have let Brendan in the tub with Sheila at that age. And had that woman said *penis*, or had she just imagined it? 'Lisa and Liam,' she called, 'Come here now. I want you both to get washed.'

But of course the wild Indians did not come. She had to catch them first. As she led them into the bathroom she heard Dr Lupus' voice. 'I'm talking about the woman who takes over the breadwinner's role in fact or fantasy. The competing, aggressive type.'

'In other words, a ball breaker,' Gallery said.

'Hey, Pat, easy does it,' Brendan's voice warned. 'My mother might hear you.'

'Ah, but your mother has a darlin' brogue,' said Gallery. 'A darlin', darlin' brogue. It's a pity you've lost so much of your accent, Brendan. That is English as she should be spoke.'

Mrs Tierney shut and locked the bathroom door. Balls, did he say, was it testicles he meant? She caught sight of her face, red as a sunburn, in the medicine cabinet mirror. 'Now hurry up, children,' she said. 'Let's wash our hands first.'

'I wish Ruthie was here,' Lisa said.

'Who's Ruthie?'

'Ruthie Lupus, silly. That's her Daddy in there. He's a doctor for kooky people.'

'You're kooky,' Liam said.

'Kooky yourself.'

'Now, children,' Mrs Tierney said. 'Use the soap. Come on, Liam, let me help you.' (Gracious God, no wonder they don't have their friends in very often if that's what they're like.) 'And after you've washed,' she said. 'I'm going to tuck you into bed and read you a nice story.'

'I want TV,' Liam said.

'No, a story,' Lisa said.

'All right now, that's enough. We'll see when the time comes. Dry your faces and hands.'

She reached over to turn off the gushing taps and the cold water on her fingertips made her think of the warm, sticky holy water she had touched in the church font tonight. The priest she had seen in confession had been no use. He said she must make Brendan bring the children to church and have them baptized. As if Brendan would ever agree to the like of that. The priest had offered to call on Brendan and Jane. What good would that do? Priests lived behind presbytery walls. They did not understand.

She shut her eyes: excitement was bad for her, the doctor had said. But she had made a promise to God the other afternoon in that hospital corridor. Baptism was a sacrament: without it, these children could not enter heaven. It was a special sacrament: in case of emergency any layman or woman could do it. Jane was not at home: the children were both here. And this is water. All it takes is the words and water.

She opened her eyes and saw herself in the washbasin mirror, a woman with flushed cheeks and guilty eyes. Would the children notice anything odd about her? 'Use the towels,' she told them. 'Dry your hands on the towel.'

'I've finished,' Lisa yelled.

'Me too. Me too.'

'Wait a minute, children,' she said. Her hand trembled as she took the plastic mouthrinse cup from the shelf. She put it under the tap and filled it up. Then, turning, her heart thumping, she went to the bathtub and sat down on the edge of it. 'Now, children. We're going to do something. Come here, Liam, you're first.'

'I don't want any more wash,' Liam said.

'It's not a wash. Come here, dear.'

She dipped her fingers in the plastic cup, then sprinkled a few drops of water on his forehead, avoiding his bandage. 'I baptize thee Liam Brendan,' she said. 'In the name of the Father and of the Son and of the Holy Ghost. Amen.'

'Who's the father?' Lisa said. 'Daddy?'

'No, dear. God.'

'And who's the ghost?'

'That's God too.'

'Who's God?' Liam asked.

'O, you know,' Lisa said. 'The Jesus book.'

'Now, come here, Lisa,' Mrs Tierney said, trying to make her voice sound normal.

'I don't want to. What good is this game?'

'It's not a game, dear. Come on.'

'Can I have a candy if I do?'

'Yes, dear.'

'Me too?' Liam said. 'Me too, a candy?'

'Yes, Liam. Now come here, Lisa. Hold your braids back. That's right. Now.'

She sprinkled the water. 'I baptize thee Elizabeth Jane in the name of the Father and of the Son and of the Holy Ghost. Amen.'

'That's wet,' Lisa protested.

'All right, dry your faces. There. Now we'll go into the kitchen and get a candy.'

'Two each. You promised.'

'All right then. Two each.' She put her arms around them and hugged them, laughing. They stared at her: it must be some grown-up joke. She laughed and laughed. 'Come on now,' she said. 'Come on, my little Christians.'

*

When Jane came in she closed the apartment door and leaned against it, as though in sanctuary. All the way home on the subway she had suffered a horrible fantasy about Italiano following her. But now, as she shut the bolt in the door, a new fantasy replaced the former one. She saw him, waiting in the office, growing angry, and finally deciding to phone her at home. Had he phoned here?

She went along the corridor. Mrs Tierney was in the kids' room, reading them a story.

'Did anyone phone for me?'

'No, dear.'

'Hello, Mummy.'

'Hello, darlings. Did you have a nice day?'

Mrs Tierney, waiting for Lisa's answer, knew that her days of trial had begun. 'Yes,' Lisa said. 'We played games, didn't we, Gran?'

'Yes, and you were both very good,' Mrs Tierney said quickly as Jane in her silky dress bent over to kiss Liam good night. From where she sat, Mrs Tierney noticed a thin crucifix of perspiration spread from the points of her daughter-in-law's shoulder blades to run down the spine of her dress and suddenly she felt a quick sympathy for this girl who had come home after working all day in a hot office to find her children in bed, being looked after by a mother-in-law she did not trust, with dinner to be cooked, and three strangers in her living-room, all of them drinking too much. And more than that, behind her back, something had happened to these children.

Jane moved to Lisa, kissed her, then turned to Mrs Tierney.

'I'm sorry about tonight,' she said. 'I mean about your missing church.'

'That's all right, dear. You look tired. Let me make supper for you.'

'What's church?' Liam asked.

'Now, you go to sleep, darling,' Jane said. 'Are you coming?' she asked Mrs Tierney.

They went out together, shutting the door behind them. 'I don't know about supper,' Jane said. 'I haven't got enough food in to feed all these people. And we can't afford to go to a restaurant, at least not the kind of restaurant they'll pick. Have you eaten?'

Why does she never address me by my name? Mrs Tierney wondered. 'Yes, dear, I've had my supper.'

'Well then, let's go in and have a drink. Or did you want to go off to church?'

'No, I've been there. I mean, Brendan took care of the kids while I was gone.'

'Now, what's all this? What's this little conference in aid of?' said a loud voice. It was Dr Gallery coming out of the kitchen with a trayful of ice. 'Hello there, Janey,' he said, putting his arm around Jane who, to do her justice, Mrs Tierney thought, did not seem to enjoy it.

'Come on in,' Dr Gallery said. 'You too, Mrs Tierney. We need you to save us.'

'Save you from what?' Mrs Tierney asked, managing a smile.

'Save us from Freud. Did you ever hear tell of Dr Sigmund Freud, Mrs Tierney? Or would he be unknown in Holy Ireland?'

'Ah, now, you'd be surprised,' Mrs Tierney said, walking with them towards the living-room, thinking it was just like these Irish-Americans to take all real Irish people for know-nothings like themselves. Of course she had heard of Freud. Grattan had said the Church had condemned him. He was some sort of sex doctor like that other old cod, Voronoff, the one with the monkey glands.

They entered the living-room where Brendan was going on at the top of his voice. 'The trouble with analysis,' Brendan said, 'is that it's become a religion with a Messiah and Holy Writ and even its Judases like Ferenczi and Reich – and a whole damn priesthood.'

'That's prejudice,' Dr Lupus said.

'Is honest scepticism always prejudice?' Brendan shouted.

'Brendan,' Jane said. 'I'm home. Aren't you even going to say hello?'

'Sorry, I forgot. Welcome home, my Lord and Master.'

For some reason Mrs Tierney did not understand, they all seemed to think this very funny. Except for Jane.

'Your mother,' Dr Gallery said, 'has been telling me that even in the land of saints and scholars the name of Freud is known. Am I right, Mrs Tierney?'

Mrs Tierney nodded uncertainly and Brendan said: 'Well, Mamma, what about that drink I promised you? Here, drink this, it's good for you.'

It was neat gin, very nearly; it would take the skin off your throat. No wonder they were all squiffy. She watched the other doctor leaning over towards the red-haired girl. 'Well, that depends on what you mean by abnormal,' he said. 'Abnormality *per se* may be irrelevant to a person's functioning. I had a patient once,' he said, lowering his voice to a whisper.

'Faeces?' the girl said, interrupting the whisper. 'My God.'

Faeces. (Of course if I hadn't been a nurse, that would have been Greek, or rather Latin, to me.) *Faeces.* None of them paid any attention. Jane sat on the windowseat, looking tired and out of things. Brendan was talking to Dr Gallery who was not listening, but trying to get a word in edgeways. All the windows were open because of the heat and in the street below there was a continual squeal of cars. It was as though she were watching people in a play. They acted their parts, but did not see her. For them she sat in darkness.

Hard to believe that only half an hour ago, a few steps away from this noisy room, she had performed a sacrament: had done perhaps the most important thing in her whole life. Why was she sitting here now with these drunken shouters of balls and filth, these lunatics who believed in nothing but their own mad selves? And these were what Brendan called his friends. God help him.

Unnoticed, she got up and left the room. She went down the hall and entered her little cell, shutting her door on the roar of their dirty talk. She looked up at the bare white walls and saw that print by some heathen Chinese. I've had enough of trying to please them, she decided. Tomorrow, a crucifix goes up on that wall.

Max Bronstein's sister, Bella, put her head out of the kitchen. 'More *kreplech*?'

'Uh-uh,' Max said, his mouth full.

'So, are you ready for chicken?'

'Yuh,' Max said. He sat, solitary at his worktable in the dark little room which he shared with his cat. The room also contained two kitchen chairs, a portable typewriter, a convertible bed-sofa, an arm-chair purchased from the Salvation Army and five hundred books, most of them stolen from the Bronx, Brooklyn and Manhattan Public Library systems. On the wall was an *Esquire* pin-up calendar: on the mantelpiece were a pair of binoculars, and in the tiny adjacent kitchen (where Brendan had once proved you could not swing Max's cat) a set of Japanese erotic drawings picked up cheap from a friend who was getting married. 'Girls get a kick out of them,' the friend had said. But so far, the only girl who had seen them was Bella.

Bella was unmarried and worked as a secretary at New York University. Once a month she visited Max and made him a home-cooked meal. She considered her brother a genius. He considered her a dope. So what did that make him, he wondered.

'Now,' said Bella, coming in with the fried chicken. 'Tell about your lunch with the publisher. How was it?'

'That was *weeks* ago.'

'Okay, so it's weeks ago, have I seen you since then?'

'It's not interesting.'

'So, tell me anyway.'

'Well, Key himself was there.' Max said. 'And Sidney Gerston, a senior editor.'

'First of all, where did you eat? Sardi's?'

'Why would we eat at Sardi's? He's a *publisher*, not an actor. We ate at a place called Pierre's.'

'In Leonard Lyon's column, a lot of big writers eat at Sardi's.'

'Leonard Lyons.'

'So, anyway, what did you have to eat?'

Max put down his fork. Was it worth a home-cooked meal to have to talk to Bella? 'Who cares what we ate?'

'Now don't get mad,' Bella said, humbly. 'What did you talk about?'

'My book. What else would we talk about?'

'And?'

'They were telling me their promotion plans. Just business talk. You wouldn't understand.'

'Well, what else did they say?'

'Nothing. I mentioned Brendan Tierney to Gerston and he'd heard of him. So I talked Brendan up, I told them he's writing a novel, they should get it. And they were interested. They thanked me.'

'The trouble with you,' Bella said. 'You don't look after your own interest. Would your friend Brendan do you such a favour?'

Gloomily Max shovelled noodles and chewed them. Four years ago, when he and Brendan first met, Brendan had a job on the magazine and Max was trying to sell some pieces to the magazine. Brendan had helped him then. But now? 'He's changed,' Max told Bella. 'You know, after lunch that day I made a special trip downtown to tell him the good news. And you know something? Not only did he not thank me, he practically kicked me out because he was working. Yes, he's changed, all right.'

'I ask you,' Bella said. 'A writer with a talent like yours, why should you waste time with a *nebbish* like Brendan? Wait till your novel comes out, when you're a big success, he'll come running, you'll see.'

O, Bella, what do you know? The one thing Brendan will never do is run towards my success. Can't you see Brendan means something to me that you'll never mean? His jealousy gives me a bigger lift than all your stupid praise. Success, Bella, success is having people you once might have envied – it's having those people envy you. Success is very complicated, Bella.

'No,' he said. 'Brendan's my best friend and he's a talented guy. I told Gerston he was talented. I gave Gerston Brendan's phone number, even after Brendan behaved like a sonofabitch.'

'The trouble with you, Max, you let people take advantage.'

And the trouble with you is, you're too dumb to understand me. I need Brendan. I hate him, in a way. I hate those mean eyes of his, one bigger than the other. I hate the way he turns ugly when he drinks. I'm physically afraid of him: those big hands of his that stick out of his cuffs. I hate his mean, pricky way of talking, his ability to make an insult out of an ordinary remark. But I need him. He says all the angry, jealous things I feel but cannot say. Now, I get a bang out of his envy of me. Like that night I came to Dortmunder's with Jackson Clayburn's girl and he thought she was mine. I could see him staring at that gorgeous piece of ass and thinking I was in there. Ever since that night he wants to get even. But suppose he does? Suppose his book is a big success, bigger than mine? I talked him up to Gerston, half because I like him, half because I wanted to look big to him later. Maybe I went too far? Maybe Gerston will like his book more than he likes mine?

'More chicken?'

*

Frank Finnerty bought knackwurst because it was easy. Put it in a pot with cabbage, potatoes and a little salt and you had supper going for you. Cabbage he had already, and potatoes, although there were no potatoes in New York like the ones he remembered from Ireland. They were about all he did remember from there any more. He had lived thirty-one years in these United States.

On his way home he bought *The Journal-American* and checked his social security number against the numbers listed in the newspaper's daily contest. For years he had been a fan of Lucky Bucks and other newspaper promotion schemes and had twice won minor sums of money. He also played the market in a small way and as soon as he got home (a two-room, rent-controlled apartment in the East Fifties, close to the postal station where he was assistant supervisor) he put the newspaper down beside his Barcalounger chair, planning to look at the Wall Street Final before his guest arrived. Then, although he normally did not drink on week nights, he made himself a bourbon smash of Old Grand Dad.

Finnerty was a bachelor. He had not had a woman in his place since the gang from the station came over after last year's Christmas party. Although this was different, this woman was his first cousin, must be ten years older than him, a widow with grown-up kids. His sister Imelda back in Letterkenny had written to him saying the woman was coming here to live with her son. Finnerty had hoped he would not hear from her. Nowadays, Ireland was no more to him than Saint Paddy's Day and the odd letter from home. He didn't even wear green on the 17th. 'I don't have to advertise it,' he would say, with a look at Fred Schultz (whose mother was an O'Banion) and who wore four-leaf clovers, a tinsel harp and a green tie for the occasion. Who needed that garbage? Ireland? A dead issue.

He had told her seven but at six thirty-five, before he had finished his drink and checked on Algoma Mines in the newspaper, the doorbell rang. It was like opening up a stamps wicket and finding a line of customers shoving money at you before you got set up right. '*Okay*,' he said to the doorbell. 'Just a minute, will you?'

He rang the buzzer and opened the door. He could see her coming up from the foyer, short of breath as she climbed the stairs, a woman on the heavy side, with grey hair, and a ringed hand holding the banister. For a moment he could not remember her married name. Who was that doctor Imelda said she married?

'All the way up,' he called down to her and then as she drew level, he smiled and offered his hand. 'I'm Frank Finnerty. Nice seeing you. Come on in.'

'O, but I'd know you were a Finnerty,' she said. 'You have the Finnerty nose. We met, but that was a long time ago. You couldn't have been more than nine or ten.'

'Was that in Letterkenny?' he asked.

'In Creeslough. You came to our house with your father.'

He no longer remembered his father, except as a man in a photograph. But Creeslough rang some kind of a bell. 'Was there a waterfall there?' he asked. 'I seem to remember a waterfall with salmon jumping in it.'

'Yes, that's Pull Mor. The Big Hole, in Gaelic. It was on our place.'

'But I think I remember it,' he said. 'Well, what do you know? I remember it. There was a lime kiln near it, wasn't there?'

'There was indeed.'

'Well, how do you like that,' he said, shaking his long bald head, a pleased smile on his normally dour face. 'Pull Mor. I can see it, clear as a picture. Sit down, sit down. It's Eileen is your first name, right?'

She smiled at him. She understood his pleasure. Nowadays, scenes from her girlhood came back to her, every detail in them clear and sharp in a way that did not often happen with the places she knew from later years. She too could see Pull Mor. She saw the stone bridge over the road and the little gap in the whin bushes where the path led down to the glen at the foot of the falls. She could even remember the sound of the falling water, loud at dawn when you woke, loud at night when you were falling asleep. It was the sound of home. She looked at him with affection, for how many people were left in the world who knew the sound of her home?

Finnerty smiled back at her. Funny to think that just remembering some little waterfall you visited as a kid could give you this kind of lift. Usually, as soon as he left his office he felt like a motor that had been turned off. Weekends and vacations, the time was stale. He never looked forward to his annual vacation and once when a fishing trip with a guy from the office fell through, he spent the whole three weeks going up and down Forty-Second Street, seeing as many as four double features in one twenty-four hour period, eating in automats, ending up drunk in neighbourhood bars. Retirement was a thing he did not want to dwell on and sometimes when he could not sleep he wondered what would become of him when he was no longer Frank Finnerty, Assistant Supervisor, Station H. So the waterfall, well, you could say it kind of brought him back, connected him to the somebody he had been before the years he spent in the States. He could hear the word Creeslough and see a waterfall. And, after more talk with her, he began to remember other things about those days.

So, for him, the evening was saved. They ate in the kitchen and she complimented him on his bachelor tidiness, saying, the men at home in Ireland could never look after themselves half as well. With her memory helping his own, he got back whole scenes from that day's visit to his uncle's farm. She told him a joke her father had made, when his father was going off to a dance one Easter. She said his father had sometimes danced with her and that he was a very good dancer. And Finnerty, listening eagerly, tried to fit what she said about his father to the sepia photograph on his bedroom dresser, a photograph of a young man in academic robes, holding his B.A. scroll, standing by a Grecian pillar, a potted palm on his right. MADDEN

PHOTOGRAPHERS, 12 *Bridge Walk, Londonderry*. He had not looked at that photograph in years. After her first visit, he looked at it often.

There was just one part of the evening that went off the track. That was when he asked her how she filled in her time here.

She smiled a peculiar smile. 'I'm a maid,' she said. 'An unpaid domestic servant. They have me run off my feet.'

'Kids,' he said. 'That's the trouble. They want a lot, don't they? Sometimes I'm glad I never got married.'

'The thing I don't understand about them,' she said. 'They're so selfish. And if you never get beyond thinking of your own self, how can you be fit to be a parent?'

Finnerty looked at her uneasily. So she didn't get on with the son and his wife. 'Yes, the younger generation, you hear all kinds of stories. Some of the boys down at the station –'

'Of course, when I was a younger woman,' she interrupted. 'I'd have spoken up. But the older you get, the less courage you have. Or maybe it's just that you want peace.'

'Well, live and let live, is what I say,' Finnerty offered. 'Besides, things are a lot different here than in the old country.'

'I don't understand,' she said, 'how they can go through life without ever thinking about the things that count. Mind you, I don't blame her, I blame my own son. And I had the rearing of him, so I suppose what he's turned out to be is my own fault.'

'That's too bad,' Finnerty said. 'Though I guess if you don't like it over here, you could always go home?'

'Home?' she said. 'I have nothing to do at home since my husband died. Mind you, before that, I had a grand life, we had good times, I was always busy. I came over here, you see, because I thought I'd be a help with the children. But sometimes I wonder what help I am. If a person does nothing when a thing is all wrong, that can be a mortal sin.'

'I'd keep out of it, whatever it is,' Finnerty said, gently. 'Remember, you got to live with people.'

'Aye,' she said, smiling her peculiar smile. 'That's the sad part of it. You have to live with people.'

He looked at the carpet: he did not know where else to look. After a moment, he changed the subject. They went back to the past, to that country he half-remembered, and at ten when he walked her to the subway she was laughing and talking with him as though she had known him for years. He knew what that meant. He knew how, when you were alone a lot, you laughed and talked too much on the one night you were invited out. At the subway entrance he asked her to come again. She said she would love to come. And as he turned back towards his own place he felt a tightness in his chest. He knew what it was like.

*

Vito Italiano surfaced from underground by the side of the Times Building, danced through a downrush of traffic, side-stepped in and out of the slow clog of Times Square tourists and cut up Forty-Fourth Street, fast and foppish in his short-assed black silk suit, trousers, leotard-tight at calf and thigh, tab-collared mauve shirt, black knit tie, squared-off shoes. Left turn at the Blue Ribbon Restaurant. Opened the swing door by punching in with his hairy fist. Where's Lester?

Embattled Lester Krim, his friend and admirer, signalled from a two-stool outpost in the middle of the crowded bar. Swiftly, Vito moved to claim his rightful place.

'Gentlemen?' asked the German bartender as Krim relinquished the extra stool and Vito climbed aboard.

'Wurtzburger on draught. Two.'

'You're late,' Krim accused. 'What kept you?'

Vito smiled. He tilted himself back on the stool until it seemed in danger of toppling over, then brought it forward, landing on four legs with a loud thump. Double martini men on either side edged away, disapproving this horseplay. Krim paid for the drinks.

'Ass,' said Vito. 'Tail. The desire and pursuit of the hole.'

'You mean that chick from Birdland?'

'*Non, signore,*' Vito said. 'I do not mean any ordinary ass. I mean unlisted, private, exclusive, U.S. Choice, *hors concours* ass. To be put down, preserved, decanted and enjoyed at precisely the right moment.'

'Give,' Krim said. 'Who is it?'

Vito did not answer. First, he enjoyed a swallow of Wurtzburger. He lit a cigarette, shut his eyes and smiled. 'Vintage, a twenty-eight or twenty-nine,' he said. 'Sexual content one hundred and forty proof. Dark, full bodied, ripe. Chateau bottled, a connoisseur's choice.'

'Ah, come on, cut out the wine crap,' Krim said. 'Who is she?'

'Married,' Vito said. 'Two small *bambinos*. Husband, a writer of sorts. Location, right in my own department. Under study now for over a month. First skirmish, about a week ago. Second move today.'

'You laid her already?'

'It's not a question of laying her, Lester. It's a question of strategy. Let's say that as of today, I have a beachhead going for me.'

'But you said you've been a month. That's slow for you, man.'

Vito shook his head. 'Funny thing. She was under my nose for two weeks and I didn't read her. But then, one afternoon last week I'm sitting in my little cubicle and there she is, out on the floor, bent over her drawing-board. And *mamma mia, mamma mia*, the hots, Dad, the hots.'

'So?' Krim said.

'So I got up and went over, checking on her work, like. And then I took hold of her ass. Pow! She bawls me out.'

'So you goofed.'

'Yeah, I goofed, all right, but not the way you think. I goofed because I played it chicken. I went away, had a couple of Martins and came back to the office at seven. She was still there, finishing this job. So I ask her out for a drink. So that makes me a guy who asks for dates. Wrong? wrong. You dig?'

'Dig,' Krim said. He did not.

'Result, I let her go upstairs for a minute and I'm all stood up. Finish.'

'So what happened today?'

'Wait. All week I play it very cool. I treat her like nothing but nothing ever happened. Yet all week I'm there. When she looks up, I'm watching.'

'You're waiting, right?'

'Right. The gun is cocked. And there she is waiting for it to go off again, thinking about it going off. And the more she thinks the more nervous she gets. Dig?'

'Dig.'

'Now this is where the strategy comes in. First of all she's a personal friend of Louise Rogers, our promotion editor. And Louise is a dike. Mean, man, mean. So it's tricky. I mean, all it takes is one squawk out of Southern white married lady and this coon is facing the posse.'

Krim laughed. That Vito. 'So what did you do?'

'I meditated,' Vito said. 'And it came to me. She wants it and yet she doesn't want it. Because, believe me, by this time I know she wants it. The hots is a two-way thing. She has it, all right.'

'Same again,' Krim told the bartender.

'So,' Vito said. 'I finally decide that she wants it but she wants to be able to say it was rape. I couldn't stop him, your honour, he attacked me. Okay. So today, I waited until Dick and Patsy went out for coffee. Then I went in the back room where we keep the art materials. I made sure it was empty and then I sent the office boy to go tell her she's wanted. I waited in there and when she came in, I shut the door. Pow!'

'So give?' Krim said, anxiously. 'So, what happened?'

Vito shut his eyes, his white teeth showing in a smile of sweet remembrance. 'I never said a word. I just walked up and took hold of her. She was wearing a green dress. And under it, just panties and bra. What a shape.'

He smiled again, tantalizing Krim. 'So the first thing she does, the first thing is, she bites me in the neck. Look.'

He unbuttoned his collar, loosening his tight knotted tie. He pulled open his mauve shirt and showed Krim a weal of teeth-marks in the black hairy fuzz at the join of his neck and chest. 'It hurt,' he said. 'So I got her by the wrists and shoved her up against the wall. She could have yelled, that was the chance I took. But no. Like she fought me, but I knew she was faking it. Starts to moan. Keeps her eyes shut. Wants me to do those things to her, but doesn't want to know I'm doing it. Dig?'

'It's like this Lady Chatterley,' Krim said. He had been reading the paperback and found it dull. 'Like this broad in the book, she's not getting it at home, so she starts romancing –'

'This chick doesn't want a romance,' Vito said. 'She wants an orgy.'

'Same thing in this book –'

'Who's talking about a book? I'm telling you about this chick. You want to hear it or not?'

'Well, sure I do, Vito. I was only –'

'So I'm working her over and she's moaning and moaning and then – Pow! I push her away. I turn around and walk out.'

'But why?'

'Psychology. If I'd laid her this afternoon where do we go from there? She might have second thoughts. Besides, it would have been risky, I could have been interrupted. But this way, man, next time the gun goes off she'll help me pull the trigger. And when that happens, what a lay. Pow!'

Dolefully, Krim stared at the bar mirror, seeing his and Vito's reflections over a bank of stoppered liquor bottles. A married woman who wanted stand-up sex with no trimmings and no ties. Who but Vito could have such luck? For a hopeful moment Krim let himself stand in Vito's shoes, saw himself in the stockroom tearing the green dress off Lady Chatterley. For an envious moment he considered the possibility that Vito was lying, that it was all the kind of day-dream he sometimes invented himself. For a painful moment he compared himself with Vito, remembering his own sad sheet of hits and runs. He thought of solitary evenings in strip joints. He watched Vito's tongue licking Vito's lips, cleansing away the small froth of beer. Dirty pig.

When Jane came home she found her mother-in-law sitting in the living-room wearing hat and gloves. The children had already been put to bed, although it was only six o'clock.

'But why?' Jane asked, outraged.

'Because my cousin, Frank Finnerty, is taking me to dinner at a restaurant. I thought it would be easier for you if I put the children away before I go.'

What was the use in talking to her? Jane went into the children's room and although it was still light, the blind was drawn. The children were in their pyjamas, watching cartoons. She shut the set off and raised the blind.

'Why did you do that?' Lisa asked.

'Because. Give me a kiss, darling.'

They both came to her and she bent down to hug them, pressing their childish faces against the green silk of her dress. She thought of another face which had pressed against her dress earlier in the afternoon. She felt sick.

'Now hop into your bunks and I'll read you a story.'

'No. Cartoons.'

'Please, Mummy. Cartoons.'

'All you care about is TV,' Jane said, in a hot, choked voice. 'I'll bet you wouldn't care if you never saw your mummy.'

They stared at her, surprised.

'We want to see Huckleberry Hound,' Liam said.

What was the use? Sometimes, despite Gesell and Spock, her feelings of rage and aggression made her want to slap them. But, of course, there was no question of that. She switched on the set again and as she came out into the corridor, there was Mrs Let-Me escaping by the front door. 'Good night, dear,' she said to Jane. 'I won't be late.'

Be late, for heaven's sake.

She went into the living-room. If she had begun to scream the minute he touched her, he would have stopped. Or if she had simply threatened to report him to Louise. If it happened again, she should report him. Or something. It would happen again: she knew it and he knew it. O, sweet Christ, if only he were with me now, we would go into our bedroom – no, not *our* bedroom – somewhere else. The spare room. Mrs Let-Me's.

She went out the living-room and was going to lay the table for Brendan's supper when she passed the spare room. If Vito were with me we would go in here, I would open the door like this and on that bed, underneath that little black crucifix, I would lie with Vito. It would be the Feast of San Gennaro in the Village and this would be his room in the Village, and there would be music and coloured lights in the street outside as we lay here, under that crucifix, it's just the right note, because, being Italian, he's probably Catholic.

But this isn't the Village: this is *our* spare room.

What's that thing doing up there?

Why did that silly old woman put that up there?

Why can't she leave the room the way it ought to be?

And then, by a quick, outrageous illogic, it came to her that everything that was wrong today – that crucifix, Mrs Let-Me, the children watching TV instead of wanting their mother, Vito in the stockroom – everything was Brendan's fault. If he had not asked her to take this job, if he had not wanted to bring his mother over, none of this would have happened. None of it.

All his fault.

In the moment of her rage, she heard someone come in at the front door. Guiltily, she shut the spare-room door, sure that Mrs Let-Me must have come back for something. But it wasn't her, it was Brendan. He went straight into the living-room.

'Any calls for me?'

'No,' she said. She followed him in.

'Are you sure? Max said Gerston was going to call me.'

'Nobody called.'

'What's for supper?' he said, sitting down with the paper.

'I don't know. I haven't made it yet.'

'O.' He went back to his paper.

'Did you know she's stuck a crucifix up on the wall in the spare room?' Jane said.

'Has she?'

'Is that all you have to say?'

'Well, what about it, it's her room.'

What was the use. She went to the window. Spits of rain began to spatter on the pavement, covering it with a chain-mail pattern of drops. 'Brendan,' she said. 'What would you do if I asked you to let me stop working and come home to mind the children again?'

'What?' He wasn't even listening, he was stuck in the paper. What does he care what I'm going through?

The phone rang. 'I'll get it,' he said. He heard that, all right.

'Hello? Yes . . . yes, Max told me about you. Yes . . . Yes, that's right . . . Well, I hope to finish it by the fall . . . Really . . . What story of mine? . . . O, that one . . . You liked it? . . . Thank you . . . Yes. Max mentioned that . . . Okay. Sure, I'll send you the chapters. Of course . . . Yes. Okay then. Wait.'

He turned to Jane. 'Get me a pencil and a pad. Hurry.'

She did as he said.

'What was that address again? Yes.' He began to write. 'Okay then. I'll give it to you next week. Great . . . and thanks. Thanks very much. Good-bye.'

He put the phone down. 'That was Sidney Gerston, you remember I spoke to you about him? He's the editor who wants to see the book.'

His face was excited: she had rarely seen him so excited. 'And remember,' he said. 'Max thinks I can get a fifteen hundred dollar advance if they like what I show them. Do you realize what that means?'

'That's wonderful,' she said. 'But, Brendan, I want to ask you something. Would you be very angry at me, if I quit this job?'

'Why should you quit?'

'Because I'm unhappy there. Isn't that good enough?'

'But I don't understand: you told me you liked the job. Now listen, Jane, even if I get fifteen hundred dollars, that isn't going to be enough to keep us all until the book's finished.'

'I wasn't talking about money. I was talking about me.'

'Yes, but the money put this idea into your head.'

'It did not. I asked you before that phone rang, but you weren't listening.'

'O, darling,' he said. 'Be reasonable. With your salary and this advance, we could manage quite comfortably. On the advance alone, we'd founder.'

'Comfort. Is that all you care about?'

'Who's been complaining about having to scrimp, you or me? Darling, I don't understand you.'

'Because you never listen any more.'

She turned from him, went out of the room and down the corridor to her last, her only refuge. She locked the door and, as she had done so often before, sat on the john and waited for tears. But they did not come. She bent her head, exhausted, nervous, ready to scream. They did not come.

'Jane? Are you there, Jane?'

Yes, I'm here. And tomorrow I might be raped, do you hear? No, not raped. Laid. And I want to be laid, Brendan, I can't stop myself, do you understand that? I can't stop myself. Help me, why won't you help me?

'Jane?'

'Go away.'

Today, I made my apologies to Max. I phoned him because Gerston has at last phoned me. For the past three weeks I have gone about believing that Max, to spite me for my rude behaviour on that day he told me about Gerston's interest, had deliberately omitted to give Gerston my phone number. Then yesterday, Max phoned to say Gerston would be in touch with me.

So I have been unfair to Max.

But I cannot honestly say that it was my sense of fair play which prompted me to apologize today. Through Max, I may find out Gerston's true opinion of the chapters I am sending him. This means, of course, that Max is a person with some power over my future. I resent that. So, today, when I agreed to meet Max for a beer, I was prepared to be difficult. He wanted to go to the Cedar Bar. I wanted to go to Eddy's. I let him win the decision, but I was surly about it.

'I like it here,' he said, as we entered the Cedar. 'What have you got against it?'

'The Cedar,' I said, 'is like a thousand other bars. Eddy's is not. Eddy's has a certain atmosphere.'

'But this is a good place,' he said. 'I mean, take the people who drink here, they're unpretentious.'

'Yes. Action painters. Eddy's has Third Avenue house-painters.'

'Come on,' he said. 'That's what's wrong with Eddy's, that Irish bar stuff. Maybe it was true once but now it's strictly phony. Only squares like Gallery think it's hip to drink at Eddy's. Didn't you know that?'

He had no idea how much this offended me. How could he, or he would not say it. Like a small town Lothario who doesn't care what people think of his morals but who would be enraged if someone told him he ate with the wrong fork, I am obsessed by fears that I am insensitive to certain nuances of life in New York. I was furious that it had not occurred to me that Eddy's was what he said it was. Thinking of Gallery, whose favourite spot it is, I was sure that Max was right. But the other side of me – a wiser, more bitter self – was outraged at my own shallowness in being swayed by these fraudulent equations of in and out, hip and square.

'So, you're not square, eh?' I shouted. 'Well, that's just great. Frankly, to paraphrase Wellington, I don't know what you'll do to the squares, but by God you frighten me.'

A conciliatory smile formed so suddenly on his face that I knew my anger had caused his retreat. 'I don't get it, Old Buddy,' he said. 'What do you mean?'

'I mean do you ever stop to think how conventional your unconventionality is? It's Murger's book updated but with no imagination and no taste. You live in the Village, you wear sandals and grow a beard, you shun a regular job, you keep a cat. You're living the life of a stereotype: you're one of thousands.'

'So okay,' he said. 'So it's easier that way. I can do the Jewish bit too. People like you if you fall into the expected bracket. You see, Brendan, becoming a stereotype has a lot of advantages. You don't have to work at it. If I decide to play the Jew or the artist I have the part all made up, I have all my reading, all the movies and plays I've seen to draw from. No sweat.'

'And when Pat Gallery plays the Irish stereotype, do you enjoy it?'

'Of course. I feel superior to him. People love stage Irishmen because even though the clown may be witty, he's still a drunken, brawling Irish clown. And it pays off for the clown. You see, we're not all as honest as you are. You're a sonofabitch, I know, but at least you're no stereotype. I admire you for that, but don't be too hard on the rest of us.'

Jesus was a Jew: he turned the other cheek. Max, with that Jesus-turning, touched suddenly on all my own uncertainties. Who was I to lecture him, I who want a publisher to bolster my ego by taking an option on my work? Who am I to sneer at Murger figures, I who waited cravenly until the age of twenty-nine before finally renouncing the world of bourgeois jobs? And are my motives really so honest? Do I have some important philosophy which I must impose on the world, or am I simply trying to inflate myself by making others listen to me?

'Max,' I said. 'Why do you write?'

'What do you mean, man?'

'Why do you write? What do you want – fame, riches, immortality? Do you want to change the world?'

'Change?' he said. 'I don't know. Immortality? Am I a mystic? When they sing *kaddish* for me will I be there to criticize the performance? No, Brendan, I write because I have a basic need to be loved. Freud says the need for love –'

Damn Freud. Love, for me, does not enter into it. Approval, yes. But love – Jane wept last night because I refused to let her give up her job. I did not even feel sorry for her. I wanted her salary, that was all. Do I love her now? Do I love my children? I don't know. I think only of this book.

'I talked to an analyst once,' Max said. 'And he told me the reason I write novels and stories goes back to the time I was a kid and wouldn't help parcel the goods in my uncle's store. I felt guilty about that but I repressed it, see? So now, when I refuse to take a regular job, when I write stories, I'm playing, he said, I'm avoiding reality. And when I write crummy magazine pieces to make a dollar I'm making up parcels, I'm atoning. Get it? Now, the question is, suppose my serious writing pays off, supposing it starts supporting me? Will I stop it then because I won't be playing any more, I'll be parcelling? It's an interesting question.'

He stopped talking, picked off his dark glasses and stared past me. A tall girl, her dark hair bunched into a bouffant mop, had just entered the bar. She wore a green Chinese dress, its skirt slit high over her haunch. Max sat silent, his discussion forgotten, mouth slack, eyes fixed in an avid stare as she hoisted herself on to a nearby stool. As she did, her slit skirt opened wide and a white, opulent thigh slid out of it. I looked. I felt nothing. Nothing. And it isn't the first time. In the past weeks it has happened every time I looked at a girl. Yet before I became obsessed with the act of writing this novel, the sight of any pretty girl, any time, could upset all my meditations, reducing me to a mindless gape. I remember, with an odd nostalgia, the *angst* caused by wasted afternoons in burlesque shows, the idle hours when I sat at my desk watching some girl at a window across the street. Has that gone forever? In my new avocation am I become some anchorite who is above these things of the flesh? And if that is so and I can no longer feel these things, then how will I be able to write about feeling?

'Just look at that mother over there,' Max whispered. 'Man, O man.'

Max can still feel.

Lisa, tired of the silly old bricks game, wandered to the bedroom door and went a little way down the hall. What she saw sent her back, hand tugging urgently at Liam's shirt. 'Come and see.'

She led him into the hall and pointed to the open doorway of Gran's room. The sight of that grown-up, so big and heavy in her blue dressing-gown, down on her knees staring at the wall, silenced even Liam who always giggled and gave games away. But this was not a game. It wasn't even like watching Mr Carney, the super, peeing by the garbage pails. This was scary. Gran's lips moved yet no words came out. She seemed to be whispering to that little toy man on her wall. And why had she left the door open? She always shut her door. Perhaps she did it on purpose to scare us, Lisa thought. She writes letters to old nuns in black hoods.

Suddenly, wanting to run, Lisa pulled at Liam and ran with him back into their room. He was not afraid. 'Wunga, wunga,' he said. 'Me big white chief.'

'Shut up,' she said. She left him playing with the Build-It bricks and went back to the door, drawn by that sight down the hall. Gran was still on her knees, her lips moving, spooky old Gran, scary old Gran. Gran might be a witch who made secret spells. Lisa and Liam were alone in the witch's cottage.

'*Mummy*,' Lisa screamed. 'I want my *Mummy*.'

Mrs Tierney rose from her knees, awkward and stumbling as an animal trying to rise after being hit by a bullet. She saw the child run into the bedroom and hurried after her. When she entered the room, Lisa was in a corner, squatting monkey-fashion, hands over her face. She screamed when Mrs Tierney came near her.

'What's the matter, pet, what happened?'

'Go away,' Lisa shrieked.

'What happened to her, Liam, did she hurt herself?'

'Don't know.'

'Lisa, are you all right?'

Lisa screamed.

'What frightened you, darling? Tell Gran.'

'You did,' Liam said. 'You and your man on the wall.'

'What are you talking about, child?'

'Your toy man on the wall.'

'What toy – ? You don't mean the crucifix? But that's Jesus. Don't you remember, I told you about little Jesus?'

'How can that be a person? It's a toy,' Liam said, his voice a perfect replica of his mother's when irritated by a silly remark.

'No, it's a statue of a real person,' Mrs Tierney said.

'But Jesus is only a story,' Liam said. 'Like TV.'

Lisa screamed again.

'Lisa,' Mrs Tierney said. 'Come on, dear, get up. There's nothing to be frightened of.'

'No,' Lisa shrieked.

'Please, dear.'

'No. Leave me alone.'

'Now, don't you talk to me in that tone of voice, miss,' Mrs Tierney said.

'Go away.'

'All right then, I will go away. Liam too. We'll just leave you here. You won't go to the park with us, that's all.'

'Go away.'

Mrs Tierney turned and left the room.

'Gran's mad at you,' Liam said.

'Don't care.'

'You're scared. You're a scaredy cat.'

'I am not.'

'You are so. Scaredy cat.'

'You're too young,' Lisa said. 'She's a witch. You don't even know what a witch can do to you.'

'Do so.'

'You do not.'

'Scaredy cat.'

'Children,' Mrs Tierney said, coming back into the room. 'Stop quarrelling. Come on now, tidy up in here. I've decided to take you both to the park after all. Lisa, I'm sorry if I frightened you, dear. Now give me a kiss and let's make up.'

Lisa did not move.

'Scaredy cat,' Liam said.

'Am not.'

'Well, come on,' Mrs Tierney said. 'Are you going to kiss me or not?'

'Scaredy cat,' Liam said.

Lisa, with a look at him, unwillingly kissed the witch's cheek.

The slip of paper slid down on the tilted incline of Jane's drawing-board and came to rest beside her pencil. The message was printed in block capitals: LUNCH AT 12.30. CHINESE FOOD. MEET ME IN LOBBY.

Across the drawing-board, less than four feet away, the holdup man waited her answer. Don't scream: I'll shoot. A little to the left of him, Patsy Armstrong was telling Norma about a television show she'd seen last night. Dick Duryea and Carl Heffner were tossing for who would buy morning coffees. A perfectly normal scene. He waited.

'Okay,' he said. It was not a question: it was an order. Her hand closed on the slip of paper, crumpling it into a ball. She felt her face hot as she nodded. Yes.

He turned and walked back to his cubicle. No point in screaming now. It had happened in such a completely unexpected way: ten o'clock on a Friday morning, in full view of the staff. Patsy was still going on about television; Dick and Carl had begun to set up a layout and he, in his cubicle, was on the phone talking to one of the engravers at the plant. Chinese food? Perfectly normal thing to go out to lunch with your boss: people did it all the time.

Her hair. O, why hadn't her hair appointment been for yesterday instead of next week? And at lunch, what would they talk about, office gossip, or would it be about themselves? Where did he live, where had he gone to school, what sort of things did he do or like? She had no idea.

It was an eternity until twelve. Then she went to the ladies' room and spent twenty frantic minutes re-doing her hair in two different ways. At twelve twenty-five she took the elevator down and in the lobby it was the usual lunch-hour scramble with thousands of people hurrying out of their offices to eat. How would she find him? At twelve thirty-one, when he was exactly sixty seconds late, she went through the agony of believing it all some cruel joke, another skirmish in the war of tension he had played with her for the past week. He would not come.

He had made her commit herself and now he would not come.

But just as she had convinced herself of this, he darted from an elevator, weaved in and out of the crowd, and skated up to her with a confident smile, taking her by the hand as though they were teenagers going steady. He led her into Lexington Avenue, snapping his fingers for a cab.

'Where are we going? To a Chinese restaurant?'

He laughed as though she had said something outrageously funny. '425 West Fifty-Seventh,' he told the cab driver. He lay back on the cab seat and took her hand. 'You look great,' he said. 'Just great.'

Four twenty-five West Fifty-Seventh. When they got there it didn't look like a restaurant at all, it looked like an apartment building. As he paid the cab, she searched the façade of the block for some Chinese sign but all she saw was *Dr J. Jackson, Dental Surgeon : Al-El Productions, Recording Studio : H. Weitzmann, Wholesale Novelties.* The entrance hall needed a paint job and smelled of cleaning fluid; the elevator was a self-service one and there were rows of apartment name-plates in the foyer. It *was* an ordinary apartment building.

'What is this place?' she asked, as he led her to the elevator.

'Friend of mine has a pad here,' he said. 'I sometimes use it lunchtimes.'

Use it for what? O God. But he did say Chinese food, didn't he? Just think of Chinese food.

On the fourth floor he produced a key and unlocked a door. She read the little nameplate beside the bell: *L. Krim.* Who was Krim? As she stepped into the little foyer, she met the warm stale air of an apartment left empty all day, its blinds drawn, its windows shut. The living-room which faced her had a dim, second-hand look, with two spavined arm-chairs, horrid banana-coloured end tables, magazines on a pile on the mantelpiece, a tatty, wine-coloured rug and a ghastly amateur abstract over a sofa which seemed too narrow to serve as a bed. The front door shut behind her.

'Now,' he said. 'Let's have a nice cold Martin.'

He went into the kitchen and came back at once with a tray on which there were two frosted glasses and a cold jug of martinis. He *would* call them Martins, he was that sort of man. She could see him in some night club, the life of the party, heckling the performers onstage.

'How's that for service?' he said, stirring the icy liquid in the jug. 'You leave the gin and the glasses overnight in the freeze and then, at the last minute, add a few drops of vermouth. That way, you get them pure. No ice. Dig?'

He handed her a glass. 'Here,' he said. 'Get rid of your inhibitions. Two of my Martins are worth a course with S. Freud himself.'

If only he wouldn't talk, she thought, giving him a false smile. The doorbell rang.

'That's our food,' he said. He went to the door and a middle-aged Asiatic entered, wearing a white jacket and carrying a wicker basket from which he unloaded several differing paper containers. As he was being paid, the Chinese looked over at her, grinned, then shut his slant eye in a wink. What did he mean, how many times had he delivered lunches here, was she one of scores of girls?

'Okay,' Vito said, after he had let the Chinese out. 'Let's see. We've got sweet and sour spare ribs, egg rolls, fried rice, almond chicken and snow peas. That suit you?' He began to carry the containers into the kitchen.

It was impossible. She began to laugh, wondering for a moment if she sounded hysterical. It was unbelievable: at one o'clock on a Friday she was in an apartment not far from Carnegie Hall, eating snow peas and drinking 'martins' with her dark yet comic ravisher come to life.

He came out of the kitchen.

'What's funny?'

'Chinese food,' she said, laughing. 'There really *was* Chinese food.'

For a moment she thought she had offended him. He stopped in mid-stride, a carton of food in either hand. Then, his lips parted, his teeth showed in a bright, feral smile. 'Know something?' he said. 'You've got a mind like a sewer.'

'Have I?'

'And you know something? Me too.'

He put the cartons down on the coffee table, picked up the martini jug and refilled her glass. She was reminded of children giving a party, going through a series of adult politenesses which they knew to be merely a game. But she smiled and nodded her thanks, raising her drink in a toast. As they drank, they eyed each other over the rims of their glasses. Her amusement died.

She saw his left hand tug at his crotch and noticed the bulge in his awful, tight trousers. He was aware that she had noticed and at once he smiled in his knowing dirty way.

'That's right,' he said. 'I've got the hots.'

His hand went out, took the glass from her hand and set it on the end table. And then, O Christ, it was as in the dream, it was as though she were suddenly knocked down in the middle of the street. Time stopped: for seconds she would know where she was: she was on the sofa, but she had ruled out the sofa long ago as too narrow for that. She was on the sofa. Time stopped: she was on the floor. Something was hurting her back: it was her handbag. He came at her again and she moaned and clung to him. It was a street accident; she could not remember what happened. Her hair was all over her face. She pushed it aside and sat up for a moment. She saw one of her shoes under a table and her dress on the arm of an arm-chair. He talked to her obscenely. His hand caught her shoulder, pushed her down. And time stopped again.

She was standing now: where was the bathroom? She went in drunken dizziness across the room and heard herself giggling. She heard him laugh, then shut the bathroom door on him, who was that girl, that hag with her hair wrecked, staring, smiling like a crazy woman in the mirror? Must sit down somewhere. She felt weak.

On the shelf over the bathtub were a paperback novel, an electric razor, a bottle of Aqua Velva and a torn envelope. She examined these items as she would strange pebbles found on a beach. She picked up the envelope and saw a name: Lester Krim, 425 W. 57th Street, N.Y., N.Y. This is Fifty-Seventh Street in New York and it is lunch time and people are having lunch downstairs in coffee shops and restaurants. Right now. The MONY sign predicts it will stay fair and warm. There are cars in the Holland Tunnel at this very moment and the afternoon papers are on the street. Manhattan has not changed: everything is going on just as on any other day at lunch time. But I am here.

She ran cold water and washed her face. She put on lipstick. He knocked on the bathroom door and she said. 'Yes?' and he opened the door. He was wearing jockey shorts (he *would* wear jockey shorts). He had a carton of Chinese food in his hand and his mouth was full. 'How about some spare ribs, sweetie?'

She giggled: he was a stranger: the whole thing was a dream. When it was not lust, there was nothing: he was Vito Italiano from the office: an undressed stranger eating sweet and sour spare ribs. But the dark stranger: she looked at his dark-skinned muscular body, at the curling black hair which covered his chest and belly from collarbone to white jockey shorts.

'Come on,' he said. 'It's ten after two. Want to eat?'

She shook her head.

'What about a beer or something? I got cold beer.'

'Beer?' she said. What was he talking about? But he took it as assent and brought her a glass of lager. She sat down on that narrow sofa and drank it like a child told to drink up its glass of milk.

'Tell you what,' he said. 'If you want to stay here a while, I'll say I sent you over to Kohner and Woods to check on a layout. Maybe you'd like a little nap?'

'No.'

'Well, in that case we'd better eat and run. Louise will blow her top if I don't show up for that stupid ideas meeting at three.'

'O,' she said. So they would not stay locked up here forever: they would not look out on the night lights of the city: they would not pull the blinds and never never go back to that other world before the change. He was her dark ravisher, but he was also the Promotion Art Director; he would sit at Louise's Swedish teakwood table at three o'clock and discuss the pro-promotion for future issues. It was lunch hour. Lunch was over.

'Want some snow peas? They're good.'

She shook her head at the proffered carton. The food was cold. 'Hand me my dress,' she said.

Today, Sunday, the first heat wave of summer is upon us, a heavy, humid swelter which infects even the mind. Waking into it, I felt, not my usual anxiety to get down to my workroom, but a sluggish Sunday indolence. I remembered Jane's complaint that I no longer spend any time with the children and so had the idea to stay home and devote my day to a brilliant imitation of that paterfamiliarity I once found natural.

So much for my good intentions. An hour after breakfast I lay torpid on the living-room sofa, exhausted by sweaty horseplay, a father figure who had early abdicated. Jane was hunched on the windowseat, knees drawn up to her chin, reminding me, as she often does, of what she must have looked like as a small, sulky child. (She has been very quiet all weekend: probably still brooding on my refusal to let her quit.) The children were also with us for Good Daddy, having given up games, had consented to have the television set moved into the living-room. My mother, of course, was out at church.

Lisa played roulette with the channels.

'And on that Sunday morning,' said a television voice, 'Our Lord decided to go down into Jerusalem. Now why did Jesus –'

'No further word this morning from Bonn. From Moscow, a report that Soviet astronauts –'

'I want the Jesus programme,' Liam said. 'I want to see an idol.'

'Speaking to the National Association of Manufacturers last night in Denver, the president –'

'Lisa, turn that off,' Jane said.

Lisa turned it off.

'Brendan?'

I knew that tone of voice. It was 'Brendan, the apartment is on fire but we must keep it from the children.' In silent frustration I abandoned my *Sunday Times* Book Review Section.

'Now, Liam,' Jane said. 'What idol?'

'The Jesus idol,' Liam said. 'Jesus was a little boy like me. He was a god and he was a boy. Not a girl. A boy.'

'Who told you that? Gran?'

'Yes, Gran.'

'Lisa, what else did Gran say?'

But Lisa did not answer.

'She's afraid 'cause Gran's a witch,' Liam said.

'Now look here,' I said. 'Gran is my mother. You're not to talk about her that way.'

'But she *is* a witch, Daddy,' Lisa said. 'She writes letters to a nun in a black hood and she makes spells with her statue and water and a holy ghost.'

I looked at Jane. How much had she understood? If this was what I thought it was, we were due for the most frightening fallout yet. But she did not seem to have guessed. She said: 'Lisa, what else did Gran tell you?'

'Well, she said we're little Christians.'

'And what did you say, did you tell her we don't believe in that?'

'I said we're not religious,' Lisa explained. 'Because you told me to say that, Mummy, if people ask me.'

'That was right, dear. And you're not to be afraid of Gran.'

'But I am afraid of her. She's a witch.'

I waited. I foresaw it all: bedroom conference: tears, threats, appeals. Off with my mother's head. But none of it happened.

She looked at Lisa, sighed, and spread her hands, palms upwards, in a gesture of resignation.

'Can I have TV?' Liam asked, bless his egocentric little heart. At once I got up and turned the set on.

'And now, boys and girls, be sure that next time you go shopping with Mom you look for the box with the giraffe on top. Because for real goodness –'

Could Jane have missed it? Yet even if she did not suspect what I did, why was she taking this witch talk so calmly? I watched her, knees hunched to her chin, peering broodily at the river in a silence more disturbing than any show of tears or rage. Meanwhile, my own rage was reaching matricidal proportions. Mamma and her grim fairy tales. Wait till I got my hands on her.

Sunday was ruined. The newsprint wavered before my eyes as I sat, stunned in the television chatter, a prisoner of my worst forebodings. Was it ten minutes or was it the hour it seemed before I heard the front door open? I got up at once, spilling the sections of *The Times* all over the floor. I went into the hall and there she was in her black sailor straw and white cotton gloves, a missal in her hand.

'Mamma, can we go into your room for a minute?'

'All right, Brendan.'

I led the way. As I opened her bedroom door I saw the crucifix, that First Cause of my present difficulties. 'That's new, isn't it?'

'Is it?' she said. 'I thought it was two thousand years old.'

Perspiration seeped from the roots of my hair as I sat on her bed. My mother unpinned her black straw hat and put it on the dressing-table.

'Sit down,' I said. 'I want to talk to you.'

'O, is that what you want,' she said, smiling as she took the only chair. 'I thought you wanted to spank me, the way you ordered me in here.'

With that smile, with that remark, she forfeited the last faint sympathy I had felt for her. 'What are these stories you've been telling the children?' I asked.

'What stories, Brendan?'

'Mamma, you know very well what stories. This stuff about Jesus and little Christians.'

'Well, what harm was there in that? It won't hurt them to know something about the Christian religion.'

'Tell me,' I said. 'What would you have done if someone had come into our house at home and started behind your back to instruct us in something you didn't believe in?'

She did not answer.

'Mamma, I asked you a question.'

She picked up her missal and held it on her lap. She looked down at the missal, but said nothing.

She was afraid to answer: the next question was one I was afraid to ask. Spells with water, holy ghost, you are Christians, she told the children. If Jane had not guessed it, then perhaps I was imagining it? But if I asked my mother, wouldn't I be putting the idea into her head? I tried to approach it obliquely.

'Look, Mamma,' I said. 'What's the point in your filling the kids' heads with religious information when they're not even Christians?'

Her hands gripped her old black missal worn with thirty years of use, its thumb-marked pages interleaved with Mass cards commemorating the deaths of people she had known. Her face became flushed, angry, childishly eager to repay the hurt I had given her. At last, her mind made up, she put the missal on her bedtable. 'Yes, they are, Brendan. They're baptized.'

'Where were they baptized?'

'Here in this apartment. I did it.'

'But you're not a priest. It doesn't count.'

'Doesn't it, Brendan? In case of emergency, the catechism says that any layman or woman can do it. Do you not even remember that?'

'Now, wait a minute.'

'It was an emergency,' she said. 'Because you'd never agree to it being done in a church. But it's been done, now. You cannot undo it.'

In that moment I hated her. She was my past, with all its stubborn superstitions, its blind emotional faith. The rage we feel as children when Mummy knows best, the rage we know as adolescents when our parents deny us the conduct of our affairs, the frustration of all intercourse with the older generation; these things made my hand tremble as I pointed to the crucifix on her wall. 'Do you know that Liam thinks this is an idol?' I heard myself shout. 'And do you know that Lisa believes you're a witch?'

She smiled: that maddening mother-knows-best smile. 'Och,' she said. 'What's the world coming to when a wee boy thinks that's an idol? Would you want me to even my wit to a child?'

'That's not the point, the point is, you're frightening the children out of *their* wits. What do you think Jane's going to say if she finds out you've baptized them, how do you think I'm going to be able to keep you in this house?'

'Is it Jane is the boss here?'

'Jane's helping me while I finish my book.'

'The book,' she said. 'Everything comes back to that, doesn't it? It's not the religion that worries you, is it? It's just the famous book.'

'Why should the religion worry me?' I said. 'You stuffed me full of religion and it didn't do you any good.'

She bowed her head. 'Your own know where to put the sword,' she said.

'But you asked for it, Mamma. Do you know what you're

trying to do? You're trying to pick up two souls for the two you failed with.'

'What two?' she said in a frightened, furious voice.

'Sheila and I.'

'Thank you, Brendan.'

'But it's true, isn't it? It's your own salvation you're worried about, not Lisa's or Liam's.'

I said it without thinking, but the moment it was said I felt I had hit on, at least, a partial truth. She glared at me, too hurt for tears, too shocked for revenge.

'That's what you think,' she said. 'Now what do you want me to do? Go home?'

'I didn't mean that, Mamma. I don't want you to leave. I just want you to promise me you'll stop interfering with the children.'

'You say you don't want me to leave,' she said. 'But what I don't understand is why you ever brought me here. Why did you, Brendan? Tell the truth now.'

She waited: stubborn, proud; an old woman her grandchild thought a witch. A wrong word now and she would leave. I knew that. 'I thought you were lonely there since Daddy died,' I told her. 'Besides, I wanted your help with the children.'

'Aye, you wanted a maid.'

'I did not want a maid, Mamma, that's not fair. I wanted you.'

'Did you, Brendy?' she said, and as her dark, sad eyes slowly filmed, I was a boy again, frightened and touched by my mother's tears. I went and knelt beside her chair, I put my arms around her and for a moment buried my face in her bosom.

'Of course, I want you. Come on now, Mamma. Cheer up.' I raised my head and kissed her old, soft cheek. I held her for a moment and in that moment she was my mother; she had nursed me. But holding her, I thought of Jane waiting in the living-room; brooding, silent.

'One thing,' I said. 'I don't think Jane knows that you've baptized the kids. And I don't want you to tell her.'

I felt her go tense in my arms. She put her face up to look at me. She seemed surprised. And did I detect a certain disappointment in me?

'Is that what you want? Not to tell Jane?'

'It would be better.'

'All right, then. O, Brendy, I'm a burden to you. I hate being a burden.'

I kissed her. 'You're not,' I said.

But she is.

I left her, went out in the corridor and looked into the living-room. Jane was not there. I stood in the doorway, remembering a blind Negro beggar who sometimes gets on the subway car at Times Square. I was that beggar. He enters the car, moves with unobtrusive speed towards the connecting door, an actor positioning himself on his chalk marks. On cue – the jerk of the train's starting – he unholsters an aluminum cane and brings from his pocket a small tin cup. Then, legs wide apart for balance, his cane preceding him like a warning finger, he begins – tap-tap-tap/one step forward/pause. Tap-tap-tap/one step forward/pause – his slow march of pity and guilt.

Like that beggar I had rattled my tin cup, winning from my mother a donation of surrender. Now, still playing it by ear, I advanced tap-tap-tap/one step forward/Jane. I entered our bedroom.

A shimmer of sun high above the Hudson struck the double bed where she lay, the brooding Indian maiden, staring at the ceiling, her dark hair down. Awkward male mediator between warring women, I felt for the next step. I announced that my mother and I had just had a bitter row. I said my mother had offered to return to Ireland. I said she had given me a solemn promise that she would talk no more about religion to the children.

Jane stared at the ceiling. She did not look at me.

'Anyway,' I said. 'The kids will tell us if she breaks her word. And if she does, this time I'll take action.'

'What action?' she said. She still did not look at me.

'I'll send her back to Ireland, if need be. But don'k worry, she's cowed now. I really gave her hell.'

She turned her head and looked at me. 'Did you? What do you call hell?'

Tap-tap-tap. One step forward. At once I began to improvise a harsh, erroneous version of the interview, a version which played on my discovering my mother's selfish motives to her. (Though did I discover them to her? I doubt it. My mother is frightened, not repentant.) But for Jane's benefit it became a tale of wrong-doing sought out and punished, of humble, abject penitence. Of course, I did not mention the baptism.

'So you're satisfied, are you?' Jane said.

'Yes, I am. Now, I want you to forget it.'

Again she stared at the ceiling.

'Please, Jane?'

'Do you care whether I forget it?' she said. 'Didn't you tell me the other day that I can't quit, that I'm stuck with this arrangement for my children whether I like it or not?'

'That's not true, darling. They're my kids too, remember. I feel responsible, you know.'

'So you're going to take the responsibility, are you?'

'Of course. You have my word that if she tries a trick like this again, she goes home.'

'All right,' she said. 'Remember, that's a promise.'

And hosanna! I had won. Holy water, Holy Ghost, a laying on of hands, the worst had happened and somehow I had tap-tap-tapped my way forward to win unconditional surrender from my mother and an astonishing truce from Jane. Concomitant with this sense of triumph I felt a stirring of desire (a rare enough occurrence in the past month or so). I saw Jane's shoulders tremble under the brown and white seersucker dress she wore and, wondering which came first, the chicken of my desire or the egg of her tears, I sat down on the bed beside her, took her in my arms, kissed her, unbuttoned the front of her dress and kissed her naked breasts, making obeisance, magnanimous in my victory.

But something was wrong. The trembling I had taken for the usual tears was instead a sort of shivering, as though the touch of me frightened her.

'What's the matter?' I said.

'Nothing.'

'Well, come on, then, take your dress off.'

Obedient, she sat up in the bed and pulled her dress over her head. I drew the blind against the morning sun, locked the door against the children and then, sweating but victorious, lay down beside her. It was strange: I felt as though I was at last master in my own house and, strangely, our lovemaking reflected it. Jane held me more as one would hold a forgiving parent than a sometimes insensitive husband; she was not as she normally is, aggressive and wild in her movements, but passive, frightened, almost as though she simulated pleasure for my sake.

Of course I know her too well to believe that. Unless she gets pleasure, she complains, she wants another round. But this morning she did not ask for anything. She lay beside me, silent and still.

Acquiescent to my whim. That's more like it. As I said, I felt myself master of the situation. My earlier attempts at pater-familiarity, my role-playing of a Sunday at home now seemed an unreal, unnecessary farce. Balzac, during some crisis in his personal life, dismissed it with: 'And now for the important thing. Who will Eugénie Grandet marry?'

I sat up in bed.

'Jane,' I said. 'Do you mind if I go downtown now and do some work on my book?'

'No, I'll take the kids to the park.'

I began to dress at once.

Half past seven. Fix your face, get your clothes on and get out of here, why didn't he warn me how late it was, how many times this past month have I told him for godsakes don't let me be late getting home again. It's not Brendan I'm worried about but she's beginning to look funny about it and if she ever catches on. Besides, the kids, god, I never see them any more, poor darlings –

Compact, eyeliner, lipstick. She put them down shakily on the bathroom shelf beside Krim's electric razor, Krim must be waiting in that bar down the street for Vito to give him the all clear to come up –

Sweet Christ, look at that bruise under my breast, how did I get that –

Eyeliner, eyeliner, steady now. Is sex worth the worry and the drag of this evening when all I'll want to do is go to bed and sleep and not wake to find Brendan instead of him in the bed, Brendan going on about his book –

Lips. Steady with the line, and clothes, where're my clothes, where's my garter belt, outside?

Must be here someplace?

'Vito, where's my garter belt, did you see it?'

'Vito?'

In the kitchen, maybe?

'*Vito!*'

O, the lousy, stinking rat, I thought he was kidding. Gone. To some other bitch in heat, no doubt. That's nuts but, christ, why did I ever get into this, I'm sick, sick, sick that's what I am, I should see an analyst, it's masochistic and –

Here's my belt. Dress, where's my dress? On the sofa.

What time now? Twenty of – I've got to get out of here, damn him, he could have waited and got me a cab –

Zipper, please don't stick.

Cab. Money in purse?

I had five dollars, was sure I had, where is it, change purse, what did I do with it, less than a dollar in change, the subway'll take hours, O *Vito*, Vito, help me, you bastard, why couldn't you have waited –

The bar, bet you he's downstairs in that bar with his friend Krim, telling Krim all about us, no doubt –

Shoes?

All right now, all set. Imagine forgetting shoes, you'd forget your head these days if it wasn't screwed on. Please let him be in that bar, the subway, I won't be home until eight-thirty, even Brendan will think that funny –

'Hello there. Going down?'

Smile at him. Filthy old tomcat of a super in his felt slippers, his face ill-shaven, clotted with tiny spits of blood as though last night in some alley he was badly mauled by the other cats –

'Hot enough for you?'

Smile. Nod. Does he know me, he's seen me often enough, does he think I'm Krim's or does he know about Vito, he's always here, every time you come in or out, he *is* this building, its spirit made flesh, he never leaves it –

Ground floor, thank you, smile, and run now, run, O, let him be in that bar, make him be there –

But, in the bar at the end of the block there were only the neighbourhood fruit sellers, truck drivers, delivery men and postal clerks. And on a stool at the far end of the bar, a glass of draught beer in his fat hand, a folded copy of *The New York Post* in front of him, she saw the Dutch cheese shape of Lester Krim. As she approached, she looked for another glass on the bar counter, Vito's glass, with Vito just stepped out to the men's room or to phone. No glass.

'Hi there, sweetie.'

How dare you call me sweetie.

But in her high spike heels, in her fawn cotton knit summer dress, too tight this year, her hair still half mussed, her walk slightly shaky, she knew very well what she must look like in that bar, and she was no better was she, O sweet Christ, don't think of that now. He eased around on the stool, shifting on fat hams, all powdered and neat in his ballooning blue summer suit, a white hanky edged with his initials stuck up like a placard in his breast pocket, his hairless shanks showing over thick white collegiate socks, his fat man's feet in loose black loafers. He patted an adjoining stool in invitation. She did not sit.

'Have you seen Vito?'

'I thought he was with you, sweetie.'

'He was, but didn't he come in here a moment ago?'

'No. What gives? I thought you were both up at my place?'

'Yes, we *were* up there but –' How could you go on with that sentence, it looks to him now as though Vito and I had a row, or he ran out on me, he thinks, O, why did I ever come in here? Go.

'Anyway, I'm late,' she said. 'I must run. Will you tell Vito I had to rush if you see him?'

She turned, half-running –

'Hey, wait a minute.'

He said it so loud she had to stop. Everyone was looking.

'What?'

His eyes, large and distorted behind misted hornrims, floated up from her legs to her face, and then floated down again in horrid inventory. 'Can I get you a cab or something?'

A cab, O god, I forgot, he could lend me but I don't want to owe him anything, Vito could pay him back –

She pretended to look in her purse. 'As a matter of fact, I wanted to borrow cabfare from Vito.'

His smile was like folding white dough. 'Well, that's all right,' he said. 'I can lend you some, sweetie.'

Hams shifted on the stool, fat hand beckoned, willing her to come close. She stepped forward. He was above her on the high stool. 'Look, how's about a drink, hah? I mean, one short one before we get a cab?'

'No, I have to run, I'm late already. Could you possibly lend me a couple of dollars? Vito would give it to you tomorrow.'

He wagged his hand in the air. 'Hey, Harry. Some service here. Now, come on. One drink, sweetie?'

'No.'

'Two Manhattans,' he told the bartender.

'Are you going to lend me cabfare or not?'

'Like how much?' he said. 'Fifty dollars?'

'You bastard,' she said. Vito and Vito's world where men say things like this. Get away now.

'Hey? Hey, Jane?'

'Let go of me.'

'Hell, I lend you my apartment any time you want it, you might at least have one drink with me, what's the matter with you?'

'Let *go* of me.'

'What's going on?' said the bartender, coming back.

'Nothing,' Krim said, letting go.

She ran into the street.

*

It was mortifying for Mrs Tierney. The one night in the past fortnight that she wanted to go out, Jane was late home again. Mrs Tierney had to wait until seven-thirty when Brendan came in and then spend her own few pence on a taxi downtown and even so it meant her cousin was half an hour standing on the street corner in all that heat, and him, poor man, after a hard day's work.

So was it any wonder she was a bit flustered now, faced by fruit desserts, watermelon, cottage cheese, salads, roll-mops, tongue, sandwiches of liverwurst, pastrami, chicken livers, salmon and lox, Swiss cheese, baloney, meat loaf, Yankee pot roast, baked ham and noodles, pork chops, liver and onions, roast beef, corned beef and cabbage, spaghetti, ravioli, macaroni and lasagne. Pumpernickel and rye bread, caraway, poppy-seed and cinnamon rolls. And all this only a beginning for the counter was sixty feet long and behind the glass display shelves were dozens of alternative dishes. Bewildered by such choice and intimidated by the counterman's impatience, she selected just a cup of tea, a ham salad and a slice of cream cake which Frank Finnerty put on a tray and carried to a table.

The cafeteria was in Times Square. It was crowded and when they found an unoccupied table it was littered and dirty. A floorman came to clear away, beginning by dumping two ash-trays of cigarette butts into a half-used portion of food, then stacking all the dirty dishes on top of each other without clearing them off first. It sickened her, the waste and carelessness of it. The cafeteria was air-conditioned and had rows of green plants which were not plants and tables and chairs which seemed to be made of wood but were some plastic stuff. Finnerty told her he often ate here. The food, he said, was first class. But as she bit into the cake she suffered a familiar disappointment. American food was for show, not for taste. Like the false wooden tables and the plants which were not plants, it was as though no one remembered what the real thing had been like.

Finnerty went off to get them some ice water. As she looked

down the vast bright aisle of tables, Mrs Tierney noticed how many of the people were eating alone.

Alone. When Brendan kissed me that day last month and asked me to stay on regardless, I was sure things would change. He would be nicer. Kinder. I had a right to think that, hadn't I?

I'm not imagining things. The minute I come into a room, don't both of them pick up books and newspapers to avoid having to talk to me? And sometimes when I make some ordinary remark, Jane draws in her breath as though I had stabbed her. Or worse, looks at me across the table with eyes that say you old nuisance you, yes, that and nothing else. I'm not imagining it. It happens.

Alone. Isn't it boycotted I am this past month? Why should I put up with it? Life's too short, as the man said.

They say it's a sign of age when you start feeling put upon. Old people are always imagining they're being insulted, when that's not the case.

But I'm not imagining it.

O well, here's Frank coming back, no sense worrying him with my woes. It's nice of him to ask me out, nice to talk to somebody for a change. 'Well, Frank, and how's the work going?'

'Slack. Volume of mail always drops off in the summertime. Mind you, we have lots of change of address headaches when people go off on vacations.'

'And what about you? When do you take your holidays?'

His long pale face grew uneasy and he stared at his plate as though he had eaten something sour. 'End of July. Me and another guy go up to Canada to fish.'

'That must be nice.'

'Well,' he said. 'Tell you the truth, I don't care much for vacations. Three weeks is a long time away from work.'

'I didn't know you liked your work as much as that.'

'I like the company,' he said. 'I mean, living the way I do, it's the company that counts. Five years from now when I go on pension, I don't know what I'm going to do to fill in the days.'

She nodded, for she knew. Dromore Estates and that wee bungalow. 'But maybe you might find another job, Frank?'

'Not at my age, not in this town. Anything I'd get would be leavings.'

'You know,' she said. 'I've been wondering if there isn't

some job I could do, once Brendan no longer needs me to help with the children.'

'You mean you want out of there?'

Now, why did he say that, what did he guess? 'O, no, I was talking about the future, not now.'

'But you don't like it, living with Brendan, do you? They're giving you a hard time there?'

She stared at him, trying to put a smile on her face. 'Brendan? Not at all, Brendan's very decent to me. I was only asking about jobs for later on, when my grandchildren are more grown-up. I thought I could take a full-time job baby-sitting for someone else's children.'

'At a buck an hour? You wouldn't make a living.'

'Well, I could always do other things, Cooking or something.'

'A domestic? At your age, a woman like you? If that son of yours ever lets you, he should be shot.'

'Now, don't misunderstand me, Frank, I never discussed it with Brendan. I was only wondering –'

'Sons and daughters,' he said bitterly. 'I'm glad I never got married. One thing about me is, I can take care of myself. I don't have to ask anybody for a thing. Yes, I only have myself to worry about.'

No sense losing your temper with him, he doesn't understand, he's the sort that insults you without knowing he's done it. How could he know that you can love your children, even when they no longer love you? How would he know that one kiss or a kind word from Brendan, even now, is a sign that I am still wanted here on earth. Poor Frank.

Outside the cafeteria window golden advertising lights bled into a red haemorrhage, blacked out, became golden once more. On a huge billboard, a painted face advertised Camel cigarettes. Every five seconds, through the hole of its mouth, a large, wavering smoke ring floated out across the square. Like Frank, the billboard face stared out through eyes that did not see, it blew out smoke, simulating life. It felt nothing. It would go on blowing smoke until the day when, dirty, showing signs of age, it was pasted over and replaced by a new billboard face which, in turn, would simulate life but feel nothing. Frank lived for his own self. Was that life?

O Brendy, that day you kissed me, I asked you if am a

burden to you. 'You're not,' you said. It was an answer but what does that sort of answer mean? It reminded me of the times I used to ask Grattan if I was getting old-looking. (And I was getting old-looking.) 'Of course not,' he would say.

An answer.

From the omphaloskepsis of my writing I have been dragged back into life. Gerston, the editor to whom I sent those chapters six weeks ago, wrote me the day before yesterday to say that he had read them, was 'most interested', and that he and Gardiner Key, his chief, would like to have lunch with me at the Harvard Club today. Would one o'clock be convenient? These simple words had the ring of poetry. I could have improved on it, of course, but after six weeks filled with unease at the possibility of rejection, it was joy. I have not been myself since.

And so, *me voilà*, at two minutes to one on a hot July day, pausing on the corner of Forty-Fourth Street in a childish panic: is my hair untidy and do not notice the smudge on my shirt, it was an accident: is this grey silk tie which I bought in emulation of those gentlemanly English actors I see in movies, a mistake? My blue summer suit does not fit: as always the sleeves seem too short. My shoes are dusty although they were clean when I left home. If they think I am provincial or poor, they may try to take advantage of me by offering me a smaller advance. Couldn't I call the whole thing off and write them a letter instead?

In this indecisive state I passed the Harvard Club twice without finding it, my panic increasing for, by now, I was three minutes late. Finally, by a process of counting street numbers, I decided that the unobtrusive doorway, unmarked by any plaque, must indeed be the club. I entered and was at once noticed by a hall porter who asked my business. I am unable to describe the hallway: I remember only that it seemed to me that the club servants looked as though they belonged there while the members (men in ordinary business suits) did not. I know that I was asked to wait and wait I did, cap-in-hand and bomb-in-the-other-hand, while a porter who had taken my name went down a long hallway, through a room where men played chess and into another room where men sat in dark leather armchairs, reading magazines and newspapers in what seemed to be semi-darkness. The porter emerged from this room followed by a person who proceeded up the hallway under the gaze of oil portraits of former Harvard alumni as though he were a visiting chief of state and the portraits an honour guard of troops. At sight of this person (was he Key or Gerston?) I wanted to hide. How could my work interest this sort of man; what had I in common with a denizen of this established deep? But, as usual, the arrogance of my insecurity won over my fears. I stood my ground as the porter whispered, pointing me out. The porter stepped aside. The prince came on.

At first sight I mistook him for English. His summer suit, cut for him in London, seemed in New York foppish, tight-waisted, faintly homosexual. He was English too in his hairdressing arrangements, for he wore his hair unusually long, curling down in grey locks near his collar. Erect and senior, he advanced towards me, a Hogarthian figure with bluish, pouting lips, choleric cheeks and a large signet ring on the hand which shook mine. 'How do you do? I'm Gardiner Key. Good of you to come.'

The phrasing might be English but his voice set me at ease for it was Southern, folksy, professionally warm. His grip was dry and firm, his hand slid from mine to pat my shoulder, turning me in the proper direction, easing me on to the premises. He looked around as though daring any member to object, then deftly steered me into a large bar where drinks were served. We stood at the bar: there were no chairs. 'Sid Gerston will be along in a minute,' he said. 'Now, what will you have to drink, Mr Tierney? Gin and tonic? Hot today, isn't it?'

I said it was. The front of my shirt showed it.

'Do you work here in the city?' he asked.

'Yes.'

'You have a job?'

'No. I gave up a job to finish writing this book.'

'Umm.' He turned from me and looked along the bar. 'There's Sid.'

Sidney Gerston, who came hurrying up, was short, dark and impeccably tailored in a black suit of the style favoured by managers of Ritz hotels. He refused a drink, whereupon Key led us into the other room, sat us down at a table, rang a bell to order me a second gin and tonic, then leaned back in an armchair, his grey lion's mane ruffed against its head-rest. 'Now, Sid,' he said. 'Tell this young man what we think.'

'I have some notes here,' Gerston said. His notes, which he produced from an inside pocket, seemed to be written on the back of a business envelope. I felt a quick prick of irritation.

'Well now,' Gerston said. 'First off, if the ending of the book matches what you've already shown us, Mr Key and I believe it's quite possible we'll have a best-seller on our hands.'

'That's right,' Key said. 'If you keep this pace up, I'm willing to bet you'll emerge as one of the most successful young novelists on our list.'

Best-seller. Successful. My dear Mr Bach, these church pieces aren't church pieces at all, they're good music hall tunes and they'll make you a great hit on the boards. I, who had come to them, tailwagging, rumpswitching in eagerness for their caress, had instead been kicked twice in the head. For wasn't this proof positive that they thought my book had no literary merit, but was simply the rough stuff of one of those wish-fulfilment chronicles which, properly packaged and marketed, would bring riches to the house of Key?

I drank my second gin and tonic at a gulp. Gerston was still talking, but who cared?

'... One or two small points, questions of taste. However, that's all very minor ...'

(So all my life I had been deceiving myself, I had imagined myself to have talents I did not. ...)

'... for the important point, of course, is that while we do get the odd book which has definite literary merit, most of them, I'm sorry to say, don't find a wide audience. In your case we feel we have a book that will be more than just a critical success, there's every chance it'll also reach a fairly large readership and *that*, mind you –'

'Wait?' I said. 'Did you say critical success?'

'Of course. The book has very high literary merit. The writing is very exciting.'

'Indeed it is,' Key said, tossing back his lion's mane. 'Beautifully done. And as for it's being exciting, why, I read the whole thing at a sitting and now I can't wait to read the last part. I gather you're pretty far on with it?'

'Yes, I've been working on it for two years and since I quit my job to finish it, it's been coming along at a great rate.'

'And when do you hope to finish it?'

'September, I think.'

'Splendid. Well, supposing we give you an advance of five hundred dollars now, as an earnest of our interest. And when you deliver the completed manuscript, we can let you have another fifteen hundred. How would that suit you?'

'That would be fine,' I said, and what I said after that, I no longer remember. The gin hit my head in a sudden rush of euphoria and I have never, I swear it, felt anything like the bliss that followed. We had lunch and they talked and I pretended to listen but my mind was far away in the sweet realm of speculation. A critical success *and* a large readership. My short stories had not been a flash in the pan. I was at last, officially, a writer.

Is it any wonder that when I said good-bye to them at a quarter after three, I was a little delirious? I remember wandering over to Sixth Avenue and pausing to stare in the window of a back-date magazine store, wondering if, one day, collectors might be searching stores such as this for issues of the little magazines which had published my early stories. And yet those stories no longer seemed important. This was important. I was born today, today I have at last had some proof that my life's search has not been a delusion. For, all my life I have been a seeker: no Hound of Destiny has pursued me down the nights and down the days. I am the hunter, I seek the hound, yet until today, no tracks have appeared to show that he has indisputably passed my way, and the rumours of his presence which I have followed over the years have often seemed garbled, the road empty, the spoor faked. But there, staring into the window of that back-date magazine store on Sixth Avenue, I knew that I had at last found the track. I was Brendan Tierney, a free man and a writer, and in that moment, I would not have traded places with anyone else who lives or lived. I was young: I had justified my boasts. The publication of my book would change my life. My entry into Jerusalem had begun.

If misery loves company, then triumph demands an audience. Maybe I'd phone old Max. You'd better treat me with more respect now, Max, I'm going to get a bigger advance than you did. They think I'll be both a critical success and have a wide readership, d'you hear me, Max? You and your girls in orange suits.

I found a phone.

'Max?'

'Brendan, that you?'

'Yes, listen, Max, I'm uptown, I just had lunch with our publishers. How about meeting me at the San Remo for a beer?'

'So they're going to do your book,' Max said.

'Sure, they're going to do it, they're high on it, they think I'm going to be the most successful young novelist in the country. Key said that. Now, come on, let's meet and have a celebratory drink.'

There was a silence at the other end of the line.

'Max?'

'Look, Brendan, I'm working.'

'Ah, come on now, don't do that to me. Just one drink?'

'You did it to me,' Max said. 'So long, Brendan.'

He hung up.

Success breeds jealousy: one must be prepared for that. And I felt his jealousy was intelligent: I would be jealous of me, if I were Max. After all, I had warned him that one day he would fear me.

Well, who else would be impressed? Pat Gallery, but Pat has patients in the afternoon, he's never free before five, no good telling him on the phone, I needed him facing me at Eddy's bar, telling others that he knew me when. Pat was for later. But it was only half past three. Who?

Jane. Her office was close by; she could come out and have a drink. She wanted a goddamn bestseller, didn't she? Well, Jane, you'll get what you want, and I'll get what I want. Critical success and a large readership, dammit.

I found another dime.

'Mrs Tierney? Do you mean Jane Tierney?'

'Yes. Mrs *Brendan* Tierney.'

'One moment, please.'

'Hello, who do you want to speak to?'

'*Mrs Brendan Tierney.*'

'You mean Jane? Hold on. Hey, sweetie, you're wanted on the phone. Take it on two.'

(Who's that calling her sweetie, who's he?)

'Hello?'

'Jane, this is Brendan.'

'O, it's you. How did your lunch go?'

I told her.

'But that's wonderful, Brendan, just wonderful. I'm so happy. Did he really say all that?'

'Of course he did.'

'O, that's the best news in ages. Aren't you excited?'

'A bit,' I said. 'Now, look, I want you to come out right now and have a celebratory drink with me.'

'But that's impossible, darling, I'm in the middle of a rush job.'

'Well, drop it. This is the biggest day in our lives.'

'I can't drop it, they're waiting for me to finish this layout so that it can go to the plant. Supposing we celebrate later on when I get home?'

'No,' I said. 'I want to see you now. To hell with the job.'

'You said we needed the job.'

(Well, of course, that was true. Five hundred was all very well, but –)

'All right,' I said. 'I'll see you this evening. Will you be home early?'

'I'll try. And congratulations again.'

She rang off.

And who did that leave? There were other friends, of course, but all of them were working. Besides, my news would have greater impact if dropped casually. Phoning seemed gauche. And who did that leave, what enemy could I strike dumb with this tale? 'What makes you so sure you'll do something great in the future?' Those words came to me in the telephone booth and, decided, I went out again into the swelter of Sixth Avenue. She would probably be in the park with my kids. Children, your Daddy is a great man: one day you will know it. And you, mother, with your maternal smile of disbelief, wait till I tell you this.

Heavy with drink, wet with perspiration, breathless in the heat – yet happy, light-headed, ready to sing – I signalled a taxi and told the driver to take me to Central Park at Ninety-Sixth. Tomorrow, back to my cell in the Village for the last lonely weeks of toil, weeks that will be shortened by the knowledge that I am no longer writing into a void. By Brendan Tierney, a young author who has sprung fully-armed, in our opinion Brendan Tierney is the most promising, a talent of whatsit proportions, a book which stands out among the dead trees of contemporary, etcetera, etcetera. By Brendan Tierney, foreign versions including the Japanese, copies in all the great libraries including Alexandria –

A tiny white puffball yap-tapped at my ankles as I came up the path to the playground. Dogs dislike me. When I menaced him with my foot, a black crow flapped at me, her hag's features contorted with rage. 'Here, Bubbles, here, Bubbles – you leave that dog alone.'

'Make him leave me alone.'

'A little dog, what harm could he do you?' Scooping up her hideous baby brute, scuttling back to her bench, giving glare for glare as we pass. On a bench a little further on, my mother in earnest conversation with an art nouveau figure whose neck and arms were adorned in grotesque ceramic jewellery, and on whose lap, so help me, I saw a copy of Suzuki's *An Introduction to Zen Buddhism*. Zen? Mamma? And I, in my innocence, worried that she might be lonely here in New York. I stopped. She had not seen me. She listened to her companion, who, seeming to recognize me, whispered and pointed. My mother looked up, alarmed.

'Brendan, what are you doing here, what's wrong?'

'Nothing, Mamma. How are the kids?'

'They're on the swings.'

Liam's little butt falls from the sky to meet Lisa's twohanded shove. Up he goes to the treeline, his tiny figure etched against the distant towers of Manhattan, swinging free, innocent of his future, of the father he must surpass. My children. I feel a sudden surge of love for them. But my books shall be my true children. Sickening memory of my arrival in America, the customs officer coming up as I waited on the pier with my suitcases open. The customs officer put his hands in, found some manuscript folders of stories and poems: beginnings, all abandoned. 'What are these?'

'My children,' I said, babbling it out, sick of shame and shock at having said it. 'What?' said the customs man.

'Personal papers, I'm a writer.' And I will meet him in hell and tear his throat out for the way he laughed, then leaned across the table, telling his colleague what this lunatic had said. But after all, who was to blame but myself, what sort of writer would say such a thing except some old Bloomsbury Lady-poet, twittering at the Society of Verse Speakers' annual meet? Of course, if M. Gustave Flaubert said it, Mr Francis Steegmuller would record it. To achievement, all is forgiven. But who will forgive me, young and naked in the marketplace, my wares unproven, the knife-blade of public contempt already half-way in between my shoulder blades? A familiar nightmare, but as I relived it, there on the path to the playground, I remembered that today I *was* forgiven: remembered Key, Gerston, that talk of ours –

'Mamma,' I said. 'I have great news. They're going to publish my book.'

I had forgotten the Zen mother. 'Well, isn't that marvellous,' she told my mother. 'Congratulations, you must be so proud. And congratulations to you, of course,' she said, smiling on me. 'How wonderful, wonderful, wonderful to know your creativity is recognized.'

'Brendan, this is Mrs Hofstra, a friend of mine,' my mother said. 'Mrs Hofstra is very interested in the arts.'

'Not only interested. Engaged and involved. Of course, only as a student and amateur, you know. Not a creative talent like yourself.'

Mother, I screamed in silence, mother, I must talk to you, I am bringing you the most important news of my life, I do not want to meet this friend of yours, come with me –

'Mamma,' I said. 'Could you spare a moment?'

'All right, Brendan.' She stood up. 'You'll excuse us, Mrs Hofstra?'

'Of course, dear. I must get back to my book. Nice to have met you, Mr Tierney. An honour, I should say.'

'Are you interested in Zen?' I asked her.

'O yes. Such a wonderful man, Dr Suzuki. Nearly eighty and such a fount of energy and activity.'

'Do you understand Zen?'

'Well,' she said smiling. 'The sound of one hand clapping. That's pretty deep, wouldn't you say?'

'I would.'

I took my mother's arm and steered her down the path.

'Brendan,' she said. 'I'm ashamed of you. You could have been more polite. Goodness knows, Mrs Hofstra was dying to meet you. I don't know where you got these manners.'

I was ten years old and we were in the park at home and I had failed to salute one of her friends. The news that I had come uptown to deliver had not penetrated that fond, obtuse mind which still saw me as wee Brendy, a child of Liam's age. And I, in turn, felt with her, not the irritation I would feel with an adult, but the exasperation of an adult faced with a balky child. Is it any wonder that, in this impasse of confused identities, I was too angry to speak?

'I mean,' she said. 'You might at least have thanked her for her good wishes.'

'And what about you, Mamma, I came to tell *you*, not some stranger. And what did you care? All you care about is what some complete stranger thinks.'

'That's not true, Brendan.' She stopped in the path, half-turned to face me and put her hand on my arm. 'Of course I'm pleased, you've done well. I'm proud of you. Here' – she put her face up and kissed my cheek – 'I remember that even as a wee boy, you always wanted to write a book. I'm very glad.'

But was she? Was this the moment I had waited for all my life, was this the final, unconditional surrender of the forces that had predicted my fall? My mother was my mother: I was still her child. I was in a temper: I demanded her love and respect. Knowing this, she kissed and calmed me. There, on the playground path, I relived my memory of that long-ago school fountain. I shivered and, as then, I felt I might weep. Was this the final fulfilment? Was this all there was?

'Have you seen Jane?' she asked.

'I told her over the phone. We might go out tonight and celebrate. Is that all right?'

'Of course, dear.'

'Well,' I said. 'I just wanted to tell you. I'll go now.'

'Good-bye, Brendan. That's good news.'

Good news.

And then? There is a time I do not remember, the time which elapsed between my leaving the park and phoning Pat Gallery to meet me in Eddy's bar. I went downtown: I remember walking along Fifth Avenue and stopping outside Scribner's window, trying to visualize a pyramid of copies of my novel behind those panes. I was not satisfying as a fantasy: after all, thousands of bad novels must have been pyramided there over the years. My mother was glad for me, that was all. I was wee Brendy and I had been rude to some old woman who was her acquaintance in the park. I had not won my battle with her: I would not win it in my lifetime. One book did not prove me right. I was not revenged.

But Pat – Hibernophile Patrick O'Sullivan Gallery – now there was my man for praise. I wanted to see his face, so I did not tell him the news over the phone. I waited in Eddy's, waited two gins and tonic worth for the first sight of his grey crew cut, his tycoon spectacles, his neat collegiate suit. This then, would be the moment. This would be the joy. But was it?

When he came in, I bought the drinks. 'Why?' he said. And I told him. I was modest, yet I left nothing out. As I talked, I watched him grip his glass, his eyes on me, his lips parted. I waited for his shout of glee.

'Great,' he said, in a voice flat as stale soda water. 'That's just great, Brendan. That's good news, all right.'

I waited. Surely to Jesus we would at least have one whoop, one hyperbolean statement, one yell to Eddy to come and hear?

'Yes, you must be pleased, all right,' he said.

What was wrong, why did he seem so down, was he in the middle of some personal crisis, or did he just not believe me? 'What's wrong, Pat? I thought you'd be happy. It confirms your judgement, after all.'

'Nothing's wrong. It's all great.'

Again, that flat 'great'. Was he, could he possibly be jealous, what was there that worried him in my story, was it the best-seller thing? That was it. 'Is it the best-seller bit that worries you?' I asked, and as I asked it I saw that it was not that, for he lit on it like a man finding an argument.

'Best-seller, yes, that worries me a little,' he said. 'I mean, let's face it, no work that has any real merit finds immediate acceptance with a large public, now does it? Nothing that's really new. Obviously, Key thinks this book of yours already fits some neat publishing groove.'

O, that wasn't it at all, he was jealous. He had lost his right to patronize me and feed my ego, that was it, I saw it in his face. But he had made a fighting remark: I had to answer it. 'Now, that's just not so,' I said. 'There've been a lot of good books which immediately appealed to a large public.'

'A certain public, yes,' he said. 'But best-sellers? Name me some.'

But for some reason I couldn't think of one, off hand. Of course, I was dulled with drink, duller with disappointment. One book would prove nothing, I could see that now. Not even with Pat. And it was then, looking back on the afternoon that I remembered Max cutting me off, my mother being 'glad' for me. (Jane now, while she wouldn't have a drink with me, had been nicer than that.) Jane had been really glad, hadn't she? I no longer wanted Gallery; I wanted my wife. 'Just a minute, I said, avoiding that bestseller question. 'I've got to phone Jane, she's going to meet me here.'

'Go ahead,' he said. He did not seem to care if I ever came back.

So I phoned Jane's office. The phone rang and rang. After a long time, some cleaning woman said everyone had gone home. I phoned home. My mother told me Jane was not there.

*

At five fifteen, Jane tidied her desk, took the elevator down to the lobby and pushed through the revolving doors which led to the street. It was the evening rush hour: all over Manhattan men and women were going home. A right turn would take her towards her subway. She turned left. She walked one block down and half a block across and went into a restaurant called *The Little Danube*; a long dark room, lit in this pre-dinner hour only by the strip of fluorescent lighting over the service bar. Behind the bar the restaurant section stretched back towards two doors marked *His* and *Hers* and, in the murky shadows, tables loomed like rows of tombstones covered by white shrouds. It was hard to see if anyone was there. Sometimes he was: sometimes he was not. She never knew.

When he did not come he left no message, no excuse. He behaved like a secret agent, ignoring her in the office, enjoying the elaborate subterfuge of note-passing, the selection of rendezvous, the precautions of separate arrival and departure. It was as though he took pleasure in the contrast between their abandoned private behaviour behind the locked door of Krim's flat and the formality of their encounters in public. He never kissed her here. In taxis he did no more than hold her hand.

For Jane all this was a painful excitement; painful because she could never be sure of him. Sometimes after receiving a note from him arranging a rendezvous, she would sit for an hour in the gloom of *The Little Danube*, despising herself, hating him, leaving in a rage. Sometimes, he wanted her to come to Krim's place at lunchtime and again, after work, on the same day. But sometimes no note would pass for two or three days, and stare as she might in the office, he would ignore her. He did not love her: he used her. At first, she had been glad for it meant that there were no messy complications: now, it dismayed her.

Tonight, he had come. Of course. He *would* come on the one night she must refuse him. He sat in the shadows in a booth by the wall, a martini glass on the naked tablecloth in front of him. He did not get up when she came and as soon as she sat down, he hissed at the waiter, a trick she hated. The waiter raised one finger to show he understood and they sat in silence until the drink was served and the waiter had retreated. Vito did not trust waiters.

'I can't come tonight,' she told him.

'What's up?'

'Remember that call for me this afternoon? That was my husband.'

'So?'

'His book is going to be published. He wants me to come home early so that we can celebrate.'

'So, you'll be home a little late, is all.'

'No, Vito, I can't.'

'Why not? You afraid of him or something?'

'Of course not. It's just that I don't want him to become suspicious. I don't want to spoil what we've got.'

He was silent for a moment. Then he leaned across the table and said in a sudden, furious whisper: 'Janey, you've got nothing, do you hear me, nothing, unless you come with me tonight.'

Under the table she locked her hands to stop the trembling that had started. It did not stop. 'You're a bully, Vito. You're a stinking, lousy bully. You *are*.'

'But you like it. You told me you like it.'

'No, I didn't. Not this sort of bullying. Anyway, it's not fair. Think of all the times you've stood *me* up.'

'We're not married, are we?'

'Please, Vito. O, please, I don't want to fight with you.'

'So, don't fight. Let's go to Krim's place for a while.'

'But I can't. It's impossible tonight. Now, that's final.'

His hand reached out across the table, caught her bare forearm. It hurt. 'Wait,' he said. 'Let's make sure you know what you're saying, sweetie. If you don't come with me now, I won't ask again. Dig?'

'But that's not fair.'

'Who's talking about fair? I'm telling you I'm not going to stand around and wait for you while you go off with your husband, understand? That's not my style, kid.'

'O, for God's sake,' she said, pulling her arm away in irritation, 'stop talking like some second-rate Brando.'

He picked up his drink: she thought he was going to throw it at her. He drank it in a swallow, put the glass on the table, stood up –

'Vito, wait, I'm sorry, please Vito –'

'Bye,' he said. He went to the bar, put a five-dollar bill on it, did not wait for his change, walked out. Yes, just like some imitation Brando tough, that's all he is, that's just what he is – In panic she scrabbled on the banquette for her handbag (it had fallen under the table), found it just as the waiter came up with change from the five, rushed past the waiter and out into the street. He had reached the corner. She saw him put two fingers in his mouth and give the piercing whistle with which he habitually signalled a cab.

'Vito, Vito?'

She began to run, crippled on her spike heels . . .

'*Vito.*'

. . . saw a quick wriggle of his hips in the tight, grey silky suit as he bent to enter the cab . . .

'Vito, I'll meet you at Krim's –'

The cab door slammed shut, the long, yellow body of the cab slid forward and she saw his face in profile; that dark feral face, staring at the back of the taxidriver's head. Had he heard her? The cab merged in traffic and she was alone, suddenly perspiring in the muggy heat of the street, a strange man looking at her as he passed. She turned, lost, walked to the street corner, wondering where the cab had taken him, O, please, darling, please come back, you lousy bully.

Perhaps he had gone to that bar to tell Krim he would not be using the flat after all. Or perhaps, hearing her shout, he had decided to go to the flat and wait to see if she would come running. Yes, I'll come running. She waved to a cab, but the cab passed on. She walked down the block, signalling several cabs before she had any luck.

'Where to, Lady?'

Yes, where to, Lady? What if he isn't there, why did I make

that Brando crack, who'd ever have guessed he'd be so insecure? Or was it just that he's been waiting for an excuse to have a row with me?

He's tired of me.

When she paid off the cab at West Fifty-Seventh Street, she hesitated for a moment. The bar, or Krim's place? The bar would be easier. She went in. Four men in shirtsleeves at a table at the far end. A drunken old woman sat on a high stool, trying to get the bartender's attention. There was no one else. Not even Krim.

Vito lived on Delancey Street. She knew that. She had never been to his place and he seemed reluctant to talk about his home life. One Sunday afternoon, thinking of him with such longing that she prepared to risk his anger, she looked in the phone book and dialled his number. There was no reply. Would he have gone home now? No, she thought not.

She left the bar and went out into the street. She walked down the block to Krim's apartment building. The apartment super sat by the door in felt slippers, surplus store pants and transparent nylon shirt. He was smoking a White Owl cigar. 'How're ya,' he said. He got up and followed her into the foyer. He rang for the elevator, why didn't he leave her alone, filthy old tomcat. 'Hot enough for you?' he asked. 'Over on the East Side last night some woman went crazy in the heat, ran out in the street, naked as the day she was born, with a big butcher knife in her hand. Stabbed two fellas and a cop before they got her in the wagon for Bellevue.'

He acted this out as he told it, making an obscene breast-hugging gesture when he said 'naked', menacing her with an imaginary butcher knife as he described the stabbing. He winked at her as he held the elevator door open. Mad old tomcat, this city was full of lunatics, people who went into muttering fits on the bus, others who shouted obscenities in automats, lost souls who walked the pavements alone, caught up in imaginary conversations. And I am one of them, running like a madwoman after the likes of Vito, humiliating myself –

She went down the corridor quick as a thief and jammed her finger on Krim's bell. No one answered. She rang again. She rang a third time. She was just about to turn away when she heard a footstep in the tiny foyer inside. 'Vito?' she whispered. 'Vito, is that you?'

No answer.

Had she imagined it? She listened, but heard no sound. 'Lester,' she said. 'Is that you, Lester?'

No answer.

But then she heard an inside door shut, she could swear it. 'Vito, I know you're in there. *Vito.*'

(Mustn't shout.)

Across the hall, slightly to her left, a door opened. A tiny girl in a stained playsuit stood looking at her.

'Vito, do you hear me? It's Jane. I'm sorry. I said I'm sorry.'

'A Mr Krim lives there,' the child said. 'You have a wrong address.'

'Go away. Close your door.'

But the child did not move.

'*Vito,*' Jane said. She hammered her fist on the door.

'There's no Vito lives there,' the child said.

'O, go away. Vito?'

(O God, I'm not going to cry, am I, I mustn't cry. He *is* in there. Maybe he's not. I'm not sure.)

Only one way to find out: that was the super downstairs. He had probably been sitting at the doorstep all afternoon. She turned from the child's stare and ran to the elevator. She went down and there, sure enough, the super was still sitting in his chair, smoking his White Owl. 'Excuse me, I wonder if you saw that man I sometimes – a young man who sometimes comes here with me. I mean, did you see him go upstairs today?'

'You mean that dark guy, friend of Mister Krim?'

'Yes.'

'Let's see now, I *think* I seen him. Or was it last night? Comes in and out of here all the time.'

'I know,' she said. 'But this was just a short time ago. He probably came here by taxi.'

'Well, I was down in the basement for a while. But, I think I seen a fella looked like him get in the elevator just as I was coming up the basement stairs.'

'Thank you.'

'Whyn't you ring his bell, see if he's at Mr Krim's place?'

'I did,' she said. She went down the steps of the building. Trying to hide from me in there, sitting in the living-room like a statue, hoping I'll go away. Well, we'll see about that.

Further down the block she found a candy store. At the back

of the store she shut herself in a phone booth and consulted the directory. *Lester Krim, 425 W. 57.* She dialled the number. I'll be smart for once.

'Hello?' It was his voice, she knew it.

'Is Lester there?' she said, using a sort of Bronx accent.

'Lester, no, he's not back yet. But I'm expecting him any moment. Who's calling?'

'Jane Tierney.'

There was a moment's pause. Then: 'Can I take a message?'

(O, the gall of him.)

'Yes, Vito,' she said, 'you can take a message. You stink.'

She slammed the receiver down.

At once, she wanted to call him back. She had to leave the booth to get dimes from the candy counter, but the man at the counter looked the surly type, so she bought two O'Henry bars for the kids. When she returned to the booth a teenager was in there, receiver cradled in the crook of her neck, settling down for a long conversation with some friend. Frantic, Jane ran out into the street again, ran down the block, found a tea-room and went in, looking for a phone. But the clock above the cashier's desk in the tea-room said six forty-five. She would have to tell Brendan she'd gone to Macy's to buy a girdle after work. Something like that. But first, just one more phone call.

'Excuse me, is there a phone here?'

'Sorry.'

Out into the street again and back up to the candy store. The teenage girl was still in the booth. Jane rapped on the glass with her dime and the teenager turned, still talking, and stuck her tongue out. At that point, Jane began to weep. The teenager hung up at once and came out of the booth. 'What's the matter, it's an emergency?'

'Yes.'

'So, okay, you should of told me.'

She had forgotten Krim's number; she had to find it again. She dialled. For a long time, no one answered. Then Krim came on the line.

'Hello?'

'Lester, this is Jane Tierney. Please let me speak to Vito?'

'He's not here, sweetie.'

'But I *know* he's there.'

'Sorry, sweetie –'

'Please, Lester, it's important.'

'Look, I told you, he's not here.'

Someone else took the phone. Vito. 'Hello,' he said.

'Vito, please, I'm sorry. I want to talk to you –'

'Get off my back,' he said. 'Stop phoning. We're busy.'

'O, darling, please if I could only see you for a minute, just one minute?'

'Get lost.'

He put down the receiver.

It was half past seven when she got home and her mother-in-law was waiting for her as soon as she got in the door. 'O, Jane, I'm glad you're back. Brendan has called you three times.'

'Where is he?'

'He's in someplace called Eddy's. He wants you to meet him there. I'd say he has a drop taken.'

'He got good news today,' Jane said. 'He's celebrating.'

'I know,' Mrs Tierney said. 'He came to the park to tell me about it. He wanted to celebrate with you.'

'Well, I had a rush job to do. I was held up at the office.'

She stared at Mrs Tierney as she said this, as though challenging Mrs Tierney to contradict her. But the older woman gave no sign that she either accepted or denied the explanation. She merely said: 'Would you like to see the children? I just put them away.'

Jane nodded. She went into the children's room and found Liam already asleep. Lisa was colouring in a colouring book. 'Mummy, will you take us to the Museum of Natural History?'

'I thought you were there last week with Gran?'

'But it's not fun with Gran, the way it is with you. Please, Mummy?'

'All right, darling, we'll see.' She bent over and kissed Lisa. Poor kids, stuck here all day with an old woman they hated. She remembered the O'Henry bars and took one out of her purse. 'Now, don't make a mess. I have to go down-town again to meet Daddy.'

'Gran says Daddy's going to have a book and he might be famous some day. Is that true, Mummy?'

'Yes, dear. And promise you'll go to sleep as soon as you've eaten your candy.' It probably is true, she thought. My husband's going to be a famous writer, I don't need you, Vito, you imitation Brando. I'm finished with you forever. Never again.

She went out into the corridor, considered changing her dress, but decided she didn't have enough time. Although she had spent a fortune on cabs tonight, another cab was indicated. She must try to get to Eddy's by eight.

'Jane?'

Now what did that woman want? Unwillingly, Jane went into the living-room. Her mother-in-law was sitting in a canvas and iron butterfly chair. She did not belong in a butterfly chair; she looked as though she was trussed up in some sort of sling. 'What is it?' Jane said.

'I just thought I'd mention –' Mrs Tierney said, then stopped. She spread her hands on her lap and inspected them carefully. 'You see, the first time Brendan phoned here it was half past five. I said to him maybe you'd been kept working late and he said he'd already phoned your office and a charwoman told him everybody had gone home. So I said maybe you had to do some shopping. You mentioned you were going to get some T-shirts for the children?'

She stopped, still keeping her eyes nun-quiet on her hands. 'I just thought I'd mention it,' she said. 'Have a good time, dear.'

Jane stood for a moment without speaking. What was there to say? There *was* one thing to say and at last, uneasily, she said it. 'Thank you.'

'That's all right, dear. Good night.'

Brendan, Pat Gallery and Yvonne, David Dortmunder and Anna – they were all in a booth at Eddy's. Brendan and Gallery seemed quite drunk.

'Well, here she is at last,' Pat Gallery shouted, as Jane came down the bar.

She faced the booth, faced the hot faces which looked up at her, as though they were not sure of the welcome she would receive. Brendan, she surmised, had been complaining.

'I'm sorry I'm late, everybody,' she said, hoping she sounded unconcerned.

'Where the hell were you?' Brendan asked.

'I had to go to Macy's to try to find new T-shirts for the kids. I couldn't find them so I went over to Gimbels.'

'You weren't working late?' he said in a policeman's voice.

'No, I left at five. But it took me ages trying to find the right kind of T-shirts.'

'Well, anyway, she's here,' Yvonne said. 'Now, we can eat. Isn't it wonderful news about Brendan's book?'

'A hell of a night to go shopping for the kids, wasn't it?' Brendan said.

'Give her a drink there,' Pat Gallery shouted. 'Just one more drink and we'll all head over to the San Remo for veal scallopine.'

'Brendan, I'm sorry,' Jane said, sitting in beside him.

'Sorry?' he said. 'I'll bet you are.'

'It's too hot for veal,' someone said.

'Brendan.' She bent towards him and whispered it. 'Brendan, don't you believe me?'

His face perspiring, his eyes glazed with gin, he turned to her. 'Believe what?' he said in a puzzled voice.

'I don't know. But you look as though you hate me.'

'Why should I hate you? But, goddammit, you might have done your shopping some other night. I wanted you here. This is my big day, after all.'

'Of course it is,' she said. 'And I'm sorry. I thought the shopping would only take a minute.'

'Prosciutto and melon and iced Frascati,' Dortmunder was saying. 'How does that appeal to everybody?'

'To hell with the shopping,' Brendan said to her. 'Jesus, what a day it's been.'

He put his face close and said, in a drunken, slurred whisper. 'Some friends I have. Every one of them is jealous of me. Only person who cared was you. When I phoned you this afternoon, you were the only person who was really happy about it. That's why I wanted you here.'

'Well, I'm here now,' she said. 'I'm here and I'm proud of you. I always knew you'd do it.'

Drunkenly, he bowed his head, in acknowledgment of her praise. His brow touched her brow. His face was wet and he smelled of gin, but she was so relieved, so grateful, that she put her arms around his neck and kissed him, first on his lips, then all over his neck and face, ignoring the ironic cheers of the others. Suddenly, she did not know why, but holding him, kissing him, she began to cry.

'Hey, you shouldn't be crying, Janey,' Yvonne said. 'This is your celebration.'

'Yes, come on, Janey,' Dortmunder said. 'Live it up.'

'Tears of happiness,' Pat Gallery declaimed, 'are tears of regret for things past. The beauty queen cries at the very moment they put the winner's crown on her head. She foresees her old age and the end of her beauty. Cry, Janey, cry. Your world has changed.'

*

The Christ figure drooped on the wall, as though it too suffered from the heat. She did not kneel to say her night prayers. She lay on the bed in her nightdress, her body already dampening the sheet, and hurriedly ran through the minimum of Our Fathers and Hail Marys. When she glanced at the crucifix, the Christ face seemed to turn away from her, disgusted. But I only warned Jane not to tell a lie. You offered her a better lie, the Christ face said. You thought of days when you told lies to your own husband. But You, Jesus, showed pity for the woman taken in adultery? You tell us that what God hath joined together, let no man put asunder. I was trying to keep the peace tonight; that was all.

She shut her eyes against the crucifix and turned towards the wall. I must try to sleep. O, this heat, this heat – There was a great flight of steps, like the main staircase of a palace. Below was hell. The judge sat at the top of the steps: it was the judgment seat of heaven. He had a reddish grey beard and was her father. The witnesses waited in a circle at the bottom of the steps. She saw Grattan and Rory and Sheila and her sister Taddie, long dead. Taddie was younger looking than Rory, yet she was his aunt. 'Call Frank Finnerty,' the judge said. Frank came forward. 'I'm an American now,' he said. 'I'm not married. I live for my own self.' He blew a smoke ring and his mouth stayed open, a charred black hole. 'He cannot help you,' said the judge, her father, in a Donegal accent. Frank was her only friend in America but he was dead. Brendan came up to the steps with a book in his hand. He showed the book to everyone. He was very happy. He held the book up for the judge to see, but the book slipped from his hand. It fell into the flames beneath the steps. 'This is your son,' said the judge. 'He lives for his own ambitions. His children do not know God.' Brendan did not seem to hear the judge. His face was happy: she wanted to slap him. 'But I baptized those children,' she told the judge. 'It is a sacrament: once done, it cannot be undone.' The judge shook his head. 'Call Father Byrne,' he said. A priest came out of a confession box. 'I am Father M. J. Byrne of the Church of the Most Precious Blood on Amsterdam Avenue. Mrs Tierney, who is a new parishioner, came to me in the confessional. I advised her to bring her son to see me. She said he would never see a priest. I offered to visit him. She promised to speak to her son and return to me. She did not return. She put herself above her church and baptized the children herself. The baptism was not a true emergency. It is not valid.' Christ, naked and blood-stained, appeared in a cloud above the steps, His arms out-stretched in the pose of crucifixion. 'Is that an idol?' the judge asked. 'From bad to worse,' said the priest. 'She helped her son's wife tell lies to deceive him.'

'But I don't know if Jane's carrying on with someone,' she said. 'Why would I think that of her, now why would I?' The judge held up his hand. 'Wait,' he said. 'Why did you stay in a place where things were done which were against your beliefs?'

'I was lonely,' she said. 'I had come all this way, I'd sold my furniture in Belfast. Where else would I go? I did my best, I tried to help the children, I tried to tell them about God. But everything is different in America. How could I change them?'

They brought Pilate. He was Sir Cedric Hardwicke. He called for water and washed his hands. He smiled. He screamed. Two angels cast him down to hell. 'Look over there,' the judge said. 'That is Limbo.' She looked and it was a quiet place like an airport lounge with green plants that were not real and food on a buffet that was not real food. There were many old men there, old men in white robes with long white beards. They were the just men who had died before the coming of Christ. They sat hopeless and silent, for they knew they must stay forever in oblivion. There were many children there too, including un-baptized black babies who had died in Africa. She looked among the white children but could not find Lisa or Liam. 'You baptized them,' the judge said. 'You denied them even the consolation of this place of neglect. You made them Christians, but you did not prepare them as Christians.' Lisa and Liam were brought forward to the foot of the steps. They wore white robes but the robes were stained with filth. 'Better,' said the judge, 'that a millstone be tied around your neck and that you be cast into the depths of the sea than that you should harm one of these, my children.'

'But I thought I was doing the right thing,' she said.

Brendan came forward. He looked up at the judge. 'She promised me she would not interfere any more,' he said. The priest came forward. 'She never came back to confession,' he said. Jane came forward. 'I am their mother,' she said. 'She did this thing behind my back. She hid it from me. Later, she kept my secret.'

'Is it true,' the judge said, 'that you baptized these children to atone for your own sins, for Brendan and Sheila who are lost to us? Did you do it for your own self, Eileen?' asked the judge, her father. 'Look at yourself,' he said. 'You're a sight.' She looked down. Her white night dress was all stained with filth. Christ appeared again at the top of the steps. He wore white robes. He was sorrowful. 'She abandoned me,' He said, 'for her own self.'

Two angels with long wings took her, each one holding an arm. She tossed and turned and cried out but it was no use, they were pulling her towards the edge. 'Grattan?' she screamed. Grattan's dead face, surrounded by calla lilies, came up close to her. There was a fine arch to his nostril which she had not seen while he was alive. He did not open his dead lips, but a voice came out all the same. 'Sometimes,' it said, 'I believe you have a filthy mind.' O Grattan, the flames, Grattan come back, I need you, the flames, the angels, flame at my neck, Grattan? –

It was night and she was wet with perspiration and in the darkness she heard a high, tiny noise. Her neck stung. She traced her fingers over a swelling on her flesh. There was a mosquito somewhere in the room.

When Jane went down to the office next morning she had made up her mind to speak to Vito Italiano once and only once. That would be to tell him it was over. Just who in hell did he think he was. She was going to tell him *what* he was: he was a tart, a cheap, male tart and she had used him and if he ever fooled himself that at any time in their relationship he really meant anything to her, well, he was one sadly self-deluding imitation Brando, that's all. She put from her mind the things she had sobbed out to him in Krim's flat, things about love and being crazy for him, for it wasn't love at all. He must be told the difference. She planned to let him know that there were times when, after leaving him, she'd gone into guilty fits of laughter at his dumb opinions and his outrageous manners. And those clothes of his, those disgusting, male tart's clothes, pathetic really. Yes, pathetic, my tough monkey. Did you know that you're a joke to the other people in the office? No, of course you wouldn't know. You're not very bright, are you, Vito? I'm used to men with more brains. My husband, for instance. Yes, Brendan Tierney, the writer. They're going to do his book very soon. When that happens, I'll be leaving, of course. Yes, we'll probably travel a lot. Europe. Maybe the South Seas.

But as she stood at her drawing-board, with Patsy Armstrong on her left and Dick Duryea shouting something across the room, she saw him come in and go to his cubicle and, when he stripped off his jacket, felt a guilty thrill, for he had belonged to her and no one here knew. Worse, when he sat down and picked up the phone to call Louise Rogers, ignoring her as though she were not in the room, she realized that her anger and resolves were dead sticks. He held the whip: he was still her dark ravisher. In a second of time as measured by clocks, she saw the humiliations, the endless appeals to him, the complete self-abasement she was capable of to win him back. At the same time she knew her only hope of salvation was to walk out, quit now, good-bye. Of course, she could not do it.

At ten-thirty, under pretence of asking him about a copy

change, she went into his cubicle. She had picked her time carefully. Dick and Carl were in the other room and Patsy was coffeeing in a corner with Norma. She went in without any idea of what she must say. He would apologize: she would forgive him.

'Vito?'

She saw that he was reading the sports page of *The Daily News*, under pretence of checking some copy. He turned in his swivel chair, looked up, said nothing.

'This copy for the banana diet promotion sheet, it won't fit.'

'Let me see.'

He took it, read it, and put it aside. 'I'll get Dick to work on it,' he said. He swivelled in his chair and picked up *The Daily News*.

'Vito?'

'Vito, I want to talk to you.'

He put his paper down, looked at her over the top of it. 'Okay,' he said. 'We better have a talk. That Hamburg Heaven on Lex, you know it?'

'Yes, the one we –'

'I'll be there at twelve-thirty,' he said. 'See you then.'

She went back to her desk and sat down. Her coffee grew cold. It will be all right, yes, it will be all right, O please, make it all right. Vito, we both said things we shouldn't have said, I know, darling. I'm sorry. We had a row, everybody has. Vito, I only left you last night because I don't want to lose you. And listen, I meant that Brando thing as a compliment, you're even sexier than he is, you've always reminded me of him.

No, better not mention that at all. Unless he brings it up.

Patsy Armstrong was coming over for a chat. 'Hi, Jane, what's new with you today?'

(New? We're going to have lunch. And, yes, Brendan's got an advance on his novel, the publisher's very impressed. Patsy would be impressed too, but she would immediately tell everyone in the office and that would include *him*. He would hear that she was proud of Brendan. No. Nothing must be said to make him jealous.)

'New? Nothing.'

Patsy sat down on the desk, leaned forward confidentially. 'Listen, when's your vacation?'

'I haven't been here long enough,' Jane said. 'I'm not on the roster.'

'Well, you know what's happened? I've just been screwed.'

'How?'

'You see, they give vacations on a seniority basis,' Patsy said. 'Like, Vito and Dick have priority over Carl and me and Norma. So, a month ago, I put down for the first two weeks in August. And this morning, I've been moved to the middle two weeks because somebody else decides he wants to go off next week. Last week in July, first in August. We'd overlap by a week.'

'Who?' Jane asked. Her heart hit, then stopped.

Patsy jerked a thumb at the cubicle. 'Says he's got some deal to go down to Acapulco next Monday. He sneaked in this morning and first he cleared it upstairs with Louise Rogers, then he came to me and said: "Patsy, honey, listen, I have this great deal, would you mind switching?" Mind? Of course I mind, I told him. I mean, after all, I have plans too, I made my reservations. I said to him, I don't think that's nice, Vito, you're just pulling rank –'

'Monday?' Jane said.

'Yes, Monday. I mean, it's such short notice, it only gives me this week to change all my arrangements. I'm going to speak to Louise. Don't you think I should?'

'Of course. Yes, speak to Louise.'

'Because, after all, it isn't fair,' Patsy was saying, but Jane's mind said Mexico and a Cinemascope short subject she had seen last winter started up in De Luxe colour; lush America-plan hotels, fishermen bringing in sailfish, glamorous girls in beach clothes, native boys diving from cliffs, cocktails, cha-cha-chaing it all night, in a dozen nightspots, and she could see him, he fitted it perfectly in his tight, silky suits with his dark skin and his smile. Lonely, rich women in those places. What deal? She looked at his cubicle. He was with Dick. If he had made arrangements to go away next Monday, it must be because of last night's row. He was running from her. That should be comforting, shouldn't it? He was running away because he was hurt. Or was he tired of her?

The coloured man slid two hamburgers from the great steel hotplate, flipped them on to two buns, added french fries and put them on the counter. The waiter brought them over. Hamburg Heaven was air-conditioned but in that noonday rush of lunchers Jane felt her face come out as in a heat rash. The waiter placed the hamburgers in front of Vito who opened his first bun, squirted ketchup, smeared mustard, dolloped relish. He had arrived before her and had ordered. The waiter lingered. 'Yes, miss?'

'Just coffee.'

'Coffee,' the waiter said. 'Nothing else?'

'No.'

'You got here early, Vito. I didn't see you leave the office.'

He took a big bite of his hamburger, began to chew, speaking, as usual, with his mouth full. 'Yeah, I left early. I got to get back soon.'

'I thought we were going to have a talk.'

'Okay, let's talk. We've had a nice time but it's over. Now's the time to pick up our winnings and check out.'

The roar of the air-conditioner behind him, the noise of plates and cutlery, the people talking at the next table, and his words, flat and casual, how could they really talk here, it was hopeless. He was still insulted: that was what was wrong with him. All right, tell him you're sorry. Say it.

'Vito, listen to me, I'm sorry about last night. I was in a panic, darling, I did and said all the wrong things, I know that you were rude, but I started it. I know it can't be nice for you to stand aside for my husband but honestly, darling, he doesn't mean anything to me. You do . . . O, stop eating, will you?'

He looked at her, surprised, then squirted ketchup on his second hamburger. 'See what I mean?' he said. 'It's getting to be a drag. That happens. Listen, Janey, it's not last night that counts. This has been coming for weeks.'

'No, it hasn't.'

'It has, don't kid yourself. I'll be honest. I've been waiting for the right moment to finish it and last night, you gave it to me. You wanted to go back to your husband. Okay, go back.'

'But I don't want to go back.'

'Save it,' he said. 'I don't care what you want. As far as I'm concerned, the party's over.' He closed his second hamburger over, picked it up, and took a bite. 'Look,' he said. 'We had fun, didn't we? Now that it's over, we might as well stay friends.'

'Friends? Good God, do you think I ever was friends with you, do you? Do you think I'd be able to go on working in the same room with you after this?'

'I've taken care of that. I moved my vacation up a couple of weeks. Sort of a cooling-off period for both of us.'

'Yes,' she said. 'Mexico, isn't it? Tell me, if I don't mean anything to you, why are you running away?'

'Who's running away? I just decided to take my vacation now, that's all. Just trying to make it easier for you.'

'Thanks a lot,' she said. She was reminded of her schooldays when 'Yah, yah, yah,' was the only riposte she could muster.

'You'll see,' he said. 'A couple of weeks will make all the difference.'

'How little you know about women.'

He put cream in his coffee. 'I know women, all right.'

'Well, you don't know me.'

He grinned, as though she had said something obscene.

'Why has no one ever stuck a knife in you, Vito?'

'Some girls have tried. Take Norma.'

(O God, not Norma too?)

'Norma and I had a romp a couple of years back, when she first came to work here. I had to cut it off. She acted like a crazy woman for a while but she got over it. Now we're good friends.'

(Norma, fat Norma, and how many others?)

'You're such a lover boy.'

He grinned. 'You'd be surprised.'

(What did he mean, was he hinting at someone in particular? He was such good friends with Louise. Louise? Impossible. Brendan always said Louise was a Lesbian.)

'Just tell me one thing,' she said. 'Is Louise a former "romp"?'

'Louise is our leader. And I'm a gentleman, Janey.'

'*You're* a gentleman? Now I've heard everything.'

He was so pleased with himself. He looked around as though he hoped the people at the next table were listening. He wiped his mouth with a paper napkin and crumpled the napkin into a ball. 'Trouble with you,' he said. 'You're not honest with yourself. You won't face facts. This kind of thing swings for a while and then it stops. It's over. Get it? Finish.'

He stood up. He picked up her coffee check and, idiotically, as though it was the final insult for him to pay for her coffee, she plucked it out of his hand. 'Okay,' he said. 'If you want to be friends, all right. If not, it makes no difference to me. Suit yourself.'

He went up the aisle of tables to the cashier's desk. A black face loomed over her. 'That gentleman coming back?'

'No.'

The waiter cleared the dishes and an old man with a tremor in his hands sat down in Vito's place. She looked at the man and, sick, got up and went out of the restaurant. She wandered along Lexington Avenue, crossed over on to Fifth and began walking somnambulistically towards the park, ignoring traffic lights at intersections, drifting in the tide of lunchtime shoppers. At Fifty-Third Street, she crossed the street as though by instinct, walked past a large church whose name she had never bothered to know, and entered the foyer of the Museum of Modern Art. In her art school years she had come here almost every day and now, still in a trance, she paid and wandered through the cool, yet violent rooms of abstracts into the quiet sanctuary of the sculpture garden. She ignored the people lunching on the terrace, went to a bench and sat. A rapacious, knowing pigeon stalked the base of Lachaise's massive female nude, then, cautious, came to her bench. The pigeon bothered her: its cocked eye was cunning, yet stupid; there were no thoughts inside that sleek, tiny head. Scavenger and predator, its cold eye was Vito's and for a moment its presence almost drove her to leave. But why should she run: this garden was her place, not his. She stamped her foot and the pigeon, startled, flew up and out of the garden. Heartened, she began to plan.

Today was Thursday. She would not go back to the office this afternoon, and tomorrow she would stay home sick. On Monday, he would be gone for fourteen days and by the time he returned from Mexico, she would have herself in hand. Besides, Brendan would finish his book in the next six weeks or so, and then she could quit this job forever. Somehow, they would get rid of Mrs Let-Me, and with Brendan a successful author, life would be quite different. She would treat this thing like an illness: two weeks – almost three – to convalesce. Tomorrow, she would spend all her time with the kids, those poor kids, how she'd neglected them. Their lives were starved with that old woman. Why, they've never even been in this garden.

She got up from the bench and walked slowly down the garden. In her mind the children were with her and as she looked at Guimard's metro station archway, she was telling Lisa about *art nouveau*. Lisa was perhaps a little young for that, but a start must be made somewhere, otherwise you developed adults like Vito. She supposed that with his training as an art director Vito might know something about *art nouveau*. But in her mind, she saw Vito knowing about it only as a promotion gimmick. He cheapened everything. He. . . .

No, she mustn't think of him. She tried to bring the children back into the sculpture garden. Look, Liam, do you see that statue? That is a statue of a famous writer called Balzac. Your father might be famous too, one day. Do I love my children, of course I do. I'd throw myself in front of a subway train to save their lives. Yes, but admit it, I wanted a rest from them, I wanted a job, I wanted excitement. *Excitement.* Krim's apartment and that vulgar brute in his jockey shorts, wearing his gold wristwatch with the gold-linked watchstrap, he wears it even when he's naked. He wore it while he laid fat Norma. And Louise, sexless, dried-up Louise, who got me this job. Thank you for nothing, Louise.

The children; she must forget him and think of the children. Tomorrow she could spend all day with the children. She could bring them here and show them everything. We'll have lunch on that terrace. Cokes and hamburgers.

No, not hamburgers.

At five o'clock the following day, the heat wave broke in a thundershower. On Fifty-Fourth Street, a woman who had ventured out under the sidewalk awning of an apartment house turned and ran back to the shelter of the doorway. At that moment Jane and the children, having left the Museum of Modern Art by way of the Whitney, found themselves caught in mid-block. They ran towards the sidewalk awning. When they reached it, spattering raindrops, wetting even the strip of pavement under the awning, forced them back into shelter beside the woman in the doorway. Beauty's cripple, fragile in beige chiffon, sheer bone stockings, white suede pumps, the woman faced the building, shielding her elaborately made-up face, her coiffed and lacquered hair, discomfitted as though the rain would break her brittle bones, melt her dress, wash her hair and features down into the gutters.

As Jane and the children approached the woman looked up and Jane smiled at her in the common, rueful camaraderie of people caught in a shower. The beauty reciprocated by crooking her mouth in a vague parody of a grin. O, to be her, Jane thought, as the apartment house doorman ran past them into the street, vainly blowing a whistle on non-appearing cabs. But on a second look she added ten years to the rich beauty's age and the heavens, confirming her judgement, sent forth a blind of lightning which lit the doorway, the pavement and the beauty's face in the same magnesium flash of unreality. Liam huddled close to his mother, burying his face in her skirt and as she patted his head and fondled the back of his delicate, childish neck, that mother love which all day she had tried to summon amid her miseries, came on her, filling her with peace. She felt only condescension towards the rich beauty. She was a mother: the beauty should envy her. 'There now, darling,' she told Liam. 'It will be over in a minute.'

It will be over. Like the shower, it will be over and I will take up my life again. The children will save me.

Again the doorman blew on his whistle, but the cab rushed

past in a grey curtain of rain. The doorman spat his whistle out, letting it fall on his chest. He walked back under the awning and said: 'Sorry, Mrs Lebel. We'll have to wait a minute.'

The beauty, her back to him, nodded in silent misery. Lisa danced out under the awning.

'Lisa, stand in,' Jane ordered.

'Rain, rain go to Spain,' Lisa chanted. She stretched out her hand from under the awning and watched it get wet. Then she danced over to Liam. 'Want some rain, some rain, want some rain?'

'Lisa,' Jane said. 'Stop that.'

'She's going to wet me, Mummy, she's going to make me all wet.'

'Lisa, stop it.'

But Lisa had already smeared Liam's face with her wet hand. She danced around in a hop and skip. 'I baptize thee,' she chanted.

Jane's heart jumped.

Just then the doorman ran past them, blowing frantically on his whistle. A cab slowed down. The elegant lady traversed the length of the awning in a hobbled walk, giving Jane a bony smile as she passed. The doorman held open the door and the beauty entered the cab.

'Stop it,' Liam protested. 'Mummy, she's made me all wet.'

'I baptize thee,' Lisa chanted.

'Lisa. Come here.' She spoke quietly but there was something in her tone which brought Lisa to heel as her previous threats had not.

'What, Mummy?'

'Darling, what do you mean, I baptize thee? Where did you hear that?'

'Gran said it.'

'When?'

'O, one time,' Lisa said, skipping up and down.

'Stop jumping. Listen to me. Tell me what Gran said.'

'It was one time in the bathroom,' Lisa said. 'She did this spooky spell and she wet our face with water and she said "I baptize thee in the holy ghost".'

'Me too,' Liam said. 'She did it to me too.'

'And why didn't you tell me?' Jane said.

'It was a long time ago, Mummy.'

'How long?'

But even as she asked the question, she knew she would not find an answer. At five years of age, time is long in a minute, short in a week. 'A long time ago,' Lisa repeated.

'And what else did Gran say?'

'She said we were little Christians.'

Lightning came. Lisa skipped back into the shelter of the doorway, frightened despite herself. Thunder banged and banged across the city and the rain came down in grey walls. Baptism, that was something a minister did in a church. You brought the baby in a christening dress and they put water on its head. Brendan had insisted that the children be registered and not baptized. A minister must do it but perhaps with Catholics it's different. You're little Christians, she said to them. Little Catholics?

And while it happened I was probably naked in that room with him. Even today I would have been with him at the office, going off to Krim's at five: I would never have known about this; selfish, disgraceful mother that I am. Behind my back she has changed them, done damage that may only come out later in their lives.

The wall of rain became a curtain, then thinned. The sky lightened and the sun shone through. The shower had stopped. Jane took each of her children by the hand and marched them down the block to the subway. She thought of *The Turn of the Screw*, of the corruption of innocents by those into whose hands careless guardians have given them. Quint and Miss Jewel were no worse than the blarneying, put-upon tricks of Mrs Let-Me. Wait till I see her.

When she got home, there was Mrs Tierney on her knees in the hallway of the apartment, dusting the baseboard with a rag. Nobody asked her to, Jane decided, as, staring down at her mother-in-law's hindquarters and the soles of her black, sensible shoes, she restrained an urge to kick her. The children must not hear, so she put them in their room and promised them a lollipop each if they would play there until she called them. Brendan was not home and it did not occur to Jane to wait and talk it over with him first. She asked her mother-in-law to come into the living-room.

'Did you have a nice day at the museum, dear?'

'Sit down, please,' Jane said. 'I want to ask you something. Is it true that you went through some baptism rite with the children?'

Mrs Tierney, dustrag in hand, moved uncertainly to the long black sofa and sat on the edge of it. 'What was that, dear?'

'You heard me.'

'Did – have you spoken to Brendan about this?'

'What's that got to do with it?'

'I – I just wanted to know if you'd spoken to him.'

'Not yet. And you haven't answered my question.'

Mrs Tierney, after pretending to inspect her dustrag, folded it in four, put it on her knee and looked at Jane, an open hostility in her dark eyes set in their tired sacs of skin. 'Look here, Jane,' she said. 'I'll have you know that I'm not your servant. I won't be spoken to in that tone of voice. Do you know that you never address me by name?'

'That's not the point, you didn't answer –'

'One moment,' Mrs Tierney said. 'When you talk to Brendan and the children, you always refer to me as "she". I have a name, you know, I'm not the cat.'

'All right then, *Mrs Tierney*. What did you do to those children?'

'I baptized them as Catholics.'

'You *what*?'

'O, I'm not certain that it's a valid baptism,' Mrs Tierney said. 'I think it is, though. I admit it wasn't nice to do it behind your back, but with Brendan the way he is, I had no other choice.'

Jane stared at her. She felt herself tremble, felt the beginnings of a rage so terrible she thought she would faint of it. 'When?' she said.

'When did I do it? In May. But, after that, I gave Brendan my promise that I'd not interfere with the children any more. I've kept that promise.'

'O, you have, have you?'

'Yes, I have.'

'But you didn't tell him you'd already baptized them, did you? You didn't have the nerve to tell him that.'

Mrs Tierney was silent.

'No, of course you didn't. Because you knew he'd have thrown you out on the street, that's what he'd have done.'

'Jane,' Mrs Tierney said, 'I realize you're upset by this and I think, from your point of view, you've every right to be. But I'm Brendan's mother, I'm entitled to some respect in this house. I won't allow you or anyone else to talk to me in this way.'

'O, *shut up*. Who cares about you, how dare you, how dare you frighten my children, the nerve of you –'

'Jane, control yourself.'

'I didn't want you here, I never wanted you to come, life's miserable with you on top of us all the time and then you go interfering with my children, you sneaky, deceitful old – *poop*.'

Mrs Tierney made a move to get up, but did not. She bent her head, closing her eyes. The dustrag fell from her lap.

(Old faker, old faker, Jane raged.)

Mrs Tierney remained bent over for a moment, then caught her breath and straightened up again. She seemed quite recovered from whatever it was. 'Well,' she said. 'There's nothing more to discuss, is there?'

'There's plenty more,' Jane shouted. '*Plenty*. And Brendan will say it to you when he gets home, don't *you* worry.'

'I'm going to my room, Jane. Will you tell Brendan I'd like to speak to him when he gets home.'

'Don't worry, he'll speak to you all right –'

Mrs Tierney moved. With a speed astonishing in one so heavy and old she rose, crossed the room and slapped Jane's face.

Open-mouthed, wide-eyed, Jane stared –

'You're hysterical,' Mrs Tierney said. 'I was a nurse, you know. Now, get a hold of yourself. You don't want the children to see you like this.'

'The children, a lot you care about the children,' Jane began; but her cheek stung; she felt stunned. Mrs Tierney took her by the arm and sat her on the sofa.

'I think you're under a strain this last while,' Mrs Tierney said quietly. 'Sit here a minute and calm down.'

She turned and left the room.

Sisyphus. Each time I labour to push the stone of my domestic difficulties up and out of sight, it falls back and crushes me. Tonight, that meaningless non-sacrament performed months ago in the sanctity of our john has become our be-all and end-all here.

First, Jane. Waiting for me in the living-room when I came home, in appearance still the Jane I knew, but inside her, as though some demoniac possession had taken place, a Judith in the tent of Holofernes.

'Your mother wants to see you. I think she's leaving us.'

'What the hell are you talking about?'

'I found out today that Liam and Lisa have been baptized as Catholics. Your mother admits she did it.'

Need I say that this announcement put the heart across me? Thoughts of my mother's betrayal of our secret ran into other thoughts that perhaps, behind my back, she had taken them to a church and had the job done again. 'Baptized?' I said feebly. 'How? Where?'

'Here in the apartment. Lisa let it out today. Now, you promised me that if she did anything like this, she'd have to leave. And this is it. She's got to go.'

'But she did it before I made that promise,' I said, and no sooner had I spoken than I felt a cliff crumble under my feet.

'How do *you* know?' Jane asked.

'I don't. I mean, I was just supposing.'

'Well, you suppose right, as a matter of fact. It happened in May. But that's not the point, Brendan, the point is she never told us and she never would have told us. She and I have just had the most awful row. She actually *hit* me. I can't have her here after that.'

'Ah, now wait, darling. I mean, what about the kids, what about your job?'

'I'm quitting the job.'

'O, no you're not,' I said. 'What will we live on?'

'You'll have to go back to doing mag pieces, that's all.'

'Like hell I will. I'm on my last chapter and I've promised to deliver the manuscript at the beginning of September. I can't down tools at this stage.'

'That's your problem, Brendan.'

'Darling, you're not being sensible. You want to get rid of my mother. Do you realize that if we paid her fare home now, it would take most of the five hundred that Key gave me? And if you quit, it might be weeks before I find a freelance assignment?'

'But I've got to quit, Brendan, there's no other solution.'

'There must be. If you hold on until September, I'll have the book finished and I'll have that extra fifteen hundred and then, I promise you, I'll find some free-lance stuff to tide us over.'

'No.'

'Be reasonable, Jane.'

'I am being reasonable. There are other reasons why I've got to quit.'

'What reasons?'

'I don't want to go into them now.'

'O, for christsake,' I said. 'You know how long I've worked on this book. All I'm asking for is six lousy weeks. My future depends on it.'

'The kids' future is just as important.'

'Of course it is. But they have their whole lives ahead of them. This is my one chance.'

'All right,' she said. 'All right.' She went to the window and stared down at the street. 'Look,' she said, at last. 'I have an idea. Suppose I phone my sister and ask her if she'll take the kids for the next six weeks? It would be a vacation for them up there in Saratoga.'

'But I thought you and Barbara weren't even on speaking terms?'

'I'll make it up with her, if I have to. God knows I loathe doing it, but it's better than leaving the kids with your mother.'

'Are you sure Barbara will take them?'

'She will if I explain what's happened.'

I had never seen Jane so determined. My mind raced. Six weeks' grace. By the end of next week I'd have finished my last chapter; a month for final revisions and when I delivered the manuscript I'd get fifteen hundred dollars. Besides, in six weeks she might change her mind about quitting. A lot could happen before September.

'But you've got to do your part,' she said. 'You've got to back me up. Momma doesn't live here any more.'

'Ah, have a heart, Jane. How can I tell her that?'

'I've already told her. Maybe she thinks she can get you on her side, but I'm warning you, Brendan. If she stays, I won't go through with it.'

'Some choice.'

'Take it or leave it. Now, do I or don't I phone my sister?'

'O, all right, phone her. But, Jesus, you're really twisting my arm.'

'Somebody has to twist your arm – What is it, Lisa? I thought I told you to stay in your room?'

'Gran wants to speak to Daddy.'

'All right,' Jane said. 'Your move, *Daddy*. And remember what I said. If you back out, the deal is off.'

*

When I knocked on my mother's door, I had no idea of what I would say to her. In the *realpolitik* of the situation Jane, not my mother, was the indispensable ally. Perhaps, because of their row, my mother had already decided to leave. But if not, if she pleaded with me?

'Come in, Brendan.'

Her room was confusion. Her bed, a stall at a church rummage sale with little piles of blouses and underthings arranged on the coverlet. Drawers open: her suitcases on the floor. My cowardly heart rejoiced.

'What are you doing, Mamma?'

'Just sorting things out a bit.'

'Why?'

'I want to see if I can get everything into these cases.'

'You mean you're packing?'

'Yes, Brendan.'

'Surely, there's no need for that?' said St Brendan the Hypocrite.

'Have you spoken to Jane?'

'Yes, Mamma, I have.'

'And did she tell you what she said to me?'

'Well, I know that she's found out about the baptism and that she's very upset.'

'Did you tell her that you knew about it all along?'

'No, I didn't. That would have been a bit awkward.'

'It might have made it less awkward for me, Brendan.'

What could I say? I watched her pick up a slip, fold it and lay it on a pile of garments.

'O, sit down, will you?' she said. 'You make me nervous.'

So I sat on the edge of the bed and, as I did, a photograph album slid off a pile of books and fell on the floor. I picked it up and there, neatly tacked down by passe-partout stickers, the dead past eyed me. Beside the seaside, beside the sea, on a windy promenade walk, my father, heavy and jaunty in white ducks and blue beret blinked at the camera, head cocked to one side, armlinked with his young wife who smiled and held a hand to her summer straw. In another snapshot, two children in bathing suits stood in the rush grass of a dune, on the rim of a cold Irish sea. Rory and Sheila. Portstewart 1929, my mother had written beneath this snapshot in her neat convent hand. I was not born then. My father blinked, my mother smiled, my dead brother looked out at the world with the clear, condemning eye of innocence. The past could not be cajoled: the snapshots, fixed in time, accused me. I closed the book.

'Brendan,' my mother said. 'Do you remember the first day I was here? You said I could always go home if I wanted to.'

'Yes, Mamma.'

'Well, I'd like you to get me a ticket as soon as possible. Next week, if you can manage it.'

'Why, Mamma?'

'Why am I going home?' She smiled but her sad dark eyes did not smile. 'Och,' she said. 'Let's say the climate doesn't suit me.'

'Mamma, Jane sometimes says things –'

'And you never say anything. I don't know which is worse. Let's not talk about it, what's the use. I'd like to go home. Will you help me?'

'Of course. I just wanted to say that I'm sorry about all this.'

She raised her hands, palms upwards, in a hopeless gesture. I felt she despised me, and this gesture of resignation touched some nerve of memory, bringing back the sudden, wronged impotence I had felt as a boy. Why was it always my fault, never hers? Why could we never talk to each other, she and I?

'But how will you manage if you go home?' I asked. 'You'll have no place to live.'

'O, there are plenty of places. I won't need much more than a room and a kitchen. I have some money due to me from the sale of the furniture and silver from Drumconor Avenue, and there's my old-age pension coming in a year or two. If you could just send me the same as you used to, I could manage very well.'

'Of course. We'll talk about it, we'll see what can be arranged.'

'There's nothing to talk about, Brendan. Just get me the ticket. And in the meantime, I'd like to move to Frank's place.'

'Finnerty's? But there's no need for that.'

'I'd prefer it, that's all. You see, Frank has gone off on his holidays; he goes up to Canada to fish. He left me the key and asked me to keep an eye on the place, water his plants and so on. If you're worried about the children, I could come and pick them up here in the mornings and, of course, I'd babysit for you two if you were going out at night.'

'There's no problem about the kids. As a matter of fact, Jane's sending them up to Saratoga.'

'Well, in that case,' my mother said. 'You have no further need of me here.'

'But, Mamma, I don't want you to feel you have to move.'

'I'd like to.'

She smiled at me, the smile of a rider facing a stiff jump. In that moment I remembered her as young and pretty, quick to laugh, quick to scold. I remembered her waltzing with me in the drawing-room at home. How could we end this way? 'O, Mamma,' I said, and moved across the room to kiss her.

'I have a lot to do now.' She stood up, avoiding my embrace. 'I want you to help me move my things when I call the taxi. And could you lend me a few dollars for my expenses at Frank's place?'

'But you're not moving tonight?'

'I want to, Brendan. Now, leave me.'

She left at eight. None of us had eaten supper. Jane talked for a long time on the telephone to her sister in Saratoga and it seemed that things were arranged. Between us, we had gotten together forty dollars which I brought to my mother in her room. Jane put the children to bed and when my mother came out into the corridor with her suitcases and odd parcels, I expected that she would ask to see them. She did not. She hesitated at the doorway of their room, but did not look in. She turned to me.

'I'll see them some time before I go,' she said.

'Yes, of course.' I looked around for Jane, but she was hiding in the bathroom. 'Jane?' I said. 'Mamma's leaving.'

'No, no,' my mother said quietly. 'Don't disturb her. Come on now, Brendan.'

We did not speak in the elevator. We said a few words in the taxi, but I do not remember what they were: they were things said only to fight the silence. I remember that as we turned off Madison into the East Fifties (I was surprised that Finnerty lived at such a good address) she said, suddenly: 'The plants. I forgot.'

'What plants?'

'The plants at Frank's place. If I'm going home next week, I'll have to get somebody to come in and water them until he comes back.'

'You mean at his apartment?'

'Yes. They need watering twice a week. Would you do it, Brendan?'

'All right.'

'Thanks very much. I'll show you which ones when we go upstairs.'

I paid off the cab and carried her bags up. As she unlocked the apartment door I saw a small, dun living-room, centred around a television set and a huge red Barcalounger chair. A bedroom; a dark, narrow kitchen, its sink full of dirty dishes; a skylight in the tiny hall. She showed me around, pointed out the plants which were in the living-room, and in a window box on the fire escape. 'It's a lovely little place,' she said. 'I wish I had one like it.'

Did that mean that she did not want to go back to Ireland, did it mean that if only she had a place, she would stay in New York? I was afraid to ask. I opened the small refrigerator and saw that it was empty. 'Tell you what,' I said, 'I'll run down to the corner and get you some milk and tea and stuff.'

'No, don't bother. I can do it in the morning.'

'It's no bother.'

I had to escape. I went down to the street and searched for three blocks before I found a store that was open. As I walked the hot pavements, past lonely boutiques, locked showrooms, shuttered specialty stores, Ted Ormsby walked into my mind, flat cap on his grey, curly head, his thick-lensed glasses iridescent against the light. 'So, you're getting rid of your mother, eh, boy? Another sacrifice for your art, I suppose?' What gave him the right to judge me, what had he done with *his* life? He taught in some backwater: his poetry forgotten. Ted Ormsby stood in Lavery's pub, his long back leaning against the bar. He sucked on his pipe then took it out and examined the stem. 'Yes, Brendan, you'll sacrifice other people for your work. But will you sacrifice yourself?' What did he mean by that? Besides, I did not sacrifice my mother: Jane did. Ormsby smiled and spat in the fire. 'Aye, blame Jane,' he said. 'Sacrifice Jane.' But I had to go along with Jane, don't you see? It wouldn't have made any difference if I'd taken a stand. Jane and my mother have never hit it off: this break was bound to come. Why must I blame myself?

When I got back to Finnerty's place, the windows had been opened, the little sitting-room had been tidied and my mother was in the kitchen. She had stacked all the dirty dishes and the sink was filled with water and suds. It was almost dark. 'Thanks very much,' she said as I unpacked the things I'd bought and put them in the refrigerator. She did not look at me. She was washing the dishes.

'Anything else I can do, Mamma?'

'No, no, you might as well run along. I have to finish cleaning up this place.'

'Maybe I could help you?'

'No, go on home. And you'll phone me as soon as you find out about the ticket?'

'All right, Mamma. Are you sure you'll be okay here?'

'Positive. Good night, son.'

Would she let me kiss her? Would a kiss absolve me? But her hands were wet and in the sink. 'Good night,' she said again.

The Greyhound coach from Saratoga Springs was air-conditioned and new, its windows tinted green to keep out the sun's glare. But at midnight, as it cruised half-empty towards the night lights of New York, Jane felt shut off as in a hearse. The day had been interminable, from the dawn start at West Side Terminal on Eighth Avenue, when she and the children boarded the bus, a tiresome journey broken only by 'comfort' stops to take Liam to the toilet. At high noon, in Saratoga, they transferred to a two-tone station wagon driven by Barbara's husband and in the back seat, in Bad French, Jane had tried to explain to Barbara, *devant les enfants*, what exactly her mother-in-law had done. After lunch at the farm (her brother-in-law was upstate New York manager for a farm equipment company: his farm was his showroom), they walked across fields to a barn where the children were introduced to a bull, a visit interrupted when Liam, afraid of the bull, set up a howl. Four years old, and she was abandoning him for six whole weeks. She sensed Barbara's disapproval: knew that Barbara and her husband had always thought Brendan an incipient beatnik and that this business of making her take a job while he finished his book must seem to them a confirmation of their worst suspicions. But what could she do about it, how could she explain to people like them, just what was involved?

And, when at last it was time for her to take the bus back to New York, Liam cried and wouldn't be comforted, not even by her promise to come and visit him every weekend. She could see Barbarra whisper to her husband as they waved good-bye from the Saratoga bus station, and knew that Barbara was probably drawing some terrible Spock-and-Gesell conclusions. She could not blame Barbara; she'd have thought the same thing herself.

On the bus, going home, she tried to remember the cheerful side: she remembered the joy of waking up Saturday morning and knowing that Mrs Let-Me was gone forever and – after Brendan had spent Saturday phoning around like mad trying to get a tourist flight going to Shannon, but finding the soonest he could book a seat was in two weeks' time – the relief of knowing that they wouldn't have Mrs Let-Me in the house for two weeks of put-upon silences and reproachful glares. Thank heavens for that cousin of hers. Two weeks. Vito flies to Mexico tomorrow for two weeks of lolling on some beach, drinking his 'Martins' and eyeing bikinis. In two weeks he could forget me. I *mustn't* be there when he comes back.

It was ten minutes to one when she came out of the bus terminal and started to walk towards the Seventh Avenue subway. Tomorrow morning he would leave for Mexico: she would probably never see him again. It was so hot tonight: her brow was damp and her dress was crushed and she felt so tired she could weep. She could tell Brendan she'd spent the night in Saratoga, missed the bus, he'd never know the difference. Or care. Delancey Street, it would be mad to go at this time of night, what if (like the time at Krim's apartment) he refused to open the door to her? Or came down and told her to get lost, shouting out, humiliating her in the street in the middle of the night. It was crazy to think of going there. Completely crazy.

Twenty minutes later she got out of a cab on Delancey Street. In the hot summer night, four teen-aged boys sat on the steps of the house she was going to. They were the sort of boys who sprawled in the Washington Square fountain on Sundays humming illegal folk songs with one eye on the police. One of them had a guitar and as she went up the steps among them he murmured something, probably obscene, in Italian, or was it Spanish? The others laughed. She did not look at them, she was looking at the nameplate: *Italiano V. M.* (what did the M. stand for?). She rang the bell and held the door handle, ready to open it when someone released the spring upstairs. One of the boys whistled as if he were calling a dog. The guitar struck a sudden plangent note. She rang again.

I was just passing by, I mean, I was downtown and I thought of you, no, I mean I had a chance to come tonight because my husband thinks I'm out of town, no, don't mention Brendan at all, that might annoy him. I had to come, one last time. All right, so I'm a nymphomaniac. So what.

'Sweetie?'

Pay no attention.

'Hey, lady?'

Ignore them.

'Lay-dee?'

Upstairs, the buzzer blipped. She turned the handle but was too late: the door did not open. She had to ring again.

'Like she's in a hurry, man.'

The buzzer blipped and she turned and pushed and the door opened suddenly, sending her stumbling into the dark inner hall. The guitar sounded a deep note. What floor is he on, I never thought to look? It was a house converted into three apartments, one on each floor. She began to go up but no door opened to receive her. Why don't I go home? Those Washington Square minstrels waited outside, they might follow her to the corner and mug her, or worse. New York was a jungle: just read the papers. But I came here to be raped, didn't I?

Light spilled across the banisters above her. One flight up, at an opened doorway, wearing only his pyjama bottoms, his feet bare, sleepy-eyed, scratching his head. Under the harsh light, his chest with its familiar curling mat of hair, his muscular shoulders, his strong neck, a pulse beating in his throat. And his fly was open, wasn't it just like him to appear like that, showing it to any female who might be on these stairs. In sudden jealous rage at his shamelessness, she ran up into the pool of light.

'What's up?' he said.

'Nothing . . . You're leaving tomorrow.'

'So?'

'I wanted to see you.'

But he blocked the doorway.

'Can't we go inside?'

'My mother's in there.'

O, the liar.

She tried to push past him. He caught her arm. 'All right,' he said. 'Take your shoes off first. And keep it quiet.'

It was a family parlour, no other way to describe it, a worn, plum-coloured living-room suite, lace doilies on the table and dresser, a rubber plant in a pot in the corner, framed photographs everywhere. (Young men in U.S. military uniforms; brides in white and grooms in rented morning clothes; a Garibaldi father figure from the old country; babies in christening robes; the Pope.) She saw the parlour only from the hall for he led her down a passageway and carefully opened a door and there in a double bed that filled the room, nightdress rucked up over heavy veiny hips, yellowish grey hair spread like sea wrack across the bolster, an old woman who snored, twitched in the heat, moved a varicosed ankle across the expanse of bedsheet. He shut the door.

'Satisfied?'

'I'm sorry,' she said.

'Shh.' He pointed to a second door which was open, light coming from inside. He cupped his hand around the cheek of her buttock and pushed her gently forward. This room was his: all his boy's enthusiasms were on display, a museum of his growing up. Boxers and baseball heroes stared at a Buffet print; copies of his first layouts were displayed in glass-covered prominence; an N.Y.U. pennant, a tennis racket in a corner; a closet full of his awful suits, ties and slacks. No pin-ups. But then, he lived with his mother.

He shut the door, motioned for silence, then pointed to his open window. He picked up two shabby cushions from a chair, and helped her out of the window on to the fire escape. He spread the cushions on the iron step. Somewhere in the street she heard the guitar.

'Can't talk inside,' he said. 'Might wake her up.'

He reached inside the window, found a pack of cigarettes on his bedtable, lit one for himself but did not offer her one. That was just like him. As he cupped his hands around the match and sat down on the step beside her, she slipped her fingers into his fly.

'How'd you get here?' he asked, pretending not to notice her hand.

'I took the kids up to Saratoga to my sister's. I just got back. My husband thinks I'm spending the night there.'

With her other hand she stroked his bare back; like a whore, she thought, working him up like a whore. Below, in the street, the guitar twanged. 'This time tomorrow,' she said, 'you'll probably be in Mexico.'

'Mehico,' he said. He shut his eyes and let her stroke him.

'How long have you lived with your mother?'

'Since my father died,' he said. 'Five, six years.'

The guitar stopped. He threw his cigarette down between the iron rungs of the ladder, turned to her, caught her by the arm, and bit her hard in the hollow of her neck. She cried out with pleasure.

'Shut up,' he said.

'I'm sorry.'

'Look,' he said. 'I never before in my life shit on my own doorstep, you know what I mean.'

'Of course, darling.'

'My mother's my mother, know what I mean?'

'Yes, darling.'

'So, if we go inside, I want it quiet, okay?'

'Yes, darling.'

'And you got to be out of here before six. She wakes early.'

'Yes.'

'And another thing. This doesn't mean we're going to start jazzing again on a regular basis, right?'

'Vito, please,' she said. 'I know that. That's why I came. I probably won't even be working at the office when you come back from your vacation. I've decided to quit.'

'Why?'

'You know why.'

He nodded and stood up. He motioned to her to come in. 'No noise, see?'

His bare back receded into the bedroom and she followed, jumping down awkwardly from the window ledge. He caught her and held her, her hair damp, her body hot and trembling. His hands slid down her sides, caught at her skirt and began to tug her dress up over her head. Hastily she unzipped it at the side (he had torn two dresses this way). Bending down, her arms extended to help him remove her dress, she again heard the guitar and wished he would put out the light. They could be seen from the house across the way. But she did not speak. She was afraid of him.

A moment later she stood, naked, awkward and vulnerable, and gestured at the opened window. He went towards it, pulling at the drawstring of his pyjamas, letting his pyjamas fall about his heels as he tugged the curtain shut. He did not switch off the light. He turned to her, smiling as at some coarse private fantasy, and in that moment she heard the old woman snore in the next room, saw in her mind's eye those heavy veiny old thighs which long ago bore this brutality into life. How could anyone ever think of him as a son, this hairy male who closed on her now, the street accident happening all over again, time stopping, the cruel rhythm easing, then increasing. Time stopped. Their bodies wet and glistening with sweat, they came to consciousness on the floor and lay listening to the old woman snore. This was the last time, she might never see him again and so she turned to him, clung to him and again he revived. Time stopped.

She was lying on his bed and he had switched off the bed lamp. He got up, went to the window and drew the curtain. A grey wash of light diluted the darkness and she heard the birds which sing only in the pre-dawn hours, the never-seen birds of New York. He stood over her, hairy and urgent.

'Come on, get up. Show's over.'

Fifteen minutes later she stood on the bottom step of the apartment house, looking up. He did not kiss her. He grinned, patted her lightly on the cheek and ran back up the steps, using his key to open the door. And, O God, there must be something she could say, some way to make him say it, it just wasn't going to end without a word, was it?

'Vito?'

'What?'

'Have a nice vacation,' she said foolishly.

'Thanks.'

'And, Vito?'

He stood, holding the door open, in a hurry to go back up.

'Think about me.'

'Be good,' he said. The door shut. She walked slowly away from the house, from the street accident, her mind blank, not knowing she was crying until a cold tear touched her lip. She licked the salt taste and opened her purse. Her watch said four-thirty, it must have stopped, mustn't it? How can I go home at four-thirty? Is there a night bus from Saratoga, could it get in at this time?

At the corner of Eighth Avenue a private sanitation company truck stood outside a warehouse. Three men in green coveralls were feeding the contents of garbage cans into its noisy, churning maw. The sanitation men did not look at her as she drew level: they saw many odd sights at this hour of the morning. Her steps slowed and she stopped and looked at the huge maw of the machine. Cans, cartons, food, paper, all revolved in there: the maw churned and sifted, reducing all to waste. Things no longer wanted were tossed out. She walked on.

Time and privacy. Nothing can be created without them, and this week I have both. I live each day for the hours of reality in my workroom. There, I do not notice the heat, the street noises, or my surroundings. In a few days I will write the last paragraph of my book.

When I leave my workroom I enter into a state of waiting. At home, I walk from room to room, I pick up books but do not read them, I sit in a chair and stare. I no longer know what is happening in the world. I never read a newspaper. The apartment is blessedly peaceful; no rows, no children, no television. The children are in Saratoga and my mother, of course, is at Finnerty's apartment. She will be going home at the end of next week. That reminds me. I must call her. As for Jane, she is strangely silent. She misses the children, I suppose. She will be going back up to Saratoga to see them again this weekend and I'll have the apartment completely to myself. Peace, it's wonderful.

I am happy. I cannot explain this happiness except to say that I wake each morning sure that there is no place in the world I would rather be than here, nothing in the world I would rather do than get on the subway and go down to that shabby, airless room. I feel a sense of excitement which I would not have believed possible. I am not bored or lonely. I wish this state to last forever but of course, it is almost over. I am nearing the last paragraphs and the rest is revision. On Sunday, before I start those revisions, Sidney Gerston wants to read the last two chapters. I am not worried about his verdict; not in the least. I know the book is right. I have never been so confident of anything in my life.

Jane, who has read the book several times in its embryo stages, is supposed to sit down with the completed manuscript as soon as I finish. But I don't feel she's in the mood for it just now. It must be the absence of the kids. She has actually taken to sleeping in their room. (Perhaps she thinks that by denying me herself, she can make me bring the children home. She's wasting her time. I no longer feel a need for sex.)

On Saturday night, while she's in Saratoga, I plan to drop the book off at Gerston's. I shall sleep late on Sunday and by Sunday evening Gerston will call and tell me what he thinks. Monday, I'll pick up the manuscript from him and start on final revisions –

No. Monday I'm supposed to bring the airline ticket over to my mother. I must take her out next week, I must spend some time with her because she's leaving. That reminds me. I should call her.

Aschenbach's whole soul, from the very beginning, was bent on fame. That sentence from Mann now strikes me as false. Fame is not the prize: the prize is in the doing of the thing itself. The other day on Eighth Street, I met Max and we went to Howard Johnson's for coffee. Max's book is coming out any day now, but he complained that on his last meeting with Key and Gerston they talked more of me than of him. He said Gerston tells everyone that my book is the most 'exciting' thing that has happened to him in his years as an editor. Once, Max's jealousy would have warmed my blood. Now, it seems irrelevant. Even the thought of my book being read by strangers in a strange country no longer excites me. The writing itself is the whole joy. *Passionate and absolutist youth can only be enthralled by a problem.* Mann said that too. It is closer to the truth than his Aschenbach.

And yet, when I think back to the years of fits and falls on this book, it was not just fascination with the act of writing which kept me at it. Ambition played a part. Secretly, I am writing it for someone. Secretly, I hope for someone's praise. But who? Not Gerston, not Max, not Jane, not Gallery, not even some ghost from the past like Ormsby. Who then? Some old Dog-God Father who will look down and tell me he is well pleased?

That reminds me. I should phone my mother.

All oyster heads roman, Dick Duryea had scribbled across the rough. Jane picked up her brush, but at that moment someone passed dangerously close to her elbow. People should be more careful. She looked up and the careless one was Norma Malcolm the typist who worked for Dick and Carl. And it started again. In *The Little Danube* he faced her across the table, smiling: 'Norma and I had a romp like this a couple of years back.' Norma, heavy-breasted, thick-thighed, dark patches of perspiration under the armpits of her Klein's basement cotton print, Norma who wore heavy spectacles as she typed, whose upper lip carried a down of dark hair. Of course, Norma. And who else? Girl-to-girl in the john, what tales could be told? She looked over at his cubicle and he materialized in that empty chair, smiling a ghostly ravisher's smile as he ticked off his conquests. Patsy Armstrong? Marlene? Sue Anne? Had them all and laid them end to end. And in six months, in *The Little Danube*, who would he tell: 'had a romp with Jane a couple of months back.'

Neatly now. OYSTER. Take up your brush and letter that and stop thinking about anything else.

PINK. I'll tell Louise this afternoon, I'll explain that I have to quit because Brendan's mother's going home next week. And tonight I'll tell Brendan that Barbara phoned from Saratoga and said the kids want to come back to New York. His book's nearly finished, another month for revisions; we'll manage somehow.

Steady now. SHADES. I'm tired. Sleeping in the kids' room the last four nights, or not sleeping's more like it. When the kids come back I'll really try, I'll be the best mother in the whole of New York, they'll forget old Mrs Let-Me and her baptisms and mumbo-jumbo. Yes, I did the right thing getting rid of her, there was no other choice.

PINK SHADES ARE FORECAST FOR FALL.

Besides, with the kids to look after every day, how could I see him again, how could I *do* anything? Back home in Riverside Drive, taking them to kindergarten and the park, showing them things that will be useful to them later, like the Museum of Natural History and the Met, and teaching Lisa to read, I'll forget all this. Life will be exciting. Brendan's book will come out, he'll be famous, everyone seems to think. I wonder what that will be like? Sinclair Lewis' wife wanted people to know her as Mrs *Sinclair* Lewis, not just any old Mrs Lewis. And Frieda Lawrence was the woman behind all the women Lawrence wrote about. Or nearly all. I should have kept Brendan's old letters.

OYSTER GREY TOO WILL BE FEATURED.

But supposing Brendan drops me? Writers all seem to marry twice, they get rid of the women who helped them up the ladder. And there are girls who collect writers, so that they can boast that they slept with them. That bitch Jean Revere who kissed Brendan in the kitchen. She's the type.

ACCESSORIES WILL FOLLOW THE NEW

Not that he's worried about girls these days, he's dead from the neck down, all he thinks of is his book. Isn't he supposed to have dinner with his mother tonight? Shall I tell him before he goes to dinner or after? Better after.

ALL OF THESE FEATURES AND MORE IN THE NEXT EXCITING ISSUE OF

'Hey, Jane.'

Patsy Armstrong coming across the room with a postcard.

'Card from Mexico,' Patsy said. The card slid down the incline of the drawing-board, as his notes used to do. She put away her brush and turned the card over.

Even out of season, this is the greatest. Best to all the gang.

Vito.

To all, to all, to all. To Norma Malcolm and who else? Marlene and Patsy and who? And me.

I *won't* be here when he comes back. Right after lunch I'll speak to Louise.

The air-conditioning unit in Louise's office gave off a noisy hum, making Louise's voice sound scratchy and strange as an old Caruso record. 'Ten days' notice? But, sweetie, that just won't do.'

'I'm sorry, Louise, but I have no other choice.'

'O, come on now. Your kids are up at your sister's place, you said. It's not as if they were with some stranger.'

'I know. But they're not happy there. I can't just abandon them, can I?'

Above Louise's head Japanese paper birds stirred slowly in their French birdcage. Louise's jade earrings shook as Louise jabbed a thin, silver paperknife into her flower-embroidered desk pad. 'That's fine for you, sweetie, but what about me? If you quit now you're going to foul up the vacation schedule for the rest of the kids here.'

'But why?'

'Because I've promised to let Marlene and Carl off the first two weeks of August, that's why.'

'But Italiano – (had she blushed as she said his name?) – I mean, he'll be back just about the time I leave.'

'Sure he'll be back,' Louise said. 'But Vito's work and yours don't overlap. Look, Jane, when I hired you it was partly on the basis that I needed someone to help out over the vacation period. You're letting me down.'

'I'm sorry.'

The earrings shook. 'Sorry isn't enough. Surely you can leave your kids in Saratoga just for the first two weeks of August. That way, Carl and Marlene will get their vacations. Honestly, sweetie, I don't think that's asking too much.'

But it was. That was two weeks in the office with him.

'I'm not asking you to decide right now,' Louise said. 'I want you to go home and talk it over with Brendan. And remember, I did *you* a favour when I hired you. I expect you to do at least as much for me, in return.'

What could you say? She looked at Louise's thin shoulders and flat chest and could not help wondering if they had lain on some floor underneath Vito's weight. Was Louise a veteran in the emotions she herself was going through? She remembered how grateful she had been when Louise hired her. She would have to pretend to think it over.

'All right,' she said. 'I'll talk to Brendan.'

There was no phone in Brendan's workroom so, at five when she finished work, she took a Seventh Avenue subway down to Twelfth Street and walked over to his building. And it began again, a memory of the last time she had walked in the Village, at five in the morning. She remembered how he had turned away and run up the steps, so eager to see the end of her. And suddenly, for the first time, she wanted to tell someone how awful it had been; to have someone listen and be shocked and sympathetic. Mostly sympathetic. But who could she tell? Once she might have told Louise, but that was out. No, the person she most wanted to tell it to was the person it would shock most. But of course, she couldn't tell him.

Why not?

She stopped right there in the street when she thought of it. In front of her, unnoticed, a spastic teenager on aluminium crutches waited impatiently for her to pass.

Why not?

The spastic, giving up, moved around her, angry, twitching, affronted.

It would stop any nonsense about *why* she was quitting. He would see that she had to quit at the end of this month. It would end her fears that Vito might gossip and that the gossip might somehow come home to roost. She had been unfaithful, all right, she had had an affair, all right, and he would have every reason to feel mad about it, but wouldn't he also feel threatened, wouldn't it make him worry a bit more than he did about his ability to keep her?

Of course, she needn't tell him *all* the details. Or any, come to think of it. Just that this man was in love with her and had made passes and that she was getting out now to avoid something worse. It would serve Brendan right to be told: it would give him something to think about besides that book of his.

Well, she said to herself. We'll see. She walked on.

But going upstairs to the cramped fourth-floor room where he worked, her thoughts moved again towards the drama of telling it. She saw his face, naked in shock, anger and fear. She saw herself, as on a stage, the light shining down on her, a woman taken in adultery, and in the wings Brendan wept, his book, his ambitions, forgotten, wanting to bring her home, give her back her children, shield her from all further harm.

Or would he?

She opened his door and in the dusty sunlight from his dirty window, saw him hunched over the long trestle table, writing in longhand. He did not look up as she entered the room although her footsteps were loud on the uncarpeted boards. There were sheets of paper everywhere and a huge bowl filled with cigarette ends. My god, she thought. Suppose he really *is* a great writer?

'Still at it?'

He turned in his chair slowly focusing on her, as though irritated by the interruption. 'What time is it?' he asked.

'Five thirty, quarter to six, I guess.'

'That late?'

'I thought we might have a drink downtown before I go home,' she said. 'I want to talk to you.'

'All right. But what I'd like to do is have a hamburger downtown and come back here to work tonight.'

'I thought you were going to see your mother tonight?'

'O god, I forgot. I have that money for her.'

'What money?'

'That fifty bucks I was supposed to give her on Tuesday.'

'Do you mean to say you haven't seen her since she left?'

He looked uneasy. 'Well, I meant to give her the airline ticket and this money on Tuesday, but I was working so I phoned and made a date for tonight instead.'

'Then you must go tonight.'

He turned back to his table and looked longingly at the handwritten sheets in front of him. 'But I haven't got time,' he said. 'Why don't you do me a favour, darling, and run over with the money and the ticket?'

'Me? She's your mother. And she's leaving next week.'

'I know. I know. But this is a crucial part, I'm coming up to the end of the last chapter. Look, I'll phone her and make it for tomorrow night.'

'You'll do no such thing,' Jane said, furious. 'That poor woman has been all alone ever since she left our place. My god, Brendan, I've never heard of anything so heartless.'

'Look, you don't understand.'

He picked up a pencil and in that moment she wanted to lift her handbag and smash him in the head. What was the use in talking to him? That poor woman, all alone since Friday.

'Give me the tickets,' she said.

He looked relieved. 'Yes, sure.' He got up and took an envelope from his jacket. 'Thanks, darling. And tell Mamma I'll be in touch with her tomorrow, okay?'

'What's her address?'

He pencilled it on the envelope. 'I really appreciate this.'

'I'm not doing it for you. And when you come home tonight, we're going to have a real talk, remember. I'm quitting my job at the end of this month.'

'Not that again.'

'Yes, that again. I spoke to Louise today. Tomorrow, I'm going to make it final.'

But, even as she spoke, he sat down at his table, longingly shifting the manuscript sheets about. 'Well, we'll talk about it later,' he said, vaguely. 'And thanks again, darling.'

Darling meant dearly beloved but what did it mean to him? If she no longer suited his needs would she, like his mother, never hear from him again? She slammed the door, and went out into the street. Down the block, a group of Puerto Rican families had placed chairs and tables outside their tenement and sat, in a sidewalk scene as crowded as an opera stage, playing cards, reading Spanish-language newspapers, the smaller children running in figure-eight formations in and out among the adults. A woman in a kimono leaned out from an upper window and shouted down to her card-playing husband; a grandfather sat on a stoop, holding a transistor radio to his ear as though it were a sea shell. No one looked up as Jane passed and, ignored in that thick familial atmosphere, she found herself wondering why in all New York it was only these poor, unwanted immigrants, imprisoned in their alien language and customs, who still lived a life in real community. She thought of Brendan's mother, waiting almost a week in some stranger's flat for a son who was too busy to call and, to her surprise, walking in the street, she felt like crying, crying for an old woman she had never liked, for a mother whose son had forgotten her, whose son had changed, who could not change him back.

In the East Fifties there were no Puerto Ricans and many of the apartment dwellers had left town, fleeing the summer's heat. The street in which Mrs Tierney was staying was empty save for two businessmen who stood under the canopy of a small, expensive restaurant while the doorman hunted down the next street for a cab. As she passed these men, they turned to look at her, their eyes congealed in a martini glaze, their pink, locker-room faces sprouting like plant bulbs from summer uniforms of grey lightweight suits, white button-down shirts, narrow, small-patterned ties. One of them turned to the other and said something in a whisper. She heard the other man laugh and guessed it was something about her.

When she rang the bell in the hall of the apartment building, an answering buzz sounded at once and she had a vision of Mrs

Let-Me, dressed to go out, standing by her doorbell upstairs in readiness for Brendan. As she went up the stairs she decided that unless her mother-in-law's attitude was one of complete hostility, she would deputize for Brendan and take the poor old thing out to supper. And at that moment she realized that ever since she had set off on this errand of mercy she had banished Vito from her mind. Good deeds were good therapy. But, didn't knowing that take all the good out of them?

On the landing above her Mrs Tierney waited by the open doorway in her green dress, white cotton gloves and black sailor straw. Her expression, as Jane came around the bend of the staircase became fixed – a *Daily News* photograph of a mother being told.

'Where's – what's happened to Brendan?' she said in a rush.

'Hello,' Jane answered, still climbing. 'I'll tell you about that in a moment.'

'He's all right, isn't he?'

'Yes. He's just working.'

Mrs Tierney closed her eyes as though offering up a prayer of thanks. 'Come in, dear,' she said.

The cousin was a postal clerk, Brendan had said, and Jane could see that this apartment, odd in such an area, was furnished at the postal clerk level. In the small living-room, a big blue television glare, sound turned off, voiceless singers mouthing in a snowstorm of interference. The windows were open but it was still stuffy. Mrs Tierney, preceding Jane into the room, raised her hands to her head began to unpin her black sailor hat.

'No, please keep your hat on,' Jane said. 'I hope we'll be able to go out and have a bite of dinner together.'

Her mother-in-law did not answer. But she did not take off her hat.

'Brendan's terribly sorry about not coming tonight. He asked me to bring the ticket and some money. It's in here.'

She took the envelope from her bag and held it out. Her mother-in-law took it, still without speaking, and put it down on the coffee table. Something more must be said. 'You see, he's finishing the book this week and he's terribly involved with it.'

'Aye, the book. The famous book.'

'I know,' Jane said. 'He hardly even has time to speak to me.'

Her mother-in-law went to the television and turned it off.

The blue glare contracted to a white, tiny circle; died. Neither woman sat down.

'And how have you been keeping, mother?'

Why had she said mother? When the word came out it startled her as much as it did her mother-in-law who looked up as though recognizing a sound in some foreign tongue.

'O, I've been all right. It's very hot though. I must say I won't be sorry to go back to a bit of rain and cold. Sometimes, coming up the stairs in this place, I haven't a breath left in me.'

She turned to the coffee table, picked up the envelope and opened it. 'Is this the ticket?'

'Yes. It's for a week from tomorrow.'

'And money. You shouldn't have.'

'It was Brendan sent it. I'm just sorry there isn't more of it. I mean, you must have shopping to do, things to buy.'

'No,' Mrs Tierney said. She put the envelope in her purse. 'There's a restaurant called Schrafft's not far from here,' she said uncertainly. 'It's not too bad.'

'Would you like that?'

'Whatever *you* like, dear.'

'All right then, let's go to Schrafft's. Are you ready?'

'I'll just close the windows first.'

'But won't it be very hot when you come back in?'

'Aye, but it's not my place, you see. I wouldn't want anything stolen.'

Not her place. Where *is* her place now, Jane wondered. Brendan had said something about her getting a little council flat back in Ireland: he said she would be no worse off than before she came. But she sold all her furniture, didn't she? Imagine how I would feel at her age, sent home by Liam, living on a miserable little allowance I couldn't even be sure of, with nothing of my own left.

'Ready now, dear.' Mrs Tierney locked the door and they went downstairs. In the street, walking towards Schrafft's, Jane said that Brendan had promised he would phone tomorrow.

'O, if he's busy, let him not bother,' Mrs Tierney said.

Was she not even angry? Her face showed nothing. It was as though, in the seven days she had lived apart from them, she had completely lost her persona of mother-in-law. The woman who now sat down opposite Jane in Schrafft's was an elderly stranger, uninterested and uninteresting, a stranger who politely asked after the children, how did they like living in the country, wasn't it nice for them to get away from this heat, how long did they expect to stay up there? When Jane mentioned Brendan and tried in a roundabout way to criticize him for not coming tonight, Mrs Tierney interrupted to ask the waitress for a glass of water, then changed the subject with some talk of meeting some ladies she knew in the park. 'I still go to the park every day,' she said. 'It's very restful.'

But what *did* she do all day? What had she done all week in that apartment with nobody to talk to? She did not say. When Jane turned the subject to Ireland and her future plans, Mrs Tierney merely smiled in a vague, uninterested way, and said: 'O, we'll see when I get there. A friend of mine – he used to be a friend of Brendan's, a man called Ted Ormsby – he'll look out for a place for me. I wrote him last Saturday, you see.'

'I'm sorry,' Jane said, touched despite herself. 'I wish things hadn't worked out this way.'

'No need to be sorry, dear, it's probably just as well. The children missed you when you were working, you know. Naturally, they prefer their own mother to a stranger, and who can blame them? You'll be happier back at home.'

'I know,' Jane said. 'If only Brendan would finish this book. It's next month, I'm worried about, leaving them up there in Saratoga –'

But Mrs Tierney signalled the waitress. 'Do you want tea or coffee, dear?'

'Coffee. Black. I was saying about next month –'

'I'll have tea,' Mrs Tierney told the waitress.

And that was all. Jane fell silent and they drank the hot liquids in a hurry. Mrs Tierney offered to pay for their meal, but Jane insisted. When they went out of the restaurant, Mrs Tierney hesitated on the pavement. 'No need for you to walk me back, dear. Your bus is the other way.'

'O, but it's early yet.'

Mrs Tierney smiled, her dark eyes suddenly alert and wary, the smile of a stranger. 'No,' she said. 'It's quite late.' And with that she bobbed her head, held out her hand and said: 'Good night, now. Thank you for coming.'

'But we'll see you very soon, Brendan will call you tomorrow and when I come back from Saratoga, on Monday maybe you'll come over for supper?'

Again that smile. 'We'll see,' Mrs Tierney said. 'Good night, Jane.'

'Good night, mother.'

As she said this Jane moved towards Mrs Tierney, reaching out both hands to take hold of the older woman's shoulders. The kiss she wanted to give was kiss-and-make-up: it would be forgiveness for baptism and interference, in exchange for forgiveness for coldness and abandonment. But Mrs Tierney avoided her arms, as a politician moves past a too importunate voter. She turned, looked up towards the sun-dulled traffic lights on Fifth, then down in the other direction. With the caution of old age her foot hovered like a mine detector before it risked the step off the pavement. Shabby, dumpy, slow, she made her way across the street, then turned, waved, and was gone, a cleaning woman on her way home. But Jane did not wave back. Ungrateful old Apple Annie, and here I was trying to be nice to you, forgetting my own problems to come and help you out when your own son wouldn't lift his finger, yes, even offering to forgive you for the harm you did the kids. All right, Mrs Let-Me, if that's the way you want it. All right.

She arrived home in a thoroughly bad temper. Brendan should have gone, it was *his* mother, the whole lousy mess was his fault. And – the last straw – he wasn't even home when she got there.

Was that why, when he did come home, she told him about herself and Vito?

She remembered looking at the clock when he came in. It was ten after ten. Yet the first thing he said to her was: 'Hey, how about something to eat?'

His seersucker suit, as usual, seemed too small for him; it should have been sent to the cleaners days ago. His dark hair needed cutting and the Napoleonic lock which fell over one temple seemed foolish and affected. His face was pale, as though he had not spent one moment in the sun all summer, and his eyes had that familiar I'm-writing-in-my-head look which warned her that he had not thought of her or of his mother all evening. As for thinking of his children, when had he last done that? Days ago, most likely.

'Eat?' she said. 'I thought you were going to eat something downtown?'

'I forgot. You see, I was finishing the draft of the final chapter and I wanted to go straight through. It was just a rough draft but it means that, at last, I've written the ending.'

'I saw your mother tonight.'

'O good. I must call her. You know, it felt very peculiar to be writing those last pages –'

'Look, Brendan, can't we talk about anything but your damn book?'

He looked hurt. 'What's the matter? Are you mad at me or something?'

'Yes, I am mad. I'm supposed to tell Louise tomorrow about leaving the job at the end of the month. I've been waiting all evening to discuss it with you.'

'But what do you have to quit for? I thought you were staying until September so that I could finish my revisions.'

'No.'

'But that's not fair, that's not what you promised when I agreed to get rid of Mamma.'

Rid of Mamma. That's how he sees it, rid of Mamma.

'All right,' she said. 'Let me put it in words of one syllable. Unless I quit at the end of this month, I'm going to have an affair with a man.'

'What man?'

'A man at the office.'

'You'll go to any lengths to force me back on the treadmill, won't you?' he said. 'Even to threats of adultery.'

'Brendan, they're not threats. I'm trying to prevent something happening.'

'You serious?'

'Of course I'm serious.'

'I see. Have you slept with him already?'

She did not answer.

'*Have you?*'

At least he was angry, at least he looked worried now. And face to face with him, how could she tell him the whole truth? Be cautious. 'No,' she said.

'Then how do you know you're going to sleep with him?'

'I know it, don't ask me how. Please, Brendan, I'm asking you to help me. If I quit now, you can still do those revisions somehow. But if you make me stay on with Louise, it'll be the end of our marriage.'

'I'm sorry,' he said. 'I have to have that month.'

Month – month – month thundered senselessly in her head. For a long moment she had no thoughts at all: it was like fainting with your eyes open.

'So to give you your month,' she said, at last, 'you want me to sleep with Vito?'

'Is that his name?'

'Yes.'

He got up, went to the table and poured himself what was left in the bottle of gin. He turned and went into the kitchen and she heard him take ice from the refrigerator. He must think she was bluffing or something. He must.

He came back into the living-room with a gin and tonic and stood looking down at her, rubbing the tumbler of gin and tonic back and forth across his forehead as though it were a cold compress.

'Well?' she said.

'I've been thinking. You know, when people write about this sort of situation, they get it all wrong. They tend to write about the willed moral reaction, not the real one. They decide that a man's supposed to feel angry and hurt and vengeful when he hears his wife's planning to be unfaithful. So they write it that way. But I don't feel vengeful at all.'

'What *do* you feel?'

'Well,' he said. 'I *was* angry, at first. But, back there in the kitchen, I began to think of divorce. I decided that, even though I'd miss the children, you'd better have them. You need them more than I do.'

'Wait a minute. You needn't think you're going to ditch us like you ditched your mother.'

'You ditched her,' he said. 'Not me. And you're ditching me for some office Lothario.'

'O, Brendan, listen to me. I don't love this man at all. In a way, I hate and despise him.'

'Then it shouldn't be hard to give him up.'

'You wouldn't understand.'

'No? Maybe if I have a talk with your boyfriend tomorrow, I'll make *him* understand.'

'He's on vacation. Besides, it's not him needs talking to, it's me.'

'What's that supposed to mean?'

'Look. Why don't you go to Gerston and ask him for that fifteen hundred dollars now? Then I could quit.'

'No. It's in the contract that I get the money only when I deliver the manuscript. All I need is five more weeks. Surely you can hang on –'

'Hang on,' she said. 'God, Brendan, you'll throw anybody to the wolves to get what you want.'

'That's funny. Someone else said something like that to me a long time ago.'

'Well, whoever it was, they had your number, all right.'

'It was Ted Ormsby. And he was exaggerating, just as you are. You're missing the point. The point is, you're asking me to jeopardize my work, and that's not fair. You promised me a month. I'm holding you to that promise.'

Month, month, month: it thundered in her head. You promised me a month. Japanese paper birds stirred above the desk as Louise thanked her for staying on another month. Vito came back from Mehico, he had the hots again, he dropped notes on her drawing-board all month, she went out with her diaphragm in her handbag all month – month – month, the old woman with veiny thighs snored next door as they rolled on the floor and sad Krim waited at five in the bar downstairs, all month – month – month, you promised me a month. And at the end of the month she could have an affair with someone else, why not, for marriages do not end in jealousies and fights, they end in indifference and permissiveness. And this marriage would end. It was just a matter of time.

'Anyway,' he said. 'Let's not panic. All that's happened so far, is you've developed a crush on some guy. There's no need for it to go any further. Besides, you're jeopardizing a lot of good things that are coming up.'

'What good things?'

'Well, Gerston says when I publish this book I'll be in line for a foundation grant. That means we could go to Europe for a year, the kids too. Once the book is finished, I'll apply right away. Gerston also thinks I can get a part-time teaching job. All sorts of things will open up if the book's a success. Life's going to be very pleasant.'

Life's going to be pleasant. Sleep with Vito and life will be –

'Well?' he said. 'Look, it's only five more weeks. Then, if you want to, you can quit and see what –'

'All right,' she said. 'Only, please, *shut up*.'

He reached out for her but she dodged past him, running to

the bathroom like an animal to ground, locking herself in as so often in the past, sitting on the throne facing herself in the full-length mirror on the bathroom door – a girl with her dark hair in braids, a girl whose face seemed pale, too pale – and suddenly she was sick. She knelt over the bowl and retched, and in the act of retching she felt purged and relieved, as though all her rage had come out at last. He knocked on the door, but she pretended not to hear. She sat on the bathroom floor, her brow cold and damp, her body drained and weak.

'Are you all right, darling?' his voice said. 'Jane, are you all right?'

Don't answer.

'I'll be in the living-room,' he said. 'Or can I get you anything?'

Yes, I'll have a foundation grant, thank you. Buy me a ticket to go away, anywhere. I'll walk hand in hand with Lisa and Liam past those naked stone nymphs at the back of the Paris *Opéra*, going to American Express to get the mail from home. I'll sit on the terrace at the *Deux Magots*, sipping my *café crème* while the children drink grenadines. I'll write cards: *best to all the gang*. Like Vito. And you'll be upstairs in the hotel writing a book, for I'll have promised you another month, another year, another lifetime, and in the afternoons, I'll take the kids to the Louvre, I'll walk them up the stone steps, past the Winged Victory of Samothrace, and down those shiny parquetry-floored corridors past the huge Davids and Ingres I remember from the days I went there, Jane Melville, just out of college. What would Jane Melville think of me now? In Mallorca for the summer months, on the little beach at Camp de Mar where two dollars a day paid for the hotel, three meals and wine and at night I sat with you drinking Calisay liqueur on the terrace. A second sick honeymoon it will be this time, with the children asleep upstairs in their room and the night porter paid to look in on them while we two take the bus to Palma and re-create that first night we ever made love to each other, behind a rowboat on the beach with the Cathedral across the bay, wet sand in my underwear, and you would never ask me for a month. But now you ask me and I say yes because I'm afraid to make a break. There are the children, remember? Yes, we were happy that night on the beach. We didn't see the years ahead; the baby carriage, the prison afternoons in iron-barred playgrounds, the years of sit-ins because baby-sitters cost so much.

Castles in Spain. If we go back, all he will think of is a book, a damn book. He's obsessed now, he doesn't care about anything but that. Maybe he never will again?

'Jane,' his voice said. 'Come to bed.'

'You go on. I'm sleeping in the kids' room.'

'No, you're not. That's over. You're sleeping with me. Now, open up.'

Sleeping with him. Like dead mutton she would sleep with him.

'Open up.'

She opened the door and he lifted her up in his arms and carried her down the corridor. Dead mutton. She let herself go limp.

*

When I carried her into the bedroom, she went dead on me. I remembered that in the first year of our marriage I used to undress her as a preliminary to sex, and as I began to unbutton her blouse I wondered about this office Romeo of hers and what might have taken place between them. Kisses in the corridor, a cuddle in the coffee shop? What did he look like? And, suddenly jealous as I had not been when she told me, I began to kiss and fondle her. She did not repulse me. She simply lay on the bed like a mother enduring the caresses of an overly affectionate child. And I, in turn, found my attention beginning to wander. As I gently bit on her breasts I thought of Gerston and wondered what he would say about the last two chapters of my book. While my tongue explored the recesses of her ear, I was speculating on whether my absorption in writing was a substitute for the waning of a more primal urge. I wanted to roll over and go to sleep but instead, I went on kissing and caressing her. I foresaw a new version of hell in which I would endlessly make love to her. Endlessly, she would not respond.

'Do you want me to stop?' I asked at last.

She raised herself on her elbow, her other hand chastely between her thighs. In the moonlight, naked except for her necklace of green stones, she reminded me of Manet's *Olympia*. I was her blackamoor slave.

'Do *you* want to?' she said.

But I wanted *her* to call pax. 'Maybe you're tired?' I suggested.

'No.'

I felt myself go limp. Frightened, I got off the bed and went into the bathroom. I switched on the light (why do bathrooms seem so harshly lit in the middle of the night?) and as I bent over the washbasin, two cockroaches came up out of the waste pipe and ran across the white porcelain surface of the basin: lost, blinded, two small stupid creatures, terrified by this brightness into which they had blundered, this white, stark world from which they might never escape.

I watched them for a moment, then turned away. Across the street I saw a lighted checkerboard of windows at Union Theological Seminary. But the theologians were abed: there was not even a cleaning woman to be seen among the empty desks. I switched off the bathroom light and stood in darkness, trying to arouse my desire by summoning up images of other times, other girls. I remembered myself at twenty-two, rigid and excited in the front row of the stalls at Concert Mayol on my first visit to Paris. An opening chorus of eighteen naked girls paraded down the ramp, each turning to present to the audience her bare bottom and a placard with a capital letter; the whole spelling out GAIETÉS PARISIENNES. I mourned my hot youth. Dejected, I returned to the bedroom and my fellow cockroach.

She was not asleep. She reclined, her back to me, and now she was the Rokeby Venus, beautiful and untouchable. As I lay down beside her, I told myself that this was temporary, it was unimportant – wasn't it de Maupassant who believed that one night's sex robbed him of fifteen days of writing? It was better that I fail. Tomorrow, I must work and now I must go to sleep.

'Well?' she said, her back to me. 'Have you finished?'

And so, in the pitiless foreknowledge of failure, I tried again.

The photograph of Frank Finnerty's father said good morning from its place of honour on the cheap yellow dressing-table across the room. Uncle John Finnerty (he had been an old man when he danced with her in the parish hall in Creeslough) was young and raw in this picture. He stood by a photographer's Grecian column in rented academic robes, holding in his right hand the sheepskin which would enable him, all his life, to teach Latin, Greek and History to small Irish boys. Funny how that photo caught her eye each morning she woke here, reminding her that she was not in a strange place; that here was her mother's older brother; that outside this room and across the sea there was a country which was home; that going back would not be so bad after all.

And that brought her to the airline ticket Jane had given her last night and the day and the date and the hour of flight. Next Friday, just one week from today. And it was a Friday night – last Friday – that she moved over here. A week alone – a long time. And not once has he been to see me, would you credit it?

But I'll not think of that, I'll not torment myself sitting in all day, waiting for him to ring up when he has no notion of ringing up, and no wonder, isn't it his own bad conscience that's bothering him. Och, he's not worth upsetting yourself for, just wait till *he's* old and his own children give him the back of their hand, and they will, God forgive me, they will. Everything comes to him who waits.

Her grey hair fell about her shoulders as she got out of bed. She had forgotten to put on her hairnet. The moment she put her foot on the floor she felt the sun roasting the bare boards. Another scorcher. She remembered that Mrs Hofstra from the park – now there was a decent skin – had asked her over to tea today. A stranger, a foreigner that she'd not known four months ago, had asked her to tea but her own flesh and blood wouldn't even –

Don't excite yourself, it's bad for you. Go and get the paper.

Frank had forgotten to stop the newspaper. *The Herald*

Tribune was the name of it and it was left outside the door every morning. She liked to read it with her morning cup of tea. She also liked to turn on the telly: there was a programme called *Today*, run by a very nice big chap with glasses: it had the news and weather and a lot of chit-chat about things that happened in the world. She always woke at seven, too early when the day was so long, but what could you do about it?

Before she went to the front door to get the paper she slipped on her blue wool dressing-gown for decency's sake. The paper had come, but the milkman had not yet left his half pint of milk. She could hear the wireless from the flat downstairs. The lady downstairs played wireless music from dawn till night.

She went into the sitting-room, opened all the windows, then pulled the blinds down again to keep out the sun. As she crossed the room, she switched on the television set. In the kitchen, the two bananas she had bought yesterday and left on the counter were on the turn already. What a silly she was not to have put them in the fridge. She drew water and put the tea on. A voice from the sitting-room said that a rocket had failed to go off at that Cape Carnival place. It was the voice of that nice chap, the head man of the show.

While the tea was drawing, she made a bit of toast. The butter in the fridge was hard as ice, and she let it sit in the sun on the windowsill. She unloosed her dressing-gown, then decided to take it off. The blinds were down in the living-room and the kitchen window looked out on a blank wall. Nobody would see her in her nightie. The telly was too loud now, she must lower it. In the dark in there, she saw the blue picture and the head man was sitting at a big table with a pretty girl on his right and another man on his left. They were all looking at some toy on the table. They were laughing. Too loud. Somebody would hammer on the ceiling from above if she did not hurry and turn it down. She went in, in a hurry –

The fall took the breath out of her. She hit the side of her face on the floor, almost knocking herself senseless. A crucifixion of pain shot down her leg from the thigh.

Pain. Her head was light. Lie still a minute and it may go away. Rest a minute. *Pain*. Please, God, nothing's broken –

– I fainted now, that's what I did. I tripped on that blue rug and I came a terrible tumble and something is broken. Now get a hold of yourself, Eileen, don't lose your head. Move a wee bit.

Pain. – I feel sick. The pain is up very high. Old people's bones break, they're brittle. Move. *Pain.* O, it's my hip, I think it's the hip –

– You fainted again. Lie still now, you're a nurse, where's the fracture? If you've broken your hip, neck of the femur, isn't that it? you'll not be able to move, you'll have to be lifted. And who says it's your hip, isn't it just like you, you gloomy woman, to think the worst. Hold on to yourself. See if you can turn. Now . . . *Pain.* Come back where you were. *Pain* –

– You were away again there. I feel deadly sick. Mustn't vomit on Frank's good rug. Imagine him – someone – coming in finding me like this, in my nightie, O please, I mustn't vomit, make a mess, sick, I feel sick, O –

I must clean the rug, as soon as I get up I must clean it, wash it with soap and water, get some rug cleaner, put it out to dry at the kitchen window, nobody will know. Move away from this mess, it's in my hair as well, wash my hair. Frank's rug. What –
She lay, just inside the door of the sitting-room, on her left side, her arms raised as though she had been shot down in the act of putting her hands up. She had moved her head clear of the vomit on the rug and her face rested on the floorboards. Her hair fell over her eyes, her nightdress was rucked up, baring her buttocks and lower abdomen. It was dark in the sitting-room with the blinds down, but a shaft of sunlight from the kitchen window fell across her calves. The television picture changed and a voice said:

'And now, the latest on the morning's weather. Time: eight forty-six. And here's Frank.

'Well, it's going to be another hot one, I'm afraid. Estimated high is in high eighties with a low of seventy-one forecast for tonight. Humidity around eighty per cent. Temperature in downtown Manhattan at the moment is seventy-five with a humidity reading of eighty-one. On Long Island Sound –'

– happened? Floor. Leg dead. My hip. Listen, somebody talking.

'And now back to Dave.'

Telly, that is, but there's somebody on the stairs. The milkman? Help me. But if he came in, lying in my nightie, mess everywhere, no, no, can't let him come in like this.

Have sense, woman. Call out to him.

But the telly is too loud, he won't hear.

Listen. Clinks of bottles.
Call him now.
Late. Call.
– Hello? Help? –
(Did I call or did I just dream it?)
Footsteps. Hall door. Gone?
'We have in the studio with us this morning Miss Fumi Watanabe who has come all the way from Tokyo to dance the title role –'
On the kitchen windowsill the quarter-pound of butter began to melt. The toast grew hard.

When we woke this morning, I thought of those cockroaches. We dressed in silence, breakfasted in silence, and as we waited on Riverside for the bus downtown, the silence was broken by the jungle chatter of pneumatic drills at a demolition project down the street. The wreckers' ball and chain swung sullenly across a rubble of bricks, smashing old walls. I had to shout to make myself heard.

'Are you going up to Saratoga tonight?'

'Yes,' she said.

'What time are you leaving?'

'Six.'

'Well, supposing I meet you at five-thirty at the bus terminal. We could have a coffee or something?'

'Why?'

'No special reason. Just to see you.'

'And to make sure I didn't resign?'

'Don't be bitchy. I just thought we could spend half an hour together. We won't be seeing each other until Sunday night.'

'What do you care?' she said. 'You won't miss me.'

Well, the bus came then and it was crowded as usual and we had to stand. She stood with her back to me and for a moment I really hated her. But I remembered the cockroaches. Before she got off the bus, I told her again that I would meet her at five-thirty. Will we ever get back to that warm, dark drain.

*

The queen for the day began to weep as the pretty girls showed her prizes: a fitted vanity case with a year's supply of beauty aids, a console television set, a set of matching cashmere sweaters, a spin-dry washer with a year's supply of detergent, a simulated leather coat and then, with a roll of drums, the grand prize of tourist air tickets to Hawaii and two weeks in a beach hotel, all expenses paid. The queen was a thin, ageing woman from Scranton, Pa, with a large wen on her right jawbone and two fingers splayed from a childhood accident with a hammer.

Her story (husband crippled fifteen years with Parkinson's Disease, seven children to support on a cleaning woman's wage, sick sister in California, eldest child stricken by polio) had rated highest on the applause meter and now, as the master of ceremonies led her forward, the centre camera dollying in for a close-up, her face grew huge on the television screen in happy, confused, weeping ugliness. Off camera, a young man raised a card which read *applause*. The studio audience brought their handclaps to crescendo.

The applause woke her and for a moment she thought they were applauding her. She was coming along. Awake, the pounding headache returned: it had started soon after she began to move. She was much closer to the telly now and from where she lay she could see the front hall, the little table and the telephone on it. Each move brought the pain, and afterwards, while she rested, she fell into long dozes. But she had moved a good three yards. If she stuck it out, she would reach the phone.

And I will stick it out, she told herself. I am not Shaun Moynahan's daughter for nothing. I stuck out the pain of Rory's death, I stuck out the years of Grattan's illness, I will manage this.

She braced her hands underneath her breasts, moved slightly so that the toes of her good leg could gain purchase on the floor-boards and then lifted herself up. Eyes shut, sweat running down her brow and neck, she strained forward. Her body lurched a few inches. She fell on her face. Another wee bit nearer. *Pain* –

– They were all in the room with her: Grattan wore the brown Donegal tweed suit he had worn on their honeymoon, Sheila wore the yellow dress she had on the day she ran off to Australia, Moira was in her black novice's habit, Brendan in his wrinkled American suit that looked as if it were made of pyjama material, Rory in his Air Force blue. Her father was there too. Although he wore his beard, he reminded her of Uncle John Finnerty, for he was in Uncle John's academic robes and stood by a photographer's Grecian column. They were all on the other side of the room. They were waiting for her. They were all dead.

And a voice spoke: 'My Father's house has many mansions. Enter ye faithful into the joy of the kingdom prepared for you. This is my beloved daughter, Eileen, in whom I am well pleased.'

They all clapped for joy. And she cried out in her happiness, for it had all come out in the end, all of them were saved and in heaven. Even Brendan. And old Father Hanlon was sitting in the middle of the room. He said: 'This world is a vale of tears, a testing ground. We must suffer here on earth so that we will be worthy to stand before the judgment seat of heaven.' She had doubted God's goodness, she had thought that God punished her for Denis: Rory dying, Grattan's illness, Sheila running away, Brendan's godless life. But God was good. He understood. Lisa and Liam came across the room to her, little angels, both baptized. They held out their hands to her. Her father also crossed the room and his beard tickled her cheek as he kissed her. 'It's all right, Eileen,' he said. 'You did your best.'

'Even with Brendan?' she asked. 'I tried to bring him up to believe in the things that matter, but he doesn't, he believes only in his own self, he never came to see me in Frank's flat. Was it America was to blame? Or was it me?'

'Come,' said her father. And he took her hands and joined them with the hands of her grandchildren, and her grandchildren led her across the room into heaven as everybody clapped and clapped and clapped –

It was the telly, they were clapping on the telly again. She could see the phone, so far away. The pounding started again in her head and her lips were dry, O for a sup of water. She felt she would vomit. It passed. It was God's will that she fall and hurt herself like this. God was punishing her for doubting Him these last few weeks. He was testing her. Thy will be done.

Again, she put her hands underneath her body. One-two-three. She lurched up and leaned forward. She fell on her face. Like a slap. *Pain* – Easy now, it will go away. She listened, amid the pounding, to the voice on the telly. An organ was playing.

'And now,' a voice said. 'Edge of Night.' She knew that programme, it came on late in the afternoon. She remembered that Mrs Hofstra would be waiting to give her tea. Mrs Hofstra would be wondering what had happened to her. Would Mrs Hofstra ring her up, or perhaps come over to see what was keeping her? No, you're not to think that; no one will come. The phone is there. Not so far. Another half-dozen moves or so. Now. One-two-three.

At six, when the news came on the telly, she was close to the living-room door. As she lay, half dozing, head pounding, she heard the telephone ringing. It rang and rang and could it be Mrs Hofstra, or was it – please God it is – Brendan? If there's no answer, he might decide to come over and see what's happened to me.

But why would he? He hasn't come all week.

The phone stopped ringing. Could have been a wrong number, that happens all the time here. One good thing though: the phone is in working order. I must get to the phone.

*

Kierkegaard and Camus, Dostoievsky and Gide – I spun the circular racks at the bus terminal paperback stand. Would there be room for me? On the other racks were detective stories, how-to-do-its, Norman Vincent Peale, Westerns, animal stories. Who read all these books?

I had arrived at five-thirty precisely but she had not shown up yet. At the coffee shop doorway, two Negro servicemen (just up from the South?) hesitated for a moment before entering. The loudspeaker announced the departure of a bus for Chicago. In the air-conditioned cool of the concourse my damp shirt stuck to my skin.

Tomorrow afternoon I deliver the last two chapters to Gerston. Despite the fact that I had little sleep last night, I worked well today. Now, if only I could patch things up with Jane. Where was she?

At a quarter to six I saw her high-heeling it across the concourse, her overnight bag and three parcels in her arms. As she came closer I looked at her face: sullen, pretty, pale. I felt sorry for her. Then why did I snap at her in my first sentence?

'You're late,' I accused.

'I had to buy some things.'

'What things?'

'Some toys for the kids, from the five and ten. And something for Barbara.'

'Barbara, all right, but the kids don't need any toys. They have far too many already.'

'They need something They have no father.'

'Look, Jane. I came here, trying to be nice to you.'

She sighed. 'All right, you came. Thank you. Now, why don't you go back to your goddamn book. I'll get a seat on the bus.'

'But we have fifteen minutes. Time enough for a coffee?'

'No. I don't want to stand all the way to Saratoga.'

'All right. Which platform is it? I'll walk you over.'

'Eight.'

We began to walk back across the concourse. 'You might at least take my bag,' she said accusingly.

'I'm sorry.'

So I took her bag and the parcels, thinking to myself that we never used to fight like this. Well, not quite like this. I thought of a verse from James Stephens and, trying to win her back, I quoted it: 'Jane,' I said.

> 'Some day, when this is past,
> When all the arrows that we have are cast,
> We may ask one another why we hate,
> And fail to find a story to relate.'

'A story?' she said. 'O yes, we'll find a story all right.'

'What's that supposed to mean?'

'I'll tell you next month.'

We went out on to the loading platforms and, reaching over, she took the bag and parcels away from me. 'Good-bye,' she said.

'But what's your rush?'

'Look,' she said, turning towards the bus. 'If you want to do something useful, why don't you call your mother?'

'Yes, I must. Jane?'

'What?'

'Ah, how did it go at the office today?'

'I thought you'd ask that. I told Louise I'd stay on. She was delighted.'

She got into the bus: the bus windows were coloured dark green so I could not see where she was sitting. I walked up and down looking in, but could not find her. I waited around awkwardly on the loading ramp, knowing she could see me. As the bus pulled out, I waved good-bye.

How many times in the years I worked for Downes did I dream of a weekend like this one? Alone in the city. Wife and children away, alone with my book. And yet, minutes after she took the bus I was lonely for the first time in months. I called Pat Gallery, hoping that he and Yvonne would ask me over to eat with them, but they were out on Long Island at their summer place. I phoned Max but he was having dinner with his sister. I phoned Dortmunder but there was no answer. I even thought of phoning my mother but I was not in the mood for reproachful silences and so, at last, I simply wandered back to the Village. The idea came to me that if I worked all evening, I might be able to deliver those last two chapters to Gerston at lunchtime tomorrow. If he reads them tomorrow afternoon, we could spend the evening discussing them. A splendid idea. I went into a coffee shop, ate a ham sandwich and within an hour was back at my desk.

*

The bluish-grey light from the telly spilled across the living-room into the hall, but the telly was quiet. It must be the middle of the night, she decided. I must have dozed a long time, I don't remember. I remember falling and I remember moving, but how long ago was all that? The pain is as bad as ever and the pounding in my head is worse. I am weaker. O, for a sup of water. It's worse than a pilgrimage to Lough Derg: the penance of fasting all night and going around the island in bare feet on those sharp stones was nothing to this. How long have I been here?

Hard to remember; maybe I lost track. That pounding in my head is my heart. Don't exert yourself, Dr Brady said, don't excite yourself. He should see me now.

As her eyes became accustomed to the semi-darkness she saw that she was in the hall. Dimly she saw the outlines of the little table where the phone was. A few more moves and I'll be there. But I must wait. If I knock it over in the dark, I might have to move again to find it. And not find it. O merciful God, I'm afraid, I'm afraid. I could die here.

Now stop that, woman dear. Why would you die, what are you talking about, you're a nurse, you should know better. You broke your hip. You'll not die from that. You could live a week or longer. And you'll get to the phone, somebody will come, Brendan or Jane or somebody will be over this weekend. You'll phone, dial O, and get the police or the operator.

Can I talk? Have I my voice?

'Hello,' her voice said. 'Hello.'

The phone is in front of you someplace. Move now while you have the strength, who knows how long you'll be unconscious the next time.

She put her hands underneath her breasts and raised her torso. Sweat stung her eyes: it was hot here, even in the middle of the night. One-two-three. Up. She fell forward, fell on her face. *Pain* –

– She was at home in Creeslough, she was a little girl, she had gone down the loaning to the waterfall and a salmon jumped up in it and she leaned over to see and fell in, she was in the water, she could not swim and the waterfall sucked her nearer. She looked up and Brendan and Jane were sitting on the bank at their kitchen table, eating their breakfast. She called to them but they were not speaking to her, they pretended not to hear. She called to the children (Liam! Lisa!) but they would not come, they were afraid of the water, they did not want it on them. And all the time she was carried along until she was under and the waterfall fell down like stones on her head and filled her mouth and –

I was sick again, I vomited. Rest a minute. Rest.

'In South Viet Nam,' a voice said. 'Viet Cong guerillas last night attacked several government positions and inflicted severe casualties.'

Above her, she saw the bright sunlight from the skylight in the hall. The light hurt her eyes, so she closed them. Pain seeped through her abdomen in an exquisite, sickening wave. Another voice came on the telly.

She knew that voice, it was the nice chap with the glasses who was in charge of *Today*. So it was daytime, it was the morning. She had just gone to lower the telly and she had tripped. She opened her eyes. Then why am I here in the hall? Yesterday, it was. Or sometime. The *phone*.

I am near it now, that's what I moved for. Very near. A couple more shifts and I'll be at it.

But as she slipped her hands underneath her body, she knew that she was much weaker. No food, nothing to drink and the pounding all day and the pain. She knew it would be all she could do to make those last moves. She braced her good leg and strained but her arms trembled and she fell flat again without moving forward. She rested. Our Lady would help her. She asked Our Lady to help her, just as she had asked her when the children were being born. She tried again. One-two-three. *Pain* –

She had moved a little bit. Her arms trembled even when she lay flat. It was going to take longer than she had expected. But she would do it.

*

Gerston, *en famille*, was not the same man I had met over lunch at the Harvard Club. For one thing, his apartment was West Side, shabby and badly furnished. There were toys in the hallway and before he shut us into his den he shouted: 'Dorothy, keep the kids out of here.' His den was books. Books on bookshelves and on tables, books in bright jackets, books in manuscript, books in galley form, in page proof, in boxed format, in fine bindings, books arranged in irregular pyramids through which we picked our way as in an attic. He cleared books from two chairs. 'Now,' he said, expectantly.

I too was expectant. I had delivered the manuscript at noon and had been told by his wife to return at six. I had spent the afternoon shaving, showering and priming myself on three bottles of Heineken's beer. In memory of his elegant appearance, I had worn my good blue suit and the grey silk tie I bought for our first meeting, but when I presented myself on his doorstep ten minutes early, he received me in a sweatshirt, army suntans and loafers. He was unshaven and his dark hair was uncombed, showing that in reality it was sown with long grey hairs. In his habit of peering at me over the rims of his glasses, he reminded me uncomfortably of my first Latin tutor. My confidence ebbed.

'All right, let's start with the last two chapters,' he said, picking up some ruled foolscap sheets from the floor. I saw that these sheets were covered with tiny, pencilled notes.

'First of all, I like the ending, I think it's very fine.'

'O, good,' I muttered foolishly.

'There's really nothing to discuss in those chapters. I think we can leave them. Let's talk about the book as a whole.'

(As a whole?)

'It's a wonderful book,' he said. 'But I think, in places, it could do with a little cutting.'

'Well, of course, I intend to go over it –'

'I have some notes here,' he interrupted. 'They represent Mr Key's ideas and the ideas of two other editors who read the book when you first sent it in. And my own notes, of course. In other words, this is the gist of our best editorial opinion. Well, then. First of all, while we all admire the book enormously and have great hopes for it, we all agree there are a few things which could be cut. Now let me explain –'

He began to read from his notes, but I did not hear him. Parents, a spinster has just told you that your child is deformed and definitely a problem for the school, but told you also that if you have some surgery done to its nose, have the eye operated on, and cow its independence, there is a possibility, just a possibility, mind you, that it will be accepted and trained to be like all those other dull little children you despise. His persuasive tutorial voice went on and on, but can it be that his peroration and my silences took less time than it takes me to tell it now? If so, I believe in the eternity of hell.

'Well now,' he said. 'What do you think? It doesn't amount to very much, does it? But without those few redundancies it would be improved, I think.'

He waited.

'Look,' he said. 'I know that to a good writer, every word he writes seems important to him. I know how hard it is to make even small cuts like these. But believe me, I wouldn't be asking you to do it unless I was very enthusiastic about the book. I don't usually take the trouble I've taken with your book unless I feel that the author really has a future.'

'What sort of future?' I said bitterly. 'Best-seller?'

'Not at all, Brendan. Some of the best writers on our list have taken far more drastic editorial suggestions than this.'

'Such as who?'

'Well, Sol Silver for one.'

Solomon Silver is one of the few American writers of my generation whose work I admire. I couldn't believe it.

'You mean you cut things out of his books?'

'No. He cut them out, on our advice.'

'Well, I don't want your advice,' I heard myself say. 'After all, I wrote this book, I spent two and a half years writing it, it's the most important thing in my life. It wouldn't be my book if I let other people decide what went into it and what came out.'

He sighed. 'Of course it's your book. And of course you must do what you think is right. But quite frankly, I believe that these few small cuts could make the difference between a very successful book and one which might drop like a stone in the publishing lake. Look,' he said. 'I'll give you my notes – I hope you can read them – and you go home and think about it. Try to visualize your book with these things missing. Just a few paragraphs, that's all. I really think you'll see it's improved. Will you do that, Brendan?'

I could not speak: I wanted to hit him. How could it be true that Solomon Silver had agreed to 'far more drastic editorial suggestions than this'? He must be lying.

'Now let's see,' he said, standing up. 'Where's your manuscript? What a mess it is in here.'

My book is my child. I can pick it out amid innumerable others. I saw it on the table behind him, half of it in the box, half of it in the box lid. I went over and reassembled it. He fixed his sheaf of notes in a paper clip and handed it to me. 'Read it over tomorrow,' he said. 'And call me Monday. Then we can have another talk.'

He said a lot more, he started at once to praise the book and the writing and so forth, but I did not listen, my mind said Solomon Silver, was he lying about Silver, could it be true that any good writer would let them remove one word? As he showed me to the door, stepping over the abandoned toys in the hallway, I suddenly blurted out: 'Silver? Does he live in New York?'

'Yes, he has an apartment on Lower Fifth. Nice guy, you must meet him.'

'Yes.'

'Well,' he said. 'Call me on Monday. And cheer up. You have a great book there, Brendan. I'm really excited about it.'

We shook hands. I turned towards the elevators and behind me I heard his apartment door shut. I pressed the elevator button and as the red light went on, signalling that the car was coming up, an ambulance siren screamed past in the street outside, like a cry of terror.

I went down. *Excited. Successful. Drop like a stone in the publishing lake. Gist of best editorial opinion.* You pompous money-grubber, you towering tunnel of hot air, you fluting Philistine, writer-destroyer, gelder of Solomon Silver, may your grey locks strangle you!

But, there on the sidewalk in the full head of my rage, I shivered as though I had a fever. Rage was easily summoned but fear came uninvited. Hadn't the house of Key made a reputation as publishers who knew real talent and who could instinctively judge a book's true worth? If I did reject their judgement, then I must also suppose that their praise of my book is meaningless. But if I grant them judgement, then I must deny it to myself. If Gerston is right then he, not I, will be the arbiter of my work: the book will no longer be wholly mine. This isn't journalism, dammit. Unless every single word in the book is there because *I* have decided it, how can I go on believing in myself?

Genius cannot be discouraged or dissuaded: genius surmounts all obstacles, ignores all setbacks. How often have I read that, or some similar variant of the biographer's myth. But there on the pavement, clutching the battered cardboard box containing my manuscript, I understood something that the biographers have missed. The fuel of genius is a dream of achievement, a dream whose abandonment means a lifelong surrender to the counting house, the customs office, the treadmill of a routine existence. And since those who are not geniuses are not studied by biographers, there is no control to balance the assumption that only genius cannot be discouraged. How many awful mediocrities ignore all setbacks, continuing endlessly in their useless work simply because they lack the courage to give up their dreams?

Am I, too, a prisoner of my dream? Have I the courage to withdraw my manuscript from Gerston, pay him back the money he has advanced me, throw my manuscript on the open and indifferent publishing waters, and start rowing back up that long lake that leads to recognition? And even if I do all this, can I honestly say that it is my daemon which has driven me to it? Could it not be pride, a pride which fears that Gerston is right and I am wrong? Surely greater writers than I have profited from a wise editor's advice; offhand, Eliot is the example that comes to mind. And I remember that when I discovered his *miglior fabbro* was Ezra Pound, Pound rose in my esteem: Eliot fell.

So I stood on the sidewalk, confused, peering at the hateful yellow sheets covered with Gerston's notes. It was seven o'clock. I had not eaten and was not hungry. Again, I wondered if it were really true that a writer of Silver's reputation and ability had allowed Gerston to advise him. If he trusted Gerston, shouldn't I? I decided, in fairness, that I must go home, read the notes, then re-read my book and reconsider. Perhaps it was not fairness. Perhaps it was simple cowardice.

*

Five horses came around the turn into the home stretch, bunched like knuckles on a fist; knuckle extending to pointing forefinger as Sword Dancer drew away. The crowd's roar drowned the television commentator's excited chatter, fusing his voice in an allvoice.

It was raining outside. The raindrops fell on the skylight above her head. Her left hand held the leg of the little table on which the telephone rested. She had waited a long time, all through this last programme, before trying to topple it. She wanted to be strong enough for this move.

'What do you do when headache strikes?' asked the television set.

Now. Carefully she began to tilt the table leg, catching her breath as she felt the receiver above her begin to slide. She lay propped on one elbow, ready to let go of the table and grab at the receiver if it slid off close to her. It was coming, she could not stop it, saw it teeter – going to fall on her – *now.*

In a sudden convulsive effort she lunged up towards it, dragging her whole body forward. The telephone receiver fell on her wrist, with the force of a hammer blow. The bell jangled –

– She lay. Could not see. Could not get her breath. Slowly she turned her head, focusing her eyes in the mistiness, seeing it come clear, the telephone receiver, the fallen table. Nausea washed over her, left her limp. Something went wrong. I strained something, I am not well, I am trembling, the pounding in my head like blood bursting out –

The phone is there. One more move and you'll have it. See the wire? Reach out and pull it towards you.

Her brain ordered her arm – her hand – her fingers. The order, transmitted, moved down to her hand which did not move but trembled, trembled, did not cease to tremble when, in panic, the order was cancelled. The order to move went to her right leg, her good leg. The order, transmitted, moved to the good leg but the leg did not move. Panic. Again, to her other arm and that arm moved slowly, but it moved. It was under her; it came out but it was too far from the phone and she forgot the phone for panic brought her eyes back to that other hand and arm, willing them to move, but they would not move: they trembled, they shook. Her leg on that side shook. Her face felt numb. Wet came from the side of her mouth: it was nice for she was so dry in the mouth. Drool. But the drool was not on the side of the mutinous, shaking hand and arm, the leg that would not move. *Grattan.*

– When she came into the sickroom, his eye warned her. He knew something was wrong. But his words, when they came slurring from the good side of his mouth, showed that like any sick person, he thought only of himself. 'Ba' news? Wha' Case'men say?' Dr Casement was attending him. Tears threatened in her eyes. He thought she wept for him, not for Sheila who now, according to that boy's mother a minute ago on the phone, was on a boat with that boy, going God knows where, running away. 'Wha'?' Grattan said again. 'Nothing,' she said. 'Just time for your medicine.' She wiped the drool –

The phone, I think of the phone, like Grattan I cannot get to it. The drool is on the good side, the side that is not paralysed. But my hip is broken on that side. My broken side is now my good side. Unless Brendan comes, I will die.

I may die in days, I may die in five minutes, O my God, I love You, I am sorry for having sinned against You, I am sorry for my sins because they are displeasing to You, my God, who art so good. I firmly resolve by the help of Thy holy grace, never to sin again. Amen.

I cannot sin again. I am dying.

Wasn't it the bad luck though, when I was almost at the phone?

Funny the things you think of. They say your whole life comes before you, but I mustn't be dying yet, I can't think of a thing. My headache, Grattan's wireless set, Mrs Hofstra asked me to come to tea, won't she get a shock if she reads in the paper about me being dead. They wouldn't put it in the paper here, it's far too big a place for one woman dying to matter. I never saw a hearse in the streets here, where will they bury me? And Brendan and Jane when they hear, when they find me, their faces shocked, a priest (will they get one?) and a funeral here, will they send my body home and will they cry, yes, they'll cry, they'll be sorry to their dying day they left me here like this. God forgive me, but I'm paying them back now and Lisa and Liam will come into the sitting-room and see their faces and ask what happened. Gran's dead, Gran is dead. And a letter he'll have to write to my sister in Derry, what will she feel after all these years to hear that Eileen is dead. She never thinks of me, nor I of her, she hardly knows me any more. And Moira in the convent in Pinks Lane in Manchester (Pinks Lane, a funny name), called down to the parlour by the Reverend Mother, Sister, I have bad news for you, your mother is dead. God rest her. We will all pray for the repose of her soul, a whole convent will pray for me but what matter, I will be judged by then. Who else will hear? Sheila will. Sheila, you wore a yellow dress that day you ran away to Australia, I see you still in your yellow dress, your children around you there in Australia, as you open the letter, my grandchildren they are, although you never even sent me a photo of them, will you cry for me now at the end of the world in Australia, will you cry when you hear that your mother died on the floor with nobody near her? Will you be sorry, Sheila, for the way you treated me, not one letter in all these years, not one line since that cheeky postcard from the Suez Canal, December 29 (I have it still, I keep it still). *Married here today on our way to Australia. Sheila.* No love. Why did you write letters to Moira, but never to me, it is five years since that postcard, Sheila (I keep it still), surely five years have punished me enough? We must make up now, Sheila, you and I. I am dying.

I want: my own room in my own house, my own brass bed, my own good sheets, a nice nightie on me and my hair done. I want the house tidy and drink and food downstairs for the people coming in. I want a priest, I want the last sacraments, I want Mass cards and a funeral at home and my place beside Grattan on the hill. I want to die in my own place, not here. *Not here.*

Poor Frank Finnerty, when he comes back from his holidays and sees the rug, he'll think twice before he lends his place to a stranger again.

But my place is gone. The day before they put Drumconor Avenue up for auction I went back there, the house was empty, not one stick of furniture in it, went upstairs to our room, Grattan's and mine, that room where (with only Miss McGarry attending me) I bore every blessed one of them, the old brass bed was gone, all the dressers gone, the walls looked bare and dirty with the marks on them where the pictures once were and that room is now the sitting-room and the house is a Home for Fallen Girls run by the Sisters of Mercy, was that a judgement on me, a home for fallen girls, my home? Is Denis dead now? I heard he was married –

– Pain. I had forgotten the pain, there is less pain now because the stroke has dulled it. How long does it take, a stroke like this? Five minutes? Ten hours? How long to die?

Who's that, somebody talking, somebody?

It's the telly. Fancy me lying here and the people on the telly looking at me, talking away, smiling at me, the telly is like the world, people looking at you but not seeing you. O that's right, that's a good one. I could laugh only my mouth is stiff.

My heart I feel the thump worse, is this another str –

– Oooo . . . get my breath. I am still here. Tired, I want to sleep, I am sleepy, I am going now. Death is not bad, all the fuss they talk about it, it's easy, like sleep, easy. Let it all go . . .

I'm not *dying*, O my God I'm not *dying*, help me, somebody come, somebody *please* come, somebody, help, Grattan – Brendan – Rory – help me?

Somebody, *please*?

The thump, I feel it, afraid, O please, I'm worse, I know it, worse, my breath, can't get my br –

Love me?

Today, I did something so embarrassing that I can hardly bear to remember it. Even now, I cannot credit that I, of all people, made such an abject fool of myself. My pride – that arrogance of my insecurity – has, in the past, demanded that unless I can meet people on an equal or superior footing, I shall not meet them at all. But today I betrayed my pride. I went to see Solomon Silver.

I had spent Saturday evening studying Gerston's suggestions. I slept badly and when I woke this morning the question of to cut or not to cut seemed the most important moral decision of my life. Sitting in the kitchen, drinking cup after cup of coffee, I worried back and forth in my mind Gerston's remark about Solomon Silver, for to me, Silver's work seems a perfect whole. Was Gerston lying? There was only one way to make sure. I must talk to Silver.

Now, apart from my jealous avoidance of the famous, I cannot tell you how unlike my normal hedgehog self was the performance of that person who at once buried his independence and his pride, shaved and dressed as though he were off to apply for a job, looked up Silver's address in the telephone directory (lower Fifth Avenue, just as Gerston had said), took up the hateful editorial notes and ran out of his apartment to catch a downtown bus. On Sundays in summer, lower Fifth Avenue is almost an evacuated district and as my bus moved into this somnolescence of tall, empty buildings, my journey began to seem Kafkaesque, a search for a truth which could not be revealed to me. I had not phoned Silver because I felt unable to explain my predicament over the phone and now I became convinced that Silver would be out of town. My trip was simply a device to postpone a decision which I and no one else could make.

But when I rang the bell in the hallway of Silver's surprisingly elegant apartment building, an answering buzz immediately warned me that someone was at home. As I crossed the mirrored foyer I saw, reflected, an untidy, big-handed farmer in his best blue Sunday-go-to-meeting suit. Mother of God, perhaps

Silver would think I'd put on my best togs on his behalf? And I had, hadn't I? While waiting for the elevator, I removed my gentlemanly grey silk tie and stuffed it in my jacket pocket. Then, as the elevator rose and my nervousness rose with it, it came to me that perhaps I could pretend to be a magazine writer, use the name of my old publication, and try to winkle the information from Silver in the guise of an interview. I pulled out my tie once more and was caught with it half-knotted when the elevator doors opened automatically on the seventeenth floor and there, facing me, was Solomon Silver. I recognized him at once from the photograph on his book jackets, but in his working clothes – jeans, check shirt and sneakers – his head seemed unreal, a handsome false face, purchased with his success.

'Yes?' he said. He did not sound welcoming.

At once, drawing on my protective carapace, I announced myself as Brendan Tierney, magazine writer; I told him I wanted to write a piece about him. 'I'd just like to have a few minutes preliminary talk with you,' I added. 'Just to go over the project and get your approval. I won't keep you long.'

'Why didn't you make an appointment?' he asked and, mercifully, answered himself at once. 'Ah yes, the phone. I forgot. Well, come in.'

Light: space: the insect crackle of air-conditioning. Beyond the large windows, a penthouse terrace bordered with green shrubs, and above the terrace wall, a shimmer of mid-town skyscrapers. I walked on a blue Bokhara rug, passing a white sofa and white, slip-covered armchairs. Books, pictures on white walls, red gladioli in white vases, more books. And a table to which my guilt went at once; a table, a typewriter, sheets of paper: work suspended.

'You were working?' I accused him.

'That's all right, I feel like a break. Sit down. What would you like, iced coffee or a drink?'

'Whatever you're having.'

'I'll get you a drink,' he said.

I nodded my thanks and clumsily backed to the white sofa, producing Gerston's notes as I sat down. Cool, dry, artificial air struck at my damp shirt front. Sweat grew cold as it ran from my neck into my collar. There were ice sounds in the small, bright-metalled kitchen and my host reappeared carrying an ice-cold silver goblet.

'Here you are.'

(Where was *his* drink? And how would I pretend to interview him: I hadn't even got a pencil.)

'Well,' he said, sitting opposite me. 'Shoot.'

'Have you been in town all summer?' I began.

'No. In June, I flew down to Houston to see my kids and last week I got a special visa to go to Cuba and look over the revolution. Spent some time with those bearded pards. Fantastic set-up. Of course, Cuba always was fantastic. I remember in the days before this puritanism set in, it was completely corrupt, everything was for sale, jobs, women, murders, anything. Did you know they used to make pornographic movies in cinemascope and technicolor? Fantastic.'

'That so?' I said, trying to appear interested, although what was he to Cuba, what's Cuba to me, I had my future to settle, I wanted to settle it.

'And are you working on a novel now?' I asked.

'No, a play. My first and last, if this experience is any clue.'

'Why?'

'Well, it's the *chutzpah* of these theatrical people that gets me, it's their invincible combination of arrogance and ignorance. I write alone, not in committee, and that's something they'll never understand. That's why I've had my phone disconnected. You did try to phone me, didn't you?'

I nodded, ashamed of my lie, but anxious to keep him on that 'working in committee' tack.

'Yes, the theatre's a madhouse,' he said. 'It makes publishing seem sane after all.'

'Does it? You mentioned working in committee? Well –'

'Do you know Jack Clayburn?' he interrupted.

'Jackson Clayburn? I've met him.'

'There's the perfect theatrical object lesson,' Silver said. 'He started out as a good writer, a small writer, mind you, but good. Now, he writes everything in collaboration with his director. He's just a Broadway whore.'

'Yes,' I said. 'That's one of the things I thought we might talk about for my piece. I mean, do you think a novelist should ever listen to an editor's suggestions?'

'Some writers need editing, I suppose.'

'But you yourself wouldn't tolerate anything – any interference, would you?'

'No, not really,' he said, getting up, taking my goblet. 'I'll get you another.'

'No, wait –'

But he was already in the kitchen. I had to shout. 'Do you know Sidney Gerston?'

'Yes, of course,' he said.

'I was talking to him yesterday about your work.'

'Were you?'

'Yes, we were discussing just that point and he said that, sometimes, you *had* accepted his suggestions.'

'Gerston told you that?'

Back he came from the kitchen, my replenished goblet in his hand. He put it down beside me. 'He told you *that*?' he repeated.

'Yes.'

He digested this in silence, his handsome, threatening face stony as Michelangelo's David poised to hurl the sling-shot. I picked up the goblet and drank gin as though it were Seven-Up. I had betrayed Gerston; I had got Gerston in god knows what sort of trouble. I must rehabilitate him. 'Mind you,' I began. 'He said it very nicely, very respectfully –'

'O did he?' A small stony smile.

'I mean,' I said. 'He admires your work tremendously. So do I. Whether there've been cuts or not, the end result is always a very good book.'

'Nobody cuts my work,' he said. 'Nobody but me.'

'Of course. I'm sure Gerston probably meant that, he probably –'

'I don't know what he meant, nor do I give a damn. I must have a talk with Gerston.'

'No, I don't want –' I began, then caught myself. 'I mean, this wasn't part of the interview. You see, I've written a novel myself and Gerston's going to publish it. He just mentioned this in conversation.'

'So you've written a novel, have you?'

'Yes. And Gerston gave me some notes suggesting one or two cuts and I was worried about making them and so –'

'Wait,' said he, with an avenger's stare. 'Did you come here to interview me, or is that just a front?'

'I, no, not at all. But this question was extraneous to the interview, so to speak. I was worried about the cuts and while I was here I thought I'd ask your advice –'

'Dammit,' he interrupted. 'Gerston has no right talking to you or anyone else about my methods of work.'

With that, he turned away from me, as though dismissing me, and as I stared at his handsome head silhouetted against those bright windows, his two large gins hit me suddenly in the head. On top of the world he was in this cool eyrie, the city stretched before him like his prey. From here he flew out to Texas to visit his children, to Cuba to chat with revolutionary leaders, to Broadway to snub directors who begged to see his maiden play. Why should he be so damn lucky, why should he have everything while I had nothing? Because he was corrupt, that's why. There was, come to think of it, something bland and controlled about his work, wasn't there? Weren't his denials a little too angry, weren't they tinged with a furious guilt, how could he live like this and be a good writer? I no longer envied him, for it seemed to me that his sort of success would destroy my impulse to write, leaving me like a millionaire with a ruined stomach. I had asked for truth and found a Judas. No wonder he was angry with me, for wasn't I there to remind him of his original sin, a sin which, if I committed it myself, would bring me cool eyries, flights to Cuba and all the pleasures of Faust?

Convinced, I jumped up from the sofa in furious, foolish rage.

'I don't believe you,' I said (and no sooner were the words spoken than a sickening second guess warned me that this was not conviction; it was my old weakness of jealousy. Maybe I had made a mistake, a terrible mistake?).

'Frankly, I don't care what you believe,' he said. 'And I think we'll forget the interview. If you'll excuse me, I'd like to get back to work.'

'But look, Sol . . .' I made a step towards him but stubbed my toe on the coffee table and the step became a shameful stagger. After my insult, my calling him by his first name seemed a final and utter gaucherie.

'I'm sorry,' I said. 'I mean, of course I believe you.'

'Sorry?' Again that small, stony smile. 'Thank you. But I guess I'll manage to live, no matter what you believe.'

'I said I'm sorry. What more can I say?'

'So you did. Excuse me, there's my bell.'

It was true. I heard it ring. He was Solomon Silver; he willed me to be gone and since he was Solomon Silver, the bitch goddess heeded his needs. He went out to the hallway to press his buzzer and in the Empire mirror over his desk I saw my flushed, angry face, my cheap blue suit, my ill-knotted tie. I was out of place in that mirror and in the room it reflected. I knew I would never be in place there.

'Sol, darling.'

'Hello, Tanya.'

Silver kissed her as she stepped over the threshold. She was tall and young with a dark chignon and spectacular legs. 'Hello, Sol,' said the man who came with her.

'Davis, how are you?'

The man did not answer. His eyes went across the room, found me, agreed with me that I did not belong. Davis? He must be Davis Deal, the critic: I had read his books. And Tanya Zaharovna, the ballerina: I had seen her dance at City Center. O yes, they were the names we know better than our own, that bloodstock of celebrity.

'Are we interrupting something?' Deal asked.

Silver turned to me. 'No, this is Mr – ah – Cherney. He's just leaving.'

They all waited. I moved towards the door.

'Nice to have met you,' Deal called after me.

'Good-bye,' Silver said.

I did not speak. I opened the door and he shut it behind me. I stood in the carpeted hall, willing the elevator to come at once, to take me down and out. I wished I had been able to think of one crushing remark for all of them.

Behind the shut door, the girl laughed. 'Who?' she said. I could not hear Silver's answer, but they all three laughed again. Then Deal's voice said: 'If I were you, Sol, from now on, I'd have a special signal. Three long and one short ring on your bell. And enter friend.'

'Three long and one short,' Silver said. 'I'll remember that.'

'Anyway, darling,' the girl's voice said. 'Now that we're alone, I have the most wonderful news to tell you.'

I did not wait to hear her news. The red light appeared above me, the soundless elevator doors opened. I entered and came down to earth. They had laughed at me and their laughter washed away my self-loathing and self-doubt, making me sure once more that Silver was a liar, a man destroyed by his success. Time would avenge me. Years from now, Davis Deal would sit at his typewriter and recall for his readers how, paying a call on a minor novelist of the day, he caught his first fleeting glimpse of the legendary Tierney. As for Tanya Zaharovna, she would live to regret that she had not been my mistress instead of Silver's, heigh-ho Silver, who by then would be forgotten.

What nonsense. They hadn't even got my name right.

I went out of the building and into the street and, at once, the sky darkened and emptied on me in a sudden summer cloudburst. I ignored it, walking as once I had walked across the school yard at home, ignoring the rain because I was already too wet for it to matter, while behind me still grouped around the fountain where they had ducked me, my enemies laughed uneasily over the essay in which I had declared my aims. I could not go back then, I cannot go back now: I must prove my boasts; some day it will be my turn to laugh. I walked down Fifth Avenue, sopping wet and as I passed by Washington's Triumphal Arch, I was a Caesar, marching out to order a massacre of all who opposed me. But how will I be able to order anything if I refuse Gerston and am thereby denied publication? Won't I again become Brendan Tierney, the unknown and unregarded nonentity? I must decide.

And then – why didn't I think of it before – I remembered Max.

As Max Bronstein entered the Dortmunders' apartment, he removed his dark glasses and unbuttoned his raincoat, revealing himself in a bird-of-paradise sports shirt and bright yellow chino slacks. 'What a day, what a day,' he told the Dortmunders. 'Our boy, Brendan, *what* a performance.'

Dortmunder, plump and perspiring, took Max's coat and went back into the kitchen where he was helping his wife prepare supper. Max moved at once to the dining nook which was set for two. He sat down hopefully at the far end of the table.

'Get another plate, dear,' Dortmunder whispered. And then: 'You'll stay to supper, Max?'

'Sure. Thanks a lot.'

'So, what's with your friend Brendan?' Mrs Dortmunder asked from the kitchen.

Max tapped his index finger against his right temple. 'What a performance,' he said. 'About two o'clock this afternoon, I was still in bed –'

'In bed?'

'Well, I was reading the Sunday papers, you know how long it takes, I wasn't watching the time –'

'So you're lazy,' Dortmunder said. 'Is that news?'

'Anyway, I was in bed and there was a knock on the door and in came Brendan, soaking wet, like he was just taken out of the river. So I asked him what's up. And he said: "Max, if I ask you an honest question, will you promise to give me an honest answer?"'

'Well, I made some crack, like, not if it's about my sister. "I'm serious," he shouted. "This is important." All right, I said, what's on your mind? Then he said "Tell me the truth now. Did Gerston ask you to make cuts in your novel?"'

'A few', I said.

'"More than this?" he said, and pulled out a bunch of notes. "Go on, read," he said. "Tell me what you think." Now, the joke is, he's never let me read this novel of his, even though I asked him. So, what's the use of me reading these notes, they were notes about something I'd never read. So I told him that. And you know what? He went berserk.'

Dortmunder winked at his wife over the sink. Max? An exaggerator.

'I'm not kidding,' Max said. 'He came at me, dripping wet, and half pulled me out of the bed. "Read it," he yelled. So all right, I took the notes, what could I tell from them, except it looked to me they were nothing much, just little picky bits about a word here, a word there, and some little bits of philosophizing they thought slowed the narrative up. It was nothing; it was a lot less than I was asked to do. I told him that. I pointed out to him that Gerston and Key are very hot for his work, they think he's a great new talent and all that jazz. And then I said again that it wasn't fair to ask me for an opinion when I hadn't even read his book. And then . . .'

Max paused for emphasis, took out a tin box and popped a lozenge in his mouth. '*Then*, Brendan said, "What good would it do if you read it? What do you know about writing a book?"'

Mrs Dortmunder wiped her hands. 'You should worry,' she said. 'Jealous, that's his trouble. You remember the night you brought Jackson Clayburn, the playwright, here, you remember the way he acted that night?'

'I remember,' Max said. 'Anyway, I kept my temper. I said,

Brendan, you asked me for my opinion, I didn't offer it. "I must have been crazy," he said. "I might have known you'd agree with them." All right, I said. I agree with them. I think you're making a lot of noise about nothing. "O, you do, do you?" he said. "Well, let me tell you something, Bronstein" – get that Bronstein, all of a sudden – he said "Bronstein, you never had any talent, you can't write. They probably cut your book to pieces and they got some senile old hack like Carnovsky to write a blurb for it and the whole thing is a lousy swindle, because it's not your book any more, it's their book, not yours and you've sold out, you're chicken and corrupt, you're a lousy, phony, no-talent fraud."'

'Oi,' said Dortmunder. 'Sick.'

'But wait,' Max said. 'Right in front of me, after he'd said it, he started to cry. Tears. It was embarrassing. I mean, I've known him four years, he's the last guy in the world you'd expect to see in tears.'

'He's Irish,' Dortmunder said. 'He was drunk.'

'No, he was sober. I think.'

'It's something else altogether,' Mrs Dortmunder said. 'The Irish are the worst.'

'Anti-semite,' Dortmunder said. 'Now it comes out.'

'No, no, not Brendan,' Max said. (But could it be true, he wondered?)

'David is right.'

'*Bronstein*. Right at the crucial moment,' Dortmunder said. 'You pointed it out yourself. It's obvious.'

'Anyway, there he was. Crying. Brendan Tierney crying. "You don't understand," he said to me. "It's not the same for you."

'What's not the same? I said.

'"Writing," he said. "My book for me," he said, "is the belief that replaces belief. I'm changing from the person I used to be –"'

'Changing is right,' Dortmunder said.

'"Now my whole life has a meaning and a purpose," he said. "It's as though I'd been waiting in the wings all these years. I'm happy," he said. "You wouldn't understand," he said.'

'So how does he know?' Mrs Dortmunder asked.

'And then he said – this is the interesting part – he said: "I've sacrificed other people for my work. I've always thought there'd be no question that, when the time came, I'd be ready to sacrifice myself. That time is now," he said. "And I don't know, I don't know." Then he picked up the notes off the bed and ran out of the room. What did he mean by that?'

'Who cares?' Mrs Dortmunder decided.

'All the same,' Max said. 'I feel sorry for him. He's a strange character, Brendan. I wonder what he meant by that?'

On Sunday night when Jane came back from Saratoga Springs, she found all the lights on in their apartment. In the living-room, surrounded by a huge circle of typescript sheets Brendan squatted, shirtless and bare-foot, consulting a crumpled wad of yellow foolscap notes. He did not look up when she came in: he would peer at the notes, crane his body forward, find a place among the typescript, and read to himself in an unintelligible mumble. After watching him for a moment, she realized that he was not ignoring her; he simply did not know that she was there.

She did not speak to him. She turned back from the living-room doorway and went down towards the kitchen, her skin still burning from the sunbath she had taken on the farm that morning, her hair coming loose about her neck, her dress crumpled from the long bus ride. Despite the fact that she wore only a brassiere underneath her dress, she felt burdened, and as she opened the refrigerator to get a glass of cold milk, she absentmindedly began to undo the buttons down her front. She sipped at the milk and then, holding it as a child does, forgotten in her hand, she wandered back to the living-room to look at her husband. He craned over the typescript, muttering, searching, and as she moved in front of him, she noticed the puffy, reddish appearance of his eyelids. Brendan weeping? Impossible. But back into her mind, as it had all weekend, came her last sight of him, Friday night, standing on the bus loading platform, waving hopelessly at the bus. I would have wept if I were him. Why doesn't he look at me now? Is he trying to pay me back?

'Brendan?' she said.

Their eyes met.

'I'm tired,' she said. 'I'm going to bed.'

'No, wait.'

'I have to go to work in the morning.'

'No, no,' he said, clumsily getting to his feet. 'I want you to read this.'

'At this time of night? Are you crazy?'

'No, I've been waiting for you, I've laid it all out for you. you won't have to read the whole book, just these little bits I show you. They want me to take them out and I don't know what to do.'

'Who's *they*?'

'Gerston and Key. They've given me all these notes. God, you don't know what a weekend I've had.'

Into her mind came a memory of the weekend *she* had had: false maternal smiles as she played with the children in the droning summer quiet of the farm, endless pretending to the questions and hints dropped by Barbara and Barbara's husband, sleepless night hours when she tried to shut out the picture of the weeks ahead. She thought of the one hope she had held on to. It was that, after the way she had ignored his caresses, after the despair she had seen on his face next morning, after her cold farewell at the bus terminal and a weekend alone and remorseful in the city, he would meet her tonight shamefaced and repentant, tell her once and for all that he had been wrong. When she remembered that hope and balanced it against this man in front of her – puffy-eyed, half-naked, trembling – a mindless fury came. Her hand obeyed.

He flinched, shut his eyes, turning his face sideways, and for a moment she saw the bloom of her slap on his cheek.

'What's wrong, what have I done?' he asked, surprised.

'If you don't know what's wrong, then I can't help you.'

'No, no, wait,' he said. 'Look, if you promise to read this stuff now, I'll make a deal with you. You see, if I agree to these cuts, making them will be very easy, you won't have to work in August. I could edit the book in the evenings – and – and in the meantime, I could take some assignments, get money somehow, we'll manage – and you can bring the kids home at the end of the month, you can have everything the way you want it. Honestly, Jane.'

Month, month, month: it thundered in her head. To suit his own plans he could make the sacrifice he had denied her when she begged him. *I could take some assignments, get money somehow, we'll manage.* If only he had said that last Thursday.

'But there's one condition,' he said. 'You've got to tell me the truth now, you've got to tell me if I'm right to go along with their suggestions.'

'Will it make a great difference in the book?' she asked. (It was like asking Liam if he wanted to colour pictures or play with blocks.)

'No, I don't think so. It's a matter of principle. I'm worried about how good their judgment is. I'm not sure whether I should agree to any cuts at all, I've gone crazy all weekend trying to decide. You've got to help me. Look' – he grabbed at her wrists, led her into the circle of typescript – 'you sit here and I'll read you each suggestion in turn and then you read the parts they want cut. Okay?'

(Want to play with me, Mummy? All right, Liam.)

'Now, here's their first suggestion. Listen.'

Listen? Listen to what? If I tell him they're right, I won't have to go back in September, it will be over with Vito, I can bring the kids back from the country. And *he* wants me to be honest.

'Well, there it is,' he said. 'Now read the passage. Start here.'

Words, skimming across the copy paper, words jumbling in her brain as she sat crosslegged among the sheets of paper, forcing herself to read. She was back in college and this was an oral examination: she must concentrate and get high marks. In the past six years she had talked to him dozens of times about his ideas and his characters. Now, she must pass with honours, remember all his vanities, use them to convince him. She must be careful: to prove impartiality she must disagree with his editors on certain small points. Above all, she must save his dignity, make him feel that the cuts would not destroy his work. *His* dignity.

So she began to read. When she spoke, phrases came with the rapidity of multiplication tables. 'No, I think he has a point here. The rest of this section is written in such a way that – I think this slows the narrative – it's unnecessary, and besides, you imply more subtly elsewhere, the thing you state here . . .'

He sat on the sofa, haggard, anxious, interrupting: 'You think so – but don't you think – No? – well, perhaps – yes, maybe so, but – all right, let's take the next point – read this.'

And on and on, for he was insatiable, he wanted to argue every word, yet he wanted to be told what she told him and, as they read and talked, hour merging into hour, she wondered in a far recess of her mind whether, like an actress living a part, she had really come to believe what she told him. It seemed irrelevant. She played a role: outside that role her judgements would have been those of another person. She watched for his shifts of mood, gave ground when it seemed dangerous, pressed home

Gerston's views when he seemed to waver. After a long time, she asked him to make a cup of coffee and when he had gone, looked at her watch. It was two in the morning. The viva voce had been successful. He had simply needed reassurance. It was only when the last sentence, the last note, had been dealt with that she emerged from her mimic trance and wondered: *what have I done?*

'You're sure that it won't cheapen the book?' he asked for the umpteenth time that night.

How should I know? she thought, I'm no critic. But now that the acting was over, the changes they asked for seemed very minor to her. It occurred to her that it was only his colossal vanity which had made them seem otherwise.

'Perhaps I should put it aside for a week or so,' he suggested. 'Then we could go over it again.'

'That's just hedging,' she said. 'I think you're afraid of publication.'

'Jesus, Jane, you don't think that, how could you?'

(I don't think anything. I don't care any more. You never once asked about the children tonight. Or about me.)

'Of course I want to be published,' he said. 'But unless I'm a good writer, I might as well give up. And how can I be a good writer if I need editorial help?'

'What help?' she said. 'My god, Brendan, they haven't asked you for one important change in the whole manuscript. You're behaving like a nut. I'm sure lots of good writers get far more editorial quibbles than you've had.'

'Gerston says Silver does,' he said. 'But when I went to see Silver this morning, he denied it.'

'*You* went to see Solomon Silver?' she said, astonished. 'But you don't even know him.'

'I barged in. It was a crisis, after all. He lives in a plush apartment on Fifth Avenue and you can keep him, I can tell you that. He was lying, I'm sure of it now.'

'What else did you do this weekend?' (Imagine him barging in on Silver. He's gone crazy.)

'Well, I went to see Max and asked him about his book. He's agreed to cuts, all right. But what does that prove? I never thought he was any good, anyway.'

(Gerston, Max, Silver. So that was his weekend. And what about his mother?)

'Did you call your mother?'

'My mother?' he said, looking surprised. 'No, no, I hadn't time. I'll call her tomorrow.'

'You should have called her. You should have gone to see her.'

'This was a *crisis*,' he said, irritably.

What was the use in talking to him? 'It's after two,' she said. 'Let's go to bed.'

But, in the bedroom as she took off her dress, she remembered their last time together and looked over at him, wondering if he would try again tonight. She could pretend when it was just talk about his work. In bed, could she also pretend? He stripped off his trousers and shorts and lay down, shading his eyes from the light bulb overhead. 'You do think I'm right to make the cuts?' he asked again.

'Yes. Go to sleep.'

'Yes, I must,' he agreed. 'I'm exhausted. I must be fresh for tomorrow.'

He must be fresh. Yes, he was quite right: he must be fresh because he was about to become a success. He would be a success, she had no doubt about it. He would write more books, he would be praised, he would be a Solomon Silver all over again. As she unhooked her bra, she looked down at him. He had turned over on his stomach and lay, his head sideways on the pillow, his eyes shut. I have married a man who will be famous. Naked now, she moved across the room and switched off the light so that the famous man could sleep in peace. She sat down in a chair by the window, but the famous man did not miss her, did not ask her to come to bed. After a few minutes she heard him begin to breathe heavily. She listened, making sure, and soon he began to snore.

She turned towards the window, hugging her breasts as though she cradled a baby. Downtown, a red neon glare rose like a fiery halo over the buildings as though the centre of the city were ablaze. In the bed the famous man was asleep, a person strange and familiar to her as her parents had been strange yet familiar when she was a little girl: a figure without whose protection and help life would be uncertain and difficult. And that is all, she said. Vito stole the one little United Nations forum we had left: bed. He took it away and what is left? Yet, I do not want Vito, I cannot follow Vito to recapture that thing

I lost to him. Who, or what, can I follow now? She stared at the red glow, the city on fire. Who do I love, she wondered? Is there one person in the whole world I really care about? She thought of her sister, Barbara. Yesterday, on the farm, they had tried to recapture their childhood. But the door was closed: Barbara was a stranger. I love my children, she told herself, but that is not the same thing. They are my children. Isn't there one adult person I care about now?

She could think of no one. At twenty-eight, wasn't it an admission of failure to have no person, no thing which you loved more than you loved yourself? I do not love myself, she thought, but if I do not love others either, then I am no better than Brendan. She sat in the chair, stroking her thighs and staring out the window. She remembered herself at sixteen when she had hoped to become a painter. She remembered herself at twenty when she had wanted to make a career as an illustrator. At twenty-two she had lost faith, even in her talents for that. She wanted babies: motherhood would give her life a meaning. At twenty-four, married and a mother, she had felt she needed some other cause to live for. She did not find one. Perhaps now is the time to look for a cause, she thought. Perhaps I could join the Peace Corps and live in Africa, or crusade against the Bomb, or something? But with two children, would she be able to give her time to a cause? And wasn't it true that she did not feel very strongly about these causes, wasn't she considering them only as therapy?

Still, there must be something I could do. For a time she sat staring at the city's red glow, feeling cheated, remembering the rag-bag of articles and books she had read in the past ten years, her mind dithering among the catch phrases of her time: affluent society, beat generation, existential decision, nuclear holocaust. But somehow she could not feel that the plight of her generation could really be called tragic. Her generation was not tragic, she decided: it was pathetic. And in college she had been told that pathos was an inferior emotion. Perhaps that is our tragedy, she thought. We have lost our dream and are therefore pathetic. No, that doesn't make sense. Pathetic is not tragic. I should go to bed.

But she did not. She sat until the darkness faded, the red neon glow behind the buildings died in a grey milk sky. The city was no longer on fire. It seemed dead.

Atkin left his partner at the wheel of the squad car and went into the building to check the nameplates over the occupants' mailboxes. He had no apartment number to go on, and no last name. The slip of paper in her purse said: *Brendan. 468 Riverside Dr. Mon* 6-8707. Her British passport listed her name as Tierney and there was another phone number, a Mrs Hofstra, no address. They had phoned the Hofstra number but there was no answer. As for the Monument number, it was all the time busy, so Atkin and his partner decided to take a run over there. Atkin, searching among the nameplates with his bandaged finger, found a Tierney in Apartment 8A. That must be it. He turned towards the elevator.

Atkin was a heavily built man in his late thirties and he found the heat hard to take. His uniform shirt was crumpled and his police belt, weighed down by the pistol, chafed against his belly, leaving a welt of reddened skin. Two nights ago he had hurt his hand while checking through an empty loft where some kids were supposed to be and now, as he went up in the elevator, his index finger began to throb painfully. He looked at the bandage which was getting grimy and wondered if he should check out after this call and get the police doctor to change the dressing. Would that help? He did not know.

He rang the bell at 8A, waited, then rang again. Maybe they were still on the phone: some women could yack for hours on the phone. Tentatively, he tried the door and it opened and they were on the phone, all right, but it was no woman, it was a young guy in pants, shirt and sneakers. The living-room floor was all messed up with some typewritten report or other, there were goofy paintings on all the walls and a million books in the place.

Most times if you came to a door, when people saw you – a cop – they dropped what they were doing and came running. But this character looked at Atkin as he came in, then went right on talking.

'Yes, I know, Sid,' he was saying. 'Now that cut seems a good idea to me, yes, that one's all right. But in chapter fourteen, the paragraph about childbirth you don't like, I'm not sure about it, I think I'd like to leave it in . . .'

'Excuse me,' Atkin said. He made signs to the guy saying he should hang up.

'Yes,' the guy told the party on the phone. 'I see what you mean. O well, I've agreed to most of the others, so I suppose I can do this one too. But there are one or two things, I must keep . . . Yes, of course . . . What? . . .'

'Excuse me,' Atkin said. Again he made signs that the guy should hang up.

'Hold it a moment, Sid,' the guy told the party on the phone. Then, in a grouch voice, he told Atkin: 'Look, officer, I'm very busy right now. What is it?'

Atkin did not tell him.

'Sid,' the guy said to the party on the phone. 'There's somebody at the door, I'll have to answer it, but, briefly, I'm agreed with you on the cuts, it's all right, don't worry. I'll call you back as soon as I get rid of whoever it is.'

O, no, you won't, Atkin thought.

The guy put the phone down, turned to Atkin, and said: 'Well, what's up?'

'Do you know a Mrs Eileen Tierney?' Atkin said.

'Yes, she's my mother. What about her?'

But Atkin made sure. No sense telling the wrong party: that could mean trouble. 'Living at 488 East Fifty-Fourth, apartment 19?'

'Yes.'

'Well,' Atkin said. 'I'm afraid she had an accident.'

'What kind of accident?'

'We're not sure. We figure she had a stroke. At least, that's what she died of. It looks like she fell sometime over the weekend and broke her hip – we're not sure yet about the hip, it looks that way though – and then she got a haemorrhage while she was trying to get to the phone. Coroner's office will check on it, of course, but that's the way it looked when we found her.'

'She's dead?' the young guy said. Funny, they always wanted you to tell it to them twice.

'Afraid that's right,' Atkin said. 'Old people, living alone, it sometimes happens that way.'

Then Atkin remembered the woman's passport and took it out of his hip pocket, opening it at the passport photo. 'Is this her?' he said, showing it to the guy.

The guy nodded, yes.

'Well, we'd like you to come down to the precinct and give us some particulars. And then we'll take you over to the morgue to identify the body, okay? Her husband alive?'

'No.'

'Are you the nearest relative here?'

'Yes.'

'Okay,' Atkin said. 'Want to get your jacket? We have a car downstairs.'

The guy went off to the bedroom to get his jacket. Puerto Ricans, Jews, Italians, they mostly acted up right away. Others, it took longer, it sunk in gradual, it hit them down at the station and then you had trouble getting rid of them, they wanted to tell you their life story.But when this party came back he was knotting his tie; he shut the living-room window and then asked Atkin to wait a second while he picked up his papers. He picked up all the sheets, stacked them careful and tidy and put them on a table. 'All right,' he said. 'I'm ready now.' Real cool, Atkin thought as they took the elevator down to the squad car. But in the car another story. The guy sat in back, looking out the window, and after a minute he began to ask questions.

'What time did she die, do you think?'

'Must have been sometime yesterday. She was dead quite a while when she was found.'

'Who found her?'

'Milk delivery man. He came by about seven this morning, saw that the milk wasn't picked up from Friday, it was gone sour, see, so he rang the bell, wanted to check before he left another bottle in this heat. Nobody answered, so he tried the door. It wasn't locked. He found her in the hall. The phone was knocked over. She must have been trying to get to it when she died.'

'So you think,' the guy said. 'She might have died yesterday morning? Sunday morning?'

Yes, they always wanted you to tell it to them twice. 'Looks that way,' Atkin said. 'We figure she was dead maybe twenty-four hours. Say, that wasn't her apartment, was it? Janitor told us he didn't know her. Said the apartment belongs to a man called Finnerty, he's on vacation now.'

'Yes, he's her first cousin.'

'She just visiting him, or she lived there permanent?'

For a while the guy didn't answer. Then he said: 'She was supposed to go home to Ireland this week.'

Atkin took a look at him through the rear-view mirror. It had hit him now, all right. 'That's tough,' Atkin said. His finger throbbed. Maybe it was infected.

*

She died sometime yesterday said the angel of death, that sweaty, improbable angel, his badge a tin heart on his crumpled uniform shirt. He held up his bandaged finger, nursing it: he made no judgements. She lay dying on the floor of a strange apartment while I, her son, ran senseless about the city, quibbling over words. Telepathy, like the telephone she tried to reach, did not warn me of her danger. I did not call her.

And later, at the police station, a man in shirtsleeves (a detective?) looked up from the report he was writing and asked: 'When did you see her last? When were you last in contact with her?' And, a guilty criminal, I have no alibi. It is over a week since I saw her, over a week since I turned her out.

'My wife saw her, they had dinner together on – I think it was Thursday.'

'Was she all right then, I mean was she in good health?'

'Yes.'

He wrote that down. I, not Jane, was supposed to visit her. I had promised to come. And later as she lay dying on the floor, her only hope of help was in my coming. If I had thought to phone her she might be alive today. The detective did not write that down. He made no suppositions. But if there is justice anywhere, there is a judgement.

'So, she's been about four months in this country, right? Was that on an immigrant or visitor's visa?'

'An immigrant visa. We brought her over to live with us and help look after our children.'

Immigrant visa, he wrote. I brought her here: she worked as my unpaid servant. In all those rows, I did not once take her part. She was shocked by what she found here. She thought it her duty to do something and so she baptized my children in a meaningless ceremony in the bathroom; she told them foolish myths about her God. It was for those crimes that we banished her. If there is, as she believed, a heaven above us, will her God recompense her for our coldness and indifference? Will He reward His clumsy handmaiden?

'Yet at the time she died, she wasn't living with you?' the detective said.

'No, you see our children were up in the country and Finnerty – he's her cousin – he went on vacation, so she moved into his apartment to look after it.'

He wrote that down. She is dead: she cannot contradict me.

'How about that airline ticket we found?'

'Yes. She was going home.'

'Why was that?'

'Well, she was lonely over here. I mean, she didn't like it much and we'd decided we could get on without her.'

'She wasn't depressed, was she? I mean, she wasn't likely to – ah – do anything?'

'No, no.'

Did he believe me? Was I, after all, on trial here? But he wrote it down.

'We'll have to have an autopsy,' he said. 'That's standard procedure in cases like this.'

'Does that mean an inquest?'

'No, I don't think so. Right now, it looks like she died from natural causes following that hip injury. An autopsy will just make sure.'

There will be no inquest. Indifference, it seems, is not a crime punishable by law. I am merely someone they need to supply details and identify the body. 'We'll run you over to the morgue,' they said. 'It won't take a minute.' To call her over the weekend would not have taken a minute.

In the place where the dead are kept, I waited in a room which stank of formaldehyde. The door was not closed and in an adjoining hall I saw row upon row of what seemed to be brown wooden iceboxes. An attendant wheeled a trolley up to the iceboxes, opened one and pulled out a long tray. I turned away. After a minute, he wheeled the trolley into the room where I waited. A policeman who accompanied him lifted the sheet.

The face, yellow; the grey hair matted with dried vomit; there were bruises on the cheek and jaw as though the face had been banged with an iron shovel. The eyelids had been drawn shut but did not fully conceal the dead eyes which, slitted, stared accusingly at the ceiling. I nodded to the policeman and the sheet was replaced. The trolley was wheeled out. I was told I could go.

I went out into a summer's morning, into streets quick with people. Death had infused the living with a heightened look of life. I remembered that Jane did not know and this led me to an inventory of those busy details which obscure the fact of death: telegrams to be sent to my sisters in England and Australia, a cemetery to be found, a grave bought. A coffin, a priest, a hearse.

Jane did not know. I decided to go to her office and as I took a bus over to Lexington Avenue it occurred to me that in all the months Jane worked there I had never gone to pick her up. In a waking nightmare I saw her lying on an office floor, waiting for me to come. And when I entered her building the guilt of my news drove me to telephone her from the lobby and recite the facts in the reassuring anonymity of a public call box. She said she would come down at once.

But it was a good ten minutes before she joined me, ten minutes in which I circled the lobby, purposely numbing my mind with trivial funerary details. She had the pale, queasy look of someone who is about to be physically sick and, seeing her, I was sick with empathy. But I remembered that yellow, bruised face: I remembered that it was Jane who insisted. Let her suffer: she deserved her penance.

Part of that penance was that it must all be gone over, the details repeated, the litany of death retold. 'But how did it happen, when, couldn't she, do they think her hip, O God, and they think it was a stroke, I remember she said once that she had high blood pressure, is that painful, a stroke, how long, how awful, O Brendan.'

As she questioned me I took her arm, walked her down the block, steering her towards a quiet spot where we could sit and talk. It was a restaurant called *The Little Danube*, the sort of place which has few customers before noon. 'Let's go in here and have coffee,' I said.

She jerked her arm. 'No.'

'Why not?'

'I don't like this place. Let's go somewhere else.'

Insensitive bitch. Imagine caring where we go, at a time like this. But I guessed that she was about to be sick. I took her arm, hurried her across the street and dragged her into a Hamburg Heaven. Again, she protested. 'No, not here either.'

'Come on,' I said. 'You're going to be ill, aren't you?'

She nodded and fled to the ladies' room. I sat down and ordered coffee. She was a long time in the ladies' room, and when she returned, I saw that it had happened. Her face was white and she was trembling. She refused the cigarette I offered her. She put her head down and wept.

'It was an accident,' I said. 'It could have happened anywhere. After all, she was sixty-eight.'

'No. It's our fault.'

'It's nobody's fault,' I said, angrily. 'Nobody planned it. It was just bad luck, that's all.'

'It's our fault,' she repeated, and again she wept while, all around us, people pretended not to see her. And as I watched that absolution in tears, I remembered that I had not wept, would not weep, for what I felt was guilt, not sorrow; shock, not loss. I told myself that Jane's tears had nothing to do with sorrow for my mother. Jane put her out of the apartment; Jane was the one who did not forgive the baptism. Her tears now were tears of guilt. Who then will weep honest tears for my mother? My sister Moira will weep in her Manchester convent, but won't her tears be tears of regret that she no longer has a parent to love her, to write letters and send presents from that world which Moira has renounced forever? And Sheila, who ran away to Australia, I doubt that Sheila will weep. Yet my mother's life was what is called a success. She was pretty; she married a successful man; she lived in a large house; had maids, a car and holidays abroad. She bore her husband four children and nursed him through his final illness. She had known in her lifetime perhaps a thousand people and some of those people loved her. Yet she died alone in the limbo of a strange apartment and lay dead until, by accident, a stranger found her. I see that yellow face.

My mother believed in God: I do not. She believed in hell and purgatory, penance and indulgences, baptism and extreme unction. She believed that God placed her in this world for a purpose; that in this testing ground she must, by her deeds, prove herself worthy of heaven. The temporal life was, for her, a secondary thing. For me, it is all there is. Because of this difference in belief, a gate shut between us. Because of that gate, she died alone, trying to reach me. And yet, as I sat in that coffee shop, denying and despising my wife's tears, I asked myself if my beliefs are sounder than my mother's. Will my writing change anything in my world? To talk of that is to believe in miracles. Is my motive any different from hers? Is it not, as was hers, a performance of deeds in the expectation of praise? And what is that praise really worth; how many of the praised living do I, in my secret heart, admire? To wish to join their company is to desire admission to a book of saints, the true facts of whose lives and achievements bear little resemblance to the public legends. As for the verdict of posterity, is it any more deserving of belief than a belief in heaven? How many of the illustrious dead do I honour with lip service, knowing nothing of their deeds and works? Is my belief in my talent any less an act of superstitious faith than my mother's belief in the power of indulgences? And, as for the ethics of my creed, how do I know that my talent justifies the sacrifices I have asked of others in its name? O Mamma, I sacrificed you; I see your yellow face. Jane, I abandoned you: I look at you now and know that all is changed. Am I still my mother's son, my wife's husband, the father of my children? Or am I a stranger, strange even to myself?

Who is that stranger? I met him at my mother's funeral. It was the least of funerals; a hearse and one limousine creeping through a glut of midday traffic on Long Island towards a cemetery which, when we reached it, lay on either side of the six-lane highway, plinth on plinth in telescopic foreshortening, like some huge photographic mock-up designed to warn the reckless driver of death on the road. As in the skyscrapers which house the living, so the dead of New York are crowded layer on layer, cramped even in death.

We moved on to a bypass and as the hearse entered the cemetery grounds, the priest who sat in front of me on the jump seat of our limousine, took from his pocket a stole, touched it to his lips, then draped it carefully around his neck. Beside me in the back was Jane, wearing a black dress, white gloves, a white hat and too much lipstick: she might have been going to a cocktail party were it not for her swollen eyes. In the three days preceding the funeral, she wept often. Our conversations grew more distant as though I stood helpless on some shore as she was carried off by the tides. Finnerty occupied the other jump seat; dour, ill-at-ease, his stiff back a measure of his contempt for us. But I was glad of his presence: he made small talk with the priest.

When we got out of the limousine we were less than a hundred feet from the grave. Two gravediggers stood by it, neat young American workingmen in clean overalls, their workshoes unstained by mud. The grave itself seemed unreal: neat tiles of grass were laid along its edge, ready for replacing, and a lowering device, topped by a steel platform, was in position, ready to descend the coffin into the neatly dug pit. Discreetly, the undertakers' men came forward with their burden, placed it on the steel platform, then retreated to a middle distance, removing their grey cotton gloves, wiping the backs of their necks with white handkerchiefs. The priest walked towards the grave, followed by an undertaker's man who held a bowl of holy water and a sprinkler. The priest stopped and looked around as a conductor does before he raises his baton to begin the overture. We, the triumvirate of mourners, obediently moved closer.

From his side pocket, the priest produced a prayer-book and I wondered if, in this service, I would hear those dread words of warning: *memento homo quia pulvis es et in pulverem reverteris.* But the old man, breathless and hurried, his sparse grey hair lit like a halo by the sun at his back, mumbled the words so indistinctly that I did not catch the phrase. Beside me, Jane crumpled her white gloves, shifting uneasily from one foot to the other as her stiletto heels sank in the turf of the lawn. Finnerty, hands clasped behind his back, inspected his toecaps. The priest droned on.

An undertaker's man came forward, squatted beside the coffin and looked expectantly at the priest. When the priest shut his prayer-book, the undertaker's man released a winching device and the steel platform on which the coffin rested sank smooth and silent into the grave. Remember this, said the stranger within me; remember this mechanized last descent. The priest stepped up to the edge of the grave and a gravedigger handed him a shovel. On it were a few dry clods of earth and, as the priest shook the shovel over the pit, the clods made a rumbling sound as they struck the coffin lid. Remember, man, that thou art dust. And remember this. Some day you will write it.

I was no longer a mourner. I watched the priest take the sprinkler and shake some drops of holy water into the pit. I noticed his impatient gesture as he waited for the undertaker's man to bring up the bowl so that he could replace the sprinkler in it. I turned to see if the others had seen this, and, as I did, I caught the hearse driver and the chauffeur of our limousine lighting up for a furtive smoke behind the hearse. Once more, the undertaker's men crowded around the grave: skilfully removed the winching device. The priest opened his prayer-book and turned a page.

Surreptitiously, I watched the mourners. Jane now stood stocking-footed in the grass, her shoes, their high heels marooned in the turf, waiting one pace behind her, humble and almost human in their plight. I saw her raise her face to the sun; saw tears spill down her pale cheeks. A little to her left, Finnerty raised his hand, and as a cat cleans its eyes, wiped his knuckles across his face. I noticed the small, brown liver spots of age on the back of his old man's hand, and as I stared, unashamed and fascinated by the fact of his tears, a stranger's tears, the stranger within me said: remember this.

They were filling in the grave. I remembered that yellow face, the jaw bruised, eyes slitted: that face which stared up from the pit as clods of earth fell noisily on the coffin lid. Above the pit, their shovels moving as one, the grave-diggers dug, filled; dug, filled. Earth fell on earth. The wood was silent. The priest shut his prayer-book. Remember this.

And then, as though he had come up beside me, that drunken, revengeful Brendan (was he alive only four months ago?) repeated in my ear his angry words at Dortmunder's party: '*Standing by his wife's bedside watching her face contort, the better to record her death agony. He can't help doing it. He's a writer. He can't feel : he can only record.*'

The priest put his prayer-book in his pocket. He removed his stole, folded it carefully, then nodded to us, indicating that it was time to leave. And as we turned from the grave, Jane, Finnerty and that other curiously vulgar watcher, I knew at last the answer to Ted Ormsby's question. I have altered beyond all self-recognition. I have lost and sacrificed myself.

Now you can receive these outstanding newpress CANADIAN CLASSICS right in your home

- **AN ANSWER FROM LIMBO**
  by Brian Moore
  ". . . Moore's genius is as exuberant and inventive as ever and the book lives on in one's memory through its wealth of colourful and well-built scenes, both comic and pathetic." – *The University of Toronto Quarterly* **$3.95**

- **BADLANDS**
  by Robert Kroetsch
  "It's a splendid novel . . . I loved it." – *Margaret Laurence* **$3.95**

- **COMING THROUGH SLAUGHTER**
  by Michael Ondaatje
  "A spectacular breakthrough . . . for the crazy swinging world of Buddy Bolden, it's perfect." – *The Globe and Mail* **$3.95**

- **THE EXPATRIATE**
  by Matt Cohen
  "These short fictions show perhaps better than his larger works the variety of Cohen's capabilities and his technical versatility." – *George Woodcock* **$3.95**

- **FAT WOMAN**
  by Leon Rooke
  "A triumph of empathic imagination . . . memorable for its portrayal of an exemplary and enduring love." – *New York Times Book Review* **$3.95**

- **KAMOURASKA**
  by Anne Hébert
  "A rich mixture of love, hate and violence . . . (that has) touched off an extraordinary critical response." —*Time* **$3.95**

- **JENNIFER**
  by David Helwig
  ". . . so beautifully written, so expertly plotted, and so rich with insight, that it is hard to know what quality to single out for praise." – *Canadian Forum* **$3.95**

- **MY HEART IS BROKEN**
  by Mavis Gallant
  "Mavis Gallant's insights into her characters are achieved with breathtaking economy and rightness of detail." – *Margaret Atwood* **$3.95**

Complete and Mail this coupon today!

BOOKS BY MAIL
30 Lesmill Road, Don Mills, Ont. M3B 2T6
Please send me the books I have ordered below. I am enclosing my cheque or money order for $________.
(Please add 75 cents to cover postage and handling. No cash please.)

NAME____________________
ADDRESS________________APT._____
CITY________PROV.______P.C.______

_______ **An Answer From Limbo** . . . . **$ 3.95**
_______ **Badlands** . . . . **$ 3.95**
_______ **Coming Through Slaughter** . . . . . **$ 3.95**
_______ **The Expatriate** . . . . **$ 3.95**
_______ **Fat Woman** . . . . **$ 3.95**
_______ **Kamouraska** . . . . **$ 3.95**
_______ **Jennifer** . . . . **$ 3.95**
_______ **My Heart Is Broken** . . . . **$ 3.95**

☐ Please send me your FREE CATALOGUE.

Brian Moore

The Luck of Ginger Coffee — most famous

The Emperor of Ice Cream

The Mangan Inheritance

- Also one about a doctor's wife - maybe that's the title - I can't remember

The Victorian Collection (very odd + very good)